CRUCIBLE

B.B. REID

Published by Bloom Books, an imprint of Sourcebooks
1935 Brookdale RD, Naperville, IL 60563-2773
(630) 961-3900
sourcebooks.com

Originally self-published in 2024 by B.B. Reid.

Cataloging-in-Publication data is on file with the Library of Congress.

Printed and bound in the United States of America.
WOZ 10 9 8 7 6 5 4 3 2 1

For those who are okay being the villain in someone else's story if it means finding happiness within your own.

CONTENT WARNING

Crucible contains themes that some may find upsetting—including but not limited to—violence, dubious consent, kidnapping, dissociative identity disorder, and primal play.

Q: I don't know if I have triggers. Is this book for me?

A: This dark romance unfolded in the safe space that fiction provides, which means I controlled the outcome. As we know, reality is rarely safe or predictable. If you understand that, then please press forward. If at any point this story becomes too much for you, please bow out and feel no worse for it. I care about your mental health.

Happy reading!
Please scan the code below for a complete list of triggers.

PLAYLIST

Paint the Town Red—Doja Cat
Rockstar—Cleotrapa
Stupid Hoe—Nicki Minaj
Frozen—Madonna and Sickick
Toxic—Britney Spears
Nothing's Going to Hurt You Baby—Cigarettes After Sex
Dangerous Woman—Ariana Grande
Let Me Fall—Kaeli & Paulie Preset
Halo—Beyoncé
Where Is My Mind?—Pixies
I Feel Like I'm Drowning—Two Feet
She Will—Lil Wayne ft. Drake
Poison—Bell Biv DeVoe
Archangel—MEJKO & Rose Ghould
Fallin 4 U—Nicki Minaj
Valley of the Dolls—MARINA
Neon Brother—Nothing but Thieves
Marilyn Monroe—Nicki Minaj
Take Me Back to Eden—Sleep Token
Photograph—Ed Sheeran
Pretty Hurts—Beyoncé
Muddy Waters—LP

Whenever I'm asked to recount the most terrifying part of the crash, I tell them it was waking up on that mountain, being the only one who survived, and knowing I was going to die too.

But that's bullshit.

The most terrifying part happened after—after I found that cabin and after I found *them*.

Because of Thorin, Khalil, and Seth, I met myself for the first time. Nothing else compares. Nothing else was more frightening and yet…freeing.

CABIN RULES

Rule #1: Show us some fucking respect.

Rule #2: We own you.

Rule #3: Swallow every drop.

Rule #4: Do what we tell you.

Rule #5: Have our dinner ready on time, or we'll have *you* instead.

Rule #6: Run, and we *will* let you die.

Rule #7: Keep those pretty fingers away from our pussy.

Lauren S @NapQueen 1m
The only thing cringier than @aurelia singing is her acting. #canceled
♡ 💬 14 ↪ 1 ▽

KP 🌈 @rainbowgang 1m
CANCEL @aurelia !!!
♡ 1 💬 10 ↪ 8 ▽

taurus princess 🐂 @kaylaaaaa 1m
Never liked her anyway 💅 #aureliagofuxurself
♡ 💬 1 ↪ 1 ▽

Amy 🌸 @cherryblossoms 1m
Way to lose a fan @aurelia. So disappointed. Hope you die
♡ 1 💬 14 ↪ 1 ▽

Britt Britt @brittany_twin 2m
Am I the only one who never got the hype? 🙃 @aurelia sucks
♡ 29 💬 15 ↪ 5 ▽

beautiful dreamer @shannonlrose 2m
America's sweetheart not so sweet? 😤 #cancelAurelia
♡ 80 💬 90 ↪ 2 ▽

Gabby Gab @ticklemepink 2m
@aurelia really said that to @taniabradshaw? Ew, gross, vomit 🤢
♡ 1 💬 3 ↪ ▽

Kristy @moonpie99 3m
UNFOLLOWED! #cancelAurelia
♡ 11 💬 10 ↪ 5 ▽

SexxxyYanna @jadoreyanna 3m
Welp… won't be supporting @aurelia anymore.
♡ 28 💬 25 ↪ 7 ▽

cheyenne 🌙 moneee @iamchemonee 3m
@taniabradshaw we love u! #aureliavstania
♡ 100 💬 150 ↪ 109 ▽

holly ray xoxo 💕 @cowgirl_texas 4m
I always knew that bitch was fake. That's why I never bought any of her music @Aurelia
♡ 35 💬 24 ↪ 3 ▽

thee Kim K @notkimkardash 4m
@aurelia is an insecure c-u-n-t. @taniabradshaw is better. I said what I said 😎
♡ 2 💬 4 ↪ 8 ▽

Pretty Ari 💋 @brattybaby 5m
Just found out @aurelia is a bully. Whoa 😯
♡ 122 💬 110 ↪ 3 ▽

Matt got da D @urmomishot 5m
Watching @aurelia career go up in flames is 100x better than suffering through her concerts with my girlfriend 😄 #byeaurelia
♡ 2 💬 3 ↪ ▽

PROLOGUE

AURELIA

I shouldn't look, but I can't help it.

As that last tweet so eloquently put it, my life is going up in flames, and the whole world has tuned in to watch it burn. At least *they* have the luxury of no one giving a shit when their own lives are in shambles.

Besides, I never claimed to be perfect.

I never even claimed to be *nice*.

That glowing label was bestowed on me by the very people dragging my mutilated carcass across socials.

Sweet Aurelia.

The girl with the golden voice and the heart and hair to match.

It's bullshit.

First of all, my hair is dyed, my heart is black, and my voice has never been my own.

The person the world fell in love with was nothing more than a PR stunt, and now they're blaming me for them being gullible fools.

None of those people talking shit know me.

The *real* me.

If they did, they wouldn't be surprised that I don't shit rainbows and charm innocent woodland creatures with my song. One less-than-perfect moment in twelve years and my reputation takes a nosedive while my character gets slaughtered.

Fuck 'em all.

"Aurelia," my publicist calls with an exhausted sigh. "Aurelia, are you even listening?"

No.

"Yes. People I don't know hate me. Blah, blah, blah. I'm supposed to care and apologize. Blah, blah, blah." I look over my shoulder at Joanna. "I heard every word, and I'm not doing it."

"It's one interview. Avery Shaw—"

"I'm not going on live TV to discuss something that should have been *private*. I'm not going to explain my side to people who've already told me to fuck off. Well, you know what? Fuck them too. Fuck everyone. And *fuck* Avery Shaw. That messy bitch can scoop someone else's shit."

Joanna, in her tailored white pantsuit and Valentino pumps, quirks a brow from her seat behind her glass desk. She isn't at all surprised that I'm kind of a cunt. She is too. It's why we work well together. "Don't you think your temper is what got you into this mess in the first place?"

"Tania is a brainless, generic imitation of me, and she knows it. That's why she *baited* me—"

"And you bit it, Aurelia," Bennett, my agent, interrupts. "This time, more than you can chew. Now swallow it and let's get in front of this while we still can. You think the media isn't offering Tania the same chance?"

I shrug, staring out the window of the high-rise while Joanna stands to pace behind me and Bennett reaches for the gin. I'm pretty sure I'm the reason my agent can't stay sober. "I don't care. She's the one who needs the press. Let her choke on my crumbs."

Joanna huffs and silences her ringing cell. A few seconds later, the phone on her desk starts ringing off the hook. Calls regarding me, I'm sure.

"Oh, really?" Joanna snaps. "Well, I've got news for you, Aurelia. No one's untouchable. Not even you. You can't hide behind your fans this time. You've got to face this."

"Why?"

She huffs, and through the reflection in the window, I see her turn to my silent uncle for help.

Marston George, my dad's younger brother, is a light-skinned Black man in his early fifties with a short beard, bald head, and eyes so dark they appear pupilless. I can't tell you how many times he's been mistaken for the actor Stephen Bishop. Alas, I'm not that lucky. My uncle's sitting on the sofa, twirling the brown liquor in his glass, but I know he's far from indifferent.

I've been professionally singing since I was fourteen. Uncle Marston has been at my side every step of the way. He held my hand before every performance, through my first music deal, and when my dad died.

My mom is another story.

She was a junkie turned housewife turned junkie again before she died. My dad used to be her dealer and, ironically, was the one who got her clean after they fell in love. He stopped dealing once she became pregnant with me, and they both became law-abiding, taxpaying citizens.

Sounds too good to be true, right?

That's because it was.

When my dad was murdered over a decade-old grudge, my mom went right back to her old ways. Uncle Marston wasn't having it, though. He threw her into rehab, and before the ink on the court-ordered papers was even dry, he moved me out here to Los Angeles, where he put me on a stage for the first time and told me to sing.

I wasn't used to performing for a crowd back then—for family, yes, but never for total strangers and never competitively. At first, I wasn't sure it was what I wanted anymore. It felt like a betrayal to my parents. Uncle Marston used to be a bigwig executive at Savant Records before he quit to manage me.

Before that, he had been trying for years to convince my parents to let him work with me, but they weren't going for it. My parents' only dream for me had been that I never grew up to be like them—which, for my mom and dad, meant walking the straightest line ever.

Singing had distracted me from my grief. It gave me an outlet for the pain of losing them, and for a long time, I didn't look back. I didn't care what the other kids my age were doing. I didn't mourn the experiences I missed out on. I didn't even care if the pressures and powers my fame gave me stunted my emotional growth.

"Move on, Joanna," my uncle finally speaks. "Aurelia already said no, and no one here is going to force her."

Without turning around, I smile victoriously.

Some may say having my every whim catered to has made me rotten, but I don't care. I learned early on that the "grown-ups" weren't going to rock the boat or bite the hand that fed them, so I've been walking all over people long before I was old enough to drive.

The money and fame are great, but the power is what I really live for.

While Joanna and Uncle Marston bicker about me, I study my perfect manicure with the Pretty Girls Wear Pink gel nail polish in shade number eight.

Two years ago, I rocked pink nails for the entire month of October in my publicist's feeble attempt to show my support for breast cancer awareness. I was only permitted poses that kept my hands visible in photographs—no matter how awkward—until I was finally asked about it during an interview. I then recited Joanna's prepared statement of solidarity, and just like that, I became the face of breast cancer.

A month later, I signed an annual eight-figure partnership deal with the largest cosmetic company in the world. In exchange, they slapped my face and name on as many overpriced products as they could and made a mint selling to people who could barely afford to walk through the door.

A multibillion-dollar company got richer, and I was exalted in the media for making it happen.

I fucking hate pink.

A trip to the nearest salon may be a flimsy excuse to leave, but I take it. Spinning on my Dolce heels, I finally give my team my full attention. "I'm not doing any interviews, nor am I apologizing for something I'm not sorry for."

"Aurelia—"

"I'm talking now. The public may not like this new me, but it's the me they're going to get from now on. Find a way to fix this that doesn't include me sacrificing my last shred of integrity."

I feel my uncle's gaze on me, but I avoid it because I know if I look at him, I'll back down. I always back down.

I see my chance for the first time—an open window while the walls are slowly closing in on me.

I run for it.

Freedom.

I refuse to apologize to Tania, but I will express my gratitude. Thanks to her scheming, I'm free.

I finally get to drop the act and maybe, just maybe, find out who I really am. And if it's the villain everyone thinks I am, well, so be it.

CHAPTER ONE

AURELIA

I t feels like I'm on the lam.

The moment I step out of the chauffeured car in the dead of night, my uncle takes my arm in a harsh grip and ushers me across the tarmac as if I'm an errant child. Cassie, my newest assistant in a long line of failures, silently follows like a meek little mouse, the tail of her blue-and-purple-striped scarf flowing in the wind behind her.

Wresting my arm free once we're on board my private plane, I drunkenly stumble over to the closest reclining seat and give my uncle a mocking smile once I slump into the cushy leather.

"Whisking me away and out of sight," I taunt. "A bit dramatic, don't you think, Uncle Mars?"

Cassie keeps close, but my security team takes their seats far away from me. The only face among them I recognize is Ty Westbrook, and what a handsome face it is. He's the only one of my bodyguards who hasn't been fired by my uncle for selling my secrets or quit because I'm kind of a bitch.

"Aurelia, goddammit," my uncle swears at me. "You leaked a sex tape of yourself and then called your cohost a tone-deaf sheep!"

"One, I didn't leak it. I was *hacked*," I correct. The lie works for other celebrities. Why not me? "Two, my face wasn't in it, so it could have been anyone. And spare me the lecture, Uncle Mars. Tania needed to learn why taking things that don't belong to her and crossing me is bad for her health. Need I remind you she stole my song? And even you have to admit that Tania sounds like a sheep when she sings. Baaaa-baaaaa! I wish I could be like Aurelia. Baaaa-baaaaa. See? Spot on."

I hear a cough behind me and know it's Tyler smothering his laugh, but I don't dare look across the aisle with my uncle watching. One whiff that my relationship with the former soldier transcends professional indifference and I'll never see him again.

My uncle considers the idea of me having a meaningful relationship with anyone beyond my accountant, voice coach, and the stage completely frivolous and forbidden.

"It was on live TV, Aurelia. Your outburst was seen by millions."

My smile feels more like a sneer when I cock my head. "Would it have been better if I'd treated her horribly where no one could see, Uncle Marston?"

The question hits close to home and ruffles his old feathers like I knew it would. Knowing my uncle won't answer for his sins, I snap my fingers, and after a flurry of confusion, a champagne flute is hesitantly placed in my hand by the flight attendant.

"What's your name?" I ask after she makes the mistake of making eye contact with me. I've perfected the art of appearing poised even when I'm lit up like a Christmas tree. My elbow is braced on my crossed legs as I sip my champagne.

"Susan."

"Susan. What an awful name for a child. What were your parents thinking?"

"I…I don't know."

"Well, you should ask them."

"They're dead."

"Susan, do you think I should have to beg the help for a refreshment?"

"Oh." The flight attendant's cheeks redden. "No. I'm so sorry. It's just that your uncle—"

I already know what she's going to say—that my uncle called ahead and ordered them not to serve me any alcohol. "You don't work for him," I tell my uncle's spy. She's one of many, but I hate her no less. "You work for me, Susan."

"My apologies, ma'am."

"Ma'am? You're older than me."

"I didn't mean—"

"Aurelia, leave the stewardess alone and let her get back to work," my uncle orders.

My smile is sharp when I regard my uncle. "I believe they're called flight attendants now, Uncle."

Susan apologizes before excusing herself.

The back of my neck prickles, and I feel like I'm under a microscope, but that's nothing new. The only difference is the way *this* particular gaze makes me squirm. Tyler's attention feels like he's trying to pierce my thorny exterior and see into my soul. He wants to believe that I'm really good deep down, and that's why I know we'll never work.

"This bratty behavior cannot go on," Uncle Marston lectures. "My God, I'd hoped your acting out was a phase, but you seem to get more intolerable by the day."

"I appreciate that, Uncle Mars. Really, I do. I was taught by the best."

His almond-shaped eyes narrow immediately. They remind me of my father's, and though I loved him, I'm glad I took after my mother in that regard. My eyes are upturned like hers, so it's one less thing that connects me to the man before me.

"What did you say?"

Knowing just how far I can push my uncle and come out unscathed, I throw in the towel and look away. "I said I'm sorry to disappoint you."

"Good. You've already been locked out of your social media accounts to give you time to *think and reflect*." I roll my eyes, which my uncle chooses to ignore. "Cassie will let me know if there is anything you need. I'll see you in a few weeks."

"Wait." I sit up, something like panic spearing my chest.

I don't necessarily enjoy my uncle's company, but he's never been more than a stone's throw away, managing every aspect of my life. It's been that way for *thirteen* years—my entire adult life and teenage years.

I wouldn't even know what to do with my independence now if I had it, which is why I haven't fought harder to take back my life. I've gotten too comfortable—too used to being controlled—and now I'm terrified of living without it.

"Where are you going?"

"I'm staying behind to clean up your mess, Aurelia. *Again*."

"Why?" I brush invisible dust from the white ruffled apron on my dress. I'm still wearing the sexy milkmaid costume from the studio. It has a dark green frilly pleated skirt, brown corset with yellow daffodil embroidery, and a white ruffled sweetheart neckline.

The dress is over-the-top if you ask me, but no one did, and that's the problem. Joanna and my new stylist thought dressing theatrically on the show would keep the attention on me instead of Tania, the other judges, and even the contestants.

Because everything is always about me, me, me.

"They'll get over it," I say dismissively.

"Don't be so sure of that."

If only. "But why Canada?" I ask instead of voicing the intrusive thought. "Why so far north? At this time of year? Can't I go to Ibiza or Cabo? I don't like the cold, Uncle Mars. You know that."

"You need to lie low and not in some place where you'll be easily recognized or followed. I invested in some property near a town called Hearth. A ranch with a view of the mountains. It's remote, but you'll be comfortable."

"You mean, *I* invested in property. It's my money, Uncle Mars." I prissily sip my champagne as I watch him over the rim of the glass. My uncle hates being reminded that he's at my mercy and not the other way around.

"Stay inside where no one can spot you, and you won't notice the cold," he snaps. It's my uncle's only response before he storms off the plane.

We take off shortly after, and the moment we reach cruising altitude, I stand, ignoring Cassie's startled squeak as I make my way to the bedroom at the back of the plane.

I puke my guts out inside the tiny bathroom and then brush my teeth as I stare at my reflection. This is probably the part where I'm expected to feel sorry for myself and say I don't recognize my own reflection.

Sorry.

I'm on a first-name basis with the bitch in the mirror. We braid each other's hair and support each other's delusions. The only thing out of place is this god-awful costume.

The peasant-style dress is meant to remind everyone that I'm America's treasure—sweet, gentle, angelic, and beloved.

I want to tear it off me.

Unfortunately, there's a knock on the stateroom door before I can.

There's only one person on the plane who has the lack of self-preservation it takes to disturb me.

"Come in, Tyler."

The door opens, and my most devoted bodyguard steps inside before quietly closing it behind him.

It's unnecessary.

The plane is too small to be discreet. Obviously, whatever is on Ty's mind is worth the risk of my uncle finding out. He has spies everywhere.

"You okay?" Tyler steps into the bathroom and wraps his strong arms around my waist from behind. He pulls me into him, and I let him out of pity since Tyler fancies himself in love with me.

The problem is that he fell for the "me" that doesn't exist. He's infatuated with the charming facade my uncle dressed up and put on a stage for the label, lawyers, agents, and media to carve out pieces of until there was nothing left. Tyler covets a shell, not the person lost inside it.

"I'm fine."

"You say that," he responds while I avoid his gaze, "but you haven't been yourself."

Finally, I meet his stare in the mirror, and I wish I hadn't. The adoration in his brown eyes is more than I can stand.

Tyler's handsome with smooth brown skin, expressive eyes, high fade, and a disconnected goatee. He's what you'd call good stock. He's ex-Army with a lieutenant general for a father. Tyler joined straight out of high school, completing two tours of duty before being medically discharged and becoming a bodyguard for a screwed-up singer.

It would be easy to let him believe I'm the girl he thinks I am.

But I can't.

I nudge Tyler away with my elbow, and he follows me into the bedroom. I can feel him hovering, ready to step in, as I stumble to the side of the bed and collapse in a cloud of wool and satin.

"Tell me what's going on with you," he gently demands.

Rolling onto my side, I give him the flirty smile I've practiced a thousand times. "What makes you think anything is wrong?"

"Cut it out, Aurelia."

"What?"

"This." He gestures to me as if that explains everything. "Stop pretending you don't care what people think of you."

"I don't."

"Then why are you trying so hard to make everyone hate you?"

I playfully roll my eyes. "News flash: They already do. The entire world wants me dead. Haven't you heard? I'm public enemy number one."

"And so you think being a bitch will make you care less?"

I roll onto my back because I don't want to face him anymore. "I'm sorry to disappoint you, Tyler. The Aurelia you and everyone else are so head over heels for is really my middle-aged uncle using me to cosplay, so unless you're planning to ask *him* out, I think you should start sailing new waters." I let my head roll to the side, and I smile gently to soften the blow while he glares daggers at me. "You should ask Cassie out. She's nice."

And pretty.

I don't know if she's smart or not since I don't waste time talking to her except to tell her when to fetch. Another month or two, and she'll quit like all the others.

"Okay, I don't know where the fuck that came from, but for your information, Cassie is engaged. She's getting married next month. Don't you talk to her? Ever?"

"About what?"

"Look, when I said you haven't been yourself, I wasn't referring to that Disney princess act. I'm talking about this one. The Aurelia who thinks she needs to be vicious to protect herself."

Tyler shakes his head, and though I can feel his disappointment, I don't sense any judgment. It wouldn't matter if he did judge me. I'm not supposed to care.

"That isn't you either, Aurelia. You're hurt, pissed, and feeling betrayed because when the dust fell, you realized there was never really anyone in your corner. It probably feels easier to take the punishment when you feel you deserve it, so you lash out." I keep my gaze firmly fixed on the ceiling while Tyler tries his best to wring out all my truths. "If that's true, you're still allowing others to decide who you are."

The silence between us is deafening as I fight to swallow past the knot in my throat. "What if—"

The plane starts violently shaking before I can ask him a question I don't know if I want the answer to.

What if this is me? Could Tyler live with it? Could he love a monster?

I wouldn't blame him if the answer is no. I'm not sure I would either.

My eyes flare when the plane's trembling seems to go on forever. "What is that?"

There's a worried pinch to his brow even as he says, "It's just turbulence. It will be over soon."

I squeeze my eyes closed and wait for it to stop. "I hate flying," I grumble when the plane finally settles.

Tyler checks his watch and sighs. "It's been a long day. We have a few hours until we reach Hearth. You should get some sleep."

I hum. "That doesn't sound like a bad idea."

"Then I'll leave you to it," he says before I can ask if he wants to join me.

Once Tyler's gone, I stare at the door he disappeared through for a while. When he doesn't return, I sigh my disappointment and stand from the bed to remove my boots and costume.

I'm too tired to look for my bonnet in the luggage my housekeeper packed for me, so I keep the wide green and white gingham ribbon tied around my head. It's the only thing protecting my riot of golden 4a curls from total chaos.

Leaving my clothes on the floor, I climb back on the bed and collapse with a sigh.

I'm asleep before I even remember closing my eyes.

I'm jostled awake by turbulence.

My head is already turned toward the small oval window when I open my eyes, so I can see it's light out.

No.

Not light.

White.

There's a wall of fog so thick the sun can never hope to pierce it.

At first, I think it's the altitude—that we're soaring among stubborn clouds that refuse to part for us—but the fog seems sentient. Angry and vengeful. It knocks the plane around, growing more violent the longer we stay. After a while, it doesn't feel like mere turbulence.

Tyler bursts through the bedroom door without knocking, and I don't even think to be embarrassed about my lack of clothing.

Something is very, very wrong.

"What is it?" I groggily ask as I sit up. "What's happening?"

"Get dressed and come to the front," he orders. He makes a good attempt at sounding calm, but his voice is edged with fear and panic.

"Tyler, what is happening?" I demand again.

The plane suddenly dips, and for a long, heart-stopping moment, I think we're dropping out of the sky. My stomach reacts so forcibly that it feels like it touches my spine.

Tyler curses when I'm thrown to the side and tumble off the bed. He rushes over to help me from the floor and only lets go when he's sure I'm steady on my feet.

"We crossed paths with a rogue storm, and it's bad," he explains. "The captain is trying to make an emergency landing."

"In that?" I shriek, throwing an arm toward the window. "How? I can't see anything."

"That's why you need—" A violent updraft cuts him off. We both lose our balance when we're thrown off our feet—me backward and Tyler forward. When he lands on me, his weight steals my breath. "Get out front!" he yells once the plane rights itself, and he's back on his feet.

Ty's gone before I can beg him not to leave me, so I do what he says, swiping my dress from the floor. Tyler left the door open, so I can see the rest of the plane as I struggle to get into my dress.

It's chaos in the cabin.

Cassie is screaming, at least two of my guards are vomiting, and I can hear alarms blaring from the open cockpit.

Tyler stumbles to the front of the plane to check on Cassie, who passes out by the time he reaches her. Shoving his hand underneath the scarf still around her neck, he checks her pulse. His face is tight when he turns around, but there's no trace of devastation.

She's still alive, at least.

There's resolve in Tyler's eyes as he fights his way back to me, but it doesn't make me feel safer.

This is bad.

The plane pitches to the side while I try to tug on one of my boots. I lose sight of Tyler as I roll and collide with the wall. The impact is hard enough to stun me, but I shake it off and crawl the short distance to rescue my other boot from under the bed.

I don't even know why I bother if I'm going to die. I guess because all I can think about even now is the headlines and what they'll say when they find my body.

It's pitiful.

"Aurelia!" Tyler yells from the cabin, demanding I light a fire under my ass.

I carefully regain my feet and stumble out of the stateroom. The cabin is loud. The engines are screaming from the exertion it takes to keep us in the air. Through the windows, I can see more white. I can see the wind swirling around, and it takes me a second longer to realize it's…snow.

A blizzard?

We flew into a freaking blizzard?

Tyler manages to make his way to the rear of the plane again and holds out a hand for me.

I reach for his hand, and it feels like some invisible force keeps us apart. I stretch my arm until it hurts, but no matter how hard I try, my fingers never do more than graze his.

Finally, Ty's fingers curl around mine, and he grits his teeth from the strength it takes to tug me to him. The moment I fall into his arms, I hear a terrible screech and then the sound of metal scraping like it's tearing itself apart.

Oh, God

"Tyler!" I scream to warn him.

"You need to get strapped in now!" He helps me into the nearest seat, and I scramble to buckle the belt. There's only a sofa across the aisle perpendicular to me, so it costs Ty precious seconds to reach the nearest empty seat closer to the front of the plane.

I want to close my eyes as if that will dull the terrifying roar throughout the cabin, but I can't—not until I'm sure Tyler is safe.

He feels a million miles away when he finally takes his seat. I don't see if he gets his seat belt on because something hits the plane in a rapid barrage.

It sounds like the plane is being shot at.

Hail. It's what's pelting the plane.

The lights in the cabin flicker off, and more alarms start blaring all around me.

Someone starts praying.

I hear the captain speaking over the intercom. He sounds calm, but he's no Sully. I'm not convinced.

Why does it feel more like we're crashing rather than landing?

I look out the window, but I can't see anything except that damn white. And I can't hear the engines anymore.

The earsplitting scraping sound returns, followed by a boom and then an unbearable rush of cold air. I don't need to look behind me to know that the tail is gone.

The praying guard starts chanting louder, and I'm tempted to join him. But for what? My life? My salvation? Right now, they seem to be one and the same, so I start praying for an open field.

God isn't that kind.

When I turn my head toward the window for relief from the wind, the white finally fades just enough for my heart to sink when I see where we are.

It's not an open field or anything close to resembling a landing strip.

It's a massive snow-covered peak, and we're heading straight for it.

CHAPTER TWO

AURELIA

I wake up in a tree.

My ears are ringing, and it feels like I'm still falling. I don't even remember leaving the plane. The last thing I remember was hearing that god-awful tearing sound once more as the plane coasted over the frost-tipped forest and then feeling suction, cold, wind, and then…nothing. When the ringing finally fades, I swear I can hear the echoes of our bloodcurdling screams.

But no, that can't be right.

I'm alone.

It's the first thing I notice when I open my eyes—not the tree, snow, or debris forty feet below me. I only see the isolation.

My lap belt keeps me from moving more than my dangling arms and legs, and I claw at it in a blind panic.

"Help! Somebody help me!"

My bare fingers are frozen stiff, so I have trouble releasing the latch, which is a good thing because my vision doubles after my fourth attempt. There's blood rushing to my head from being upside down. Fear that I may pass out again terrifies me more than being stuck in a tree, but less than falling out of it.

The seat belt is the only thing keeping me from falling to my death or at least breaking a few bones. From what I can tell, I survived the crash mostly unscathed, and I'd like to keep it that way.

But I can't stay in the tree.

As strong and sturdy as it looks, the tree sways from the force of the storm still raging around me.

My seat is wedged in the V between two thick branches, and I spot something brown lodged in the snow-packed ground below me. I think my eyes are playing tricks on me, but why would I hallucinate seeing a couch?

I can't explain why seeing that damn couch excites me. Maybe because I know if it could survive—if I could—then so could others.

I look around, but I don't see anyone else.

"Hello? Hello, is anyone there? Help me. Help me, please." My breathing quickens, and my heart races when no one answers. I feel the scream bubbling in my throat until it spills free. "Help! Heeeeeeelp!"

I scream and scream and scream until my lungs and throat burn, and I can't anymore. My vision doubles again, and I know I can't stay like this.

I turn my head as much as I can, searching for more wreckage. Most of my vision has cleared, so I'm able to take in more detail, and I see it's not just me stuck in the tree. There's more debris, but not much.

I still can't see where the rest of the plane ended up.

I can barely see more than three feet in front of me because the snow and hail won't let up.

It's so cold.

I'm so cold.

I could stay here and wait for help to come, or I could find shelter and see if anyone else survived. I'm a little appalled when I waver on which course to take.

Get out of the goddamn tree, Aurelia.

Reaching for my seat belt again, I inhale quick, shallow breaths, trying to build the courage. I can aim for one of the branches, but if I miss…

The snow could cushion my fall…

Or it could break my bones.

I guess we'll see.

Closing my eyes, I take one last breath and pull on the latch. I hear the click, and I feel myself fall. My stomach smarts and the breath whooshes out of me when I collide with the thick branch a few feet below me. The bark scrapes against my bare arms when I start to slip. A few of my nails break when I dig in, grappling desperately to hang on.

"Fuck!" I hear myself scream.

And then I'm falling again.

I hit another branch on my way down, but my shoulder takes the brunt of it this time as I continue to fall. When I finally hit the ground, I immediately sink into the freshly fallen snow. More flakes and some hail pelt me from the sky I can't see above. The blizzard threatens to bury me in a heartbeat if I don't move.

I almost consider it—being buried alive. It's better than suffering for days. My chances of being rescued in this storm—of surviving it—are too slim for hope. But then I hear it.

A howl.

It's the wind.

It's the wind. It's the wind. It's the wind.

A terrified squeal escapes me when I hear it again. Another answers the call, and then another. I lose count of the howls after seven.

Wolves.

I try to gulp, but my throat hurts too much from screaming, so I settle for hyperventilating.

I should have stayed in the tree.

A laugh bordering on hysteria escapes me, and then I rise with a groan. The wolves sound far away but still too damn close.

Shelter.

Need to find shelter.

At this temperature and in this stupid costume, I'll be dead before the wolves can say "lunch."

Hope they like cold cuts.

I force myself to focus on the immediate threat and search the debris. When I don't find anything useful, I debate my next move for far too long. I waste precious minutes silently losing my shit until I hear more howls.

They're closer now.

My feet start moving in the opposite direction—running, fleeing, carrying me from the tree that saved my life.

Each step through the thick blanket of snow is laborious. I stumble to my knees every other step while my skin stings from the hail.

I feel a stabbing in my ears and fingers that I don't want to think about.

I'm not wearing a coat, so I have no choice but to keep moving. I have no idea how high up the mountain I am or how close I am to stepping off a cliff.

All I can do is follow the trees.

The destroyed canopy and fallen young aspens guide me down the steep hill like a blazing arrow. My heart and lungs burn from the exertion, but it also warms my blood and keeps me going until I reach the bottom of the hill where the forest ends.

At first, I think it's the storm wreaking havoc on my mind when I see it, but no.

It's really here.

On the edge of the cliff lies the rest of the plane.

Without the engines, it hadn't made it far.

I call out for Tyler and Cassie, but heart-wrenching silence answers back. I don't know any of my bodyguards' names. It never occurred to me to ask, and now they're probably dead because of me.

My next breath shudders out of me, and I notice it's shallower than before. I'm too afraid to think about what it means, so I stumble over to the crumpled fuselage. Thick, black, and suffocating smoke billows in the frigid air.

The front of the fuselage, where the cockpit should be, skirts the edge of the cliff, and I know what I'll find at the bottom.

Too close.

If there are other survivors, it means they cheated death a second time. The pilots hadn't been so lucky. I'm too cold to cry for them—or maybe it's my heart that's too frigid.

Rushing for the back of the plane where the empennage tore off, I stop when I see footprints leading out of them—one large set.

"Hello?"

Nothing but sparking wires and wind rattling loose metal answers me. Teeth chattering, I climb inside the fuselage. It's dark and haunted, but it's shelter. It's better than being out there.

I don't make it more than a few steps inside before I see them—the frozen corpses of my security team.

Clapping a hand over my mouth, I turn away when I realize they're still strapped into their seats. The neck of the praying bodyguard is twisted at an odd angle, his mouth forever frozen in a soundless scream. I think it was Harold or Harrison, but I can't be sure. The other two are pinned to their seats by the fragments of the plane that impaled them.

This isn't a wreck site. It's a graveyard.

God, they never had a chance.

Are you happy now?

Dropping my hand, I inhale deeply through my nose and let it out slowly. This isn't my fault. I wasn't flying the plane. I didn't cause the storm.

Not this one.

Stop it!

My bodyguards are *gone*. Cassie and Tyler probably are too. I can only help myself.

Walking deeper inside the plane, my teary eyes reluctantly travel to the seat where Tyler had been sitting, and my knees buckle when I see it's empty.

Cassie's too.

Remembering the footprints I saw outside the fuselage, my heart beats a little faster.

They're *alive*.

But it's not all good because it means they're out there. In the storm. Probably looking for me.

I turn to rush back out of the plane when the cold hits me like a freight train, and I stop at the edge of the opening. I beg my feet to move, but they won't.

Because who am I kidding? I won't survive out there.

Rescue will come soon. I should stay here where it will be easy for them to find me. I'm sure Cassie and Tyler will be back soon. Feeling something suspiciously like guilt, I turn to go back inside and wait for them where it's safe.

"Help! Oh, God! Someone help me!"

Gasping, I turn around. My gaze frantically searches the area for the scream's source, but the storm makes it hard to see anything. Maybe it was my imagination.

The scream comes again, followed by more pleas, and I can't deny the voice's similarity to Cassie's. Wind can't replicate the sheer terror in it.

She could have been hurt looking for me, or she could be in trouble. Either way, if she stays out there much longer, she'll die.

Making a decision, I turn back into the warm confines of the fuselage.

CHAPTER THREE

KHALIL

This is bullshit! There's no one here!" I shout over the wind, snow, and hail. I'm two hundred and thirty pounds of pure muscle, yet the storm raging around us has my solid frame trembling like a twig in a hurricane. Snow clings to Thorin's blond lashes and thick brows when he sends me a look to shut the fuck up, and I send him an aggravated one right back. "Seriously, I can't feel my nuts anymore, Thor! We need to make camp!"

Reality paid us a visit this morning, and we've been on a knife's edge ever since.

The trek down Big Bear, our mountain and sanctum, and across the valley to reach the crash sites took longer because of the storm. It's been hours since we've found the fuselage. Our search through the wreckage—and the corpses—before investigating the surrounding area for survivors—all the while being careful not to disturb the sites or leave evidence of our being here—proved fruitless.

The barrage of storms since the plane crashed a day ago is the only thing keeping the authorities from rallying search parties, but not for much longer.

The crash was too far away for us to see or hear, but we'd felt it. The smaller mountain had roared its anger over being disturbed, and ours answered back.

I steal a glance at the reason we're out here.

Zeke caught a glimpse of the small plane on fire and flying too low through our cabin's window and lost his shit.

He's been quiet and pensive ever since.

My cold breath billows in front of me when I release a heavy breath. I tell myself it's better than the alternative, but…

I don't like how close he's standing to the cliff's edge.

Zeke's hands are stuffed in the pockets of his insulated pants, and his shoulders are hunched—not from fighting the biting cold and harsh wind, but the voice inside daring him to jump.

Fucking Seth.

Jumping will be painless and quicker than whatever Isaac has in store for him, but I am not about to let either happen.

"*Ezekiel.*" The sound of Thor's stern voice only makes Zeke shuffle closer to the edge, and I clench my teeth in irritation. Thor and I have a difference in view on how to deal with Zeke's trauma. Thor believes charging through it like a bull in a china shop is more effective, while I believe a little patience and understanding never hurt anyone.

"No one's found us," Thor gently says after catching the look I give him. "It's unlikely anyone survived that crash, and if they did, they're dead or will be soon."

"Yeah, and good fucking riddance," I add. "Anyone who even knows we exist is probably thinking the same about us."

Zeke doesn't respond. He just keeps staring into the misty abyss. Despite the pallor of his olive skin, Zeke's cheeks are red from the cold I doubt he feels.

I keep my steps slow and quiet as I approach him like I would a startled calf. From the corner of my eye, I see Thor doing the same. There's a determined glint in his eyes that says he'll follow Zeke over the damn edge just to keep him from falling alone.

We both would.

"No one's coming. And if they did…" I ignore the pissed-off look Thor flashes me at the fumbling reminder that they *could*. "We'll kill them all this time. We won't let him take you, Ezeklel."

"You're safe," Thor promises.

A tortured sound reaches my ears, and I lunge before he can move an inch. I grab Zeke's arm and yank him to me. Wrapping my arms around him, I hold him in an almost crushing embrace while his nails dig into my back. Zeke tucks his face into my neck and sobs while Thor visibly sags with relief before coming over and planting a hand on Zeke's shoulder.

Our gazes meet, and I want nothing more than to hunt the fuckers down that did this and wipe them all out. We neutralized anyone who stood in our way of getting Zeke out, but by now, Isaac—the so-called Savior—has likely doubled his numbers and tripled his influence.

Meanwhile, Zeke's very existence becomes more and more tenuous each day. He wasn't always like this—fragile, anxious, and destructive. The opposite, actually. He used to be the strongest of us all—carefree, quick to smile, full of infectious laughter…

His own brother *stole* that from him, and we've been fighting desperately to steal it back ever since.

Never should have left him alone.

Thor and I never should have left Nevada. After high school, I went off to pursue boxing, and Thorin joined the Corps. Boxing competitively kept me on the road for years while Thor was stationed at Camp Lejeune during the rare times he wasn't deployed.

"We've got you, Zeke," Thor murmurs. "Let's go home."

Home.

The sanctuary we built, with our bare hands nine years ago, as high up as we dared on the most volatile mountain in the Cold Peaks.

We still have a few hours of daylight left, but we'll never make it back to the cabin before dark, so we head south in the direction of home until we find the familiar cave we've made use of a time or two.

It has a narrow opening that keeps predators from calling it home and a water source nearby.

Thorin rips off his balaclava as soon as we're inside, and I do the same. Zeke slides down the wall until he's sitting on his ass, knees bent, and shoving his hands through his dark hair. We give him space as Thor and I inspect the small cave.

Something doesn't feel right, and judging by the tension in Thor's shoulders, whose instincts are even sharper than mine, I know it's not paranoia.

He walks over to inspect a small pile of burned kindling, stick, and flint shavings near the rear of the cave. The ashes haven't yet scattered, telling me the hastily put-together firepit was recent.

Spotting fresh footprints in the dust, I crouch to examine them in the fading light.

"Thor," I call out since he's the better tracker. I'm ninety percent positive these tracks belong to two people—a man and a woman, judging by the size differences.

These mountains are closed to the public during winter, and we still have a few more weeks until spring, when the trails become passable.

"What is it?" Thor walks over to stand next to me when I don't respond.

I sneak a glance over my shoulder at Ezekiel, and only when I'm sure he's paying us no mind do I look up at Thorin. "I think there were survivors," I whisper.

His expression immediately becomes twisted. "What?"

"Someone's been here." He gives me a blank look. "*Recently*."

"How do you know?"

I show Thor my findings and wait for him to tell me I'm wrong. When he swears under his breath, I know that I'm not. "This is less than a day old. We need to tell Zeke."

"The hell we do."

I rise to my full height but keep my voice low. "And why the hell not?"

"Because if it is Isaac, the last thing we need is Zeke losing his shit. You know what will happen if he does."

Unconvinced, I cross my arms and stare him down. "Zeke's a grown man, Thor. He can handle it."

"Can he, though?"

"This isn't your call to make."

"What isn't his call to make?"

Thorin and I startle, not having heard Zeke move from his spot by the mouth of the cave. Thor holds my gaze, silently communicating that it's a bad idea, but I disagree.

"We think there were survivors," I answer.

The color seeps from Zeke's cheeks, and he goes utterly still.

"Shit," I mumble.

"I told you he couldn't handle it!" Thor shouts. Inside the small cave, his voice bounces off the walls.

Sucking my teeth at his dramatics, I snap my fingers in front of Zeke's face. "Zeke, man. You with us, bro?"

Zeke blinks, and I count each one. After the first one, the knot in my stomach eases a fraction. His stare is long, but his eyes are clear. He's not looking around in confusion as if he doesn't know where he is or what day it is. The large knot in his throat bobs when he swallows. Zeke's moving, and that's what matters.

"I'm here," he finally answers quietly, and though laden with fear and twisted memories of his time in his brother's cult, it's his voice that speaks.

Thorin and I take a collective breath of relief.

"This doesn't change anything, Ezekiel. We don't know who they are. They could be anyone. You're safe."

"Safe," he repeats as if the word is foreign to him. These mountains have been our haven for nine years. Far longer than he was Isaac's prisoner.

"We won't let anyone hurt you," Thorin vows. "But you have to promise that you'll stay awake. If it is Isaac, the last thing we need is Seth running back to him or Bane going berserk. The trails of corpses those two will leave ends at our doorstep."

"I don't know if I can."

As I reach for him, my heart breaks a little when Zeke flinches. Remembering that it's me, he gives me a weak smile in invitation, and I slowly curl my arm around his shoulders. I feel Thorin doing the same to mine while his free hand cups the back of Zeke's head. Our heads gravitate together, and the cave and the world outside fade away.

The endurance it takes to keep the isolation and loneliness from crumbling us from within requires *all* of us. It could almost feel like a long vacation if we didn't know these mountains for what they truly are—our prison.

"Stay with us, Zeke," I plead. "We need you. Say you'll try."

"I'll try."

The three of us drag ourselves out of the cave just before first light the following morning. Picking up the trail the survivors left is easy. They're either amateurs or aren't concerned with being followed.

It wouldn't have mattered either way.

Tracking and reconnaissance was Thor's specialty in the Marines. He would have found them anyway.

The pair are definitely headed south, and the closer the three of us get to our mountain, the more nervous Zeke becomes. He's already withdrawing. It won't take much to push him over the edge. The smallest tip in the scales could upset the balance.

Getting back is taking longer than it should because we're covering our tracks as well as following theirs. It's after noon when we eventually stop for a break.

The storm from yesterday finally moved on last night, so we have a brief reprieve before another one inevitably hits. It's always like this during the tail end of winter, as if the season is rebelling at the thought of yielding to spring.

"They might be after the tail," I blurt when I can't take the weight of my brothers' silence anymore. Thorin and Zeke haven't said a word, but I know they're thinking the same thing I am—that whoever was on that plane is searching for us, and that's why they're headed south. "It's their best chance at finding the emergency transmitter," I reason.

Neither respond. They just stare into the fire I hastily made, jaws tight, eyes dark, and mood pensive.

When it's finally time to move on again, we grab our shit and trek until we reach the northern edge of the valley where our Ski-Doos are parked.

It's just after sunset, and we know these wilds better than anyone, so we ride the last twenty miles to the base of our mountain, where we leave the snowmobiles. It's still a few miles hike up to our cabin, and the climb is steep and winding.

My eyes are on a swivel as we hike in silence. We don't talk while keeping our steps as light as possible. A mile away from our cabin, we break off into three separate directions without a word. Zeke and I take the scenic routes to scout the surrounding perimeter while Thor continues forward.

He's the first to make it to our small clearing. I can see him through the cover of trees where I wait while he stakes out our home for any sign of a disturbance. Across the clearing, I know Zeke is doing the same.

We built our cabin on the very edge of a steep cliff, so this tiny corner we claimed for ourselves is a dead end unless you're suicidal.

The three of us watch the house for twenty minutes before Thor's satisfied no one is waiting to ambush us.

After I whistle our code—two short and one long sound—Zeke and I emerge from the tree line to join Thor by the woodshed. We're still hiding in shadow, just in case.

"We should go out and look for that tail first thing," Thor suggests. "Find them before they find us."

I silently wait for Zeke to object.

"If ever there was a good time to start smoking, it would be now," he says.

"You can stay here where it's safe—"

Zeke rolls his eyes. "I know it's been a while since you've had a pretty little damsel to obsess over, but I'm not your bitch, Thor. I don't need you to protect me."

Thor's blue eyes twinkle when he winks at him. "Suit yourself, sweetheart. I'll remember that the next time you have a nightmare and try to crawl into my bed for a snuggle, little spoon."

Zeke flips him off, and I cackle as we enter the cabin. Easy moments like these between us are rare these days. I think we're all just relieved to know that our mountain is still safe for now.

After giving the cabin a thorough search, we retreat to our individual rooms—a luxury we didn't have for years—to sleep off the hard journey.

Tomorrow, we'll find the tail and figure out who the hell is trespassing on our mountain.

CHAPTER FOUR

AURELIA

I'm not hallucinating. It's really there.

A cabin.

The smoking chimney promises warmth, salvation...shelter.

A whimper pushes past my dried and cracked lips. It's the only thing I can manage after three days in the wild. It's been more than one since I had food or water. It's a Herculean feat that I make it to the edge of the snow-covered clearing. The hike up the mountain had taken the last of my strength, but I kept my eyes on the black smoke rising through the trees and curling in the air as I climbed.

Food. Shelter. Warmth.

I told myself the whole way up that if I could just make it, maybe Tyler had too.

My soul shudders at the thought of my faithful bodyguard, and it's all it takes for the rest of that first day to coming rushing back. Cassie's screams, the wolves, and then me—armed only with an axe from the fuselage—getting there too late to stop them. If it wasn't for Tyler finding me when he did, I would have been next, but his perilous plan to find the emergency transmitter had proven to be just as dangerous.

We'd found each other despite the scattered wreckage and survived wolves, brutal storms, exhaustion, and dwindling resources only to be ripped apart again by an avalanche. For days, Tyler had pushed us both to survive and for what? Nothing. His plan to find the transmitter never came to fruition.

We never even found the damn tail.

But I can't think about that right now because *I'm so fucking cold*, and hungry, and it only reminds me that I'm alone again.

The log cabin is bigger and homier than the one-room shack I'd expected to find. It even has solar panels on the roof, which means electricity. It means heat and maybe a phone or radio. There are two sheds, too, one with piles of chopped wood stored inside to keep them dry. I can't see what's inside the other and I'm not curious enough to care.

The promise of warmth eventually convinces me to approach the cabin. It's modest and unassuming compared to the garish castle I live in, yet I'm intimidated. Enough to hesitate when I reach the heavy wooden door, my bruised and frostbitten fist poised to knock.

My instincts shut that shit down.

Blowing out a breath that I can see clearly in the cold, I bang on the door with a sense of urgency that can't be ignored—at least not by anyone kind enough to help a stranger.

Please.

Please be home.

I knock and knock and knock, and then I scream for help.

No one answers.

Shivering uncontrollably, I shuffle to the window and peer inside. I can see a living room with a high, vaulted ceiling and exposed wood beams.

There's no fireplace like I expected. Instead, I see a small stove tucked inside a bricked alcove made of stone. The dark metal beam on top extends to the top of the alcove like a chimney, which explains the smoke I saw.

The bearskin rug in front of it looks so soft, plush, and inviting. It's practically begging me to come inside and wrap myself in it. I've got tunnel vision staring at the fire and rug—so much so that the rest of the house fades and the voice screaming at me to keep the fuck out disappears.

My body succumbs to another violent quake, and I know that's not an option.

I risk precious life-suspending moments waiting for someone to appear. It's pretty early in the morning, so maybe the owners are still asleep.

After five more minutes of knocking, I decide that asking forgiveness is better than asking permission.

Limping over to the door again, I try the doorknob, dumbly blinking when it twists without resistance, and the door opens. It creaks open slowly like it does in horror movies, but that feeling I had a moment ago doesn't return. All I feel is the cabin's warmth beckoning me inside.

"Hello?" I call into the dark space from the safety of the porch.

The threshold feels like a point of no return. *Crossing* it feels more dire than the death exposure promises. Especially when I spot three sets of boots lined by the door, all dirty and worn, and my stomach flips when I notice their sizes—easily three or four bigger than my own.

"Hello." My throat strangles the word until it's little more than a croak. "I…um…is anyone home?"

I wait for a breath, but no one answers.

Letting my arms fall, I decide I'm being ridiculous and step inside. If they have a phone, I can probably be gone before they return. Maybe we'll never have to cross paths.

The different scents in the house converge all at once—cardamom, mint, leather, juniper, and something a little smoky yet lighter and more sensual than tobacco.

Amber.

The cabin smells like a bachelor pad for cavemen.

Oh, God.

"My name is Aurelia," I explain, even though it's clear no one is home. Shutting the door, I gratefully leave the cold behind as I move deeper into the cabin. "I was in a plane crash and got lost. I…" I stop when I nearly reveal that I'm alone and instead say, "I need help."

If it weren't completely impossible I'd swear I was speaking to the house—begging it to be good to me.

When the cabin shudders as if in answer, I exhale my relief and rush toward the fireplace…thing. The bear rug is even softer than it looked through the window. I drop to my knees and sink into the lush fur. The fire is barely more than embers, but it's better than the sparks I was able to conjure in the cave.

I stand and shed Cassie's scarf and my dead bodyguard Harrison's heavy coat.

My boots and socks are next, though it takes me some time to free my swollen feet from them. When I do, my revulsion is a gnarled thing in my stomach.

They're grotesque.

I have painful blisters on the bottom, sides, and heels of my feet, thanks to my designer boots that were made for style, not comfort. The one on my right heel is the worst. The top layer of skin has already peeled away, and it's bleeding, while the nail on one of my big toes is black and blue.

I hesitate a moment—debating the prudence of stripping naked in a stranger's home—before shedding my peasant dress. It's ridiculously impractical for this climate, but it's not as if my stylist knew I'd be heading for Canada when she dressed me or that my plane would crash onto a snowy mountain.

Standing with my arms wrapped around my half-naked body, I spot a blanket thrown over the back of the leather sofa, so I take it and wrap it around me.

Looking around the cavernous space, I soak up as many details as I can. The small loft. The antler chandelier hanging from the ceiling. The crude workmanship tells me it's homemade. There aren't any picture frames to give me a clue about the occupants, but there are enough odds and ends to tell me someone had made this place home.

I look for a woman's touch, and my stomach twists with discomfort when I see none.

Maybe a kindly old widower lives here with his sons.

Yeah, I like that better than whatever scary version my mind can conjure. Why else would three grown men hole up in a cabin all the way out in the middle of nowhere? Nothing good, that's for sure.

Three tin cups rest among scattered bullets and oil-stained cloths on the low table, and a gasp escapes me when I see steam curling over the rim.

They were just here.

The men who lived in this cabin must have left mere moments before I appeared, and judging by the abandoned food, they left in a hurry.

Why?

The memory of snow—a huge fucking mass of it—rushing downhill toward Tyler and me flashes in my mind before I block it out.

Did the men who live here feel the avalanche? See it?

Tyler and I weren't far away when it happened, but I don't know if it's possible.

Reaching for the closest cup, I lift it from the table and tentatively sip the fresh coffee. Warmth instantly floods my veins and thaws my bones, but I make a face when my taste buds register the sugar.

Too sweet.

Setting it down, I reach for the next.

The cinnamon aroma soothes my sore nose before I take a sip, only to realize it's weaker than I like and a little colder than the first.

Grabbing the last cup, I drink from it and hum happily at my first taste of the hot—nearly scalding—brew.

It's not too sweet, tepid, or light.

It's just right.

Before I know it, the cup is empty, and I don't feel so close to death. My stomach rumbles, and I don't bother counting the hours since I last ate. I fall to my knees again and devour the half-eaten sandwich. I don't allow myself to wonder what the gamey-tasting meat is as it fills my belly.

The cabin quakes again as if telling me to hurry. I don't have much time before I'm caught trespassing.

I'm not ready to leave, so I chalk it up to paranoia and move closer to the fire once I've eaten all three sandwiches. I only need a few minutes, but as I sit and stare into the flames with the blanket around my shoulders, the minutes tick by without my realizing.

I don't even feel my eyes growing heavy until I nod off.

When it happens a third time, I accept that I'm safe for now and stand.

No one is going to walk through that door and find me anytime soon. My dress, still damp in places, is mostly dry and warm now from lying in front of the fire, so I put it back on. Harrison's coat, however, is thicker, so I leave it and Cassie's scarf in a pile on the floor.

I walk to the bank of windows below the loft, and the view I'm greeted with is… I hate it.

The cabin is built on the edge of a cliff. I know instantly why the mountain men chose this cliff. I can see all of the wilds from here, every terrifying inch and endless angles. From this vantage, it looks deceptively small, but I know all too well how easy it is to get lost in it. The valley and most of the foothills below are mostly hidden by thick, white mist, but I can see the tallest of the trees that rise above it and the outline of the smaller mountains in the distance.

I was in that.

I *survived* that.

It was terrifying at the time, but all I can think now is how much I want to burn it all down.

Forcing myself away from the windows before the thought can take root, I explore the rest of the house.

The kitchen is tucked away behind the dining room, but I find it easily enough. As I pass the dining table, I run my index finger over the unfinished wood. There's a deep gouge in the sanded oak that makes me pause.

Did someone *stab* the table?

The edges of the groove are rough and splintering, but when my curious gaze passes over the rest of the table, I don't see any more gouges.

"What...?" I rasp, but I don't finish.

My throat feels like I've been gargling gravel, so I continue my exploration into the kitchen, where I search the fridge and cabinets for water before realizing these people must drink water from the *tap*.

I shudder.

But I'm too thirsty to care for long.

I grab the only tin cup remaining in one of the cupboards and fill it with water from the faucet.

My first sip is tentative, and while it's not artesian, I'm surprised by how refreshing it tastes. Cool, crisp, and refreshing, like it was sourced straight from a spring. And most importantly, no weird aftertaste. A solid seven out of ten.

I gulp down several more cups since it's a small one before I'm finally convinced I won't die of thirst. Leaving the cup on the counter, I continue my self-guided and unsanctioned tour of the cabin.

There's a set of stairs by the front door that I missed when I broke in, but I ignore them for now as I finish exploring the first level.

The house is smaller than I'm used to, so I find the bedroom right away. I'm scratching my head over why anyone would ever *choose* this.

It's so *ugly* and sad.

Not the house—though it is hideous—but the drafty room I find myself standing in. There's a neatly made bed with four posters and a simple metal railing for a headboard, two nightstands, a trunk at the foot of the bed, and a chair shoved in the corner.

Prison cells are nicer than this. Begrudgingly, I make my way over to the bed and sit on the edge.

I give it a testing bounce, but the mattress refuses to yield. It's hard, rigid, and completely devoid of comfort—just like this god-awful room.

Maybe there's another.

I give the room one last disapproving sniff before I leave. Heading for the stairs, I cautiously descend them into a finished basement, and my eyes widen in alarm. A den of sorts takes up most of the space. There's a sofa, several punching bags, an array of weapons and a large map mounted on the wall, a metal locker, and some gym equipment.

Fighting the urge to run and take my chances with the wolves, I peek behind door number one and find a room with a farmhouse sink, floating shelves with folded linen on them, and a jute rope hanging taut between walls. I think it's a laundry room, but where are the washer and dryer? I back out of the room with a wrinkled nose.

Door number two has a full bath behind it.

My third try reveals another bedroom.

While the first bedroom barely looked lived in, this one looks like a tornado had ripped through it. The closet door is hanging on a single hinge, the bed is flipped over, the frame bent and twisted, the bedding shredded, and there's writing on the walls—in *blood*. The first two are alarming, but the last one I stare at and wonder about the person who wrote it.

Death to the immortals.

Bless the Savior.

The promise that it ends is what makes life beautiful.

The hair on my arms rise as I back out. I find a third bedroom on the other side of the den. Steeling myself for whatever I'll find, I poke my head inside the open door.

My shoulders slump in relief when I find a normal-looking bedroom.

I don't bother to take in the details this time as I rush inside and belly flop onto the four-poster bed with a groan. It's bigger than the others. A king, I think. Maybe larger. Whoever sleeps here must really like their space.

The mattress isn't too soft or hard, and it's in one piece.

It's just right.

Sighing, I flip over onto my back, and my eyes widen. "Oh, wow."

I hadn't noticed it before.

The canopy.

Short, twisted branches, no more than four or five inches thick, are nailed together in a random pattern and strewn with small lights that glow with warm light. I follow the branches to the posts and gasp at the images carved into the wood—bears, wolves, rabbits, birds, fish, foxes, and frogs. There are trees, rivers, snowflakes, leaves, sunshine, and wind.

Wow, just wow.

It's fanciful, like a fairy tale.

I'm still admiring the carvings when my eyelids start to drift shut. I know I can't fight the exhaustion, pain, and trauma from my ordeal much longer.

Rest. Reset.

Rest.

Reset.

I'm not sure how people pass their time in the wilds, but the cabin dwellers could be gone for hours.

Twenty minutes is all I need.

Just as it had the last three nights, I see the faces of those who died because of me—Cassie, Susan, Harrison, the two bodyguards whose names I still don't know, and…Tylers.

His face is the last I see before I succumb to sleep.

CHAPTER FIVE

THORIN

Khalil's the first to enter the cabin, with Zeke trailing behind him and me bringing up the rear. We silently shed our heavy coats and boots in the mudroom before we go our separate ways.

Something feels off, but I dismiss it for being gone longer than we planned. This morning, we'd been readying to set out and look for the survivors when an avalanche large and close enough to make our cabin groan in agony had us leaving in a hurry to investigate. The single male boot we found buried in the snow kept us searching for hours to no avail.

Zeke disappears downstairs to the basement to sulk, and neither of us goes after him. He needs the space to work his shit out, and since we can't keep an eye on him twenty-four seven, we learned to trust him not to do anything stupid.

Khalil stomps into the living room and beelines for the secondhand recliner with a permanent print of his ass. I'm about to head for the kitchen for a drink to warm my blood when I hear Khalil bark, "Yo, what the fuck?"

"If it's a spider, forget it," I call out as I enter the kitchen. "Man up and deal with this one yourself." I quickly locate the gin, but when I don't hear a peep from Khalil, I don't bother with a cup and carry the bottle into the living room.

Khalil's back is to me, so I can't see what startled him. I'm about to ask what his deal is when he slowly turns. There's a heavy winter coat clutched in his brown hand, but it's not one of ours.

Time seems to slow, and then it speeds up before I can process what it means. I snatch the coat out of Khalil's hand, but he doesn't seem to notice because something else catches his attention.

A pair of boots are by the fireplace, and a bloodstained scarf is lying next to it. The boots are small, too small for whoever this coat belongs to.

Whoever broke in is not alone.

I think about the tracks we found in the cave, and my gaze rises to meet my brother's.

Khalil's chest expands from the breath he takes.

"Someone's here," I say hoarsely.

Nothing else needs to be said. We race for the stairs at the same time. I reach them first, but I can feel Khalil hot on my heels as we make our way to the basement.

"Zeke!" Khalil calls.

He doesn't respond, and my heart is in my stomach, which is twisting and crumbling the dead organ to dust by the time we reach the den.

A shadow moves inside Khalil's room, so I bend and remove my handgun from my ankle holster. I creep toward the bedroom, clicking the safety off as I go. I can't see or hear it because Khalil is an apex predator, but I know he's doing the same.

The door is open, and one of the bedside lamps is on, so when I enter, I spot Zeke immediately.

He's still while he stares at the bed, and even though I can only see his profile, it's enough. The curiosity, the excitement, the mischief…

I inhale sharply.

He knows we're here, but he doesn't acknowledge us. It isn't until I'm brave enough to take my eyes off Zeke's body for even a second that I see what has his attention.

I almost forget the real threat in the room when I see her.

A girl.

There's a fucking girl.

She's passed out in Khalil's bed, her unkempt golden curls fanned out on his pillow. That ridiculous green and brown dress she's wearing makes her look like some kind of milkmaid in a porn rag. It's torn and filthy, but not nearly as much as my thoughts.

The girl obviously needs rescuing, and while my military training demands I answer the call, the darker side of me wants to be the thing she needs rescuing from.

The hem of her dress is bunched around her thighs, and my fingers curl, itching to touch, mark, and own that silky brown flesh. Her tits are spilling out of the torn white bodice, kept in place only by the embroidered corset.

She's dirty and probably terrified if she was foolish enough to wander where she's not wanted, but I still want to sink my teeth into her.

Her chest is moving up and down, so she's alive, which poses a problem.

Zeke's head slowly turns toward me, but the person staring back at me isn't my best friend.

I know that smile.

He looks like hell unleashed, like shit hitting the fan, like trouble on the horizon.

Seth.

Khalil impatiently edges around me and into his room when I continue to block the doorway. He's beelining for the closet to check for monsters when Seth speaks.

"I didn't know it was my birthday, boys."

Khalil stops dead in his tracks, his head slowly pivoting toward Zeke's body.

"The plane crash was a bit much, but I appreciate the surprise." Seth reaches out and curls Zeke's hand around the girl's ankle. She doesn't so much as twitch.

Jesus, she's out cold.

"It's not your birthday, and she's not for you." The hostility in my voice can't be shrugged away. Seth may look like my brother, but right now, he's my worst fucking nightmare.

"No?" Seth coos without taking his hand or eyes off her. "Shame." His hand slowly moves up her leg, curling around her calf. "I would have enjoyed playing with her."

Except there would be nothing fun or joyous about the games Seth likes to play—at least, not for this girl who helped herself to our cabin. We never considered needing a Keep Out sign, but I'm thinking about it now.

Maybe one that says Beware of Dog.

I've got the leash out and ready for Seth when his eyes flare wide with surprise. I watch as Seth pulls his hand back to examine the crimson coating his fingers. "Fuck, she's already broken."

My gaze searches her leg for a wound. "She's hurt?"

"Who gives a shit?" Khalil snaps. "Who is she?"

"How would I know? She's either lost or right where she wants to be. Either way, she's a problem." Khalil doesn't respond, but his expression twists as he stares past me, drawing my gaze back to Seth. "No, don't—"

Seth slips Zeke's bloody fingers between his lips and hums.

Khalil gags even as he walks over to the bed for a closer look at our trespasser. "Zeke, you know I love you like a brother, but you got to rein in the weirdness, man."

"She tastes like the sun."

Khalil's weirded-out gaze flicks to him. "Or not."

"He's not Zeke."

Khalil's frown deepens, and then he gives Ezekiel a careful once-over. He heard the variation in Zeke's tone and accent earlier but probably dismissed it.

Khalil isn't ignoring it now.

He takes in the new confident posture, the wildness in Seth's gaze that replaces Zeke's melancholy, and the dark hair now slicked back instead of shielding his green eyes before Khalil explodes.

"Aw, fuck. Fuck! FUCK! FUUUUUUCK!" Khalil takes an astonished step backward and then forward again. "Seth?"

Seth sketches a mocking bow. "Been a long time, bitches. Missed you."

Khalil just looks at me for an explanation.

I shrug a little too casually, considering shit just got exponentially worse. My head is already throbbing. "Zeke must have seen this bitch and split," I explain with a nod to the sleeping girl on the bed.

Khalil turns back in time to see Seth crawling onto the bed. He's already sneaking a hand up this foolish girl's dress.

Who the fuck does she think she is, letting herself in and making herself at home? This cabin and mountain are ours.

Khalil's reflexes are legendary, his aim precise as an arrow as he lunges, catapulting himself over the girl and tackling Seth off the bed. Khalil's arm rears back once they hit the floor, and then I hear more than I see the punch land. A rapid flurry of vicious blows follows.

"Zeke!" he calls in between punches. "Zeke, you fucking coward. Get out here!"

If only it were so simple.

Seth doesn't ever give up control of Zeke's body until he's good and ready. The only one who can make him is Bane, and that animal is an even bigger pain to deal with. Bane doesn't give a shit what problems Seth causes us as long as he isn't trying to hurt Zeke.

It's as convoluted as it sounds, but this is our life—a never-ending cycle of violence and blood.

My gaze unwillingly returns to the girl.

She has no idea what kind of hell she's walked into, but the moment she wakes her ass up, we're going to show her.

Isaac and his flock aren't the only reason we're hiding on this mountain. Zeke, Seth, and Bane don't do well around others, and we refuse to let the courts lock them up, so Khalil and I took our brother and fled.

"No can do," Seth taunts. His mouth is already filling with blood when he smiles sharply at Khalil. "Zeke's sleeping."

Beating Seth to a pulp will get us nowhere, so I walk over and wrestle Khalil off him. He hurls obscenities and threats as I put distance between them while Seth rolls onto his side and groans. I don't have to question if Khalil got in more than a few good shots.

But he's still no match for Bane, and we don't need him waking up if Khalil does too much damage to Zeke's body.

I shove Khalil to the other side of the room, back near the door, to keep them apart. Khalil wastes no time trying to put his fist through the wall. The only thing he succeeds in doing is splitting the skin around his knuckles. The moment he draws blood, I stomp over and snatch his hand away before the idiot breaks it.

Khalil shoves me away, and my spine smarts when I fly back and crash into the bedpost. The tides have turned, and we're glaring at each other now as we both try to remember why we can't tear each other apart. Unlike me, Seth won't bother trying to break it up. He'll gleefully watch us kill each other, so I quickly get my temper under control.

Khalil does the same.

"Fuck, it feels good to be free." Seth rises to his feet and stretches Zeke's muscles as if he's indeed been caged for months.

Six, to be exact.

The last time Zeke split and let one of his alters take over had been after a particularly bad nightmare—one terrifying enough to feel real. It had taken us weeks to force Seth back, and during that time, he'd nearly driven us all insane.

Hence Khalil's reaction to seeing him back.

"Yeah, well, don't get used to it," Khalil snarls at him.

Seth feigns a pout and then takes a bored look around the room. I see the moment his gaze catches on the cuffs still looped around the bedposts from the last time he visited us. For the first time, he looks nervous, casting a wary look at us.

I hold his gaze, silently communicating that we'll use them again if he steps even one foot out of line.

Seth snorts to save face and then returns his attention to the sleeping girl. "I see you two finally stopped being boring," he says coolly. "Who's the toy, and when can I play with her?"

"We don't know," I answer. "We just found her here, same as you."

Seth hums, the green in his eyes turning acidic as he stares at her. And then he reaches down to adjust his hard-on.

"Don't even think about it."

"Why not?" he challenges. Seth's amused gaze flicks over my shoulder, and then he's smiling like he knows something I don't. "I'm not the only one."

Frowning, I look for Khalil and see he's gravitated back to the bed again. He's got one arm resting on the canopy as he stares down at our mystery girl with this intensity that can only mean trouble. I can see him tracing her curves, making a road map of every one he wants to explore, and there are *plenty*.

Khalil Poverly is a legend back in the States and not just from his fighting prowess. He went to the same high school as us, bedding all the girls in our town—and the neighboring ones too—like it was his mission in life to fuck himself to death.

Going cold turkey had really taken its toll on him the most. It even got so bad he begged me for a hand job once.

I...don't want to talk about it.

"Stay focused," I snap.

I don't bother keeping my voice down either. The girl hasn't woken yet and probably won't anytime soon. The cabin could collapse around her, and she'd likely sleep through it. From the way things are going, that just might happen.

The idea of fighting my brothers tastes like ash in my mouth, but we don't need the trouble this girl will inevitably bring.

We need to get rid of her.

Khalil's voice is thick with lust when he speaks. "Look at her, brother."

"I've seen her."

I'm wound tight and feeling all kinds of exposed when he drags his gaze away from the girl to hold mine. "Then *look again* and tell me you don't want a piece."

I can't.

I've been so careful not to let my attention linger for that very reason. It feels like a trap for how tempting she is. How easily she calls to my baser instincts like a dog to a whistle. It's all too convenient how she just appeared out of thin air right when the three of us were splitting at the seams.

I know I shouldn't trust it, but my dick doesn't care. Spy or not, she's a warm, wet hole to get lost in.

Unable to resist the pull, my magnetized gaze is drawn back to the bed, and I don't look away this time. I drink her in like I'm dying of thirst, and she's an oasis in the middle of the desert.

Because she fucking is.

She's everything we've been silently craving. The only thing we've been without in nine long celibate years.

She's on her back, but her head is thrown to the side, exposing the graceful slope of her neck and hiding some of her face.

The half I can see pours liquid fire into my belly and hardens my cock.

Even with her eyes closed, she's fucking breathtaking.

And her body? Fuck me. I want to commit despicable acts to that body.

There's no recognition, but it doesn't calm the violence swirling inside, pushing me to punish her for finding us and stirring this storm inside of me.

Maybe if I explore all those curves, I'll uncover all her secrets.

Those wide hips, fuckable tits, and thick thighs would be a perfect place to start. She's more Khalil's type than mine, but those lips… Those plump, rosy lips were molded for fucking, and I can't look away. They're parted as she sleeps, and the soft snores that escape sound like moans to my horny ears.

Take it.

She wants it.

She's practically begging for it.

Mine.

I inhale deeply, but it's a mistake. Her scent fills my nose, and I groan. Her perfume or shampoo pollutes the air, mixing with her sweat and blood and lingering terror. It's fading, but it's there. Something inside me clings to it.

Chases it.

Wants it.

"Dibs on her ass," Seth blurts, breaking the spell.

Suddenly, I'm aware that I'm standing closer to the bed, my hand reaching for… I quickly lower it before anyone notices.

"How do you think she got here?" Khalil asks. He's all business once again—at least for now.

"She came from the sky," Seth answers reverently, and I groan. He's already obsessed, and we don't even know her name.

"Seth," I force out through gritted teeth. "She didn't—"

I stop myself when I remember the plane crash. I'm too used to dismissing the shit Seth spews as nonsense, but right now, it's the only thing that makes sense.

These mountains are mostly uncharted and closed to tourists for most of the year. No one else lives here or even comes this far up. It's too dangerous. We've been the only ones desperate enough to take our chances with the mountain rather than what's waiting for us the moment we step off it.

Wanting his thoughts, I look to Khalil. Feeling my attention, he finally tears his gaze away from the girl's tits long enough to shrug noncommittally before going right back to ogling her.

I'm pretty sure he's already worked out what position he wants her in first. As for how much he'll take before he's satisfied, there's no telling.

"All right. Well, whatever. We need to get rid of her," I announce firmly.

Both of their gazes snap to mine, and the sheer panic in them tells me that getting Khalil and Seth to see reason will be an uphill battle. And whenever it's two against one, blood is almost always shed.

"Why the fuck would we do that?" Khalil barks. "She looks so...so fucking *ripe*."

Ripe for fucking, he means.

And he will. Khalil always finds a way to charm even the sharpest of thorns. I don't know this girl's story, but I already know she doesn't stand a fucking chance.

"She's a gift," Seth whispers from my right. I turn my head toward him to see that he's inched a little closer to the bed. *Fuck.* "She's ours." He reaches a hand out for her, but my voice stops him.

"No." He looks at me and tilts his head in question. I shake mine and sigh. "We can't keep her, buddy. I'm sorry."

"Why?"

My lips part, but when no words come, I look to Khalil for help. He only cocks a brow at me.

Asshole.

Khalil's better at getting through to Zeke and his alters because while I'm more disciplined than him, Khalil is far more nurturing.

"She might be one of them," I remind these idiots. "She could be a spy for Isaac."

Seth stiffens and then backs away a step. I hate myself for it—using Zeke's trauma against him when Seth himself is a product of the horrors Zeke faced at his brother's hands. Seth being there for Zeke when we couldn't and taking his pain is the only reason we let him stick around.

At least for a little while.

"All the more reason to keep her here," Khalil retorts. "She can't tell him what she knows with my dick in her mouth."

My anger surges as I whirl on him. "Can you think about anything else?" I snap.

Khalil blinks at me and, with absolutely no fucks in his tone, says, "No."

"*Try*. And in case you didn't notice, she's a problem, not a plaything, Poverly."

"I can smell her pussy from here," Seth says rabidly.

The sheer hunger in his voice has me spinning around in time to see him climbing on the bed, his hand unzipping his snowsuit, and his gaze intent on the girl still sleeping soundly and blissfully unaware of the danger she's in.

I'm no one's goddamn white knight, and frankly, I don't give a shit what happens to her. I'm trying to shield my brothers from the fallout of biting into forbidden fruit.

I grab Seth's nape with one hand and his jaw with my other, and I don't bother with being gentle when I haul him back off the bed.

"I said no, Ezekiel."

"Not Ezekiel!" he yells. "Seth!"

"Fine," I concede, silently cursing my slip. "Seth."

"To reject this gift is to defy Death," he immediately babbles. "The Savior won't like this. He'll punish us. He'll—"

I've heard enough. "Keep that murdering nutcase out of your head and take your meds!" I roar.

"This is stupid," Khalil grumbles. "Why can't we do both? Use her and then get rid of her. Everyone wins."

I let Seth go to face Khalil.

"That may have worked back in the real world, but out here, women aren't lining up to fuck Khalil Poverly. There's only one. So, can you really do it? Can you use her once and then toss her, knowing it will be another nine years—maybe more—before you get another?" I lean in, my voice almost taunting. "If ever?"

Khalil's brown eyes glow possessively now at the thought of his new toy being taken so soon.

Behind me, Seth's breathing quickens.

I thought so.

"We both know Zeke can't handle it out there, and Isaac will never stop looking for him. We're trapped here," I remind them both. "It would be so easy to trap her too. We could talk her into giving up her sweet pussy, make her believe it's the only thing that makes sense, abuse that ridiculously lush body, and there's nothing she'll want to do about it. No one to hear how we make her scream. Nowhere she can turn to but us." My voice dips lower. "A few more days and what's left of that plane will be buried under snow until spring. No one will ever find her. You know they won't. This is *our* mountain." I can feel myself growing harder with every word, but I don't stop. God, I don't think I can. "So, can you really do it? Can you give that up? Give her up?"

Khalil drops his head and rubs a callused thumb over his torn-up knuckles. He gives himself away, though, when he steals another peek at our impudent intruder.

Khalil is a certified pussy fiend. A fighter and a lover.

One hit is all it will take to make him an addict.

"That's what I thought," I say smugly.

Khalil rolls his eyes and crosses his arms. "You made your point, asshole, but tell me this," he demands before I can give the order to dump her ass off the nearest cliff. "What exactly were you trying to accomplish with that little speech? Who were you trying to convince? Us to let her go? Or you to keep her?" Khalil's gaze pointedly falls to my crotch and the not-so-subtle hard-on I have for this girl.

"She goes."

"Sure. But we should probably question her first," Khalil suggests sarcastically. "See what she knows."

Questioning her means risking the chance that this spell of hers takes root. On the other hand, my male ego can't handle the idea of running scared from this slip of a woman.

"Fine. I'll do it and let you know what I find out. You two can go." I nod to the door.

Khalil's glower returns, and Seth begins his agitated pacing. "Why do you get to question her?"

"Because I'm the only one thinking straight."

"Yeah, Thor. I'm sure she'll tell you everything she knows with your boner in her face."

"It'll go down!"

"When?" he taunts. I want to wipe that smug look away with my fists. "I bet you're thinking about fucking her right now, aren't you? Admit it."

"The sun is rising," Seth cuts in, sounding uncharacteristically panicked.

Khalil and I ignore his useless babbling. "It's not enough that you're obsessed with your own dick, but you have to be obsessed with mine too?"

"Get the fuck over yourself," Khalil barks. "It was one hand job, and as I recall, *I returned the favor,* so you can just—"

The sudden rustling of sheets and movement from the corner of my eye shut us both up. At first, I assume it's Seth making a play for the girl again while I'm distracted. I'm mid-sigh when I realize he's frozen where I left him.

Oh, fuck.

I turn toward the bed in time to see the girl sitting up.

Her frostbitten arms are stretched wide above her head as she yawns. Slowly, her eyes open, revealing dark brown irises. She blinks one, two, three times, and then her gaze widens when she realizes she's not alone.

If I were capable of finding anything about this funny, I'd laugh at how the three of us are frozen like deer in headlights while this girl, easily half our size, takes her time assessing which one of us she'll eat first.

"You're here," she greets, and if her voice weren't filled with sleep, there would be no emotion at all. She speaks as if *she's* in charge. Fucking laughable. "It's about time. I've been waiting."

CHAPTER SIX

SETH | ZEKE

Fuck, she's perfect.

Thanatos, bless you, Savior.

Her gaze falls on Khalil first. No surprise there. He's not just the biggest physically but also has the biggest presence.

Picture a live wire—untamed and exposed—with untapped frenetic energy and nowhere to go, so he charges the air and everyone around him until they're as miserable as he is.

Khalil Poverly equals pretty plus an insufferable ass.

I try to see him through her eyes, as if he isn't Zeke's best friend and I haven't suffered his company for far too long.

Khalil is Black with semi-dark brown skin, warm brown eyes, and shoulder-length hair braided into plaits. At the moment, the top half of his braids are pulled up in a ponytail, showing off the sharp angles of his cheekbones and jaw and letting his full beard steal the show. Inevitably, though, the girl notices that a pretty face isn't all he's packing.

His broad shoulders and massive pecs are straining against his gray thermal. Zeke told me once that Khalil went pro right after high school and retired early as an undefeated champion. He also spent some time working for his dad's construction company. Needless to say, Khalil's body has been honed into a lethal weapon of mass distraction.

Despite the fact that Khalil wants to fuck her, his game face is on as he scowls at her. That lasts until her attention shifts to his arms. I nearly facepalm when that narcissist notices and flexes a little.

The girl doesn't seem intimidated by his brute strength. Instead, she nods once as if telling herself something or giving her approval.

Who *is* this girl?

She looks barely twenty but comports herself like a queen.

Fuck. Is she? Do I kneel? Call her Your Majesty? Swear a vow of eternal knighthood?

When her gaze travels to Thorin, I panic a little, knowing I'm next. I chuckle under my breath when she looks Thor over and moves on, dismissing him a lot faster than she did Khalil.

Thor's gaze narrows to slits, and despite the fact that he wants to murder her something bad, he's jealous too.

It's not that he isn't hot.

He looks like a Nordic god, for fuck's sake—flowing blond hair, blue eyes, a straight nose, high cheekbones, thin lips, pointed ears, and a prominent forehead. He's also the tallest and almost as big as Khalil. Thor's a real-life dreamboat with the personality of a wild boar.

Unlike the egomaniac, Thorin was a little *too* successful in scaring her. I can tell by the way her brown cheeks redden, and she subtly clutches her dress hem a little tighter.

I can't stop myself from standing a little taller when our gazes finally connect. She's everything to me, and I don't even know her name. I want her to like me. We could have so much fun together. Thorin and Khalil are so boring.

What does she see when she looks at me?

Or rather, Zeke.

He has olive skin, courtesy of his Portuguese mother, dark brown hair, and green eyes, courtesy of his Italian father. On his right bicep is a tattoo of a skeleton hand holding a new moon between the pointer and thumb and two smaller half-moons on either side.

Zeke's gained more muscle tone in the years since he defected, and as much as I don't care for Thorin or Khalil, I can't deny how much they care for him.

Despite my attempts to please the Savior, Zeke's punishments came often, and Isaac's favorite was starvation. Zeke had nearly withered away to nothing when Thorin and Khalil showed up and rescued him from the compound.

The memories of that place fade away when the sun speaks and I hear her voice for the first time.

"You're here," she says while tucking a loose curl behind her ear. "It's about time. I've been waiting."

If she's a spy for Isaac, then she's really bad at it. Khalil and Thor move closer to me while I move closer to *her*.

"Thanatos sent you?"

She gives me a slow, unimpressed blink. "Who?"

"Death."

"Riiight," she draws out slowly.

Ah, hell. I've freaked her out.

"He allowed you to escape him and find us," I can't help but say. "You must be very special."

Reaching for her hair, she casually frees it from the ponytail at the top of her head before tucking the tie between her teeth. "That's what they tell me," she retorts around it dryly.

Her golden curls, which have seen better days, fall around her shoulders and down her back. She shakes them out and makes a face when she brings a strand to her nose and sniffs. Glowering her displeasure, she grumbles to herself before starting the process of tying her hair up again.

"So then, you're here for me?"

"Uh-huh," she absently answers when she's finished gathering the huge mass of curls in her small fist and grabs the hair tie from her mouth with the other.

My heart races from excitement. If this girl is here, she must be a gift from him.

Thanatos hasn't forsaken me after all. Death is coming for me.

"Who are you?" Thorin demands when she doesn't say more.

I don't think any of us expected her to answer so quickly and without a fight.

"Aurelia." She waits expectantly as if anticipating some recognition or reaction. It's quiet and awkward for several moments. When she doesn't get the response she's expecting, she repeats slowly, "Au-re-li-a."

I think I hear an owl hooting in the distance.

"Are you suggesting we've met before?" Khalil inquires with a grimace.

It's Aurelia's turn to frown. "Surely, you've heard of me. 'You, Me, and Heartbreak'? 'Flowers in February'? 'The Lovescape'?"

I swing my gaze to Khalil, hoping he knows and can clue me in, but he bucks his eyes at me, silently telling me he's as lost as I am. Even Thorin has stopped scowling to stare at her like she has two heads.

"Are you...having a seizure?" Thorin questions.

"No." Thoroughly put off and confused, Aurelia starts fussing with her appearance again as if that would somehow help us recognize her.

"You said you were here for him." Khalil points at me instead of saying my name, and I know it's intentional. He doesn't want to confirm who we are until we know for sure that she's one of Isaac's. "Who sent you?"

"My uncle."

"Aurelia..." Thorin sighs impatiently. "Stop fucking around and tell us who your uncle is. You've got five seconds."

She looks amused, leaning back on her hands and tapping her feet together as she smirks at him. "Or what?"

I smile a little at her bratty response.

I have no idea if Aurelia is who she says, but one thing she can't fake is that she is a c-u-n-t.

I like her even more because I know she'll piss off Thorin and Khalil to no end.

Thorin leans forward to plant his hands on the foot of the bed while holding her gaze. "We show you why you picked the wrong cabin, Au-re-li-a."

Her chin lifts haughtily as she stares down the length of the bed at him. "If I picked the wrong cabin, it's because I thought civilized people lived here. Was I mistaken?"

"Very," Khalil answers.

"It will be your biggest mistake yet," Thorin promises.

Growing bored now, I yawn but don't chime in. If those two idiots want to piss off Thanatos, I won't stand in their way. They're Zeke's friends, not mine.

"Is he Isaac?"

"Who?"

"The so-called Savior," Thorin chews out. I don't think he's buying her wide-eyed confusion for a second.

The sheep in Isaac's cult would never dare call him or acknowledge his real name. I was one of those sheep. I didn't care much for Ezekiel's half brother, nor did I buy what he was selling about living forever, but I did find the idea of dying rather satisfying.

"Uhh, I don't know who that is either. I'm *Aurelia*," she tells us again. "As in the singer? America's sweetheart? The girl with the golden voice? I have twenty-three Grammys. Are you guys like…okay?"

Khalil steps forward, drawing her gaze. For the first time, she has the sense to look nervous as he curls his lip sarcastically. "You're humble too."

Aurelia returns Khalil's withering look. "Humble is for basic bitches who only have being liked going for them. I'm the shit, and I know it. Fuck you if that bothers you."

Damn.

"Okay, Aurelia, the singer, why are you here?"

"I'm in need of assistance," she says primly.

Something tells me she's used to getting her way. I sneak a glance at Khalil and Thorin, who are both watching her like they can't wait to tear her apart with their teeth.

I want the same but for different reasons.

Aurelia scares them, but she excites me. She makes me want to live, at least for a little while.

I feel a bone-deep need to ravage her soul as well as her body.

"I own some property not far from here. I think. A ranch near some hovel called Hearth. I was flying there for a little R and R when my plane crashed on this mountain. I don't remember most of it. Just the plane coming apart midair and then waking up in a tree."

"Were there other survivors?"

She pauses and then shakes her head slowly, almost reluctantly. I get the sense that she's neither being truthful nor deceptive. She doesn't know that Khalil, Zeke, and Thorin have been tracking her since the crash.

"I tried," she says brokenly but doesn't explain further. What had she tried? To find them? To help them? "We—I, um, looked for the tail, hoping to find the emergency transmitter, but I ended up here instead." Aurelia wrinkles her nose as if she finds the accommodations more inconvenient than the crash.

Of course, Thorin and Khalil don't miss the slight and bristle at her impudence.

I snort, and the sound draws her attention. When I smile and wink, she looks me up and down and then dismisses me just as quickly.

My gaze drops, and I rub at the tight feeling in my chest. I'm no stranger to pain, but this kind is a novelty. It feels like my—Zeke's—heart is breaking.

I wonder what they call it?

"So, you're alone?" I ask.

She stares straight ahead but doesn't look at me when she responds. "Yes."

"That must have been scary."

Aurelia gives me her attention once more, and this time, she doesn't look away. "It was."

"If you're alone, then whose coat did we find upstairs by the fire?"

"Harrison's."

Harrison? My brows dip. And just who in the hell is he? Her boyfriend?

Not for much longer.

I'll skin him alive if she so much as whispers his name again.

She's *mine*. Death spared her for me.

"He's my bodyguard."

Oh.

Well then, in that case, I guess I'll kill him quickly.

"He's dead," she clarifies.

"Thanatos has him then. He's making his final journey to the underworld."

Aurelia casts a bewildered look around the room. "Is there someone sane here, or do I need to find another cabin?"

"You could try," Thorin answers, "but we're the only ones who live in these mountains."

She doesn't look happy finding out that we're her only option.

Tough.

She's lucky she made it this far dressed like that. If the wolves didn't get her, exposure should have. Unfortunately, her luck ran out when she found our cabin.

Something else Aurelia mentioned pulls at me to act on it, and it sends blood rushing to my dick as I think about chaining her to that bed.

My gaze meets Thorin's and Khalil's, and I know we're all thinking the same.

Aurelia doesn't realize how far she's wandered. She doesn't know that she's not on the same mountain or that she knocked on the wrong door looking for rescue. She doesn't know that she gave three drowning men a life raft, and we'd be fools to let go.

"What are you doing this far north?"

"Reflecting and thinking," she responds with a sneer.

Thorin shifts uncomfortably. Nothing this girl does brings her any closer to convincing him she isn't an agent of Isaac's. "What the fuck does that mean?"

"It means I'm supposed to stay out of sight until no one cares that I pissed in their cornflakes. Because of who I am, I had to go really fucking far."

Clearly, it was a good plan because I still have no idea who this girl is. We're completely off the grid here. No Wi-Fi. No phones. No people.

It's perfect.

We tried normal for a time after Zeke was rescued, but it did not go well. I had no knowledge of the world beyond the Savior's sadism. Bane and I caused problems faster than Thorin and Khalil could solve them, so they brought us out here where we couldn't be a danger to anyone.

"So, what did you do?" Khalil prods like a gossiping whore. He sits on the side of the bed and leans back on his elbow. Aurelia tenses at his proximity, but when he makes no move to touch her, she relaxes.

Her instincts are shit.

Aurelia's smile is back, but it isn't a nice one. It's wrapped in barbed wire, just like the woman herself. And yet, all I can feel is jealousy. She's already smiling at Thor and Khalil but not me.

"I put a dumb bitch in her place."

That causes Khalil to raise a skeptic brow. "And that upset everyone?"

Aurelia scoffs and crosses her legs, meticulously arranging her ruined dress like she's about to take a photo. "I'd say it comes with the territory, but you can be an absolute nobody and still find yourself on the business end of a microscope these days. Everyone's either miserable, scheming, nosy, dramatic, or all of the above. I barely notice anymore."

Thorin starts to pace as he continues his interrogation. "So you had a disagreement with someone—"

"A *private* disagreement," she corrects.

"You had a private disagreement with someone, and it stirred enough outrage that you had to *flee* the country?"

She shifts guiltily. "Well, that's how it started, but then it escalated."

"How did it escalate?" Thorin demands like he really gives a shit. He's just looking for holes in her story—something to prove she's tied to Isaac.

"Wellllll…"

Khalil tickles the bottom of her foot like they've known each other forever. "Don't be shy," he urges when she jerks.

"I fucked her fiancé."

"Uh-huh."

"And her brother."

Thorin swears, and Khalil snorts while my dick perks with interest. She's mesmerizing. Thorin snaps out of our mutual astonishment first and shakes his head. "Jesus, Aurelia."

"It gets worse."

"*Do* tell," he invites dryly.

"She called *me* a whore because her fiancé can't keep his dick where it belongs, even after choosing to stay with him. Can you believe that?" Without waiting for an answer, she plows on. "So I fucked him again for the hell of it and sent the recording to her before I leaked it. Anonymously, of course."

"Of course."

"So I guess a good old-fashioned catfight is old news, huh?"

She wrinkles her nose. "*Old-fashioned* would be the key phrase there, Ragnar."

Thorin stops pacing at the odd name. "What?"

"Oh, nothing."

Meanwhile, I stare in awe at this vengeful delight. "Wow… Imagine if you'd stabbed her."

Aurelia stares into the distance like she wishes she had. "I know, right?" Sighing, Aurelia shrugs like she wasn't just imagining drawing blood.

"You still can," I whisper when she pouts over the missed opportunity. "I have a knife you can borrow…or I can do it for you?"

Aurelia cuts her gaze to me like I'm weird for offering.

I guess I am.

I'm also completely serious too.

"Can't." She releases a long sigh. "Apparently, being mean is out of character for me."

"They must not have met you," Thorin can't help but say.

She glowers at him but doesn't bother defending herself. Aurelia may be a ruthless bitch, but at least she owns it. It's quiet for a few moments as we think about the state of the world we left behind almost a decade ago. I was just getting to know it when Thorin, Khalil, and Ezekiel snatched it from under me.

"Anyway." She dismisses his commentary about her character with a roll of her eyes. We've no room to judge, nor would we. Thorin just likes to give people a hard time. I should know. "You got a phone or something? I need to call my uncle and let him know I'm okay." Tension fills the room again as the three of us stare back at her. "Helloooo?" She snaps her fingers when none of us jump to do her bidding.

Instinctively, my gaze flies to Thorin, and I can see it on his face. Aurelia is begging for a hard lesson in manners, and he's dying to be the one to teach it to her.

An idea starts to take shape in my already twisted mind, and I try to push it down. I don't want to break my new toy so soon, but then her torn sleeve falls farther off her shoulder, and my eyes are drawn to the curve of her breast.

Aurelia inhales deeply at that moment, unintentionally making her tits more prominent, and then she scrambles to fix her sleeve.

"What are you willing to do for our help?" Khalil asks before I can.

Fucker's always copying me.

Thorin doesn't try to stop him from setting his trap either. He gave in to his darker urges the moment Aurelia challenged him. He just isn't ready to admit it yet.

"Fine," Aurelia says with a huff. "I'll sign whatever you want. Now, can I use your phone?"

"Sure." We don't have a fucking phone. Only a radio for emergencies that she'll never get those dainty little hands on. "But you have to do something for us," I say as I step away from the window and closer to the bed.

"And it's not your fucking autograph," Khalil clarifies. He's growing impatient, waiting to end this interrogation so he can be balls deep inside her already.

Aurelia looks at us all in bewilderment. "I have to give you something just to make a phone call? Don't you have an international calling plan?"

Khalil opens his mouth, but Thorin beats him to it just in case he tries to pussyfoot around it. Khalil has a weakness for the opposite sex, while Thorin is all brute strength and no finesse. Sometimes, he forgets that every woman he meets isn't Annalise, his drug-addicted mother who treated him like shit before she died. In my very limited experience, I've found them to be a bit tedious and wishy-washy myself, but I don't pretend to hate them like Thorin does.

Besides, Aurelia's different.

Her soul is as wonderfully grotesque as mine.

"Our help doesn't come free." Thorin lays it out sternly. "If you want to stay, you'll have to earn your keep."

"Who says I *want* to stay?"

"Oh, you'll stay," Thorin says. Aurelia withdraws, and rightfully so. It sounds more like a threat than the prediction he probably intended it to be.

Aurelia narrows her gaze, and Thorin returns the silent "fuck you."

Khalil clears his throat, easing the tension a little. "So, check this out. Even if we could get the word out, the storm that took down your plane is just the first. We'll be buried up to our eyeballs in snow for the next few weeks, long after whoever gives a shit about you gives up."

Aurelia *really* looks nervous now, and I feel my lips curve as she says, "So, what are you saying?"

"You're stuck with us, Goldilocks."

"There must be some way—"

"There isn't." It's not until Khalil and Thorin both look back at me in surprise that I realize how harshly I spoke. My carefree nature is slipping with each reminder that she wants to leave. I can't help it. It's *pissing me off.*

Leave?

No, she just got here.

She can never leave.

Ever.

I feel myself becoming a little manic, but I don't realize how visible it is until Aurelia's expression shifts, and she starts looking around for an escape route.

"Seth." Hearing my name, I drag my burning gaze away from my heartless obsession and see Thorin and Khalil watching me warily. "Do you need a nap?" Khalil warns me on the low.

"No." My jaw tightens as I turn my head, looking away from them all.

I feel Aurelia watching me. I can feel her curiosity when she had so easily dismissed me before. I brave a glance and see that she looks confused, but if we do keep her, she won't be for long. I'll have to share her with Bane and Zeke and probably these two assholes, whom I hate the most.

"Getting you down won't be possible until spring," Khalil bullshits her. I clench my teeth but force myself to remain silent. I'm all for trapping her here with us, but I know all too well what it's like to be controlled with lies. It *sucks*. "The mountain is too volatile this time of year. We can keep you alive until then, but—"

"Spring?" Aurelia sputters. "That's weeks away! I can't stay here with three creeps in a hovel until then. You could be murderers." *Definitely so.* "Serial killers." *Not enough motivation.* "Rapists." I almost snort at that. *Like she'd say no.* "No, you need to do better. I have to get out of here. I have a *life*. I don't belong here."

I swear this spoiled, gorgeous, infuriating fucking girl...

"You're welcome to leave anytime you want," I lie. "But you won't get far. Not dressed like that and not without knowing where you're going."

"I got *this* far," she shoots back.

I can't argue with her there.

Unless...

She's not one of Isaac's, that's for fucking sure. Aurelia's no sheep. She's too headstrong.

But there are some missing parts of her story that could hit us between the eyes later.

While it's not impossible that she survived that crash, she did with barely more than a few scratches. And then she crossed the Cold Peaks and all of its unforgiving wilds to find us. If Aurelia is who she says, then this pampered princess couldn't have done it alone.

"And you probably almost died, right?" Khalil points out. "A few times,

I'm willing to bet. The only access road into town is already closed off for the season, which means the only way down is on foot or by air, sweetheart."

"Okay? And?"

Thorin rolls his eyes. "You made a mistake coming this far south. You were closer to town where you crashed. It's too far to hike in this weather, Aurelia. You'll die from exposure before you even make it halfway."

"That's if the wolves don't get you first," I add with no pleasure.

Okay, maybe a little. Anything that binds her to us gives me a sickening amount of gratification. The tighter her shackles become, the more euphoria I feel.

Aurelia's brown complexion turns a sickly gray at the mention of wolves. She actually looks like she's going to cry for a moment, but then something happens that feels uncomfortably familiar.

Aurelia rallies, and then her woe is gone in a blink. She's poised and looking nothing more than put off once more, but the mask doesn't quite fit.

Yeah, this girl is definitely off her rocker. It's breathtaking.

"Fine," she agrees with her nose back in the air. I watch her look around the room and can see the gears turning in her head. "I'll take this room. I saw the others, and this is the least objectionable."

My stomach turns as I wonder if the carnage Bane and I left Zeke's room in is still there.

Thorin cocks his head to the side. "We haven't decided you can stay yet."

"But you said—"

"That you need to earn your keep," Khalil interjects. "Starting now."

"Fine. So what do you want? A picture?"

"Will you be naked in them?"

"Only in your wildest dreams, pervert." An uncertain pause follows, and then she asks, "Money?"

"We're in the middle of nowhere, and unlike you, that's on purpose," Thorin points out. "Does it look like we care about money?"

The string of tension between us grows taut, and then Aurelia snaps. "Well, that was a fun game, but I'm over it now, so tell me what the fuck you want already."

Stepping up to the plate, I ask, "Can you cook?"

Aurelia perks up. "I make an amazing cocktail."

Thorin sighs like he's exhausted with her already. "Clean?"

"You're joking, right? That's what the help is for."

"Hunt?" Khalil inquires with a grunt.

"Sorry. Cassie does the fetching." Aurelia's lips flatten, and then she grumbles, "At least she did until she went and got herself killed." No one bothers to ask who Cassie is as her gaze falls on the scarf Khalil absently left on the bed. She reaches for it and pulls it into her lap, where she cradles it. Interesting.

"Well, what can you do?" Khalil asks impatiently.

That infuriating nose of hers goes back in the air again. "I told you already. I sing."

"What do you sing, Aurelia?"

"Seriously, you *don't* know who I am? Princess of Pop? Empress of R&B?" She huffs when we all give her blank looks. "The girl with the golden voice?"

My brows shoot up. "They call you that?"

"Yup."

"Well then," Khalil says, "there's really only one thing left that you can offer us."

"Tell you you're pretty?" She gasps a second later, backing away when Khalil trails a finger over her knee, only to realize that I'm already taking up space on the other side of the bed.

Khalil's lounging on his side, and when she backs away from me—already forgetting he's there—Khalil curves his hand possessively around her bare thigh.

Aurelia stiffens when his grip tightens.

Jesus, how the fuck did she make it all the way here dressed like that? It had to be sheer will or dumb luck alone.

Aurelia starts scooting away from us both—toward the headboard. She doesn't see the cuffs and thick chain hanging from it.

"Mmm… That might help," Khalil purrs.

Instead of going for the rope to subdue her, he grabs her ankle and *yanks*. Aurelia's forced onto her back once more while Khalil sits up.

The promise of her pussy is already clouding his head.

I'm not much better.

Aurelia shoots up onto her hands, her gaze bouncing between us as she tries to find the weakest link.

An ally.

Her fearful gaze travels to where Thorin is still in the same spot—in front of the dresser by the window where he'd moved to at some point to be within arm's reach of me.

"What's your name?"

His brows rise. "Excuse me?"

"Your name. None of you told me your names."

Thorin smiles as he crosses his arms and leans against the dresser. She's trying to stall, but he'll play along.

"Thorin," he offers.

"Khalil."

"Seth." I watch her lick her lips and feel my pants grow tighter around the crotch.

"Okay. Thorin," she says, testing his name. "I'm feeling very uncomfortable."

"Oh?" he says, and Aurelia nods quickly. "Well, imagine how we felt finding a stranger making herself at home in our cabin."

"Okay. Okay, that was wrong, but that doesn't mean you should hurt me." She snatches her arm away when I trail a finger down it.

I sigh. "It doesn't have to hurt, Sunshine, but that's up to you."

"Just be a good girl for us, and we won't have to," Khalil coos. He slips a hand under her dress and glowers when Aurelia shoves it away.

"But you will...hurt me?"

Aurelia's mask is gone, and her eyes are filling with fear. The air is sweet with it. I bet her tears taste delicious. Her blood was certainly divine.

My gaze drops to her breasts, and I smirk when I see her hard nipples pushing against the bodice. "Do you want us to?"

"What kind of question is that? Of course not!"

Khalil reaches out and places a hand around her neck. He's not squeezing, but there's a flare of panic in her eyes anyway—especially when he applies pressure, forcing her to lie back onto the mattress again. "Cabin rule number one, show us some *fucking respect*."

"Get your hands off me!"

"Cabin rule number two," I say as I shed my shirt, "we own you, Sunshine. And yes, that can go both ways…if you want it to."

"Stop it!" she screams when Khalil starts tearing free the laces holding her dress together. She tries to fight him off, but she's no match. She can't stop us from looking at her body.

"Don't be afraid," I plead gently.

"Don't fight us, and we'll be nice," Khalil just has to say.

I don't see Aurelia's fight response kick in, and neither does Khalil. The moment her dress falls open and her gorgeous tits are exposed, the three of us are transfixed by the sight of her brown nipples puckered and ready for our attention.

We're mesmerized, and Aurelia uses our distraction to slap the shit out of Khalil and scramble past me. I snap out of it first and grab for her, but I swear my hard cock is weighing me down. I'm too slow.

Aurelia tumbles onto the floor, but she's back on her feet in a flash, holding her dress together as she makes a break for the window.

CHAPTER SEVEN

AURELIA

It feels like they're pushing me, leading me into a trap that I can't see, at least not until it's too late.

"Don't be afraid," the mad one says.

The look the other two give me tells me all I need to know. Fear may be the only card I have to play here.

The baleful one confirms it when he taunts, "Don't fight us, and we'll be nice."

I'm too stunned by the thinly veiled threat to stop Khalil when he works the top of my dress open. Even though they're mean and a little terrifying, the part of me that desperately wants to forget this hellscape I'm trapped in is tempted to give in.

Men like this don't exist in the real world.

They don't have deep, rough voices like gravel, strong jaws, and smoldering intensity. They certainly don't hang on to your every word while looking at you as if they're seconds from tossing you over their shoulder and carrying you back to their cave.

No, the men where I'm from have podcasts and the attention span of a gnat. They can barely bench-press a chair and think it's a woman's responsibility to make them feel like a man.

Thorin, Khalil, and Seth.

God, they look like villains. They look like every father's worst nightmare.

When I first woke up and found them standing over me, I thought I was still asleep and dreaming, but they are very much real.

My attraction to each of them is wildly different.

Khalil feels like this hot, writhing, angry gale that will sweep me up if I get too close. Thorin feels like a cold, phantom grip around my spine that threatens to paralyze me if I don't obey. Seth feels like my demons are wrestling with his and *losing*.

The fact that I want to know more weirds me the hell out.

I'm not proud of my attraction to these mountain men. It's an instinctual, impulsive thing that is no less devastating than flying too close to the sun and getting burned. Or wandering into a black hole, lost to it forever, trapped in their darkness and mine.

These men don't want to help me. They want to hurt me. But how much? More than I can take or just the right amount?

God, I need help.

Clearly, coming here was a mistake. Tyler would call me reckless, but what else was I supposed to do? I'm only alive because of him. I wouldn't last a day out there on my own. The thought paralyzes me long enough for Seth to get his shirt off and Khalil to get my dress open.

I snap out of it the moment I feel the cold air in the room breeze across my hard, *bare* nipples.

God, they weren't bluffing.

These men aren't trying to scare me into leaving and forgetting they exist. Khalil, Seth, and Thorin expect me to pay for their hospitality…with my body.

It isn't intentional when I rear back and slap Khalil for his aggression, but I'm not sorry, and I don't hesitate to take advantage of his shock.

Seth is still wide-eyed and salivating like he's never seen tits before, so getting past him is easy. In my haste to get away, I fall off the bed more than climb, but I've gotten some practice getting back up when I'm knocked down.

I'm back on my feet and backing toward the window.

It's closer than the door and my best chance at escape—*if* I really want to. But it's guarded by Thorin and he really wants *me*.

He's trying to pretend he doesn't, but it isn't really working for him. Oh, he hates me for sure. Hates me for being here. Hates me for turning his friends into rabid dogs—as if it's my fault they're creeps. But the way his gaze tracks me to the window is too focused and too territorial to be indifferent.

Thorin doesn't make a move to stop me as I reach the unlocked window and shove it open. The cold that rushes in nearly makes me reconsider. I could take my chances with the mountain men, but they're scarier than certain death, so I lift one leg to climb out.

An arm locks around my waist, and I'm lifted off my feet.

"Noooo! Let me go!"

"Calm the fuck down."

Thorin.

He grunts when I continue to struggle. I'm kicking and scratching and punching, but he acts like it's no more than a bee sting as he carries me away from the window. "Exactly, where were you planning to go, Aurelia? We're on a fucking cliff."

Oh.

He stops by the dresser again, where he sets me on my feet but quickly pins me against it. I grit my teeth when the knobs and edges dig into my back, but Thorin's hand on my shoulder keeps me there.

"Get your fucking hands off me! Do you know who I am?"

"Yeah, you're a trespasser and a rude one too." Thorin grabs my jaw, and his grip isn't gentle. "I can't imagine why, but my brothers want to fuck you," he says, making my cheeks blaze with shame while my stomach twists with nerves and want—especially when I see that Khalil and Seth are hovering nearby, and the only thing keeping them from tearing me apart is Thorin. He moves his face closer, blocking them from view, and I have to be careful not to move lest our lips meet. "Are you going to stop acting like you're too good and give them a piece of that sweet ass or not?"

I spit in his face.

"Ah shit," I hear Khalil grumble.

The dead look Thorin gives me says I'll live to regret it for the rest of my life. Swiping a hand across his face to remove my loogie from his nose and cheek where it landed, he slaps that same hand over my mouth and nose, and I scream my rage into his palm.

I don't realize his true intent until I feel a desperate need to breathe, and he won't let me. He keeps his hand in place, even tightening his hold when I shake my head back and forth, trying to free my face.

Oh my God.

He's going to kill me.

No sooner do I think it than he finally releases me. I've barely managed to suck in a single breath when he grabs my nape and starts forcing me forward.

Khalil and Seth follow but don't intervene when we leave the room. I don't fight Thorin, assuming he's letting me leave the cabin, but when he pushes me left, toward the double doors, instead of toward the stairs on the right, I panic and try to backpedal.

"What are you doing?"

"Giving you one last chance."

Reaching around me, he opens one of the doors, and all I feel is wind. A cold, unforgiving gust that barrels inside the cabin and threatens to turn me into a block of ice. I swear the deafening roar shakes the very foundation of the cabin. Outside, I can see that there is a deck. It hangs over the cliff's edge while the mist rises from the steep depths below to curl on the floor's wooden planks.

"Are you going to be reasonable?" Thorin whispers close to my ear. "It's only fucking. You've done it for revenge. Why not for survival?"

Maybe I don't want to survive.

My teeth are already chattering, but I have a feeling the shivers quaking my bones have nothing to do with the cold and everything to do with his proposal. "You w-want me to h-h-have sex with you—all three of y-you—for sh-shelter. How is th-th-th-that fair?"

"You're an extra mouth to feed, and the winters are long here. We could have a few more weeks before the passes clear or a few more months. We already have everything we need to survive. Everything except something warm and soft to make it all worth it."

"E-ever h-h-heard of a b-blanket?"

"Nine winters, Aurelia," Khalil tries to reason from behind us. "That's a long time."

Seth is quiet, but I know he's there.

"My brothers are hungry." My stomach flips when I feel Thorin butt his face against mine, pressing our cheeks together when he whispers, "Are you going to feed them or not? They need this."

"Not..." *God*, it's so fucking cold! It's only been a few hours, but I'd forgotten already "My p-p-problem."

"You're right. It's not," Thorin says in a deceptively soft voice. His hand shifts to the small of my back while his nose skims my neck. I'm staring down certain death when he inhales deeply. "See ya."

Without hesitation or care, Thorin shoves me over the threshold and out into the cold.

CHAPTER EIGHT

KHALIL

In case it isn't already clear, I think I should clarify something.

We are not good men.

Maybe we were once, but to survive out here, we had to give the mountain something in return.

Thorin came around like I knew he would. It probably happened when he got a whiff of the wilds mixing with her fading scent—peaches and daffodils.

The latter makes the most sense now that she's conscious. Aurelia has this dual personality thing going on. She can go from delicate and sweet to spicy and bitter without anyone being aware of when it happened or why. Although, it's said daffodils represent rebirth and new beginnings along with joy and good luck—none of which she'll find here.

And then there are peaches, which are said to smell the sweetest when they're ready to be devoured.

I can't get a fucking read on her, and it should frustrate the hell out of me, but the truth is that I don't care what she's really like. It doesn't matter if she's a good person or the devil incarnate. There's only one thing I want from this girl who literally fell from the sky, and it's not her charm.

I'm going to fuck the shit out of Aurelia, and I prefer for her to be on board so we can both enjoy ourselves.

Thorin meets my gaze as he turns from the doors of the deck, and I know we're both thinking the same thing. A few hours out there ought to be enough to make that stubborn wench *run* into our arms.

Thor keeps going, grabbing Seth's arm and dragging him out as they leave the den and head upstairs. I spare one last glance at the deck door and Aurelia's shadow on the other side.

Despite the fact that she tried to escape us, Aurelia pounds on the door, begging to be let back in. I wish I could say I don't give her another thought, but as I close myself inside the bathroom, strip off my clothes, and step into the shower, her face—fuck, that *body*—is all I can think about.

When I take my dick in my hand, I don't even try to deny that it's because of her. Aurelia is, without a doubt, the sexiest, most infuriating woman I've ever met.

"God," I strain to get out when I feel my balls tighten, "*damn* you."

My knees weaken the moment my dick finishes spurting cum on the shower tiles. I take my time showering the day off my skin, and when I step out and look in the mirror, I can still see Aurelia's handprint on my cheek.

I wonder what other marks she'll leave.

Ignoring the incessant pounding coming from the deck, I grab some sweats from my bedroom and then make my way upstairs. When I reach the kitchen, I walk in on Seth with his mouth open wide and Thorin peering inside. There are several pill bottles and a half-empty glass of water resting on the counter next to them.

I see another cup on the other side and walk over to inspect it. Thorin is already watching me and shakes his head at the questioning look in my eyes.

"She really made herself at home, didn't she?" I say with more amusement than the situation calls for. We still don't know if she's telling the truth, and with no way to verify…

Well, we can't let her go until we know for sure, can we?

I don't try to fight my smile or hide it. Whistling, I make my way to the fridge, where I take out the rabbit meat I left inside to thaw. If I'm stuck up here for God knows how much longer—until Zeke gains control of his alters or his brother keels over—then a little entertainment is needed desperately, or I'll implode.

"She ate our food from this morning too," Seth helpfully supplies.

"Shut up and stick out your tongue," Thor orders grumpily. The dude seriously needs to be fucked more than the rest of us.

Seth does as he says and waggles it at him.

My chest tightens at seeing him be so playful. It's not unusual for

Seth—though his brand is more mocking since he hates us—but it's just that Zeke used to be playful too. The class clown, if you will. And even though Zeke is adamant that he and Seth are not the same, sometimes it's easy to confuse him with the friend I remember.

Maybe there's hope for Seth yet, or maybe *we're* the problem—Thor and me.

Once Thorin sees that Seth's taken his meds, he storms off to his room. I hear him return minutes later and leave the cabin, slamming the front door behind him. I know he's planning to take his restlessness out on the doe he caught a few days ago, not the one that's currently marooned out on our deck.

Thorin has always been a moody son of a bitch, but these days, he stays prickly.

And yet, he can't see that the cure is literally beating down our door.

Seth also leaves to go sulk in his room when I tell him that Aurelia has to stay outside a little longer. While the two of them act like bitches, I start dinner since it's my turn tonight. Eventually, the smell of burning food and the sound of me cursing lures my brothers from their hiding places.

I can smell the dead deer on Thor, and one look from me has him pivoting on his heel before he can step one foot inside my kitchen. He heads for the shower while Seth sneaks over to the wood-burning stove and sticks his finger in the pot of stew. I send a jab to his ribs, but he dodges it, dancing out of reach with his finger in his mouth.

"Mmm, overcooked and flavorless," he hums. "Your specialty."

"Laugh all you want," I tell him, "but you just lost dessert."

Seth scoffs as he reaches for the bowls in the cabinet next to him. "Fruit is not a dessert, or so I'm told. Your training days are over, dick. Live a little."

Ignoring him, I partially close the air vent on the stove so that the wood burns a little slower while keeping the cabin warm. I then reach for the bowls Seth set out on the counter, filling each of them with the rabbit stew, but I pause when I see there's a fourth one.

I glare at Seth, who is watching me out of the corner of his eye while he drowns his portion with salt.

"We're not feeding her."

"Why not?" he immediately demands, setting down the salt. "We have plenty."

"Actually, we don't," I remind him. "Our extra stores are for emergencies, not some entitled little songbird who made herself our problem."

"Sounds like an emergency to me," Seth mumbles.

"If Aurelia wants food, she can earn it."

"Fine. Then she can have mine." Seth storms out of the kitchen, passing Thorin as he goes before I can argue.

There's a towel draped over Thorin's wet hair while sweatpants cover his legs. "What's up with him?"

"Nothing. Seth's being rational for once and couldn't have picked a worse time to be the sane one. We'll be waiting on that girl hand and foot if he has his way."

Thorin says nothing as he grabs his bowl and starts eating while leaning against the counter. If I didn't know better, I'd think he was secretly on board with the idea. His face is carefully blank, which means he's more affected by Aurelia's presence than I thought.

We don't hide from one another, so if he's keeping his thoughts to himself, it must be bad.

"How much longer do you think she has out there?" I can't stand the silence.

It takes me a moment more to realize it's a little *too* quiet.

I don't hear Aurelia banging on the deck door anymore. And then I remember Seth's last words before he stormed out. My gaze flies to where his bowl of stew should be, but the counter is empty.

Fucking Seth.

I put down my dinner and leave the kitchen.

Unsurprisingly, Thorin follows, still slurping his rabbit stew like he doesn't have a care in the world. He never seems to mind how awful my cooking is, but I'm sure it has to do with him suffering worse when he was a Marine.

Together, we quietly descend the winding stairs into the basement, and soon after, I hear voices speaking low.

Thorin and I pause at the bottom of the stairs.

From here, we can see Aurelia dusted with snowflakes and shivering violently on the sofa where she and Seth are sitting closely. There's a heavy blanket around her shoulders, and Seth has a fire in the woodstove burning already while Aurelia clutches his bowl of rabbit stew. She's pretending she doesn't feel him playing with her hair and staring at her like an obsessed maniac, but every so often, she shifts a little farther away, and he follows.

"Are you sure you don't want to stay?" Seth asks as he leisurely twirls a curl around his finger. "We could have fun together."

"Thanks, but I'd rather be two ships passing in the night."

"What about a train wreck?" Seth's dumb ass retorts. "I hear those are fun."

"Where did you hear that?"

"On second thought, that might have been a roller coaster."

Feeling Aurelia's astonishment, I curse under my breath. I have a feeling explaining the horde living inside Zeke's head with our already terrified guest is coming sooner rather than later. "You've never ridden a roller coaster?"

Seth shakes his head with a melancholy look in his eyes, and I can't tell if it's real or an act. Either way, it's so convincing that I almost feel sorry for him until I remember that time he tried to set me on fire. The only reason he hasn't forced us to tie him up again is because of *her*.

Seth's too distracted by the novelty that is Aurelia to bother with trying to kill us. We still don't know why he doesn't like us. He just doesn't and refuses to explain.

"You should," Aurelia suggests almost affably. "I haven't been on one since I was twelve, but I remember liking it. The best part is stuffing yourself with enough junk food in between rides that you want to puke while you're on one."

"Really?"

"Mhm." Aurelia lifts the bowl and slurps some of the stew. I don't think she notices the taste. The warmth it provides is enough to satisfy her after being stuck on the deck for over an hour.

"I think I'd like that," Seth says slowly. "But I don't think I'll need a full stomach to puke."

Aurelia makes a face. "Really? Why?"

"I'm afraid of heights."

But Zeke isn't. In fact, Zeke's a bit of an adrenaline junkie, something Seth didn't inherit. It's the strangest thing how they occupy the same body and possess the same mind but are wildly different.

Seth hates height, while Zeke would backflip off a bridge if you bet him five bucks.

Zeke is horrible at math, while Seth is damn near gifted.

Seth is convinced he wants to be a fucking rapper, while Zeke prefers alternative metal and indie rock.

Zeke loves broccoli, while Seth will gut you for even suggesting he eats it.

The list goes on.

"That does pose a problem," Aurelia says.

"You could come with me and hold my hand," Seth suggests. "Make sure nothing happens to me." Aurelia doesn't respond, but it's kinder than the answer I'm sure she's thinking.

I would have wagered Seth didn't stand a chance of wooing this girl or any other because he hasn't had the practice, but I was wrong. While Aurelia is wary of Seth, waiting for him to pounce and demand payment for rescuing her from the deck, her claws aren't out.

She seems as curious about him as he is about her.

When Seth realizes Aurelia isn't going to answer him, he lets her finish the stew in silence. "Want some more?"

"Are you sure Moe and Larry would approve?"

"I guess that would make me Curly, huh?"

"Seriously? You know who the Stooges are but have never been on a roller coaster?"

"I got a crash course in the classics when I left the Seeds of the Undying."

"The what?"

"It's um...where I was born."

"Oh." Aurelia frowns but thankfully doesn't pry—likely because she doesn't give a shit.

"So, more stew then?"

"Thank you, but no. If the only currency I have to offer in this hellhole is my body, I'd rather starve."

Seth stares at her for a while, and I already know what he'll say before he shakes his head and turns it to stare into the fire. "Then you don't know what it's like to be hungry, Sunshine. Not really."

"Look," she says coolly. "It's not my fault I don't have anything else you and those creeps-in-arms want, okay? All I have is my voice. It's all I know. All I've ever been allowed to be."

Next to me, Thor slurps his stew…*loudly*.

Before I have a chance to hide and pretend I haven't been eavesdropping, Aurelia and Seth's gazes snap toward us. Only Aurelia looks surprised to see us standing here.

"So, sing us something, songbird."

Aurelia's lips part at Thorin's demand. "What?"

"I want to hear the voice that made you such a big deal." A bratty little bitch is what he doesn't say.

She thinks about it for a moment—too fucking long considering the alternative—and then a cunning gleam enters her eye. "Sorry, but I don't sing for free. If you want me to perform, you've got to earn it."

"You're fun," Seth praises like their best fucking friends. "What's your fee?"

"For a private show?" She taps her chin and pretends to think about it. "How about a million dollars?"

"How about another bowl of stew and a bed for the night?" Thorin counters with a sneer.

"Just one night?" Aurelia sputters.

"We haven't heard you sing."

It's a reasonable offer and better than we'd give anyone else—which is a bullet to the brain—so imagine my surprise when Aurelia says no almost immediately.

"Why the fuck not?"

"Because I said you'd have to earn it, not pay for it. Because you're all swine, and I don't like you very much. You don't deserve to hear me sing. You deserve to be *neutered*."

Before I realize my feet are moving, I'm across the den and gripping her golden curls in my fist. I yank her up and over the back of the couch while she screams before turning her around to face me. "I'm getting really sick of your shit, you ungrateful brat."

She glowers back up at me. "You're pronouncing it wrong. My name's Au-re-li-a. And what exactly would I have to be grateful for? You expect me to fuck for watery stew and a hard bed with scratchy sheets. I'm *Aurelia*. I don't bend for anyone, so decide what you're going to do about it and take it up with management, pumpkin."

"Excellent advice."

I shove her away, and she stumbles right into Thorin's arms. He catches her, and I hold my breath as I wait for him to decide. Will he finally admit he wants her, or will he continue to pretend he hasn't been hard ever since we found her?

"Take your hands off me, and I'll think about forgetting you exist when I'm rescued."

"It's unlikely," Thorin returns.

"I swear on my parents' graves—"

"I have no doubt you'll try to forget us, but it's unlikely you'll ever succeed, Au-re-li-a."

Thorin brings her closer and then closes his eyes as he buries his nose in her neck. He inhales deeply, and his next breath rushes out so harshly that Aurelia releases a terrified whimper. I'd bet my left nut she can feel his ire and desire skating over her bare shoulder and down her spine.

She pushes against his chest to get away, kicking, punching, cursing, and growling. Aurelia's giving him everything she has, and while she's fierce, it's not enough.

Shushing her, Thorin palms the back of her head and presses it into his chest. I can see the answer in his eyes the moment he opens them and meets my gaze. For years, Thorin tricked himself into thinking he likes his women soft and pliant, but this is what he really needs—someone he can bend just to the point of breaking, someone who *will* break and then ask for more.

He shifts his hold to Aurelia's waist like they're lovers, but she's too busy scouring her nails down Thorin's bare arms to notice Seth and me tightening the kill circle.

"Looks like we're going with door number two, boys."

CHAPTER NINE

THORIN

Turning Aurelia around until her back is to my chest, I hook an arm around her neck. Her hands fly up the moment I tighten my hold, gripping my bicep and forearm. It's foolish to waste all her strength fighting me when she's going to need it. Aurelia stubbornly tugs at my arm, and when force fails to free her, she resorts to pain, digging her sharp nails into my skin.

God, it makes me harder.

"Let me go," she chokes out, although sounding a bit breathy.

"We tried to do this the easy way, but I'm starting to think you like it rough." I grab one of her hands and force it between our bodies. "All you had to do was sing for us, songbird." I press her palm firmly against the hard ridge trapped by my sweats. Aurelia muffles her disgust at the last moment, denying me the satisfaction. My dick feels like it will snap in half if I don't get off soon. "What do you think, boys? Should we give her what she wants?"

I look at Khalil and then Seth. The latter is practically bouncing from excitement. If it were up to me, I'd choose someone with fewer claws and teeth for Seth's first time with a woman, but it's not like we have options. And even if we did, he'd still choose her. Seth would beg to bleed for her.

I shove her into him, and he catches her. "Gonna give it to her good," Seth promises.

She goes to Khalil next. He catches her by the neck and plants a kiss on her lips. Aurelia squeals and tries to turn her head this way and that, but Khalil follows her, keeping their lips connected until he's good and ready. When he breaks the forced kiss, he stares down at her like someone standing over a buffet after a years-long fast. "I thought you'd never ask, Goldilocks."

When he shoves her toward me, I don't try to catch her.

I let her fall to her knees at my feet and wait while she stares at the floor for a moment, her entire body trembling as she tries to find a way out of this. I don't let her think for long before I grab Aurelia under her arms and haul her back to her feet.

"The answer is no. There's nothing you can do or say to change our minds. You're ours until we're done with you. Do you accept?"

There's disdain in her eyes when they search mine. I expect tears, pleas, or even an attempt to appeal to our good side. I even expect another loogie.

What I *don't* expect is for that cold stare of hers to turn calculating or for her to try to negotiate. "And if I do?" she asks hesitantly. "What will you do for me?"

"We'll keep you safe."

"I want to go home," she says with a tremble in her voice. It's a reminder that despite the iceberg she pretends to be, Aurelia must be terrified and not just of us. She's terrified that she won't survive on her own.

We're simply the lesser evil.

"*We'll keep you safe,*" I repeat and not kindly. She can never go home. It's best she understands that now. "All we're offering is food and shelter. Take it or leave it."

"*Fine.*" Aurelia surprises me again when she leans her head back and drives it forward as hard as she can. It's her last act of defiance. Her refusal to let us keep her forever and a promise to bend but never break.

Because she's so much shorter, Aurelia's in the perfect position to minimize damage to herself while maximizing my pain. The skin of my bottom lip splits the moment her head connects with my face. Pain bounces between my teeth like the vibration of a bell after it's struck. The last of my resistance falls away the moment the metallic taste of my blood fills my mouth. I need to have this woman as surely as I need air to breathe.

While blood is still pooling in my mouth, I tighten my hold on her arms. My grip isn't tight enough to warrant her cry of pain until I remember the second-degree frostbite on her arms. I use her distraction to press my lips against hers, but I go a step further than Khalil, shoving my tongue between her lips and making her swallow my pain.

I accepted a long time ago that there would be no redemption for me, but fuck…Aurelia tastes like the forbidden fruit that cements my place in hell.

She cries and struggles when she tastes my blood, but it only makes me devour her faster. It's the first of many times that blood will be shed—from both sides, I'm sure.

Aurelia will never know this, but if she'd kept her mouth shut and played the helpless damsel in distress, the worst thing I might have done was toss her out into the snow to die, but she had to go and make herself a challenge.

She had to prove that she could handle us.

We rarely do anything if it's not unanimous, and now it's three against one. The way it should be.

Khalil and Seth are still closing in when I finally come up for air, Aurelia leaning into the kiss more than I expected as I break away and turn her around to face them. She belongs to them, too, and though having to share is a novelty that will take some time to get used to, it already feels natural.

Aurelia pants hard, too focused on catching her breath to notice them, but then she does, her wary gaze bouncing between them when Seth and Khalil block out the rest of the den.

It might be wishful thinking or my imagination amusing itself, but I swear she presses closer to me for protection before remembering I'm her dragon, too, and there are no white knights here.

Aurelia makes a sound of distress. My dick twitches in my sweats, liking the sound, even while her gasps draw my attention over to Khalil.

I give him a less-than-amused look when I see what startled her.

Khalil has already whipped out his cock, stroking the thick length shamelessly with his gaze fixed on Aurelia's chest, which is half-exposed from her struggles. "You would be the first with your dick out," I remark wryly.

Without looking away from her breasts, Khalil shrugs. "Show us your tits, Goldilocks."

Our girl stubbornly remains motionless, so I grab her hands. She growls like a feral cat as I lead them to the top of her dress and force her delicate fingers to curl around the material. Her long, flowing sleeves hang off her shoulders naturally, so there isn't much holding her dress up except the fragile knot forming a keyhole in her bodice and the silk laces of her corset that are already dangerously loose.

Aurelia's eyes grow wide with panic when she realizes my intent. "No," she whispers, but thanks to our deal, it lacks conviction. "Please."

Finally.

Her pleas taste even sweeter than her venom.

Using our combined strength, I force her hands to shove the bodice down. The heavy globes of her perfect tits bounce free, and my balls tighten at the sight of her nipples.

Across from us, Khalil groans, and I see a bead of pre-cum leaking from his tip. Catching the pearly drop before it can spill onto the floor, he uses it to stroke the head.

Seth reaches out a trembling hand to gently thumb one of her dark nipples. His touch is hesitant and testing, his green eyes darting back and forth between Aurelia's ruddy face and her matching flushed tits to see how she reacts.

Her eyes are firmly closed in a poor attempt to keep us from seeing how into this she is, but the soft, sweet sounds she makes give her away. I can't decide if they're moans of despair or moans of pleasure. If it's despair, why try to hide it? I find myself fighting a smile.

She really is too good to be true.

"Seth." My ears perk at her whisper, and I tear my gaze away from my hand that's tugging and tweaking her other nipple, covertly showing Seth what to do. Aurelia's eyes are open again, and she's staring at him.

"I'll ride the roller coaster with you," she blurts, making me pause. "I'll hold your hand."

Seth stops mimicking my movements, and his green eyes flare with hope. "You will?"

"Yes." Aurelia licks her dry lips, which are cracked from the cold and dehydration and swollen from our kisses. "And not just on the rides. I'll even buy you all the candy apples, churros, and funnel cakes you can stand."

Seth drops his fucking hand, and I swallow a laugh when I realize what Aurelia's doing.

She's cunning. I'll give her that. But if she wants to keep this twisted game of ours going a little while longer, so be it.

Aurelia doesn't mean a word of her promise, and Seth's too green to know the difference. Somehow, she's already picked up on it.

Seth's development wasn't so much arrested as it was catapulted. He was born twelve years ago inside the mind of a twenty-two-year-old man with none of the experiences or rites of passage to guide him. The psychiatrist that Zeke saw after we rescued him believed that Seth may have manifested during childhood, but Zeke having no memories of the alter, dismissed it as a possibility, especially when Seth himself doesn't remember existing before the table.

Khalil and I have spent the last decade bringing his most willful alter up to speed with mostly promising results. Some things Seth just knows thanks to Zeke's memories and sharing his mind, but others he falls woefully short on.

Women and sex primarily.

Far away from the rest of the world, it hasn't been a problem—until now.

"She's lying, Seth."

He doesn't even glance my way when he asks, "What's a funnel cake?"

"Oh my God, it's the *best*," Aurelia gushes. She's overselling it if you ask me. "It's deep-fried batter, similar to pancakes, that's all twisted up and covered in powdered sugar and syrup."

Seth gives a curious tilt of his head. "What kind of syrup?"

"Any kind you like, Seth. Chocolate, strawberry, caramel," she lists.

Seth looks her over slowly, meaningfully, and then says, "I like chocolate."

Aurelia forces a smile to keep up the charade. "Chocolate's the best."

"Yeah, well, you know what I like?" Khalil pipes in sarcastically. "Getting my dick sucked." With a scowl tossed at Aurelia, Khalil tucks his dick into his sweats and shoves his hands inside his pockets. "Seth." Finally, Zeke's alter breaks free of Aurelia's thrall to meet Khalil's softened gaze. "She's playing you, man. Remember when I told you how girls will give guys their number and block them the moment they walk away?"

Seth nods slowly.

"Well, this is like that," he tells him gently. "She's selling you a dream."

Warily, Seth's gaze travels back to Aurelia. "Sunshine?"

I'm not sure what causes her change of heart—pity, sympathy, hatred that burns too deeply to allow her to pretend a second longer, or maybe a combination of all three—but Aurelia drops the act.

Her eyes and voice are both cold when she answers him. "Make them stop, and I'll buy you a fucking ticket to Disneyland, but I'll cut off my arms before I hold your hand, you fucking weirdo. *Sorry.*"

Hurt flashes in Seth's eyes, and even though he's tried to kill me more than once, I'm ready to make Aurelia eat those words. Who the fuck does she think she is? Out here, her name means nothing. She has no power. She's who *we* say she is.

Just as I'm ready to push her to her knees, Seth exhales and then perks up again. Aurelia squints, no doubt wondering who was playing who. Seth's hurt was one hundred percent real, but there was no way he was taking that deal with a sweeter offer on the table.

"Good. I'm sorry, Sunshine. A roller coaster does sound fun, but I'd rather ride you."

Seth reaches for her, and I give her to him.

"No!" Aurelia screams as she slaps and scratches his face until it turns red and welted. Seth's masochistic ass doesn't try to dodge a single blow. He grins through it as if he's being licked by kittens instead. "Let me go, or I swear to fucking God, Thanos, or whoever the hell you pray to that *I will end you!*"

"Goddamn, I didn't think my dick could get this fucking hard," Khalil mumbles. Inversely, his expression and voice are flat when he looks to me. "I want to go first."

Somehow, Aurelia succeeds in breaking free of Seth and throwing a punch Khalil's way, which he dodges easily. Seth catches her around the waist again and hauls her up, kicking and screaming.

"Get your fucking hands off me!"

Khalil watches her flail dispassionately. "I wish we could gag her."

"Fuck you!" she explodes.

"All right, enough." Seth lets her go when I step forward, and I wrap a hand around her jaw and squeeze just in case she resorts to spitting again. "One way or another, superstar, you're using that mouth for something other than talking back. A song or our cocks?" I offer impatiently. This game we're playing is dangerous. We don't know her limits and she doesn't know ours, but I'm too hungry for it to play it safe—to stop and see just how far she's willing to go. It's reckless. It could end with us all hating ourselves more than we already do. But I can't fucking stop. *Just this once*, I promise. "Which will it be?"

Aurelia calms down again, and I loosen my grip enough for her to answer. "I'll…I'll leave."

Such a fucking tease.

Feeling my patience slip a little more, I exhale through my nose and shake my head. "Maybe the cold froze your memory, but there's nowhere for you to go, *and* leaving is no longer on the table even if there were. Last chance. Sing us a song, or get on your knees. Your choice."

Hearing her choices, Aurelia makes one last desperate play to draw this out, but my hold is unbreakable.

It doesn't stop her from driving a knee into my nuts.

It's not a perfect blow, but it still hurts like a bitch. Fortunately, I can be bullheaded too. I grunt in pain but keep my hand where it is. "Why are you being so goddamn stubborn? It's just one lousy song."

"I'm starting to think she wants to suck our dicks," Seth muses.

An angry flush creeps up her neck, and then I let her go when she whips around to face him. "The only thing I want to do with your dick is cut it off and make you choke on it, you psycho!"

"Hmm. Bad choice of words, baby girl." I shove her into Seth's arms.

"*Stop*…pushing me!"

"Sunshine." Seth's gaze is soft and adoring as he looks down at her as if she's his entire reason for being. And then he forces her to her knees and rips open the button on the jeans he changed into at some point. "Suck my cock, Sunshine. Make it good."

Aurelia scrambles away on her hands and knees before Seth can get his dick out, and the genuine shock and confusion on his face is fucking hysterical.

Unfortunately, I don't have time for shits and giggles.

Our little tyrant is getting away.

I reach down just as she tries to crawl through the small gap between our legs and grip a fistful of her golden curls.

"No!" Aurelia screams and kicks out as I drag her ass back.

Since I'm a greedy bastard, I don't give her back to Seth. I position her until she's kneeling and trembling in front of me. I've got one hand in her hair and the other freeing my dick from my sweats, but Aurelia still has the gall to jerk back and glare up at me when I press forward.

"Put that thing anywhere near my mouth, and I'll bite it off."

I'm just protective enough of my dick to pause and silently assess if she's still playing the game or if it's starting to feel too real.

She licks her lips like she's desperate for it, and I take that as my cue to continue. Releasing Aurelia's hair to pinch her nose between my fingers, I hold her fiery gaze so that she can see the sincerity in mine when I speak. "You survived that crash with barely a scratch on you, but if your teeth so much as *graze* my dick, *I* swear I'll spank that gorgeous ass black and blue and make you suck me anyway. Now *heel*, songbird."

An interesting shiver works its way through her body despite the warm room. Aurelia's lips finally part in a desperate grab for air, and I allow her one meager breath before I shove my dick between those pouty, pretty lips and shut her the fuck up for good.

The tension tightening my shoulders melts away as I'm enveloped in her warm mouth.

She makes a gurgling noise when I hit the back of her throat, but it's drowned out by my bone-deep shudder the moment I feel her tongue stroke the shaft unintentionally. My next breath gets caught in my chest as I watch those full lips stretch to accommodate my cock.

Meanwhile, she's panicking, her hands clawing at me for purchase as I choke her with it. The hand I have on the back of her head keeps her from going anywhere, though.

Still, all her floundering is getting in the way of me fully enjoying the head.

"Breathe, songbird. Breathe through your fucking nose," I instruct. She frowns like she's confused, but then I feel the smallest puff of air blowing through my pubes. My fingers start moving on their own as I gently stroke her scalp. "Good girl. That's it. Be sweet for me, and I'll think about returning the favor."

Aurelia blinks at the praise and then does it again. It takes a while for her panic to fade, but once it does, she's leaning back on her heels, getting comfortable while her hands go still on my hips.

I almost snort at her finally giving up the pretense.

She's an enigma, though.

Not her resistance to how far and quickly we're leading her into darkness. That's natural. We've only just begun to push her into depths of depravity that she never could have dreamed of on her own—not in her safe little world where everyone kneels at her feet. Tonight, she'll kneel at ours.

It's her inexperience that confuses me. The head isn't terrible, but it's not great either.

Aurelia's got to be in her mid-twenties—old enough to know what the fuck to do, yet she's fumbling through it.

And then there's her sex appeal.

Even bruised, exhausted, dirty, and disheveled, she oozes it.

I bet if she woke up next to me tomorrow with crust in her eyes, hair all over the place, and drool dried on the side of her mouth, I'll still want to fuck her through the mattress.

Never one to look a gift horse in the mouth, I focus on busting a nut as a groan slips free.

"Fuck, I missed this."

Completely overcome with pleasure, I let my head fall back, confident that Aurelia will take heed of my warning and that my brothers are watching her every move, even if Khalil and Seth are busy stroking their own cocks and silently urging me to hurry so they can have their turn.

After a few more rounds of amateur deepthroating, I can't resist staring into those cruel almond eyes full of hate and fury as I pull all the way out. Aurelia gasps and coughs while a thick string of pre-cum and saliva keeps us connected until it lands on her chin before dripping down to her chest.

She's even more beautiful like this—used and learning her place.

"*Please*," she whispers as soon as she's caught her breath.

"What's the matter?" I gently ask as I take her chin and rub her swollen lip with my thumb. "You want me to stop?" She closes her eyes and nods. "I understand." When she opens her eyes again, there's hope there. Hope that I have zero qualms crushing. "But I haven't come yet, and my brothers are waiting, so what are you going to do? Are you going to put in some fucking effort, or are you going to stay on your knees for us all night? No one's leaving this room until we're paid in full, Aurelia."

"I…"

"Have you never sucked dick before?" I ask her.

When she shakes her head, I narrow my gaze.

No fucking way.

She's got to be playing me like she tried with Seth.

I consider choking her with my cock again to punish her, but the sincerity in her gaze makes me hesitate.

Shit. Could she be telling the truth?

No. No way.

Aurelia's already confirmed she's not a virgin, so what the fuck gives?

Annoyed, I start to shove her away. Let Khalil waste his time teaching her. But then she squirms.

Aurelia does it again, but this time, she writhes more than squirms like she's...searching for friction. My gaze narrows on the subtle movement and the way her eyes remain firmly fixed on the floor.

"Aurelia." Her gaze shoots back to me and then guiltily widens when I shift my hold to her neck. Tilting her head back, I command, "Open wide." When she hesitates, I rub the tip of my cock over the seam of her pretty lips. "Or I can tell my brothers your secret, songbird." Her brows dip further, but her gulp is telling. "I bet it's just *dripping* to be free."

She gasps at the same time Seth asks, "What secret?"

Ignoring Seth, I ask, "What will it be, my *slippery* little cocksucker?"

Aurelia's glare turns sharp, and then she slowly opens her mouth. I waste no time stuffing my dick inside with a groan, but this time I don't go as deep.

Instead, I fuck her mouth. It's a damn good thing I rubbed one out in the shower earlier, or I'd be coming down her throat already.

"Come on, you fuck," I grunt when I can feel my release hovering woefully out of reach. "Use that tongue for something other than pissing me off. *Stroke it.*"

Those little angry divots between her brows appear again, and then I feel her tongue give a testing lash. My toes curl into the carpet while my stomach dips violently at the sensation.

And then the impossible happens.

Aurelia's instincts finally take over, and she wraps her small hand around my thick shaft.

I pause to watch, partly fascinated but mostly dubious of what she'll do.

Her flushed cheeks hollow out a moment later as she takes a little more of me before pulling back. She does that repeatedly, each time taking a little more, testing how much she's comfortable with until her head begins to bob back and forth and she has a rhythm.

Suddenly, she's in charge of the pace and depth, and I don't have time to feel salty over losing control because, holy shit, I was wrong before.

She's mind-blowing.

Her mouth is like a vacuum as she sucks me up.

And for the little time that I last, she owns me.

"Goddamn… She's doing it," I think I hear one of my brothers say in awe.

Everything is muted and muddled under the roaring in my ears and pounding of my heart as I erupt, coming like a fire hose down her throat. Aurelia makes a sound of alarm at the first bitter taste of my cum and tries to pull away, but I tighten my hold on her hair and keep her there.

"Cabin rule number three," I grunt as I feed her my cum. "Swallow every drop we give you. Understand?"

Her mouth is full, so I'm not really expecting her to respond, but she nods like a good pet anyway.

Damn. I can't stop my thumb from stroking her soft cheek.

She's staring up at me through wide, vulnerable eyes, and even though hatred and fear are still very much present, there's something new there too.

"Come on, asshole. Stop hogging her."

It's not until I hear Khalil's impatient demand that I realize I'm no longer coming, and my softened cock is just resting inside Aurelia's viperous mouth while we stare at one another like long-lost lovers.

"That was almost decent," I say, breaking free of her spell. Withdrawing, I tuck my dick back into my sweats. "Lucky for us, we'll have what's left of winter to work on your skills."

It's a dick move but a necessary one.

I'm grasping for some of the distance I'd lost when Aurelia blew my fucking mind. It works, too, because the docility in her gaze is gone, and she's back to looking at me like I'm scum.

I am. I won't deny it.

Khalil stomps forward and is on her before Aurelia can catch her bearings. Some of her fight returns when she realizes it's not over yet. He drags her away, and the more she resists him, the rougher he gets. I almost snap at him to give her a moment until I remember he's my brother, and she's just some girl who picked the wrong cabin.

Sighing, I shake off the afterglow of my nut and sink to my knees behind her. Grabbing her arms, I force them behind her back before she hurts herself and lock her wrists in one of my hands. I use the other to hold her chin.

"Shhh," I soothe when she whines and tries to get away. "We talked about this, remember? Khalil is an ass, but he's not so bad. He just wants to feel that velvet mouth. You made me feel so good, and now it's his turn. Come on, songbird. Open up and show him what you've learned."

"Please," she whispers desperately. "*Please* don't make me do that again."

"Aurelia…" I kiss her soft cheek and then slide my lips to her ear. "Be a good girl," I whisper so that only she hears, "or I'll have to tell my brothers your secret."

And so that there is no doubt about what I know, I slip my hand under her costume.

Her incredibly thick thighs are as soft as I imagined, and I can feel myself growing hard again as I fantasize about tossing her to the floor and wedging myself between them.

She starts to squirm again the closer I get to the searing heat of her pussy, but I stop when I reach her damp inner thighs. I can feel Khalil and Seth watching us closely, but I keep what I find to myself—at least for now.

"Do as we say," I warn, my voice low, "or I'll show them."

"No. It's not…that's not—"

My post-nut glow fades a little when she tries to lie to me. "Don't you fucking dare."

Hooking my fingers into her panties, I wrench them aside, and she cries out from the force and lack of barrier between us now. Cupping her hot puss in my palm, I give her one last warning. "Lie to me again, and I won't just show them your pussy, Aurelia. I'll spank it."

Pulling my hand back just enough, I strike her exposed pussy once to show her I'm not fucking around. The sound of our skin connecting echoes around the mostly silent room, mixing with her surprised yelp and the crackling fire.

"*Don't. Please.*" Her lashes flutter, and suddenly, Aurelia's *dancing* in my lap. No, not dancing. Her movements are too unskilled and frantic, telling me they are fueled by impulse alone.

I hide my smile in her wild, golden curls when I realize why.

The heel of my hand is pressing into her clit, and she's chasing the friction.

My own breath shudders out of me, knowing she wants to come. Bad enough to risk us seeing, apparently.

Feeling generous, I grind my hand against the swollen nub a few times, and she stops breathing. I can feel the physical toll it takes for her to keep quiet. She doesn't want to give in, but she doesn't have a fucking choice.

I'm like a dog with a bone now, and my brothers are waiting.

Got to get her ready for them.

She needs to be as soft and eager to please as she was moments ago if she wants to survive the night. It may have been fleeting—like the blink of an eye—but it's enough for now.

"Yeah? You want to come?" I whisper when she presses against my hand. Cruelly, I shift my focus lower, away from her clit.

Aurelia's eyes fly open, but the alarm in them as I slip my fingers through her slick pussy and beeline for her opening doesn't deter me. "Wait. No!" she yelps too late.

I'm already pushing a finger inside.

Fuck, she's tight.

I'm a second from saying fuck my brothers and taking her to the floor when she yells, "I'll do it!" I'm nearly buried to the second knuckle when I pause. "I'll…I'll suck you off," she says to Khalil. "Just, please. Make him stop."

Something irrational and possessive coils tighter in my chest at her turning to Khalil. Aurelia has no fucking idea that out of the three of us, he's the least likely to come to her rescue.

Snatching my hand from her pussy, I grip her jaw. It's a testament to my jealousy that I ignore the scent of her arousal suddenly filling my nose. "You want Khalil to save you from me, songbird? Fine. What happens next is on you. You're on your own." I let her wrists and neck go to stand.

Khalil raises a brow at me in question since my anger is a little misplaced, but I just shrug off the rejection and storm out of the basement.

Leaving her alone with those two is exactly what she deserves.

For the next ten minutes or so, I pretend not to hear the sounds coming from the basement as I stomp around upstairs with no real purpose except not to be down *there*.

I clean up the mess Khalil made from dinner and then check all the doors and windows. We're alone up here, so we never worried about locking it before, but Aurelia changed all that. She showed us that we'd become too lax. Too comfortable. We'd forgotten what it meant to guard our territory, but those instincts were rising swiftly once more with her presence.

Ours.

Aurelia was ours, and over my dead body would anyone take her from us.

Eventually, I stop sulking enough to return to the basement, balancing a bowl of lukewarm stew, a glass of water, and a bottle of painkillers in hand.

The scene I'm greeted with stops me in my tracks.

Aurelia is in the same place I left her, but she's flanked by Khalil and Seth, who both have their cocks out. Right now, she's being choked by Seth's cock while Khalil has a punishing grip on her nape, holding her—*keeping* her—there. His other hand is busy stroking his dick, which is already glistening from Aurelia's saliva.

No tears though.

Huh…

If there was any part of me that rebelled at the idea of being the villain in her story vanishes when my dick goes brick-hard at the sight.

Up here, the only rules that matter are the ones we make.

Seth finally lets Aurelia come up for air, and she's briefly seized by a coughing fit. When it finally ends, I only get a glimpse of the shattered look in her eyes—her utter surrender—before she turns and eagerly swallows Khalil's dick in the next breath.

It hadn't taken her nearly as long as I thought to accept the inevitable. We're the key to her survival, and she knows it now.

While her mouth pleasures Khalil, she reaches back with one hand and wraps it around Seth, twisting and pumping his dick until he groans and fucks her fist.

Clearly, the two of them had no qualms about teaching her what they like.

I walk deeper into the den and set the items on the metal footlocker we use as a coffee table before collapsing onto the couch to watch.

Unlike when she blew me, Aurelia's eyes are squeezed tightly closed, like she's afraid of her own fantasy—as if she should be ashamed of her desires. Khalil doesn't seem to mind. He watches her like she's his already. He's got her pinned down, not just with his dick but with his fucking suffocating intensity.

He doesn't even moan or make a sound because he's so into watching *her*, but I know he's close.

It's in the tenseness of his jaw and furrow in his brow. He's wound tight, and just like any bomb, it'll be nothing less than devastating when he erupts.

Khalil doesn't stop watching her even when she releases him to take Seth. He watches her as if she'll disappear if he takes his eyes off her for even a second. Something tells me she can feel it, though, and looking away is her way of running from it.

Because she still thinks there's a chance she can escape.

I'm not aware of reaching inside my sweats and pulling my dick free. I absently stroke it with one hand and cup my balls with the other as I watch the three of them.

Aurelia is a natural cock pleaser whether she wants to accept it or not.

She doesn't give either of them a chance to get jealous or angry when her attention lingers for too long. She's already picking up on their cues and alternates between them like she's been mastering our cocks for years.

Khalil likes his head enthusiastic but unhurried. He gets off on having his cock worshipped like it's magic while he looks on like some sort of god.

Seth is an incurable face fucker, just like Zeke. The latter was always about chasing the high and getting off sooner rather than later, which is why Seth comes first.

"Fuck, I knew it," he babbles as he roughly fucks her mouth. "I knew you were it. You're the one, aren't you, Sunshine?"

Aurelia's brows dip in confusion, but she doesn't have time to wonder for long what he means. Seth shoves his cock to the hilt and comes. Aurelia gags but takes it, swallowing his cum like I told her to.

The moment his long cock slips free of her lips, he's smiling down at her like they're old friends.

She doesn't return the gesture. This is just a business arrangement for her after all.

Aurelia just turns to finish off Khalil, but he has other plans.

For a moment, her mask drops, and shock erases the haunted look in her eyes at the first drop of Khalil's cum landing on her cheek. The only sound he makes as he comes is a single strangled groan while his entire body tenses like a tightly strung cord from the effort it takes to hold back the rest.

"Oh, *fuck*," I curse, my hips rising from the cushion as I join him. My dick gushes cum, watching Khalil vengefully pump his length—his cock as angry looking as his face—as he loses himself on her.

Of course, he does.

Khalil will want to stake his claim his own way.

I glance down at the mess I made of my hands, sweats, and the couch—irrefutable proof that once won't nearly be enough to slake my lust.

The basement is eerily quiet once we catch our breath.

Aurelia doesn't run off like I expected, and I'm impressed. She's frozen in place, staring at nothing with cum on her cheek, nose, and tits, and the taste of Seth and me no doubt lingering as well. I cringe a little at the sight, and because I'm not completely apathetic to her plight, I force myself to rise and head for the bathroom. Feeling my cum already drying on my skin, I make quick work cleaning up and then grab a fresh cloth and wet it with warm water.

I carry it back into the den in time to see that Aurelia's been moved to the couch, and Seth is draping a blanket around her shoulders to soften the blow of pushing her so far this quickly. Showing her that we'll be here to catch her when she eventually falls out of subspace is all we can do.

Crouching in front of Aurelia, I reach out with the cloth to clean her face, but she flinches, and I feel something shatter inside of me before I remember that our relationship is purely transactional. She didn't *want* to do it. She *had* to do it. For survival. It's what she's telling herself rather than facing the truth.

The truth is she fucking *loved* it.

Since I suck at this part—wooing and being gentle or deceitful like Khalil, I spit out a terse, "Suit yourself."

Standing, I toss the cloth in her face.

It's sopping wet, just like her pussy, so it lands with a satisfying slap as I put some much-needed distance between us.

Aurelia snatches the cloth from her face and shoots me a withering look. I don't give her the satisfaction of returning one as I watch her use the cloth to clean her face and chest.

She's too damn quiet.

There should be tears and hysteria, but she doesn't bother with either. We'll have to make quick work of breaking her in if any of us hope to get a good night's sleep anytime soon. I've heard it only takes a matter of days in some cases for Stockholm to set in.

First, we make her fear our wrath, and then we confuse her with random acts of kindness—make her feel safe until her brain is so scrambled she doesn't have any choice but to trust what *we* tell her is real.

Honestly, it'll be the most effort any of us have ever put into a woman—especially Khalil. Since my ears are still ringing from that slap, I don't have to wonder if she's flattered.

"Aurelia," I call once she's done cleaning Khalil's spunk from her skin. If he feels guilty about what he did to her, he doesn't show it. In fact, Khalil looks upset that his mark is already gone. If only on the outside.

I wait until Aurelia's gaze rises to meet mine, and then I hesitate a moment longer because I'm about to make her wish she'd kept going when she stumbled across our cabin. This time for her own good.

"The confusion you're feeling right now is understandable. I won't make excuses for what we did when the truth is simple. We used you. We took advantage of your desperation because we're desperate too. But I want you to remember that we have a deal and that won't change when you wake up tomorrow. Your pussy, mouth, ass, and whatever else we demand of you for our protection and home. You will never leave us. *We won't let you.* Understood?"

"Answer him," Khalil snaps anxiously when she takes too long to decide. "We're not fucking around, Goldilocks."

Aurelia sighs and drops the cloth on the floor next to her. "Okay."

The three of us still because we have no idea what to make of her easy capitulation. If it's meant to fuck with us and put us on the defensive, bravo. She's clearly better at battling for power play than I anticipated.

Good.

It means we won't get bored of her anytime soon.

"One chance, Aurelia," I feel the need to warn one last time. "Prove to us even once that you're not worth the trouble, and we'll make you wish you perished in that plane crash."

Aurelia doesn't respond for the longest time, and then she gives the tiniest nod.

Khalil exhales heavily.

Out of the three of us, he's the only one hell-bent on keeping her. Seth is too, but his attention span is shit.

Tossing Aurelia out would be as good as killing her, which would be the point.

And such a waste of a good piece of ass.

Aurelia sucked our cocks as if it gave her meaning, and she doesn't even know us, despises us even. Imagine what a few months with nothing else to do but wait for the snow to melt will do. Imagine if she *fell* for us.

Seth helps her stand and then takes her face in his hands, bending a little to peer into her empty eyes—Aurelia's here, but no one's home. "Don't let them scare you, Sunshine. They're not so bad," he tells her like he didn't use her to get off too. "Thorin and Khalil are just grumpy because we're stuck up here, and it's my fault."

"Quiet, Seth," Khalil snaps from Aurelia's other side. They're flanking her again, barely a few inches of space between them.

It's unnecessary. Aurelia isn't going to run, and she's damn sure not going to ask questions. I doubt she cares what drove us to do what we did. What matters is that it happened.

Still, she doesn't reject Seth's touch as she did mine, and that acidic feeling from earlier burns a hole in my chest as I wonder if she likes him better.

It's a fucking ridiculous thought.

Why should I care who Aurelia likes better? She belongs to all of us. She'll sleep under my roof, warm my bed, and ride my dick when I tell her to, and that's all that matters.

Aurelia is still staring at the floor, but there's a furrow in her brow now, like she's wrestling with something. It's a far cry from the quiet desolation that seemed so deafening before.

I nod toward the bowl resting on the table. "Eat your stew, Aurelia. You're safe here."

I can see the question in her eyes, though—the uncertainty—when she does what I tell her.

Safe, but for how long?

Instead of asking or giving us the third degree, Aurelia exhales, her shoulders slumping, then picks up the food and starts to eat.

None of us speak, content with watching her slowly consume her second helping of stew. I don't know if it's the horrible taste or if we stole her appetite, but she eats like she's on autopilot.

When she's done, I take the empty bowl from her and set it aside before giving her two of the painkillers and making her down the entire glass of water.

"Take off your dress." Her gaze becomes wary at my command, and it's all I can do not to roll mine. "*Relax.* No one's fucking you tonight. Your dress is filthy, and so are you," I remind her. "You'll sleep better after you shower. One of us can loan you some clean clothes until your dress is sorted."

Aurelia still doesn't move from the spot she's in, and Seth waves his hand in front of her face. When he starts snapping his fingers, her eyes shift up and to the side to glare at him in irritation.

She's heard every word. She doesn't want to undress in front of us.

Tough shit.

We'll be committing far worse atrocities to her body soon enough. *Staring* will be the least of our sins.

Since I don't want to break our new toy before we're done taking it out of the box, I exhale loudly and say, "There's a bathroom by the stairs."

The stark relief in her eyes is enough to cement me as a monster.

Aurelia nods and stands, and I force myself to stay put as the distance between us grows. The blanket is still around her shoulders for protection as much as warmth, but it's ineffective. The memory of her warm mouth and perfect tits are forever imprinted on my brain.

I blame my distracting thoughts for not seeing her sway.

I'm even more annoyed that Khalil gets there first. He's already lifting her from the floor where she collapsed by the time I'm even standing.

"Aurelia." The demanding way he speaks her name belies the gentle touch he places on her cheek. He could never fool me, though. There's a trace of alarm hidden underneath. He's *concerned.*

Our songbird doesn't respond. She doesn't make a sound. At first, I think she's just being stubborn as usual, but it takes me a moment longer to realize she's limp in his arms.

My stomach sinks when we realize she's unconscious.

CHAPTER TEN

AURELIA

C assieeeeeee!"
    The mountain's gale picks up my scream and carries it off where it's lost forever. Never to be heard.

It's been five minutes since I heard Cassie calling for me, five long minutes since I chose to leave the safety of the plane to find her. With the blizzard, I have no idea which direction I wandered or if it was even the right one. Cassie's been alarmingly silent ever since.

Each step forward costs me everything.

The minutes tick by, but the storm goes on.

So do I.

I can't feel my hands, face, or feet, but I keep going because it's all I have. The hope is that Tyler and Cassie are alive, and I'm not on this cursed mountain alone.

Harrison's too-large coat is heavy on my shoulders as it sweeps my ankles. I knew I'd never survive without some protection, so I took my dead bodyguard's long coat and the axe I found in what was left of the cockpit before I set out to find my assistant.

Sucking in the thin mountain air, I ignore my ravaged throat and call out for her again. "Cassieeeeeee!"

Only the howling wind answers back.

I don't know if something happened to my assistant or if I've wandered too far. I'm already turning to switch directions when I hear a deep rumbling sound that would have sent a chill down my spine if I weren't already in the early stages of hypothermia.

Heart pounding, I take off in the opposite direction, needing to flee whatever *new terror made that sound. I rush through the woods and look for a way back to the plane.*

All I find is more debris.

Lots of it.

There's a trail that leads back the way I came—or at least I think it's the way I came.

I'm clearly lost, so I follow the scattered detritus.

Foolishly, I allow myself to hope that I'll find my way back until I see something ahead that makes me stop.

Crimson in the snow.

Blood.

An alarming amount.

I spot Cassie's blue-and-purple-striped scarf lying two feet away from it and suck in a breath.

"Cassie!" I yell again as I rush forward. "Cassie, where are you?" Reaching her scarf, I fall to my knees and slowly lift it from the ground. It hurts to move, but I stuff it inside Harrison's pocket anyway. Cassie will need it when I find her. This cold is too unbearable, too unrelenting.

"Cassie!" I croak. "Cassie, please answer me!"

Yanked free of my nightmare, the disorientation when I wake feels familiar. The lingering exhaustion that clings to me is reminiscent of my days on tour. Living on the road for months on end is a hard life, even when you're at the top, flying on private jets and staying in the best hotels.

Thinking of the day that must be ahead of me, I will my eyes open even though I can't remember what my uncle has booked for me.

A flight?

No, that's not right.

I'm supposed to be on set today for the first-ever live recording of the talent competition I'm judging—alongside Tania's scheming ass. I tell myself just a few more minutes and shift from my back to my side.

The bed I'm in is soft enough and warm, but the sheets are completely unacceptable. The fiber feels rough against my bare legs, as if it has a thread count of two.

I make a mental note to speak to Cassie.

Used to waking up in strange beds, I'm not alarmed in the slightest that the one I'm in isn't mine. I snuggle a little deeper into the pillow with my eyes still firmly shut.

The scent that greets me, though, keeps me from falling back asleep.

Amber, with a hint of juniper, but the latter doesn't feel like it belongs. Both scents stir memories that aren't mine.

Or, at least, they shouldn't be.

I add it to the growing list of things Cassie will need to fix if she wants to keep her job.

The memory of the last time I saw her pops into my head as I start to doze again. Her unseeing gaze staring up at me from the frozen ground where she's lying in a pool of crimson. I hear the *thunk* of something hard and heavy falling to the ground, and when I look down, I see a bloody axe lying next to my feet.

No.

Sure, Cassie's a shitty fucking assistant, but surely…

Lifting my hands, the white forest around me spins when I see that my palms are equally red, and then I hear that terrifying growl…

My eyes fly open, and I sit up with a gasp, my hands clutching the blanket and sheets covering me from the waist down as my gaze darts to every corner of the room. It's day, so there are no shadows to taunt me, only the ones my mind creates.

It wasn't a dream.

It was real.

Panic infuses my blood, turning it cold when it *all* comes rushing back, and I realize where I am.

Northern Canada.

The mountains.

The wilds.

The cabin.

The animals who inhabit it.

The bed of twisted branches.

Khalil's bed.

I'm in Khalil's bed, and I'm alone. I don't know for how long. I have to run while I still can—before they remember me and pick up where they left off. Fuck their rules and fuck our deal. I'm *out of here.*

Tearing the thick blanket away, I get my first glance at my bare feet and legs. I'm wearing a green-and-black wool flannel shirt instead of my dress, and it's two sizes too big, so the hem reaches the top of my thighs. On my right leg, there's a fresh white bandage wrapped around my knee, and matching ones are on both of my arms where the worst of the frostbite is located. When I feel something pulling at the skin near my hairline, I carefully reach up and wince when I touch the stitches there. The list of injuries grows longer when I discover an IV in my arm, a gauze pad taped to my cheek, and another on the back of my right hand.

I feel fine, considering, but I know I must look a mess. Even though my uncle isn't here, I can still hear him berating me for not upholding the standard of my name.

I'm never allowed in the public eye without first being plucked and primped for hours. Hell, I'm still expected to groom myself meticulously even when I'm sick and bedridden. *"You are a role model, Aurelia. It's not enough to simply appear as one. You must* behave *like one."*

Rescue could come any day now.

I need to be prepared.

I nearly drove Tyler mad during our three days in the wild, constantly picking and fretting at my clothes and hair, making him stop so I could bathe the best I could whenever we found water, and bemoaning the absence of my luggage while he fought to keep us alive.

Noticing a mirror on the dresser, I rise from the bed on unsteady legs and remove the IV from my arm before I limp to the other side of the room.

I'm horrified by what I find.

It's even worse than I imagined. The reflection that greets me doesn't look like my own.

My once-vibrant curls, which require meticulous care to manage, are now dry, frizzy, and fraying at the ends. The dark circles under my eyes make me look like I haven't slept in days, even though it feels like I just woke up from a coma. Meanwhile, the parts of my skin that aren't covered in bandages have turned mottled from bruising.

I'm still fussing with my appearance when I hear a creak on the wooden floor, and I startle, realizing I'm not alone.

I don't hear or see him, but his presence is electric—charged up and full of stifled fury, drama, and danger. He appears relaxed as he watches me from the door, but I know he's in desperate need of release—somewhere for all that pent-up energy to go. I push that thought away since I know what kind of *release* he'll be looking for.

"Women," Khalil says derisively. My only window to escape is closed now that he knows I'm conscious and moving around. "You've been through more trauma in a week than most people suffer their entire lives, and your first concern is your hair?"

I pause but don't let my shame do more than raise its ugly head before I burn it to cinders with a flamethrower. I'm proud of how unaffected I sound as I continue to stare into the mirror while using my finger to try to fluff my clumped lashes. "Who says worrying about how I look isn't just another trauma?" I speak truthfully. From the corner of my eye, I see his lips part to respond, but I'm far from finished. "It's bold of you to assume that you're the worst thing that's ever happened to me when you're not even in the top five."

"Oh? I'm all ears, Goldilocks. Tell me your secrets."

"Tell me yours," I retort. When he doesn't respond, I release a quiet laugh in case his ego can't handle being mocked. "Didn't think so." Standing back, I look over my appearance before deciding that it's the best I can do without my makeup bag or toiletries. The only useful things I'll probably find in this cabin are shaving cream and a razor.

After too much time, I finally allow my gaze to leave the mirror and travel to the door where Khalil is standing.

He's wearing a stark white muscle shirt that makes his brown skin even more striking, while the deep holes where the sleeves should be show off his muscular physique—particularly his arms and obliques. His dark plaits are hanging down today instead of pulled back like the last time I saw him. Which was . . .

The question forms on my tongue, but I stop it from passing my lips because on the heels of how long I was out is what they might have done to me while I was unconscious.

I wouldn't put it past one of them to have a Sleeping Beauty kink.

If the situation were different and I didn't despise them, I wouldn't be so opposed to trying that one out. Alas, I hate them with every fiber of my being for pushing me to exchange my body for shelter, and I'm praying minutely that I'm long gone before they get the urge to actually fuck me.

Especially since the man in front of me looks like a walking, talking fantasy as his lips move.

Villains shouldn't be allowed to look panty-dropping gorgeous.

Thankfully, I'm not wearing any.

Wait…

I'm not wearing any.

Why aren't I wearing any again?

"Did you hear me?" Khalil snaps, making me realize I didn't.

I hide the anxiety building in my belly by shooting him an equally annoyed look. "Obviously not, Khalil."

"I asked if you're hungry."

Ignoring his offer, which definitely comes with strings, I ask him a question of my own. "Where are my clothes? Why am I wearing this?"

"Aurelia," he says with an impatient sigh. "I asked you a question."

I start to tell him where he can shove his questions when his brows rise like he read my mind and is daring me to do it.

Gulping, my lips tremble as I take one breath and two steps back.

I want to be strong and pretend I'm bulletproof, but it's hard when I remember what they did to me. I can still feel their hands on me—shoving, grabbing, and taking the only parts of me I had left that were just mine.

Whatever appetite I had flees from the rising memories. Still, I'm not entirely led by my emotions. Logic tells me that if I refuse the meal, they might not offer another one.

At least not for free.

I give a small nod, and Khalil turns to walk out without a word.

I gape at the empty door where he disappeared before I realize I'm meant to follow him. Stealing a few more moments to don my armor, I leave the haven of this room where nothing bad has happened to me yet.

Entering the den, I keep my gaze pinned straight ahead and on the stairs. I don't want to risk looking around and remembering what happened to me in *this* room.

The thick calf socks I have on are too big, but they protect my feet from the cold floor as I shuffle my way upstairs. The cabin is quiet but warm, and

I still haven't seen Thorin or Seth yet, so I'm half expecting one of them to jump me out of nowhere.

I make it upstairs unscathed.

Standing on the landing, I look around but still don't see them. I hear Khalil in the kitchen, so I creep over and peer around the corner. He's got his back to me, and I can't help but notice how strong it looks.

He'll have no problem holding me down when he decides to use me again.

The muscles are bunched like he's tense, and I realize why when he says, "Stop watching me like you think I'm going to eat you and sit. Your breakfast is getting cold."

It's then that I notice the plate on the table.

There are scrambled eggs that look runny, dried meat, and diced potatoes.

"If there's no town nearby," I ask as I take a seat, "how do you guys keep from starving?"

"The same way our ancestors' ancestors' ancestors' ancestors did before the invention of markets, Aurelia. We hunt, grow, gather, and store."

I roll my eyes but don't respond to the obvious lie. I saw the deer carcass, so I know he's telling the truth about hunting, but I don't remember seeing a fucking garden on my way in. The ground is covered in snow so that would explain why I didn't, but I'm still eyeing my food like it's a bomb when he finally turns away from the counter.

"What's wrong now?"

"Last time you fed me, you put something in my food."

I'm not sure how I expected him to respond to my accusation, but I know I wasn't expecting him to laugh. It's heartless and obnoxious, just like him. "We didn't drug you, Aurelia. You passed the fuck out."

"What? I don't remember that." The last thing I recall is Thorin telling me I was safe, and then...nothing.

"Well, you wouldn't, would you? You were unconscious."

"Who did all of this?" I ask, gesturing to my bandages and clothing. My skin looks and feels clean, too, like I'd been bathed. I even have a vague memory of one of them brushing my teeth and washing my hair.

It's a kindness that, when coming from them, just feels like more of a violation.

"Thorin patched you up. He has some medical training from his time in the Marines. Not much, but enough."

"Well, it wasn't necessary. I wasn't injured." God knows what they must have done to me after I was out. My body hurts all over like someone took a bat to it.

Or dropped a plane on it.

"Yes, you were, Aurelia. Extensively. You were hypothermic, frostbitten, and severely dehydrated, among other things."

"I…I didn't know. I felt a little sore, but that's it."

Khalil shrugs as if it's no big deal. "What the cold didn't numb, the adrenaline suppressed until it finally wore off. I guess your body couldn't handle the stress of your injuries, and it shut down your brain so you could heal."

Or my mind just didn't want to deal with what they did to me.

Thorin's voice enters my mind. *"You're safe here."*

"How long have I been out?" I finally allow myself to ask.

"You've been in and out for four days."

My food threatens to come back up.

Four more days have passed, and no one's found me yet.

Is anyone even still looking, or have they called off the search already?

I try to imagine the headlines. Immediately, I hate myself for it.

How empty must my life be that it's my first thought? There's no mother, father, or boyfriend who might care if I'm found. I don't even have a dog or cat to worry about starving to death in my absence—only millions of adoring fans and critics who probably think I got what I deserved.

"You should have died," Khalil announces without care. "You shouldn't have been able to find us. We went through a lot of trouble to ensure that."

"Your point?"

"Now that I know you, my guess is you were too stubborn to die."

"You don't know me," I whisper, my voice thick with some unnamed emotion.

"Baby, I doubt you even know you."

My grip tightens around my fork. "What's that supposed to mean?"

"It means it doesn't take an expert in Aurelia George to see that you're spiraling."

The food in my mouth suddenly turns to ash. Across the kitchen, Khalil goes still. The hand he was using to reach for the coffeepot is suspended in the air, and then, as if the slip hadn't occurred, his fingers wrap around the handle. Blink, and you'd miss it.

Fortunately, my eyes are wide open.

I don't set down my fork when I turn in my chair to face him. Instead, I hold it like a weapon. "How did you know my last name?"

A soft curse spills from his lips a moment before he calmly lies. "You told us."

I so did fucking *not*. I shake my head as Khalil pours the black liquid into a tin cup. "No, I didn't."

"Yes. You did. You reminded us who you were like a thousand fucking times." My lips part to argue when he cuts me off. "Eat, Aurelia."

Khalil's tone is cold and stern, but what little appetite I had is ash in the wind, so I push the awful food away and say, "No thanks."

"Suit yourself, but it's the last free meal you're getting from us," he says calmly.

It hits its mark and pisses me off. "What's that supposed to mean?"

"It means that you've used up a lot of resources and racked up quite a tab while you were getting your beauty sleep, Aurelia. It means that you owe us, and healed or not, we plan to collect."

Lightning flashes down my spine, settling in my lower belly and heating my pussy at the promise of further degradation. But on its heels, racing down that same channel, is the ire that's been hanging over our heads like a dark cloud, and I explode. My voice is a sharp, thunderous clap as I yell, "Are you fucking kidding me?" Spitefully, I spit out the food he laid for me like a trap and wipe my mouth with the back of my hand. "You won't let me leave, and then you tell me I owe you for staying? Just let me go!"

His jaw tightens at that, and then he snatches up the coffee cup and comes at me. I brace myself for his wrath, his fury, but all he does is grab the back of my chair with one hand. The wood underneath his palm groans as he sets the cup down on the table hard enough to make me jump. "No."

My mouth falls open, and it draws his attention to my lips.

Khalil stares at them for so long that my heart tries to wring free the forbidden want like a dirty wet rag in my chest.

I lick my lips, and it feels like it's on purpose. It feels like I'm daring him to kiss me.

Khalil's pupils dilate, and he leans a little closer.

He's going to kiss me.

Oh, God. Please don't kiss me.

I don't think my tenuous alliance with my own sanity can handle that right now. Khalil kissed me that night in the den, but I don't like this need to know if kissing him back for a reason other than survival will feel just as good. It's an itch in my brain that I can't scratch.

I don't want him to kiss me.

I don't *want* to want it.

My thoughts boil over, and I make a sound that seems to snap him out of it. He shoves away from me with a similar sound of disgust, though his voice is rougher, and I feel it vibrate all the way down to my…

No.

This is bad.

It's *wrong*.

Wanting to kiss him feels like a worse violation than Khalil forcing me to.

"If you're finished, let's go," he orders sharply.

"Where?" I haven't quite caught my breath from the kiss that didn't happen, so I'm panting and holding my chest.

Instead of answering, he gives me a look. I roll my eyes as I stand to follow him like his eager new puppy that he's house training.

What's sad is that I'm not that far off the mark.

Khalil leads me into the kitchen to one of the furnaces they have all around the house. The flat top tells me this one doubles as a stove, and suddenly, it feels as if I've been transported to the nineteenth century. I stare blankly as he points out the small woodpile of logs, twigs, bark, and sticks in a basket next to it. He then goes through the motions of showing me how to light the fire and feed it.

Either Khalil doesn't notice I've tuned him out or doesn't care as he leads me to the pantry next. It's mostly dry foods and nonperishables like beans, nuts, and grains.

Not a bag of chips in sight.

Khalil wasn't lying when he said they stored enough food for the winter.

Spring is only weeks away, and yet it looks like they have enough to survive *two* winters hunkered down. I'd be impressed if I wasn't panicking at the thought of being stuck up here that long. Didn't they say the winter season lasts longer up here? I was sure they'd have to go into town sooner or later, but it was clear I was wro—

"Aurelia!"

"Aah!" I startle when Khalil barks my name, and I realize I was rooted to the spot while he had already moved on. His ungodly gorgeous face is twisted with irritation on the other side of the island as he waits for me to join him. "Sorry. Gosh. Next time, try whistling or patting your leg," I suggest as I walk over to stand at his side like a good little pet.

Khalil doesn't even try to deny that it's exactly what I am.

CHAPTER ELEVEN

AURELIA

After showing me where everything is in the kitchen, Khalil gives me a tour of the rest of the cabin. I learned that it's mainly powered by solar, with wind as backup, although they don't seem to have much need for electricity.

There's not a single TV, phone, radio, or computer anywhere.

The most modern appliance they have is the coffee machine.

They have books, though.

Lots and lots of books.

There's at least one on every subject. I even find a few *well-worn* romances hidden among survivalist manuals, cookbooks, and murder mysteries like they're ashamed of it.

I smirk at the idea of me finding their porn stash as I follow him into the living room.

Khalil absently points out the unused loft above the living room. The tip of the A-frame window serves as the back wall of the loft and overlooks the vast wilds for miles and miles. The only way up is to climb the smaller bookshelf built into the wall near it.

It's not a bad corner to stick a new pet in—it even has a view—but Khalil doesn't let me go up when I ask if I can see it.

Instead, he takes me out onto the cabin's upper deck overlooking the cliff. It looks newer and less weathered than the one Thorin imprisoned me on. I asked Khalil about it, and he told me they added it last summer. It was a project born out of boredom.

"So, you guys built this cabin yourselves?" I ask before I realize he's taking me back down to the basement.

I'm slower to follow this time, and he snaps at me again.

Luckily, we don't linger in the den.

He leads me through another door I hadn't noticed when I broke in and flicks on the light before taking me down another set of stairs. Immediately, I notice it's much cooler down here. I follow Khalil down the dark tunnel, and he turns on another light at the end.

There are shelves, but unlike the pantry, they're mostly empty. There are a few jars with pickled carrots, peppers, beets, and squash, and a basket of potatoes on the ground in the corner.

"At first, we only built one room," Khalil says out of nowhere, and I frown in confusion until I remember my unanswered question. "For years, we had no more than five hundred square feet to share between the three of us. Five, if you count Zeke and Bane."

"Who are Zeke and Bane?"

Khalil ignores me and picks up a whole carrot from the bunch, inspects it, and then sets it back down on one of the racks. "Getting materials up here without drawing too much attention was a real pain in the ass. The three of us used to sleep on cots, shit in a hole, and fumble around in the dark, trying not to invade each other's space too much. It took two years before we realized that no one was looking for us or cared that we were up here, so we got comfortable. Expanded over the years. Modernized as much as we could. Made a life."

"If you can call this living," I mutter under my breath.

Khalil hears me anyway.

I brace myself for a fight, but he just tosses back, "Why do you think we're keeping you?" as he passes me.

"You can't just keep me, Khalil." I stomp up the stairs behind him as we leave the root cellar and return to the den. "Search and rescue will find me. I bet they're looking for me right now. Once they do, it's over for you."

"Uh-huh." His dismissive agreement is all he says as we travel through the den. I glare at his back as I reluctantly follow him back up to the first floor. Why isn't he more worried that I'll escape or be found? His complete calm is having the opposite effect on me.

Khalil takes me out on the front porch, but no farther since I'm not wearing shoes, and my only clothing is this flannel. I try not to fixate on the reminder that I'm not wearing anything underneath.

It's cold as hell, and I start shivering immediately.

I don't notice that I'm shuffling and huddling toward the closest heat source until I feel warm skin brushing against mine, and then I realize that source is Khalil. He doesn't look too happy about my proximity either. In fact, he's even more tense, as if I'm the one holding him hostage.

Outside, it looks as if another ten feet of snow fell while I was out of it. The sky is clear now, and even though it's day, I can see the moon—or at least the half that's visible—so it must be later than I thought. I hear the sounds of nature all around us. The views from this high up should be stunning, but all I see is my prison.

Khalil points out a much larger cache of wooden logs a few feet away and another shed where he tells me they process and cure the meat from their kills. He then tells me Thorin does most of the hunting.

"What's that?"

Khalil follows my finger to the four wooden boards no more than two feet high. It forms a square, but I can't tell what it's meant for with all the snow covering the ground.

"Garden bed," Khalil answers with a displeased grunt. I'm wondering if he's annoyed with me for asking when he adds, "I tried my hand at growing our own produce a few times, but I wasn't blessed with a green thumb."

Huh.

Apparently, my observation skills are shitty because I hadn't noticed it when I first arrived.

I choose to blame my three days lost in the wilds.

Staring at the small abandoned garden, I ask, "If you don't grow your own produce, how did you get those vegetables in the cellar?"

Khalil's expression pinches when he realizes he's shared too much once again.

I sink my teeth into my bottom lip, biting back a victorious smile while smugly bringing my vigilance skills up from a solid four to five and a quarter.

"Thorin is good at killing shit, and I'm good with my hands," Khalil says tightly. "We sometimes trade his game and my woodwork for supplies we can't grow or make on our own. It's how we paid for a lot of what you see inside. The furniture, housewares, everything."

"With who?"

Khalil's eyes darkening is my only warning before he crowds me against the porch railing and cages me in with both hands gripping the wood on either side of my hips. He doesn't touch me, though. Thank God.

"No one comes up here, Aurelia. Stop thinking you're going to be rescued and start focusing on how to be happy here."

I snort at his lunacy. "Pass."

"You're a bitch. You know that?"

My hands ball into fists at my side. "I don't care what you think of me."

"No?"

I shake my head, but my next breath stutters out of me when his hands leave the railing and skim the outside of my thighs. They stop right below the shirt I'm wearing.

Whose shirt I'm wearing shouldn't even matter, but it does. The flannel still smells like them—warm, spicy, and woodsy, with only a touch of sweetness that you have to really dig deep to reach. It smells like cardamom.

My visceral reaction to the scent pokes at my confused brain and mocks my insistence that I hate the bearer of this flannel. *Whoever he is.*

"You ever think that if you just stop running your mouth, we'll be nicer?"

"You ever think that I don't give a shit if you're nice to me, asshole? I want you to hand me a radio and then disappear forever."

Without warning, Khalil presses his lips against mine, and I let out a surprised sound as his hands travel up the cursed flannel. My hands rise to his strong chest to push him away, but I end up gripping his muscle shirt instead. Simultaneously, he takes my naked ass in his callused palms. The rough pads of his fingers scraping against my soft skin feel like heaven.

I'm *not* thinking about the fact that my naked ass is exposed to the clearing for anyone to see when he pulls back long enough to say, "Just so we're clear, I don't give a shit what you want." He resumes the kiss before I can respond.

We're *still* kissing when I murmur, "Said every abusive asshole ever."

Khalil's grip on my ass tightens, his fingers wandering dangerously close to the arousal building between my thighs. "You think we're abusing you, Goldilocks?"

"You sure as hell aren't romancing me, asshole."

I'm rising onto the tips of my toes to reach his lips better when he utters between kisses, "Well, I think you like the way we treat you."

"*Excuse* me?"

"You heard me."

Khalil slaps my ass hard, and I yelp from the sting while he backs away from me to open the front door, holding it for me to step through. I glare at him for a long time, but he doesn't say a word. The bastard knows his silence will taunt me much more effectively than his words ever will.

Grumbling to myself, I storm past him and into the cabin with the knowledge that he's watching me with no shortage of smug male satisfaction. It's not until the front door slams shut behind him, closing off the biting cold on the other side, that it hits me.

I didn't try to run.

Freedom was *right there*, and I just…climbed back into my cage like an *idiot*.

I don't even flinch when Khalil places a hand on my lower back. He takes me back down into the basement and into the room right off the stairs. It's next to the destroyed bedroom that Khalil tells me belongs to Seth. That tracks.

There are several jumbo metal bins stacked underneath the white plastic farmhouse sink with a spigot. What looks like a metal toilet plunger is leaning against the wall next to it, along with a large wooden paddle with grooves down the length and a short handle. Tossed over the wire hanging in the middle of the room like a clothesline is my dress—clean now but still torn.

Khalil grabs a clean towel and washcloth from the floating shelves after pointing out the pile of dirty laundry waiting to be washed.

"Why are you showing me all of this?" I finally ask him. This whole morning has been one long, confusing mess of don't-give-a-fuck.

"Starting today, this is the shit you'll need to know in order to earn your keep. Make us happy, and we'll reward you. Piss us off, and we'll punish you. It's simple."

"Simple?" I echo calmly despite the shiver working its way down my spine. "Right. How?"

Khalil steps closer until I'm forced to tip my head back to keep eye contact. Leaning down until the tips of our noses touch, he rumbles, "Fuck around and find out, Aurelia."

Khalil's warning feels like a promise. It chills my bones and warms my belly at the same time. All the more reason to get out of here before I lose myself completely.

My skin pebbles with goose bumps, and I don't realize I've lowered my gaze until Khalil hooks a finger under my chin and gently forces my eyes back on him. He doesn't bother issuing more threats once he sees the submission in my eyes. He just pushes me out of the closet and into the bathroom on the other side of the stairs.

"I thought you might want to take a shower," he announces after setting the linen on the sink. "Extra toothbrushes are in the top drawer. That ridiculous dress of yours should be dry by now. I'll leave it on the bed before I go."

"Go?" I gulp. "Where are you going?"

"I showed you where everything is," he says, ignoring my question. "There's meat already thawing in the fridge. You should have no problem getting dinner started. We'll be home by the time the sun touches the horizon. Don't leave the cabin."

Khalil's gone, shutting the bathroom door behind him before I can even get a word out. For a while, I just stand there processing the last half hour until I hear the front door slam closed five minutes later.

He left.

Khalil actually left me alone as if I haven't proven more than once that I'm a definite flight risk.

Running out of the bathroom and up the basement stairs, I make it to the kitchen window overlooking the clearing in time to see Khalil step over the boundary of their property and disappear through the trees. He's covered from head to toe now in a yellow-and-black snowsuit, telling me he really does plan to be gone for a while.

Still, I wait a few minutes more, scanning the tree line to make sure he hasn't forgotten something or this isn't a trap. The three of them could be lying in wait to see if I'll run so they have an excuse to punish me.

After ten minutes, I head to the front door and take a deep breath before I turn the knob.

I fully expected it to be padlocked with thick chains and booby traps because it's the only thing that makes sense, but no.

The blast of cold air when the door actually opens is almost as shocking as finding out that I wasn't locked in.

Immediately, my mind begins to race, trying to hastily form a plan of escape among the chaos of warning bells and the sole question echoing in the background.

Why *should* they lock me in?

I remember every moment of my ordeal before I saw the smoke from the cabin curling above the trees. I only made it this far because of Tyler. I won't be so lucky on my own, and based on how thin the air feels, I climbed higher than I realized up the mountain range's tallest peak to reach the cabin.

My only hope is to wait for the cavalry.

I have this fleeting, ridiculous thought that I could get myself down before I dismiss it as lunacy.

I have no supplies, zero sense of direction, and I still haven't fully recovered from my last walk through the woods.

Heart in my throat, I slowly shut the door.

It's a few more minutes before I can bring myself to walk away from it—my autonomy, my freedom, and my certain death if I leave this prison a moment too soon.

A yawn and the exhaustion that accompanies it take over my thoughts. I've been asleep for days, yet I feel like I could sleep for a few more.

I think about going back downstairs since Khalil's bed is the most comfortable, but the idea of going back into the basement doesn't thrill me, so I eye the cracked door to Thorin's room.

I know Khalil left me a list of demands that I should probably get started on since the days are shorter in the winter, but I have no intention of becoming their twisted version of a housewife.

I choose the nap.

The bears follow me into my dreams, turning them into nightmares.

No matter how hard I run, they catch me. They hold me down and use me. They make me theirs. Sometimes, they let me get away just so it can start all over again. Each time, they take a little more until it's me gladly handing over the tarnished pieces of my soul for them to devour.

That's the most twisted part—that I don't fight all that hard.

It's my shame, my burden to bear.

Their faces are shielded by animalistic masks with gaping maws that reveal their devastatingly gorgeous faces.

They're not monsters or demons or bears. They're so much worse.

They're men—virile, deviant, lonely, and wild. They're free of the societal bonds that demand they behave honorably.

And I know who they are.

I wander hopelessly inside my own mind for what feels like days, searching for their names. Eventually, the darkest depths of my soul answer with a possession that feels perverse.

Thorin—domineering, grumpy, suspicious, and malevolent.

Khalil—passionate, vain, violent, and selfish.

I hesitate on the final name, not because I didn't remember it but because it felt wrong.

No, not wrong. Incomplete.

It feels like one side of a mangled coin. I force my mind to speak it anyway, knowing it's the key to my freedom.

Seth—mischievous, obsessive, gullible, and tormented.

It's not my first time dreaming about them, but it is the first time they speak to me.

I strain to hear, but I can't make out the angry words. The three of them are standing over me, but they might as well be on the moon. When they start to circle me too fast to tell where the attack is coming from, I try to run away again, only to realize my foot is stuck in a metal mouth with sharp teeth and an unforgiving grip.

Bear trap.

Every yank and tug at my ankle makes the trap dig its teeth in deeper, and I instinctively know that it will tear me apart before it lets me go. I hear what sounds like the crack of thunder and feel the ground trembling as if it's about to split apart just before Tyler's voice rises in my mind, screaming at me to run before he's swept up in the frozen tidal wave.

The bear trap springs open, and I'm up on my feet, sprinting away from the massive wall of snow hurtling toward me. I'm much too slow, though, and I scream as I get swept up by the avalanche.

Instead of being buried alive, I'm falling, plunging through the starry night sky. Burning debris from my plane rains down around me like meteorites until I crash through the frozen surface of a lake that pulls me deeper and deeper into its depths—

"Wake the fuck up!"

The freezing water sinks into my bones, and my eyes fly open with a gasp.

It takes a second longer to realize I'm not trapped under the ice of a frozen lake. I'm not drowning or even dreaming anymore.

I'm in a bedroom, and I'm not alone.

There are three fuming shadows standing over me in the dark, depressing room.

Thorin's expression is by far the most vicious as he holds an empty tin cup upside down that I'm guessing was filled with the cold water now soaking through my thick flannel.

Sitting up, I huff and swipe an angry hand over my face, which is also dripping water. "Was that necessary?" I shout.

CHAPTER TWELVE

THORIN

I 'm going to strangle this woman.

Besides appearing a little miffed at being woken up abruptly, Aurelia sits up like she doesn't have a care in the world. I wish I could say the same after a long day of freezing my ass off in the snow. I came home expecting a hot meal, a hard drink, and a tight pussy to warm me, but what I found was an empty table and this pain-in-the-ass girl curled up in my bed as if she belonged.

"Was that necessary?" Aurelia still doesn't meet our gazes as she peels the soaked flannel from her chest. She's all false bravado, this girl. My grip on the empty cup tightens as I try to keep my focus on her face and not her bare thighs.

"Why isn't our dinner ready?" Khalil asks. "And don't think I didn't see our laundry in the same place we left it. I gave you our instructions."

"I don't know," Aurelia answers with a curl of her upper lip while finally making eye contact. "Because you didn't make it before you left? Because I'm not your maid?" Her stomach takes that moment to grumble loudly. "Speaking of food. I'm hungry. When's dinner?"

I pinch the bridge of my nose and exhale. "Aurelia… Please tell me you're fucking with us."

We searched the kitchen from top to bottom when we arrived home before finding her belligerent ass in my bed, tossing and turning like she was having a nightmare.

If she wasn't, she's about to.

"Why would I be fucking with you?"

My body trembles with the effort it takes not to snatch her ass up. If I'm a ticking bomb, this girl is undoubtedly the trigger.

Seth takes a seat on the edge of the bed, and Aurelia eyes him warily. "Why didn't you do what you were told?" he asks her curiously, almost gently.

Aurelia would be dumb as shit to fall for it.

I may be holding on by a thread, but Seth shredded through every single one of his the moment he was born from Zeke's mind. He doesn't realize there is no such thing as gentle with this bitch. She's too damned used to getting her way.

"Did you forget, Sunshine?"

The look Aurelia gives him says all we need to know. "I thought you were joking."

Reaching out, Seth plays with one of her longer curls. "Why is that?"

Aurelia wrinkles her nose and slaps his hand away while climbing from my bed.

None of us moves to give her space.

I can tell the moment she remembers the night in the den. The night we found her. We're crowding her, circling her just the same. The fear that we might repeat that night doesn't paralyze her, though. It feeds her need to self-destruct.

"Because it's the twenty-first century, you sexist shithole? You want me to cook and clean for you like I'm your maid, and when I'm done, spread my legs like I'm your whore. What's next? Bear your child? That's basic-bitch shit. I'm Aurelia *fucking* George. I can ruin your life with one tweet. Find someone else to iron your drawers."

"Trust me, *Au-re-li-a*. You're not our first choice either. A reptile would be more pleasant than you, but I don't see anyone else around to warm our beds, do you?"

"You can't just—"

"This again," I interrupt. "We can't keep you. Blah, blah. It's wrong. Blah, blah. We're cruel caveman psycho creeps. Blah, blah, fucking blah. Now that we've established that *again,* move your ass and start showing us that you're grateful we saved you."

For a moment, Aurelia just gapes at my inability to give a fuck. "*No.*"

"No?" Khalil echoes. The dumbass actually looks shocked.

"No!" she repeats.

"Cabin rules, Aurelia. Remember? Rule number four is *do what you're told*."

She clears her throat and steps closer to me until I'm looking down my nose at her. "Fuck you. Okay? Fuck your rules. Fuck your house. Fuck your mother for having you. And fuck *that*. I'm not about to break my back washing your dirty drawers in a contraption that looks like it was made in the eighteen hundreds! You want to punish me? Fine. But do it knowing that I have a better imagination than you. Everything you do to me, you'll feel threefold. It's in your best interest not to piss me off because I *will* get out of here, and I'll *never*—"

The rest of the venom she spews is cut short when I seize a handful of her curls in my fist so hard she cries out and then reaches up to try to pry her hair free.

"Listen to me, you insufferable pain in my fucking ass. I hope you do come at us with everything you have. Go ahead. Make it interesting. We've been bored up here for nine years. These wilds haven't tamed us, and neither will you. We're overdue for a challenge."

"I'm not your entertainment!"

"You're whatever we say you are," I bite back.

I start moving for the bedroom door, but Aurelia can't fight me and keep up with my long strides at the same time, so she falls to her knees.

Ignoring the demanding pang in my chest to help her up, I keep going instead of stopping.

"Fuck." Khalil huffs. I can feel him and Seth on my heels as I drag Aurelia, screaming and kicking, through the cabin by her hair. "Yo, Thorin. Maybe you want to chill a little?"

I don't want to hear it.

This is his fault for being too soft with her.

I made it clear to him that if Aurelia stays, she needs to learn her place and fast before I change my mind about letting her stay.

Did he listen? Did any of them? Now it's up to me to be the biggest asshole.

Either we get through to Aurelia once and for all, or we give her back to the wilds. I'd rather not leave her to die when I could have her coming on my cock instead.

We reach the kitchen, and I let go of Aurelia's hair and leave her sobbing on the floor.

Khalil's soft ass walks over to help her up, but one look from me has him backing off with an eye roll.

I stalk over to the stove and feel my ire grow, realizing Aurelia let the fire go out. I hastily rebuild the fire, throwing some kindling and a log inside before grabbing the box of matches and lighting it.

For a while, I just stand there with my back to them all and watch the flames as the fire grows. I bide my time, giving Aurelia just enough to save herself. Hearing her shift on the floor behind me, I wait for her to tell us she's sorry and that she'll try harder to show us her gratitude. I already know she won't, but I stay where I am anyway.

Before Aurelia even speaks, I know her remorse has been tossed out the window.

I give myself permission to do the same.

"Okay, I'll cook for you," she says sweetly. "But only because you're such a gentleman, Thorin. Your mother must be proud."

"My mother is dead."

"Lucky her."

I laugh, and the reaction makes her flinch.

"Lucky me," I say easily. "My mother was a junkie whore without a maternal bone in her body. She had a mean streak a mile wide, though."

"So that's your secret tragedy? You got mommy issues, so you hate all women?" Aurelia snorts and shakes her head. "Your origin story sucks, dude. It's not even original."

"Stand up."

It's a command Aurelia doesn't have a problem obeying. She stands, but I don't miss the way she backs toward Khalil and Seth. I doubt she expects them to protect her from me.

Spoiler alert: they won't.

She's just desperate to get away from me.

That won't do at all.

"Come here." When she hesitates, my fingers flex with the urge to grab her, but I force myself to stay put. I didn't enjoy what I did to her just now. I'd rather not repeat it. "I'm not going to ask you again, Aurelia."

Her lips part to say something smart, but she thinks better of it and snaps them closed.

Aurelia doesn't realize it yet, but she's already starting to fall in line.

It's all I can do not to send smug looks to my brothers when she inches closer. Aurelia isn't ready to admit that she enjoys a firm hand and probably never will, so I gently take her nape as soon as she's within reach and draw her close to me until her body is flush with mine and my free hand is resting under the curve of her ass cheek. My fingers are just inches from the tempting heat of her pussy, but I ignore the distraction and focus on the task at hand.

"Now, let's try this again," I say patiently. "If you refuse to answer or I don't like what I hear, I'm going to hurt you. It won't be easy, and you won't be able to take it. Don't test me, Aurelia. I'm not in the mood. Am I clear?"

My anger slowly unfurls in my chest when she stares at my chest and nods.

"Did Khalil tell you what we expected of you today?" Aurelia hesitates a moment and then nods slowly. "Were you confused by what he told you?" She shakes her head. "So why wasn't it done?"

That defiant gleam enters her eyes again, and I tighten my hold in warning. She blinks, and then it's gone. "I–I didn't know how."

"You didn't even try," I bite out.

"Because I don't know how!"

I slap her ass hard enough for it to smart, and I swear to fucking God her nipples pebble through the flannel. "Watch that volume, songbird. I won't tell you again."

Aurelia shudders violently and then squirms against my hold when she realizes I can feel her reaction. "Don't call me that," she grinds out.

"Why not?" I whisper against her lips. "It's what you are. You don't like it?"

"*No.*"

Her response is a knee-jerk reaction. And it's a complete lie.

I'm tempted to reach under the flannel—*my* flannel—and touch her pussy to prove it.

Khalil couldn't wait to find us earlier and brag about how he kissed her, and she kissed him back. According to him, she was damn near panting for it.

It's hard enough watching Aurelia run her mouth, sleep in my bed uninvited, and walk around dressed in my clothes with nothing underneath and not do anything about it, but now it feels like I'm competing with my brothers for her attention.

"Tough. I don't like it when my woman doesn't obey me."

"I'm not your—"

I don't give her a chance to lie to me again.

She's ours, and there's nothing she can do about it. The thought sends a thrill from my fingers and up my arms and neck until it fills my head with euphoria.

Unwilling to repeat the same argument, I distract her with kisses instead. My lips are firm against hers but not demanding. I wait her out to see if she responds—to see how long it takes her to stop pretending she doesn't want my touch.

The answer: not that fucking long.

All that fuss, and I don't even have to make her kiss me back. Her eyes are closed so she doesn't see me open mine to peer smugly over her shoulder at Khalil.

He rolls his eyes and looks away.

I already know her better than the others and the thought makes my chest swell with pride. My way got her pliant, but maybe Seth and Khalil were on to something too.

Nice makes her *want it.*

Aurelia even opens that mouth of hers when I ask, and nothing but sweet comes out when she moans and claws to get closer to me.

"Do you want a repeat of your first night?" I ask between kisses.

A terrified shudder rips through her, but she doesn't stop kissing me, doesn't stop feeding me her tongue. I swear to God she even clings to me like I'll protect her...from *me.* "No."

"No?" I break the kiss to stare down at her with my fingers tightening around her hair. "Then you better get started on dinner. You've got one hour to have something edible on that table, Aurelia. I'm not fucking around."

CHAPTER THIRTEEN

SETH | ZEKE

F uck," Thorin gripes under his breath so that Aurelia won't hear. "She's an even worse cook than Khalil."

Khalil sucks his teeth at the jab. "Man, fuck you." He makes a face like he's chewing glass as he tries to stomach the slop Aurelia served us for dinner.

I can't even begin to tell you what it is.

It's bad.

Like eating animal dung would be better.

Me? I find it *hilarious*.

Aurelia literally made Thorin eat his words by serving up the worst dish known to man. I don't know what it is, but I wouldn't feed it to my dogs if I had any. I inhale it anyway to keep from laughing at these two miserable fucks.

And because Zeke will wake up soon.

I'll need my strength to keep him suppressed for a little while longer. He won't like what we're doing to Aurelia. He'll try to come to her rescue, and while I'm happy to cheer and encourage her rebellion, I can't help but want to steal a piece of her for myself—to take with me when I sleep. It could be years before Zeke loses his shit enough to let me take over.

His time out here in the wilds, away from people who can hurt him, has been good for him.

The more he heals, the less he needs me.

The more I…fade.

Thorin's gagging interrupts my depressing thoughts. "I can't do it. This shit is worse than the slop they served us in DFAC."

"There's a fifty percent chance I'm going to wake up with food poisoning," Khalil complains.

"I've got a hundred percent chance of dying if I eat another bite of this." Thorin pushes his plate away.

Aurelia notices and abandons her sorry attempt at cleaning the kitchen to walk over. "Problem, fellas?"

"No problem," Thorin lies easily. "Thanks for dinner. That was… something."

Aurelia's gaze falls to his plate, which is still full. "You didn't finish."

"I'm full."

"No. You have to eat it all," Aurelia says deceptively softly while pushing Thorin's plate back in front of him. "You were so hungry, remember? It was imperative that I feed you against my will, and now I have." Thorin glares at her while an unfazed Aurelia smiles sweetly down at him. "No dessert or getting up from the table until you clean your plate, boys."

Khalil huffs then holds his nose and starts shoveling as much as he can fit in his mouth so he can get it over with.

It's fucking hilarious.

"What about me? I'm finished." My teeth sink into my bottom lip as I sit back in my chair and eye the inner curve of her tit peeking through the flannel. This girl is more broken than I thought, letting Thorin feel her up after handling her the way he did. "Can I have dessert?"

"Of course you can. You're such a good boy." She pats my head like I'm a dog, and even though I know she's being condescending, it doesn't work. I take the opportunity to show her why I'm better than those two boneheads. I roll out Zeke's freakishly long tongue and let it hang while panting heavily like one.

Aurelia chokes on a shocked laugh, slapping a hand over her mouth when she realizes her slip. The sound is so carefree and genuine that Khalil and Thorin gape from their sides of the table like they have eggs on their faces.

Did I mention how much I adore Aurelia George?

She tries to get away, but I snake my arm out and pull her into my lap before she can get more than a step. "What?" I ask when her amusement fades, and she wears an uncomfortable look. "You said I could have dessert."

"I meant like pie or ice cream."

"Do we have ice cream?"

"No."

"Did you make pie?"

Realizing I have her cornered, she grumbles, "No."

"Mmm," I hum as I smell her neck. "Then I guess I'll have to eat yours."

While Aurelia's skin becomes cold and clammy at the thought of me touching her again, I wonder what she'll taste like. Apple? Cherry? Lemon meringue?

Our girl is sweet and tangy, so my money is on the latter.

I've been hard for her all day, but right now, there's something else I want more. She's tense as fuck in my lap, though, so I don't think she'd go for me eating her pussy.

Damn.

I would have made it so good for her.

Probably.

I could take it, but I'd rather she give it to me. I know despite all their huffing and puffing, Khalil and Thorin feel the same. They'll wait for Aurelia to come around for as long as they can stand before taking what she promised us.

I figure she's got a couple more days before one of them cracks.

"Actually, I'm pretty full," I say, letting her off the hook. "Maybe next time."

Aurelia's still rigid as fuck, but her relief is palpable.

She doesn't thank me, though, and I don't expect her to. Since I'm not a good guy and I can't have her thinking I am, I tighten my hand on her hip when she tries to rise.

"What do you say?" I prod.

"About what?"

"Skipping dessert."

"You want me to *thank* you for not assaulting me?"

"Have you ever had your pussy eaten before?"

Aurelia looks almost ashamed when she gives a small shake of her head.

"Then trust me, Sunshine. The last thing you would have felt was put out."

"I'm not thanking you" is all she says.

"You're so fucking sexy. I could fuck you right now," I offer while thrusting my hips up so she can feel how hard I am for her. "Would you like that, Sunshine? Can I bend you over this table? I won't be quick, but I'll make you scream. Promise."

"No, I—Please don't."

"Then what do you say, Aurelia?"

The dining room is taut with tension as the three of us collectively hold our breath, waiting to see if our prideful princess will bend.

"Th-thank you." Her hands ball around the hem of the flannel, and she looks like she wants to stab me with the knife I have embedded in the wooden surface of the table. She's eyeing it hard, so Khalil cautiously reaches out and removes the weapon before changing the subject.

"How are you not a virgin, but you've never had your pussy eaten?" he blurts in delayed astonishment.

"You'd have to ask the whopping four men I've fucked."

Khalil gapes and then just shakes his head like he's disappointed in our girl for not choosing better partners.

"You've only had sex with four men, and two of them were for revenge?" Thorin remarks.

"I've been busy," she says simply.

"Head should be fucking mandatory," Khalil grumbles while staring thoughtfully at the wall. He's really upset about this.

Aurelia quirks a brow. She thinks we don't see the interest she's trying so hard to hide in her eyes. "Are you decreeing so as the giver or receiver?"

His heated gaze snaps back to her as he says, "Be a good girl for us, and you'll find out." The three of us wait for Aurelia to deny that she's not picturing Khalil's head between her thighs even now. Surprisingly, she doesn't. Her gaze is a little unfocused as she stares at his mouth, and Khalil shifts in his seat while I grow a little harder under Aurelia's plump ass. "You didn't eat," he points out. "Why?"

"I'm not hungry."

"That's not what you said when you demanded *we* feed you," Thorin reminds her. He can never let anything go. Asshole still hasn't forgiven me for trying to burn him alive that one time.

My gaze narrows as it shifts between Zeke's friends.

Or was that Khalil I tried to torch?

"I've lost my appetite," Aurelia answers, snapping me out of my thoughts and my favorite subject—murder.

Khalil's gaze flicks to me when I start grinning like a maniac, but he doesn't remark on it. He probably already knows she's the reason.

Aurelia.

No matter how many times we try to break Sunshine, she dares us to push harder.

"Come here."

I roll my eyes because Thorin giving a shit whether she eats is obviously a ruse to get her out of my lap and into his. Along with holding a grudge, Thorin also has a problem with sharing. We all do, which is how I know this will never work.

I, for one, can't *wait* for it to blow up in our faces.

Jealously, I hope Thorin gets maimed the most when Aurelia stands and slowly rounds the table. Thorin doesn't speak or touch her, yet Aurelia lowers herself onto his leg without being told to.

Thorin pulls his half-eaten plate closer to himself before using his fork to pierce the tough-as-Teflon deer meat that Aurelia butchered worse than Thorin did when he killed it.

He brings the fork to her lips, but she stubbornly turns her head away.

Khalil reaches across the short distance from his spot at the head of the table and grips her jaw. He squeezes until Aurelia whimpers and turns her head back toward Thorin. The two share a look that ends with Aurelia opening her mouth the tiniest bit.

Thorin feeds her the venison.

Aurelia makes a face at the awful taste as she chews. The next portion is even larger. Having already made his point, Thorin takes one for the team and eats it.

Bite after bite, he feeds them both—with his portions considerably larger—until the plate is empty and Aurelia looks ready to hurl.

"The winters can be brutal, so we don't waste food," Thorin tells her as he hands her his water glass. Aurelia takes it from him and guzzles half of it down to wash the taste of dinner from her mouth. "There are some cookbooks on the bookshelves. They helped us; they can help you."

Aurelia pauses her slow sips to ask, "So, why didn't one of you make dinner?"

"Because we have you to take care of us now."

"Cabin rule number five," I say casually, and she glares at me. "Have our dinner on the table every night, or we'll have *you* instead."

"Oh, so you're cannibals too?" she says, purposely misunderstanding my meaning. "Wow, I'm so surprised."

None of us bother to correct her. Our grins just grow sharper as if we might truly devour her.

"And it's not just dinner," Khalil amends. "There's breakfast and lunch too. We're gone most of the day, so you don't need to go overboard for lunch. We won't always make it back before the sun sets."

Aurelia looks surprised at that. "You really trust me to stay here alone?"

Khalil shrugs. "Whether you live or die is entirely your choice, Goldilocks."

"And make no mistake, if you try to leave this mountain on your own, you won't survive," Thorin adds. "We don't care about you, Aurelia. Run, and we *will* let you die. Feel free to consider that cabin rule number six."

"But take it as a warning above all because we're not fucking around," I say gravely. "It's cleaner for us to let you perish from exposure or the impact of falling from a cliff because you can't see more than five feet in front of you."

"It looked pretty clear outside to me," Aurelia retorts.

"Wait a while," Khalil tells her.

"Today was the first time we've seen the sky since we found you," Thorin informs. "The weather here can turn in an instant."

"I can still be rescued," she argues. "I found this cabin. Search and rescue will too."

"That's true," I say with a sniff while stretching my legs under the table. Thorin and Khalil glare daggers at me, but I ignore them.

I mean, goddamn.

This girl is clinging to the tiniest scrap of hope that her old life isn't lost. Why not let her have it? Why not give her something to fight for? The three of us being willingly stuck on this mountain is depressing enough without her adding to it.

"They're looking for you, you know. The Canadian Armed Forces is all over it, coordinating with the local authorities and search and rescue team. It's been dicey with the storms, but they're out there day and night. You didn't leave a lot of tracks when you fled the crash site on account of the storms, but the men leading the teams, telling them *exactly* where to look, know these mountains better than anyone. They'll find you no matter where you go."

Aurelia's gaze brightens as she leans forward, completely unaware that she's flashing us her gorgeous tits. "Really? How do you know this?"

She's practically panting for the answer, so I give it to her.

"Oh, because we are search and rescue."

I get the sense that I fucked up monumentally.

Khalil leaves no room for doubt when he hits me with a mean right hook that has me tasting my own blood and stumbling to stay on my feet. Laughing, I spit the blood into the snow before wiping my mouth as I face them. Khalil and Thorin stand shoulder to shoulder, armed with twin glowers.

I should be used to it by now. The two of them standing against me instead of with me. Thorin and Khalil are Zeke's friends. I'm just the freak show with a high threshold for pain and no memories that exist outside of it.

Oh, boo-hoo.

The three of us came outside to "talk" after Aurelia tired herself out from screaming and throwing shit at us. Namely me. Once she passed out on the couch, Khalil carried her to his bed, and we haven't heard a peep from her since.

Huh…

I guess I didn't give her hope after all. I think I just made it worse.

Well, she hurt my feelings, too, when she called me emotionally stunted. Actually, I guess that's a fair assessment considering how dinner ended.

Thorin grabs my coat in both fists and gets in my face. "You're done. Wake Ezekiel up. Now."

"Fuck you." I shove him away. "We both know neither of you want him awake right now. Can you imagine how far it will set him back once he finds out what you're doing to that girl?" I laugh again. "Shit's going to hit the fan, and you know it, so yeah, I think I'll stay awhile longer."

"Cut the shit, Seth. Why did you do it?"

I shrug a little petulantly as I stare out into the wilds, drowning in darkness. The darkness never seems to end. Even way out here.

"I can tell Aurelia is all alone in this world. She's like me. Sunshine doesn't have anyone who cares enough to risk their own neck to save her. Not like Zeke did. She needs to accept that now so she can move on."

Khalil latches on to what I let slip and inches closer. "You're not alone, Seth."

"Fuck you!" I explode while stepping back to keep the distance between us. I can't let them confuse me like Isaac did—like they're trying to do to Sunshine. "You're Zeke's friends, not mine. You don't give a shit about me. You keep trying to make him *better*."

"Because you keep trying to kill him!"

"So? What's the big deal? He wants to die," I tell them.

Thorin and Khalil both look so pathetically heartbroken over it. Disgusting feeling creatures.

"You're supposed to protect him, Seth."

"I *am*." When they just shake their heads, I feel myself getting defensive. "You don't know him like I do. You're not in his head. You see it, but you don't *feel* it. It *hurts*. More than any of the shit they did to us."

"Then stop fighting us, and let us help you, Seth. Both of you."

I scoff and look away. "Whatever."

It's quiet for a while, and then Thorin asks, "What makes you think Aurelia is alone? She has her uncle."

We grilled Sheriff Kelly for as much information on Aurelia as we could without seeming suspicious.

Orphan.

Raised by her father's brother.

Won over the world with her voice at the tender age of fourteen.

And from the looks of it, she's been under her uncle's control ever since.

"Take it from someone whose own brother tried to kill him: Marston George doesn't give a fuck about his niece."

"You don't know that."

"She was a danger to everything he built. I wouldn't be surprised if he fucked with the plane, and it wasn't the storm at all."

Thorin blows out a breath. "That's a little far-fetched."

"Yeah? Well, what would you do for complete control of a billion-dollar fortune?"

You heard right.

Our girl wasn't kidding when she said she had the power to crush us. She's filthy fucking rich, and it's not even in the top fifty reasons why I'm obsessed with her.

Thorin grunts, jarring me back to this side of sanity where it's so fucking boring. "If she dies, he probably inherits it all," he grumbles.

"You really think she has no one? What about that kid we found? He kept saying her name when we radioed for a medevac and choppered him out. Maybe he's her boyfriend."

Ah, yes.

Tyler whatever.

Fuck that guy.

The pussy was too busy dying in the snow with a leg half gone to frostbite while *our* girl made it all the way here and found shelter.

Found us.

No. Tyler won't do at all. He's not good enough for her.

"He *was* her boyfriend. Someone ought to tell him that, like his leg, he's never getting his bitch back." I chuckle at my own dark humor.

"You just focus on keeping your mouth shut," Thorin orders. "Now is not the time to stir up trouble for the hell of it."

The sound I make is a cross between a snort and a grunt. "Pussy."

"*Seth.*"

My gaze drops to the snow when I remember the lost look in Aurelia's eyes. "I didn't mean to make her sad."

"Maybe this is a good thing," Khalil says. "It's out in the open now. We don't have to worry about it blowing up in our faces later."

I frown at that since the last thing I want is to make things easier for these assholes.

Team Sunshine all the way.

A low growl interrupts whatever bullshit excuse Thorin is about to make to continue torturing that girl. Pivoting slowly, I search the tree line thirty feet away, and at first, I don't see a thing.

And then I see two things.

Glowing eyes piercing a solid wall of black.

A lone wolf with tawny fur steps into the opening with its head low to the ground and wary eyes shifting between Khalil, Thorin, and me. There's a snarl on its lips as it slowly closes in, but the three of us hold our ground. We don't look away, and neither does the tawny wolf. It stops five feet away, lips pulling back to bare its teeth as it gives another menacing growl.

Aw, she looks just like Sunshine.

"What's the matter, girl? Where's your pack?"

The wolf snarls and rears back as if she understood me. Her pack must be a sore subject. It's then I notice her rounded belly and battle scars.

No pack, then.

Pregnant as fuck, though.

"Seth," Khalil exhales my name with a quiet breath when I reach out with my palm up.

The wolf gives a low warning growl, but I don't draw my hand back.

I wait her out.

She sniffs the air, looks away, and then sniffs the air again before inching forward. Her hackles are still raised, but she's curious too.

Just like Aurelia.

The wolf sniffs my palm, and in my peripheral vision I can see Thorin and Khalil moving into position just in case this inevitably goes south and I lose my hand. If I do, I'll make sure to gift it to Sunshine as an apology for hurting her tonight and all the nights that will no doubt follow.

The wolf is still scenting me when I sign my death wish by moving my hand through the fur under her jaw. I keep it there, admiring the untamable wildness in her gaze as she watches me back.

"It's okay, girl. Go back to your den. We won't bother you," I promise.

With one last warning growl, the wolf turns and jogs off into the trees. I guess it was too much to hope for a few palm licks before she went.

Looking over my shoulder, I smirk at the cowering pussies, Khalil and Thorin looking at me like I've lost my mind.

The joke's on them. I never had it.

"She's getting ready to whelp those pups, so her den must be nearby," Khalil remarks.

"I'll track her down tomorrow. Make sure she doesn't come back," Thorin says.

I'm still watching the tree line when I answer. "Don't bother."

"And if it's Aurelia out here the next time she comes?" Thorin retorts.

"Maybe she'll learn to stay her ass in the cabin," Khalil mumbles.

I roll my eyes at them both. "The wolf won't be back. She's not interested in us. She was just checking out the competition."

I don't give either a chance to argue. Unzipping my jeans, I pull out my dick and watch the steam from my warm piss hitting the frozen ground rise and curl in the air.

"What the fuck, Seth?"

I look over my shoulder to see Khalil pinching the bridge of his nose and looking exasperated. "*Why?*"

"Marking our territory," I explain. "Why else? If you don't want the wolf coming back..." I let my point hang since they're smart boys and continue draining the hose along the outer edges of our turf.

There's a beat of contemplative silence, and then the sound of zippers lowering as Khalil and Thorin join me.

Anything for Sunshine.

CHAPTER FOURTEEN

AURELIA

The cookbooks, which one of those creepy bastards left stacked on the nightstand for me, might as well be in a foreign language: braise, core, dredge, sauté, and brine.

I don't understand any of it.

This morning, I woke up once again in the bed of twisted branches, and it was only slightly less jarring than before. It wouldn't have been bad at all if not for the mysterious nausea and stomach cramps that roused me. The sick feeling only intensified when I realized I hadn't slept alone. Khalil was already gone when I woke, but the indentation in the pillow and the lingering warmth of the sheets told me as much.

I'd taken a much-needed shower only after making sure I was alone in the cabin, and then I donned the peasant dress because it was the only thing I had left that was mine. It was a constant reminder that I didn't belong here and that I had a life waiting for me outside of this cabin.

I'm sure if the guys knew that, they'd burn it, so mum's the word.

Despite their warning that they expected three hot meals a day, the guys hadn't dragged me out of bed to cook for them again. With great satisfaction and amusement, I wonder if it's because they weren't looking forward to sampling my amazing culinary skills again so soon.

At the moment, I'm sitting cross-legged on the unbelievably cozy bear rug in front of the fire upstairs, studying recipes for canning and making butter because it's better than dwelling on reality.

I may never leave this mountain.

If I'm not found, I'll be confined to this cabin for the rest of my life.

It's not like my captors could take me into town and introduce me as their girlfriend or anything. I'm too recognizable, and thanks to the plane crash, that now includes the people in this remote corner of the world.

Maybe in a few years, but I doubt they'll take the risk.

After reaching the end of the first cookbook without finding a recipe that seems possible with my limited skills, I don't even bother reading the others. Wiping my sweaty forehead with the back of my hand, I stand on unsteady feet and walk toward the kitchen.

The sound of something snapping and then a pained squeal draws my attention toward the side door just off the kitchen. I don't understand what could have made the sound until I search behind the trash can and see a wooden mouse trap and the gray furry rodent caught under the clamp. It squeals and wiggles to be free, but the trap's hold on it is too strong.

Join the club, Ratatouille.

Shuddering, I leave it there since I'm no fucking exterminator. I pour myself a glass of water and sip it slowly as I wait for the feeling that I'm about to vomit to fade. When I'm sure I won't pass out, I walk the cabin for the third time since my arrival.

You know how you walk into a room and immediately know something is missing, but you can't put your finger on it?

The feeling started yesterday when Khalil showed me around, but it's amplified now that I'm alone, and I don't have Khalil, Thorin, or Seth watching my every move. I don't realize what's missing until I'm back in the den, staring at the back wall in disbelief.

The weapons are gone.

The crossbow, rifles, spare hunting knives, and other shit that I can't even name are missing. There's also a noticeably empty space on the console table that I could have sworn had been occupied before.

A record player?

No.

A radio. And not the kind that gets your favorite music station.

There was also a huge map on the adjacent wall, but it's gone now.

It takes me a moment longer to piece together why Thorin, Khalil, and Seth would go through the trouble of moving all of their gear.

They *hid* it.

My guess is while I was out of it.

I eye the tall metal locker in the corner. There are chains with thick, rusted links wrapped around the handles and a padlock to secure it.

To keep me out of it?

Definitely.

Instinctively, I turn and round the couch until I'm standing over the footlocker they use as a coffee table. Was that lock there before? I don't think so, but I can't be sure. My memory is good but not photographic good.

Collapsing on the couch, I stare at the floor, but then all I can see is me on my knees that first night, so I close them until the memory fades and I don't feel so dangerously close to splintering apart.

Thorin, Khalil, and Seth didn't just refuse to help me. They stripped and locked away anything I might use to save myself if it comes to that. They stacked the deck so that I don't ever stand a chance.

Feeling this raw and angry need to fight for my survival rise inside me, I open my eyes.

As cruel as it was, Seth at least helped me see that it was weak to wait around, hoping to be rescued.

No one's coming for me.

I guess I knew that. Every day that I'm not found lowers the chance—in my eyes and the eyes of the world—that I will ever be.

If I'm going to survive this mountain and its men, I have to stop thinking of myself as the Aurelia before the crash—the pop star and the celebrity.

America's sweetheart.

I'm not that girl anymore—if I ever was.

I'm the fallen star that may not gleam brightly anymore, but I'm stronger for it. If I'm going to be saved, I have to do it myself.

I mentally run through a list of everything I'll need to make it off this godforsaken mountain.

Vengeance will come later. When I'm out of their reach, but they're not out of mine.

I'll need a map—if I can find the one they hid and figure out how to read it.

Clothes for the climate.

Food.

Water.

Protection.

A phone.

It's hard to believe they don't have one. All the way out here? It's too big of a risk, but I don't remember seeing any cell towers, so I cross a phone off my list and add a radio in its place.

When they treated my wounds, they unwittingly showed their hand.

Thorin, Khalil, and Seth are no ordinary cavemen. They're cunning and resourceful and two steps ahead, which means I'll need to be three.

Food and water.

So far, it's the only thing I can get my hands on, but it's a start.

I gnaw on my thumbnail as I continue to plot—to plan. I thought my uncle had exorcised me of the habit, but it's back with a vengeance, and I can't bring myself to care.

I'll have to find something to carry my supplies in and a hiding place to store them until I'm ready to make a run for it. Somewhere these mountain men won't think to look. It doesn't take long before I have the perfect place in mind.

Thorin's words from the night before rise in my memory with a vengeance as my mind shifts to the most challenging objective. The task that—without success—will make all the others meaningless.

"These wilds haven't tamed us, and neither will you."

Yeah… We'll see about that.

Standing, I take one step to get started on my chores when the room spins.

At first, I think I'm about to black out again, but my throat jumps, and I clap a hand over my mouth before making a mad dash to the bathroom, where I empty my stomach of last night's meal.

CHAPTER FIFTEEN

KHALIL

Leaning over with one hand braced on a tree, I try to tune out the sound of Seth retching a few feet away. It doesn't work, and I end up emptying my guts for the second time this morning before I see Thorin stumbling back to camp from wherever he'd gone to expel the effects of Aurelia's cooking.

"I think that bitch poisoned us," Thorin says under his breath so that only the three of us hear.

Seth wipes his mouth and starts weakly singing the hook of "Poison" by Bell Biv DeVoe.

Fucker.

We're currently in a camp surrounded by military personnel, local deputies, and civilian volunteers from three neighboring towns. Right after Aurelia lost consciousness the night we found her, Sheriff Kelly radioed to inform us about the plane crash and that we'd be leading the search for the pop princess and her entourage. Other than Aurelia, her head bodyguard, Tyler Westbrook, was the only one we've found alive.

And so close to our cabin too.

After that, it was easy to piece together how we came upon our infuriating captive.

Tyler and Aurelia must have wandered too far searching for the emergency transmitter and gotten separated in the avalanche. The same one that lured us from our cabin that morning. Aurelia probably tried to find her bodyguard and found us instead. She took shelter in our cabin and waited for us to come home and rescue her.

So hopeful.

So naïve.

So ours.

What *hasn't* been easy is keeping the search away from our cabin and later explaining why we insist on the long trek back to our side of the Cold Peaks every night. But with each passing day, Aurelia's chances of survival dwindle, along with everyone's morale.

Not much longer now.

Ironically, anyone with the authority to question why we've kept the search off our mountain has been too busy fielding questions from the press and assuring the public that we're leaving no stone unturned to know the actual details of the search.

Another week and it will be called off with a promise to keep looking if any new evidence surfaces.

"You boys okay?" Sheriff Kelly asks from a safe distance. The lawman's weathered cheeks are red from the cold, while his thick salt-and-pepper mustache is flaked with freshly fallen snow. "That don't look too good. Maybe you boys should head home. We can handle the search today."

"No can do, Sheriff. Our window of finding this girl alive is closing fast," I say, spinning the same web of bullshit we've been weaving since we first got the call. "This chick seems like she meant a lot to people. Hate to let them down."

"It's just a little food poisoning," Thorin adds. "We'll be fine."

"Food poisoning?" the sheriff exclaims with amusement. "You boys ain't been making good use of those books my wife sent you?"

"Of course." I force a smile. "I think we just ate some bad meat. We're good to go. Let's find this princess so we can all stop freezing our asses off."

Sheriff Kelly eyes us closely and then takes his hat, made of muskrat fur and beaver pelt, off. His face is pinched, and he looks more than just a little frustrated as he shoves his fingers through his thinning hair. "I appreciate the dedication," he whispers as he steps closer, "but can I speak freely with you three?"

"Sure." Seth shrugs, but his eyes are glazed and distant as he daydreams about Aurelia for the umpteenth time today.

I know because it's been the same for me.

I've never been so eager to get back to the cabin and hole up inside. Usually, I'm clawing at the walls to get out.

"It's already been a week, and a fancy, city girl like that…" The sheriff blows out a breath and shakes his head. "The best we can hope for is a body to give her family. It will give them closure, permission to grieve and move on."

It's all I can do to keep my grave expression and not smile.

And then Thorin surprises the shit out of us all when he says, "If *I* can be honest, I think you're underestimating her."

"How so?" The confused pinch in Sheriff Kelly's brow is genuine.

"Yeah, how so?" I echo with more than a little bite in my tone than necessary.

Thorin is seconds away from blowing our cover, and all because he chooses now to get defensive over a girl he wanted to feed to the wolves less than a week ago. It's impossible for his timing to be any worse.

"I was there for the briefing, and it was thorough."

Thorin's right. It was.

The detailed glimpse into Aurelia's life had been a real eye-opener. Let's just say I'd slept with one eye open while lying next to her last night.

"A girl like that doesn't seem ordinary to me, Sheriff. We may not understand her life, but I think you'd be surprised how far inside themselves people will dig when their back is against the wall." No one except us and Aurelia knows just how hard she fought to survive, and I know Thorin is thinking about it now. "From the looks of it, Aurelia's overcome a lot worse than a little cold weather."

The frustration in the sheriff's eyes suddenly clears, and then he straightens as Thorin's words sink in. "Yeah, son, I think you're right." Clapping Thorin's shoulders, I school my expression to an optimistic one when he looks at us all with renewed vigor. "Let's just hope for the best then, yeah?" Kelly shoves his hat back on his balding head and stomps off with a purpose.

The moment his back is turned, I drop the expression and keep my gaze forward as I watch him go.

"Way to go, Thor. I'm sure your dick was in the right place, but you just gave that old bastard hope and extended this pointless search by two days."

The three of us watch as Kelly rallies the troops and shouts orders to the shivering deputies, lingering around with tired and despondent looks on their faces.

Thorin, seeing for himself what his sudden infatuation with Aurelia fucking George has done, exhales and drops his head. "Fuck."

Seth starts singing again.

It's late when we finally make it home.

No one speaks as we trudge inside the quiet cabin. We're too on edge, wondering if we should be suiting up for a repeat of last night. I'm honestly so exhausted pretending to look for Aurelia that I don't know if I can spare the energy to fight with her again.

If she chooses violence again, I'm tapping out. She wins this round.

Thorin walks to his bedroom, where we found her last time, and peeks inside. There's a mixture of relief and worry when he finds it empty.

We finish searching the entire upper floor before I realize the cabin is warm.

The last time we left Aurelia alone, she let the fire go out, and we came home to dying embers and a frigid cabin. The fire in the living room is still burning, albeit a little wildly, for the middle of the night.

I reposition the logs inside the stove so there's less airflow before heading to the kitchen. Seth is doing the same to the larger stove we use for cooking while Thorin is eyeing the three covered plates on the counter as if they'll explode.

His gaze rises to meet mine, and I almost laugh at the panic in them as he says, "I'm not eating that."

"We have to." I chuckle as I walk over to take a closer look. "Kind of sends a mixed message if we don't, doesn't it?"

"I don't care," Thorin says. He's shaking his head and backing away. "I'll *die*."

I roll my eyes at him and then lean over the counter to study the food because it can't be that bad.

It's worse.

It looks like…shit.

The food looks like shit. And smells like death.

"How the hell is she getting *worse*?"

I'd left Aurelia the cookbooks before heading out this morning. I can see a couple of them open on the counter, so I don't have to question if she'd at least made an effort.

"Who the hell cares?" Thorin grumbles. "I'm not eating it."

"Don't be a baby. You—"

"Hey, fellas."

Our gazes shift to the opening, where Aurelia is standing with a suspiciously bright smile on her face. The front of her dress is soaked through, but I don't get a chance to ask what the hell she's been up to because she says, "You're home." There's a stumbling pause as she searches for something else to say to us. "How was your day?"

It's forced and awkward.

"Fine," Thorin snaps. The grouchy son of a bitch is glaring at her now like those things he said at the camp never happened.

The skin under Aurelia's eyes looks a little lighter, giving her a sickly pallor. Considering our struggle to keep anything down earlier, it's obvious Aurelia got sick too. She didn't eat as much as the three of us, yet she looks worse off. She's probably used to finer foods and five-course meals curated by Michelin-star chefs. She probably takes her coffee with diamonds sprinkled on top rather than cinnamon.

"Feeling all right?"

Aurelia makes eye contact with me, and I can see the indecision in her eyes before she looks away. "Yup! I hope you're hungry. I made dinner."

I rub the back of my neck. "Yeah. Um…"

Noticing my hesitation, the weird smile on her face falls. "What's the matter?"

"Aurelia, what is this?" I gesture to the food.

"Your dinner."

"Right, but what *is* it?"

"Beans."

"Beans and what?"

"Mice."

"Excuse me?"

"Mice." The practiced smile is back, and it's creepy as fuck. "I found some caught in your traps and thought, why not, you know? It was kind of tricky because they smell god-awful, and I'm pretty sure they're diseased and don't taste very good. Plus, there was no recipe for mice stew in those books you left for me. Thank you for that, by the way. Real helpful. Anyway, I managed. Bon appétit, boys."

Before any of us can think of what to say to her, Aurelia turns and flounces off back to wherever she came from.

This girl is fucking crazier than I thought.

"Do you think mice are a rich person's delicacy where she comes from?" Seth asks once she's gone. "Like caviar? Oh, shit. I think I see an eyeball." Seth points it out, and sure enough, there's a fucking mouse eye staring back at us.

I gag while Thorin swears and grabs the plates. He tosses them in the trash along with our "dinner."

But he doesn't stop there.

Thorin yanks the bag out of the bin and storms out the side door to toss it in the barrel, where we burn whatever we can't compost or recycle. I can see him pour lighter fluid over it before grabbing the matches. The flames roar to life and chase away the night until I can see his hard profile clearly through the window. The twitching muscles in his jaw tell me he's thinking about his next move and resisting it even harder.

Whatever he decides, Seth and I have his back. Well, I do. Seth is still a wild card.

When Thorin finally steps back inside, we lock gazes. "I think it's safe to say we gave our guest every chance to get with the program, don't you?"

"Yeah…" My smile is slow to come, but it grows in anticipation of the night ahead. "I'd say so. She's basically calling us out at this point. Seth?"

"Can I go first?" He jumps right to the point.

"No. You're the reason she tried to feed us rodents for dinner."

"That's debatable," Seth says petulantly.

"It's really not," I return as we leave the kitchen.

Aurelia's clearly still pissed about last night. Seth took away the only hope she had because he's desensitized to human emotion.

We find Aurelia downstairs in the laundry room.

Thorin and Seth hang back while I block her only exit. Aurelia's humming and bouncing to some tune only she can hear while hanging Thorin's flannel that she wore yesterday on the clothesline. I know I don't make a sound, but she must feel me watching her because the song in her head ends abruptly, and she turns around.

I'm standing in the doorway, leaning a shoulder against the jamb as I watch her. "How's it going?"

"Fantastic!" Her voice is light and airy and fucking weird as shit. I already know she's messing with us, but it feels like a performance she's done before. She's too good at it. I almost believe she likes taking care of us.

"I see you finally decided to do the laundry."

"It's good exercise." Aurelia grips the washing stick with both hands and makes circling motions while moving her hips. "Chugga-chugga! Chugga-chugga! Chugga-chugga! Chugga-chugga! Chugga-chugga! And whoosh!" She spins around once with her hands in the air.

Unfortunately, I get *The Stepford Wives* reference, so I know she's being sarcastic.

"Then I'm almost sorry for ruining your fun."

"Don't be sorry." She shrugs and bends to grab what looks like a pair of Seth's boxers from the metal bin. My eyes automatically travel to her round ass. "Just go away."

The hem of that obscenely pornographic peasant dress rises up her thighs just shy of showing us the bottom curve of her ass. Thorin and Seth hover silently behind me, but she doesn't see them because she's too busy trying to piss me off.

It's not going to work. I'm too hungry for her.

"Or I can stay and watch you bend over like that a few more times."

"How was dinner?" she shoots back. Straightening, Aurelia wrings out the excess water and then hangs the wet boxers on the line.

"You're quick. I'll give you that, but I can't promise we'll be the same."

She freezes, a hint of dread in her voice when she speaks. "What are you talking about?"

"You defied us again, Aurelia."

Scoffing, she grabs one of my shirts from the bin and wrings it out. "And let me guess. You're here to punish me?"

"No."

"No?"

"Cooking isn't your talent. We decided to hear you and let you off the hook."

"Oh, good. I was beginning to worry about that."

"You're doing this on purpose, aren't you?"

She still doesn't look at us as she clips my shirt on the line to dry. "What are you talking about?"

"That's why you fought so hard when Thorin tried to feed you last night. You gave us food poisoning on purpose."

"That's ridiculous."

"Cut the shit, Aurelia. No one is *that* bad at cooking unless it's calculated."

"I told you I didn't know how!"

Straightening to my full height, I cross my arms. "And the mice?"

Having no excuse for that, Aurelia shrugs petulantly. "No, wait," she pleads when I step inside the laundry room. She's backing away to give herself time, but we can't be reasoned with. Neither can she, apparently. "I… Okay, I'm sorry I tried to feed you mice. That was mean. Truce?"

My only response is to bend at the knees and lift her over my shoulder. She starts kicking and screaming the moment I turn to leave the laundry room. Thorin leads the way as we climb the stairs, but Seth's already disappeared. He's not on board with this plan but tough shit.

Aurelia's panic only grows when we reach the first floor, and I start toward the front door. Thorin beats me there since I'm fighting to keep a hold on her worrisome ass. He opens it, and the cold air gusts in. It's pitch-black out, making the sounds of the wild even more terrifying to those who haven't learned how to draw comfort from it.

It's on the threshold that I set Aurelia down.

She immediately starts shivering as she stares back at the two of us, watching her from the warmth of our cabin. It's not until Seth appears and hands her the boots, scarf, and heavy coat she came with that she realizes we're not fucking around this time. He probably thinks we won't notice the hat, goggles, and gloves he slipped her, too, but I do.

It doesn't matter anyway. The extra protection will only prolong her inevitable death—one slip, one wrong turn, one chance encounter with any of the predators that live on this mountain, and she's done for.

"Guys, please." Aurelia looks over her shoulder—to the fate that awaits her. Her shoulders slump because she thinks she doesn't stand a chance.

The memories of what it took to get here are too fresh. Nearly crippling, I bet.

Whatever fight got her this far is long gone. Aurelia's forgetting just how strong she is. *Who* she is. Maybe the reason she's stuck taking our shit is because she never really knew. Why the fuck does that bother me when it's what we wanted?

"I'm sorry, okay?" She swallows. "I'll be good."

My dick twitches hearing that. I'll be hard if she keeps talking like that, so I force myself to forge ahead and not get caught up in empty promises.

"We told you, Goldilocks. Staying means earning your keep. You haven't been holding up your end of the deal."

"I know. I'm sorry."

I'm still not convinced, and neither are Thorin and Seth. "Are you going to try harder?"

For a moment, she's frozen, the breath stolen from her, when a particularly harsh wind blows in. "Yes! Yes! God, yes!" She shivers violently. "Can I come inside now?"

"You'll try hard starting *now*," Thorin tells her.

Aurelia nods quickly. "Okay."

"Do you want to show us, Sunshine?"

"Sure. Um…" She has the good sense to look nervous. "How?"

CHAPTER SIXTEEN

AURELIA

Every time I think it will be better to take my chances with the mountain, I see their faces.

Harrison's.

Cassie's.

Tyler's just before he went over the cliff.

I don't just see their faces. I remember the cold that seeped into my bones, whispering that I'd never make it. I remember the exhaustion and pain from falling out of the sky. It felt like I was running from more than just death.

It felt like I was running from myself.

I'm not ready.

Until I am, I have to be whatever these mountain men require. I have to play their games, warm their beds, and serve them with a smile. Khalil, Thorin, and Seth think they have me where they want me.

They don't know I've been playing this game much longer than them.

"How?" I ask even though I already know.

This cabin—this false haven in the middle of nowhere—was a trap. I know that now, but I take two steps forward anyway and let myself fall into it. I don't even flinch when the front door slams shut behind me.

The brutal frigidness of the wilds is replaced by the red-hot heat of Khalil's stare as he keeps the hand he used to close the door where it is. He pushes the mass of my curls over my shoulder with the other so that I can feel the warmth of his breath on my neck when he speaks.

"You know how, Aurelia. You know what we've wanted all along."

He's not wrong.

They've made their intentions and expectations of me clear from the start—lie on my back or find another way to make myself useful.

I didn't just survive a plane crash. I've somehow traveled back in time.

"All three of you? A-at the same time?"

Khalil's mouth curves into a smile. "We can start with just one. Which of us would you like?"

Uh…none?

Knowing it's not an option and might erase any goodwill they have left, I keep my thoughts to myself.

My gaze bounces between the three of them. Honestly, I can't believe they're letting me choose.

The hard look on Thorin's face says he wants to break me in half. I think Seth's smile is meant to be reassuring, but it's a little too eager, and he just looks…unhinged.

My gaze falls on Khalil last.

His expression gives nothing away as he calmly waits for my answer, and I think it's the patience that has me saying, "You."

Seth's smile drops, and he whimpers like a dog that's been kicked. Thorin just storms into his room and slams the door. I do flinch that time.

"Smart choice," Khalil says.

It doesn't feel that way to me, especially when he backs away and looks me over like I'm some broodmare he's inspecting before mounting. I shiver.

"My room," he orders. "And don't bother wearing that bullshit in my bed." He nods to my tattered costume dress. "You have ten minutes to get yourself ready for me. Go."

"Can I watch?" I hear Seth ask as I slip past.

I don't realize I'm holding my breath until Khalil answers. "No."

Seth makes another wounded sound.

My hands are shaking by the time I reach the den, but I don't immediately go to Khalil's room.

I make a couple of detours first.

Khalil's bedroom is pitch-black when I step inside after a quick shower.

The lamps on the bedside table are off, and so are the tiny lights woven through the branches of the canopy. They're usually on, even during the day, so the darkness is jarring at first.

There's no shade over the windows, but the moonlight doesn't touch the room as if it doesn't want to bear witness to what's about to happen.

I'm still mustering the courage to drop my towel when I hear the shower turn off. Khalil was there the moment I stepped out of the bathroom, but thankfully, all he did was go inside and shut the door. It gave me time to find the weapon I'd carefully stashed inside my towel.

I quickly tuck the glass shard under the pillow I've been using, and only then can I breathe. Diving under the covers, I bring them to my chin as I peer over them with my gaze glued to the door I've just now realized is arched.

I'm being ridiculous.

Jumping when I think I see a shadow move in the corner by the window, I peer a little closer, but Khalil steps through the door, turning my brain into a puddle when I notice his glistening chest and the towel around his waist.

I swear his shadow grows larger the closer he gets until it seems like he's ten feet tall. Khalil doesn't speak as he rounds his beautiful bed. When he nears the dresser where I thought I'd seen the shadow move, he pauses and swears for some reason. I sit up a little to see what's angered him and if it's me, but Khalil drops his towel, and I get a brief glimpse of his muscled ass and long dick before he slides into his side of the bed.

His side.

The thought of owning a place in his bed has my heart skipping a beat.

Khalil leaves his lamp off, and I can't decide if he does it out of kindness. I can't see more than the outline of his body, which means I'm still thinking clearly, but I also can't see...anything.

Without a single fucking word, Khalil wraps an arm around my waist and yanks me under him.

It's so quiet in the room that the sheets rustling sound loud to my ears. My hands immediately find Khalil's shoulders to hold him off so I can think. The raw power I can feel underneath his warm skin says I don't stand a chance.

"Wait," I plead when he nudges my legs apart. "Can we...can we slow down?"

I unintentionally moan when his lips find mine, and for a while, I forget that I don't want to be here.

Khalil is an amazing kisser.

His full lips feel like pillows against mine as he shows me how he likes it. I'm not a novice to kissing, but right now, I feel woefully inadequate as I try to keep up. I can taste the mint on his tongue as he feeds it to me, and my lashes flutter as I try to keep my eyes open but lose the battle.

The moment I'm relaxed, I feel him undoing the knot between my breasts, and I come crashing back down. We're still lip-locked when I make a desperate grab for the towel, but he catches my hands and pins them to the mattress. With his free hand, he yanks my towel away, and I cry out as he tosses it over the side of the bed. Turning my head away and breaking the kiss, my gaze lands on the corner by the window again, and I swear the shadows take shape, pressing in closer.

Lifting my head, I squint to see better, but Khalil sinks his teeth into my flesh without warning, and I gasp. My gaze snaps to him, but he's already watching me with a mouth full of my breast. The possession in his eyes sends a flare of pain and heat rushing from the spot he claimed down to my toes, and I hear the silent command.

Eyes on me.

Rising onto his knees, Khalil flips me onto my stomach, and before I can regain my bearings, I feel the weight of one determined mountain man pressing into my back.

"Khalil, wait. Seriously. I–I'm not ready yet."

"You will be."

Oh, fuck. I liked that.

He yanks my hips up from the bed before I can question what's wrong with me and nudges my thighs apart with his knee. Something hard and thick teases my opening, spreading my arousal around, wonder and dread mixing when I realize how fast this is moving. Khalil runs a soothing palm up my spine like he's calming a skittish mare, and then he presses his hips forward.

My fists clench the sheets when I feel his crown breach my pussy, and I hear myself taunt in frustration, "What? No foreplay?"

He pulls out of me without a word, and I yelp a moment later when he slaps my ass in response. "You want foreplay?"

Khalil doesn't stop at one.

Holding me down by my nape, his palm strikes me repeatedly, and he doesn't hold back no matter how loudly I cry out. He never seems to hit the same spot twice, and yet before long, my ass feels red hot, and I'm dripping, writhing, and sobbing all over his sheets. God, I'm already sore and delirious, and he hasn't even begun. After what feels like an eternity, the spanking ends, and Khalil leans forward, his lips meeting my ear.

"Is that enough playtime for you, princess? Can I fuck you now?"

I'm panting like I've run a mile as he lines his dick up again without waiting for a response. It's almost mean when his hips punch forward, but it doesn't hurt when he enters me. I'm much too slick—too wanting and needy and desperate for all the wrong reasons.

Khalil swears as he sinks farther into my warmth, and I grit my teeth to keep from screaming how much I hate him. My mouth falls open when he pushes forward again, but a knot forms in my throat, so I don't make a sound.

I'm tense again, but I don't know why.

Khalil huffs when he realizes he isn't getting any deeper, not without hurting me. I'm thankful he has enough decency to stop, even if it is to bark at me. "Aurelia, enough of this shit. Just relax for me, all right?"

"I can't," I whine.

"Yes, you can. It's only fucking, baby. You've done this before." There's a beat of silence that I'm too nervous to fill, so he sighs heavily and says, "I'm not going to hurt you, Aurelia."

I want to believe him, but everything he's done to me before this moment tells me he *would* hurt me if it meant getting what he wanted.

It's not even what he'll do to me that I'm afraid of. How can I be when just the thought lights every nerve I have with excitement? What scares me is whether Khalil—or any of them—will care enough to lick my wounds after. They can break me apart, but will they piece me back together? They had that first night before I passed out, but maybe it was just their guilty conscience rather than them giving a shit about me.

"Fine," Khalil barks with equal frustration. "Fight me all you want, but this pussy is *mine*." A scream escapes me as Khalil sinks himself so deep his hips slap against my ass. He holds on to me as he pulls out almost immediately and drives forward again.

In and out. *Smack. Smack. Smack. Smack.*

My cries mix with the guttural sounds Khalil makes, and it shakes me to my core because I know this is only the beginning.

Reaching behind me, I press a hand to his abs to slow him down, but he slaps it away, and his hold shifts to my nape as he rides me even harder.

"Do *not* make me tie you down," he warns in a low voice.

I stop trying to push him away as Khalil gets lost in the rhythm he sets. Because I need his guard down, I slowly began to match it. I deepen the arch in my back and drive my hips back to meet his. I did the very last thing he expected when he took me to bed.

I fuck him back.

"Ah, shit, baby. Yeah. *Fuck*," he moans.

Taking that as my cue, I reach my arm toward my pillow. When Khalil slaps my ass in warning, I snatch it back. He does it even harder a second time and an inexplicable moan slips from me at his roughness.

Khalil's punishing grip on my nape loosens until his hand falls away and relocates to my waist. When his rhythm changes, I peer over my shoulder and see that his eyes are closed now while his bottom lip is trapped between his pretty, white teeth.

Arching my back even more to reach the glass shard I hid under my pillow, I hear Khalil say, "Yeah, I knew you fucking wanted it."

Humiliation burns through me but not as much as when I feel my pussy gushing in response. My cheeks burn from the indignity of it, and the best-worst part is that I want more. I want him to say more mean, despicable things to me.

The words that tumble from my lips burn me from the inside out with shame. "Please, Khalil. Please stop."

"No." Khalil tightens his hold on me as he fucks me harder.

Blood rushes to my middle, and I abandon the shard as my throbbing clit short-circuits my brain.

"I don't want this," I plead as much to myself as to him. I can't stop throwing my pussy at Khalil to take. I can't stop feeding this new sensation rising in my gut, curling my toes, and setting my blood on fire.

"*Too fucking bad.*"

I never in a million years expected to come from mere words.

It feels like a betrayal to myself when I bury my face in the pillow to muffle my cries. I fist the sheets and give myself over to this thing inside me that craves the depravity he offers.

Unwilling to let me hide, Khalil fists my hair and yanks my head up while I'm mid-scream. The broken sound pierces the quiet room and probably the cabin itself as I come so hard, my vision is a flash of blinding white.

I'm boneless after that.

Once I collapse onto my stomach, I can't move, but Khalil doesn't seem to care as he pulls out of me and lies on his back. "Sit on it," he orders before I can even catch my breath.

I steal a peek at his dick and shudder at the thought. The flared purple head is slick with my juices and bobbing back and forth as he breathes hard.

Khalil takes it in his hand and strokes it once before turning his head to look at me with a raised brow when I take too long.

Dragging myself upright, I straddle him with my hands on his chest. Khalil handles the next part, positioning me so that I'm hovering over his dick. The weight of his hands on my waist increases until I get the hint, and I lower on my own. As he fills me once more, I don't fight it this time—not until the pressure gets too intense, and I stop.

Khalil isn't having it. "All the way down, Goldilocks."

"You can't be serious. You're freakishly big, Khalil."

"Should I call my brothers in here? Seth or Thorin could help stretch your pussy for me."

I swear I hear a cough that sounds like it comes from *inside* the room. When I turn my head to investigate, Khalil snaps his hips, and I gasp, my nails digging into his skin when he seats himself fully inside me.

"Oh, f-fuck you. You fucking bastard."

"Aurelia."

Rolling my eyes, I start to move back and forth slowly. It's awkward at first, and I feel off balance, but it doesn't last. I focus on his face, and soon, I start to notice what it does to him when I move my hips a certain way.

Khalil bites into his bottom lip when I bounce on his dick, but when I sway back and forth, he tilts his head back and groans.

I repeat the action while watching him closely. "Like this?"

"Hell yeah, baby. Like that."

I figure out that I don't feel as full if I lean forward, so I do. It puts our faces close together, and for a while, we just gaze at one another while he makes me pleasure him. There's no sound in the room other than our heavy breaths and the sound of him moving inside of me. Khalil's hands are all over my ass, and I don't want to like it, but the way he grips and spreads it like he owns me feels so good.

It's nice when they touch me like they can't get enough.

Eventually, his eyes start to close.

I mourn the loss until I realize this is my chance. I keep one hand on his chest and my gaze on his face as I quietly slip my hand under my pillow again. This time, I succeed in pulling the shard out.

No, I'm not ready to brave the icy wilderness.

But I can take this cabin.

I'll wait until Khalil is done bleeding out and Thorin and Seth are asleep, and then I'll do the same to them. The idea of murdering anyone—even them—makes me sick, but they've given me no choice.

The moonlight that had been absent before bounces off the glass, and I pause as the reality of what I'm about to do comes crashing down on me. A week ago, I never would have imagined myself preparing to sever a man's carotid while riding his cock.

The thought of bathing in his blood makes me pick up my pace. A cold rage washes over me as I remember the night in the den and how he forced me to my knees.

He should have been the one worshipping me.

Staring down at him now and watching his face as he enjoys me, all I feel is…hmm…

It's not hate.

Hate isn't useful.

Hate doesn't get shit done.

Hate won't win me this cabin or my power back.

What I feel for Khalil, Thorin, and Seth is far more terrifying and relentless than *hate*.

"That's it," I urge when Khalil digs his heels into the bed and starts fucking me faster from below. "Come for me, baby. Keep your eyes closed and *come for me*."

My name is a string of broken syllables on his lips as our middles collide over and over. The bed of twisted branches rocks and groans underneath us like it might break in half if we don't stop, but I can't. Khalil is close, and the unintentional friction on my sensitive clit has me racing alongside him.

"Tell me again. Tell me how I wanted this."

My eyes drift closed as my head falls back, and I'm lost. I'm barely aware of my arms rising as I bounce on his thick cock. Khalil doesn't notice how close he is to death as he gives it to me.

With a strangled cry from us both, we come at the same time. It feels like I'm shattering apart, so my eyes are slow to drift open. My vision is unfocused at first, but then I can see him clearly—head tilted back, veins and tendons stretching as he comes inside of me with a groan.

The asshole didn't even wear a condom.

Holding the shard above my head with a double-fisted grip, I plunge the sharp tip downward, aiming for the center of his chest. When my wrist is seized suddenly and harshly, I cry out in confusion and pain.

The shard is snatched out of my hand half a second later, and the sting as the jagged edge slices into my palm is nothing compared to my devastating failure.

I don't even understand it at first because both of Khalil's hands are still holding onto me, and his eyes are still closed. The grip on my wrist tightens cruelly, and I feel the bones twinge right before I'm violently yanked off the bed. Khalil's eyes fly open as I fight and claw to finish what I started—to kill the first thing I can sink my teeth into.

I. Want. *Blood.*

Next to my ear, a deep voice rumbles in the dark like some terrifying beast awoken from a long slumber. "You are *vicious*, aren't you? I think we'll keep you, songbird."

I'm tossed onto the floor just as light floods the room.

Thorin is standing between Khalil and me, but his back is to his best friend as he stares down at me with a mixture of amusement and warning. If I want to get to Khalil, I'll have to go through *him*. Something tells me he hopes I'll try.

And when Thorin wins, he'll take what he's owed.

No, fighting while outmatched is stupid. I have to be smarter than that.

My previous plan was good, but I hadn't counted on an audience. Seth is standing near the bedroom door conveniently left wide open, but I'm not stupid enough to fall for that. Sitting up slowly, I stay silent and pretend my nakedness or the fact that I was caught isn't an issue.

"Anyone care to explain what the fuck is going on?" Khalil demands as he yanks the sheet to cover his dick that's still twitching and leaking cum. It figures his first instinct would be to protect that useless organ.

Lies.

It had been exceptional at turning me inside out.

For a moment, I thought that Thorin wasn't just standing between us for Khalil's sake.

What if he's protecting me too?

The moment the question is out there—at least in my warped mind—I realize how ridiculous it sounds. When Khalil finds out what I tried to do, he'll probably want to kill me, and Thorin is the last person who will come to my rescue if he tries.

The silence stretches on for too long, Khalil's question going unanswered, so he sucks his teeth and comes up with a conclusion on his own. "See, I knew I shouldn't have let y'all watch," he gripes while resting his back against the headboard, one muscled leg dangling over the side of the bed like some sort of listless sex god.

They were watching? The whole time?

"Yeah?" Thorin retorts. "Well, this bitch just tried to fucking kill you, so I'd say you're lucky as hell I even bothered to save your sorry ass."

"I knew you were upset that she chose me," Khalil blathers like Thorin didn't speak, "but cockblocking, Thorin? Really? She chose me. Get over it. What did you expect when you—wait, what?"

"She tried to *gut* you while you were balls deep, dumbass."

It's almost comical when Khalil's jaw drops, and his eyes dart to me. Then, he goes back to Thorin and then Seth for confirmation. Khalil's face is the picture of shock when his gaze finally settles on me. It's the lack of remorse he sees on my face that finally allows what Thorin told him to sink in. "Are you fucking serious? I let you come!"

Unbelievable.

Thorin tosses the glass shard on the bed next to Khalil's leg. "Seth and

I saw her hide that under her pillow before you came to bed. We waited to see if she'd make a move."

"You *saw* her hide a weapon that could kill me and *waited*?"

Seth pouts as if he's disappointed that Khalil isn't as amused as him. "I didn't want to spoil the surprise."

Thorin rolls his eyes. "We didn't see what it was, jackass."

"Yeah, whatever. You probably thought about letting her do it just to get back at me, you jealous asshole."

"Can you stop thinking with your dick for one moment? She just tried to kill you. Who cares who had her first? It could have easily been me whether she wanted it or not. The fallacy is thinking that the choice was ever really hers."

I crab walk closer to the door while they're distracted, arguing over my pussy. Seth sees me, but all he does is smile warmly and waggle his fingers goodbye. Of the three, he scares me the most.

"That little-ass piece of glass wouldn't have done more than give me a flesh wound."

"And if she'd hit an artery?"

"I *still* would have been the one she'd chosen."

I'm nearly through the door when I hear Khalil's petulant jibe and roll my eyes. They might be big, bad, scary mountain men on the outside, but they're boys on the inside.

"Get your ass back here, Aurelia."

The order comes from Thorin, who doesn't so much as turn his head to look my way. I feel the last of my fight leave me with a sigh. Of course, Thorin, Khalil, and Seth never stopped being aware of me. I never stood a chance of getting away.

Slowly rising to my feet, my gaze bounces between the three of them to gauge which one I can turn against the others.

The three of them are careful not to give a single passing thought away, but I've been practicing the art a lot longer, so I know mine are well hidden when I saunter over to…Seth.

I take one step toward the grinning maniac when Thorin reaches out a long arm and yanks me to his side.

"Explain yourself," he demands.

CHAPTER SEVENTEEN

THORIN

Aurelia glowers from the foot of the bed, where I made her sit while I wrap and doctor her hand. Khalil is still fuming and talking shit as he paces back and forth. Everyone, Aurelia included, ignores him.

It's her lack of remorse that pisses him off the most.

She doesn't fight, speak, or even look at us while we try to figure out what to do with her.

If it's mercy Aurelia wants, she doesn't ask for it.

Her spine is ramrod straight, legs crossed primly, mouth in a disappointed pout while Khalil's bathrobe drapes her curvaceous frame, and her dainty foot dangles back and forth like a queen who has given an order and waits impatiently to be obeyed. I can almost imagine a pair of designer heels adorning those pretty feet. I can even imagine her using them to step on whoever got in her way back in her world.

But it seems I'm no better than Sheriff Kelly because I underestimated her too. I never thought she'd have the stones to actually try to murder one of us.

The moment I'm done wrapping her hand, she pulls it away like she can't stand my touch while still refusing to acknowledge me.

"What do you say, Aurelia?"

"Thanks," she offers dryly.

My burning gaze narrows, but if Aurelia feels the heat of my stare, she doesn't let on. I'm too exhausted to deal with her bullshit, so I let her have it. "You want to tell me why you tried to kill Khalil?" Her lips part, and I rush to say, "Besides the obvious."

She shrugs as if what we've done to her no longer fazes her. "I told you. I want to stay—at least for a little while."

"Then why did you try to kill me?" Khalil shouts.

Finally, she turns her head from the window, and the look she gives him is so chilly that I swear the frost on the window behind her spreads. "I didn't say I wanted to stay here with *you*."

"Ouch." Seth shudders in delight. "What about Thorin and me, Sunshine?"

"You were next."

Seth's eyes widen, and then, coming to his senses, he slowly backs away.

I scoff as I begin to pack up my med kit.

I should probably show her the headlines we've seen back at the camp. I could tell her how the entire world is grieving, not praying or hoping for her safe return. Because they've already written her off as dead. I could show Aurelia just how fucked she is so that she forgets her old life and starts finding a way to make one here with us, but I don't because, more than anything, I like her fight.

Every time she challenges us, my obsession with her grows.

"You're going to have to try harder than that if you want to take us out, my wolf." I don't realize what I've said until Aurelia looks away, a flush working up her neck. Khalil and Seth are both blinking at me like I've grown a tail, but I ignore those assholes as I say to Aurelia, "Go to bed. We'll talk about this in the morning."

"Why?"

"Because I said so, Aurelia."

"Whatever."

All right. She's pushing it now. "Do you give your uncle this much trouble?"

I know the instant her gaze shutters that it was the wrong thing to say. She turns away from me to crawl up Khalil's bed.

"You got me fucked-up," he says when she tries to take her usual spot in his bed. No one moves as he disappears inside the closet and returns, carrying his sleeping bag under his arm. "You can sleep on the floor. I don't care where as long as it's not in here."

He tosses the sleeping bag at her, but Aurelia lets it fall. "Why don't you sleep on the floor?"

"Because it's *my* bed!"

Aurelia stares at Khalil, and when she sees that he's serious, she rolls her eyes as she climbs out of his bed. She snatches the bedroll from the floor and pauses. "Can I at least shower first?"

Aurelia makes the mistake of wrinkling her nose like she finds sleeping with any part of him on or inside of her abhorrent, and Khalil notices.

"Nope."

"Suit yourself. Good luck." Aurelia manages to reach the threshold before Khalil calls after her and demands an explanation for her parting words. "Well, it's simple," she says while tightening the sash on his robe before it can come undone and fall off her shoulders. "I'm guessing kidnapping an innocent woman and forcing her to be your whore is a first for you three. I'm betting you'd rather I make it easy on you and just submit, but you literally pole vault any chance of that happening *every* time. I'm even more sure you feel a smidge of guilt, and for that reason alone, you won't get a peaceful night's sleep. At least, not while I'm here."

When Khalil just stares at her, she quietly leaves the room, and I follow after a heartbeat of indecision. Seth, who had already slipped out while Khalil and Aurelia bickered, is lying shirtless on the couch in the den with one arm tucked under his head when we walk in.

"What's up?" he asks when Aurelia stops and bleakly looks around the room for somewhere to sleep. This must be what rock bottom feels like for our celebrity princess.

Unconsciously, I try to imagine what her room back at home looks like.

An image of a gargantuan bed with a canopy even higher and more ostentatious than Khalil's, sheer white curtains, satin sheets that cost a fortune, and one stubborn but sexy magnate sleeping soundly within.

And then I imagine what it would be like to sneak inside her bedroom, part those curtains, and take whatever I want.

And I wouldn't be alone.

I could offer Aurelia my bed, but I won't. She had the chance to share it but chose Khalil, so now, she can suffer his ego and selfishness.

Okay, so maybe I am jealous.

"Khalil kicked her out," I explain.

There's a beat of awkward silence, space for me to fill with the offer or demand for her to warm my bed. Bane destroyed Zeke's again, and Khalil refuses to build him another, so Seth doesn't have one to offer. Fleeing my chance to behave honorably, I disappear into the den's bathroom to store my med kit, and then I drag my feet coming out.

When I do, I find Aurelia in the same place.

"Couch for a kiss," Seth offers.

"I'll take the floor."

Grinning, Seth swings his legs over the side of the couch and stands. Aurelia stiffens, readying herself for Seth's wrath. When he starts dancing like Jack Nicholson did as the Joker in *Batman*, hopping onto the footlocker, spinning, and hopping back off, her wariness turns to…well, more wariness.

Seth is unpredictable, and I think Aurelia's catching on quickly.

Melancholy roots me to the spot as I watch him dance. Seth has never seen any of the Batman movies, which means he's pulling from Zeke's memories again. Zeke was hardcore into comics and Batman was always in heavy rotation solely because of his favorite supervillain—Bane.

Seth grabs the long poker by the fire, and Aurelia tenses again. He twirls it in the air as he dances over to her, and it's all I can do not to roll my eyes when he tosses it aside to lift her in his arms bridal style.

"What are you doing?" she whispers nervously.

Ignoring her while still dancing, Seth carries her over to the couch and places her on it like she's some gentle maiden he's sworn to protect.

One of the many blankets Sheriff Kelly's wife crocheted for us over the years is draped over the back of the couch. Seth takes the folded brown-and-blue blanket and snaps it open with a flourish. He then drapes it over Aurelia and sketches a dramatic bow.

"Sleep tight, Sunshine."

Before she can settle on a suitable reaction to his antics, Seth pries the bedroll from her and unrolls it with a snap of his wrist. He lays it out on the floor between the footlocker and couch before lowering his body onto the bedroll.

"You sure you trust her to be sleeping so close?"

Aurelia gives me a withering look before getting comfortable under the blanket and turning her back to us both.

"I trust that she's not dumb enough to try twice in one night," Seth says. "I just figured you two losers would sleep better knowing she'll have to get past me to get to you."

Except there's one problem with that theory.

Seth is a disturbingly deep sleeper.

When the nightmares overtake him, it's almost impossible to wake him. He's also twice as dangerous if you succeed because he always wakes up thinking he's back in that hellhole. It's the reason Khalil installed those lights in his bed. They sleep in there sometimes when Seth needs to be restrained or when Zeke's afraid of being alone.

Waking up in the dark can be confusing for them and catastrophic for us.

Now, it's Aurelia who's in danger with this new sleeping arrangement.

I consider warning her, but she looks exhausted and traumatized enough without me adding to it, so I tell myself it will be fine as long as the light doesn't go out.

The fire will die eventually, but there's a lamp on the side table by Aurelia's feet. I dim it just enough to keep the room lit with a soft glow, and then I take one last look at her curled up on the couch before I force myself to leave the den. By the time I reach the main floor, my teeth are gritted to the point of pain. I might actually chip one if I don't unclench.

She'll be fine, damn it.

Once I'm in my room, I strip off my shirt and, out of habit, run my hand over the raised scars marring my abs and chest before shedding my jeans too. Walking into the en suite, I turn on the shower and lament the shitty water pressure once again. It gets the job done, I guess.

Aurelia enters my thoughts not a moment later.

What does she think of the home we built with our bare hands?

I have no doubt it's nothing like what she's used to, but she could be happy here, couldn't she? What would it take to make sure that happens? Yes, it would be easier to make her *want* to stay rather than forcing her, but how would we even go about it after the start we had? First impressions are hard to shake, and Aurelia was well within her right to try to take us out tonight.

These thoughts stay with me as I crawl into bed, and I spend the night tossing and fucking turning just like she said I would.

CHAPTER EIGHTEEN

AURELIA

Someone is crying.

At first, I think it's me. I think I'm sobbing in my dream like a wild animal that's been wounded—except the voice those cries belong to doesn't belong to me. And I've learned a long time ago to cry where no one—not even me—can see.

For the longest time, I thought that I wasn't able. I thought it was just another thing my uncle had taken from me. I didn't even cry when my plane went down and I knew I was about to die.

If that's not a sign something is seriously broken inside me, what is?

Another hoarse scream jars me awake this time, and I sit up with a gasp. The den is dark, so I can't see a thing at first. My eyes are slow to adjust, so the strangled sounds are even more terrifying as I wait out the dark.

Crawling to the end of the couch where the lamp is now off, I yank on the string repeatedly to no avail.

Shit.

Bulb must have died.

Some of the darkness in the room recedes as my eyes adjust, so I search for the source of the sounds.

Seth's turned onto his side away from me, and he's shivering inside his sleeping bag even though the cabin is pretty warm. When I touch his arm, his skin feels clammy, and worry pierces my armor as I wonder if he's sick.

Oh, God. He didn't eat the mice stew, did he? Not even Seth could be that reckless.

"Seth?" I try to shake him awake. "Seth, are you okay? Seth, wake up. Seth!"

His eyes fly open, and they're frantic as they search around before finding mine in the dark. They're wide with panic one moment, and the next, I'm being yanked off the couch and body slammed onto the footlocker. My back smarts from hitting the hard surface, and it dazes me long enough for Seth to get his hands around my throat.

God, his strength, his rage...

I...I can't breathe.

My nails claw his wrists and face, but it's not enough to make him release me.

"Why can't you sick fucks leave Zeke alone?" he shouts. Seth uses his grip on my neck to lift my upper body, only to slam me back down. I almost black out right then and there. "I did what you asked! You...can't...have... him!" he yells after every slam. "You can't have him! You can't have him!"

"Seth," I struggle to get out. "P-please."

The edges of my vision are just starting to fade when the light in Khalil's bedroom flicks on.

My head is hanging over the edge of the table now, so I can see him rubbing his eyes when he shuffles into the den. "Whatever the hell you guys are doing in here, keep it down. Some of us are trying to fucking sleep."

Khalil's hand drops, and then he viciously swears when he sees us and rushes over.

"Seth," Khalil says gently. "Seth, let her go." He starts rubbing Seth's freaking back like he's the one being strangled. "She's not going to hurt you, brother. She's not one of them."

Seth tightens his hold, and I feel the fight in me fading as my eyes roll back and I start to slip away. Khalil must notice because he curses, stands, and abandons his gentle approach.

He hits Seth hard as hell in the temple.

It's only once, but it's enough to knock him off me.

I don't realize Seth's unconscious until I draw in a desperate breath. I start coughing to expel the excess air when my lungs overfill, so I roll onto my side and see Seth knocked out on the floor.

A lock of his hair suddenly falls over his forehead, and that small movement is enough to send me scrambling to get away in case he wakes up. I fall off the footlocker in my haste, and Khalil grabs me under my arms and lifts me like I weigh nothing. When he turns me around to face him, it's all I can do not to slap the shit out of him when I see his expression.

Khalil's glaring at me like this was *my* fault.

"What the fuck were you doing to him?" he demands, confirming my suspicion.

"Doing…to *him*?" I pant. I'm still trying to catch my breath. My voice cracks and grates on my abused throat, so I rub it while I regard Khalil. "He was…screaming…in his…sleep." I swallow and exhale one last time. "I was trying to wake him up!"

"He was dreaming," Khalil explains as if I should have known. "Seth gets really bad nightmares sometimes, and the dark scares him. He didn't know it was you he was hurting."

"I don't give a shit!" I scream. "You knew this could happen and didn't bother to warn me?"

Khalil's jaw locks. "It was none of your damn business."

"None of my business? He just tried to kill me!"

"But did you die? No. So stop fucking whining and join the club."

I do hit him then, but a slap is much too easy for this bastard, so I punch him in the throat as hard as I can.

Let's see how he likes it.

"*That's* for taking your sweet fucking time," I say with a growl as Khalil gags and coughs.

Recovering quicker than I did, he grabs my hair and shakes me around like a rag doll before sticking his face in mine and roaring, "Why do you always have to be such a fucking bitch?"

"Fuck you!"

Khalil's only response is to toss my ass on the couch like I'm a sack of flour. I huff and sit up quickly because it's on and fucking popping now. Snatching that useless fucking lamp from the table, I raise it in the air.

"Aurelia, don't you fucking dare," Khalil warns right before I send it sailing toward his head. He ducks, and it hits the wall behind him before shattering into several large pieces. Khalil looks at the destroyed lamp before his unamused gaze travels to me. "You're a fucking psycho, you know that?"

"I'm just getting started, Khalil."

He sighs and rubs his eyes but stays where he is. "I'm too fucking tired for this shit, baby. You can have this one. Next time Seth has a nightmare, come get Thorin or me. Don't touch him."

My lips curl despite the butterflies in my tummy at hearing him call me *baby*. It's sick how right it sounds. "Don't worry," I assure him. "I wouldn't dream of touching that animal again."

"Do *not* call him that." Khalil takes a warning step forward. "You have no idea what's he's been through!"

"Oh, boo-hoo," I mock.

A moan comes from Seth's direction, and I flinch, thinking he might be coming to.

It doesn't go unnoticed by Khalil.

"Aurelia…" He sighs again. "Go sleep upstairs."

"I don't want to share a bed with Thorin."

"He wouldn't let you if you tried. We have another couch, in case you forgot."

Relieved, I take my blanket because it's supersoft and did a great job of keeping me warm. I start for the stairs, peering over my shoulder as I go, and see Khalil hauling an unconscious Seth into his room.

When I reach the small landing midway up the switchback stairs and turn, I see Thorin standing at the top with his hands in his pockets. He's shrouded in the darkness looming behind him, but I know it's him. He looks me over and, seeing me still in one piece, turns to head to his room without a word.

The first thing I notice is that it's warmer upstairs. The sounds of the wild are louder, too, but the predators lurking beyond these walls are the least of my worries. I have my hands full with the ones inside.

I tiptoe over to the couch inside the cavernous living room and glare at the closed door of Thorin's room before making myself at home on the couch.

I can't believe this is my life right now.

I'm Aurelia George.

I shit gold and wipe my ass with money. I've convinced millions of people to worship me with only my voice, marketable face, and carefully curated persona because my real one sucks. It's like defusing a bomb with a paper clip and your eyes closed.

Total fucking bullshit, but people buy into it.

And yet these Neanderthals have turned me into their whore and made me sleep on a ratty old couch.

I get comfortable fast and start to drift, but every creak of the cabin startles me awake, and I start the process all over again.

It's been a long day, one of the longest in my life, and I still can't sleep. Somehow, I have to find a way to be up before dawn without an alarm to wake me, so I can make my captors breakfast and see them off when they leave. Then, I'll wait for them to return like a proper pet.

I eventually succumb to my exhaustion and sleep through the night.

The best part is that I don't dream.

CHAPTER NINETEEN

AURELIA

The cabin is quiet without the crackling of wood, so I know it must be morning when I feel my blanket being pulled off me. The fires from the stoves will have gone out by now, so the morning air breezes over my skin, but the cold isn't the reason for my goose bumps.

Futilely, I keep my eyes closed and my breathing even in the hopes that I won't be subjected to more of their attention, but I should have known better than to think playing dead would work.

I can't help but lock up, giving my awareness away the moment I feel the heavy weight of a feral mountain man climbing on top of me. I know who it is the moment I smell his scent—warm and spicy and wild. My eyes fly open against my will, and I can see for myself that it's morning.

I've slept for hours, but it feels like minutes.

Drawing in a deep breath, I part my lips to scream—as if anyone in this house would save me—but the sound doesn't make it past my throat. He covers my mouth with his hand, but it's the cold blue eyes of the rejected man staring back at me that terrify me.

"Am I going to have to hold you down?"

I whimper, but Thorin doesn't care if I'm scared.

"Am I going to have to get rough with you, Aurelia?"

I swallow down the need to ask him the same and shake my head.

He's not like the other two.

Thorin rarely finds me amusing or cute or any of the condescending things that make men believe women can't be dangerous. In a weird twist of irony, I guess one could say Thorin respects me more than the others. He sees me for the threat that I am and keeps me at an arm's distance.

When he uses his free hand to reach between us and pull on the worn sash of Khalil's robe—Khalil, whose cum is still dried on my thighs—I keep my promise and don't fight him.

The moment the robe is loose and the panels part, Thorin lowers his head, and his breath skates over the soft curve of my belly.

"What's it going to take to convince you that you belong here, wolf? I can take you apart one limb at a time and keep only the parts we need. But that can get messy and won't be nearly as much fun as option B."

I gulp and just barely keep the tremble out of my voice when I ask, "Option B?"

Thorin nods but doesn't elaborate as he kisses my stomach. His attention on this particular part of my body needles at my self-consciousness. It's all I can do not to snap my robe closed and hide my body from his leering. All he says is, "I like this look on you."

"What look?"

"Your belly swollen."

My gaze narrows, forgetting all about the fact that he just threatened to dismember me if I tried to run again. "Are you calling me fat?"

Thorin's gaze flicks upward, and he gives me a look full of impatience. "Out of all the things you *should* have taken from what I said, how is that what you heard, Aurelia?"

I shrug and look away.

It doesn't matter anyway. The issue isn't whether he appreciates my body. I don't care. I love the way I look. It's the fact that he'll do whatever he wants to it, regardless of how I feel.

Thorin, as if to prove a point, removes Khalil's robe and then stares at my body like it's on the dinner menu, and he doesn't know where to start—the appetizer, entrée, or straight to dessert.

"You didn't strike me as the type to be insecure," he remarks absently.

"I'm not insecure. I'm human," I say as I stare at the vaulted ceiling, waiting for him to fuck me already so he can leave me alone. "There's not a person alive who doesn't feel it sometimes. There are only those who are honest about it and those who bullshit about it."

Thorin grunts but doesn't deny it.

Looking at him, I wonder if I'm wrong.

Thorin clearly has nothing to be insecure about. He checks every box except kindness and chivalry.

As if he can tell where my mind wanders, Thorin sits up until he's kneeling over me. My gaze is unwillingly drawn back to him when he grips the bottom of his shirt. It's not until the hem shows the first strip of skin that I realize I've never seen Thorin shirtless. Seth and Khalil, yes, but not Thorin.

I realize why when the shirt clears his belly button, and I see it.

Four deep, diagonal slashes.

It keeps going, extending from the right side of his waist across his abs and stopping above the nipple on his left pec. The scar tissue is pink, slightly raised, and fully healed, but no less horrifying to see—not because of the appearance but because of what he must have survived.

Is this what I'll look like once I'm finally safe from them? Healed and alive but forever scarred?

"What happened?" I ask to keep from reaching out and touching Thorin's old wounds. And, okay, I'm also curious if his abs are really as hard as they look. Paradoxically, the scars only make him seem more invincible, and I start to waver because if whatever did *that* couldn't kill him, what chance do I have?

"Grizzly." Thorin's tone implies it happens every day. I don't know. Does it? I sure the fuck hope not.

"You fought a grizzly bear?" I echo skeptically. I give in to the impulse this time and run my fingers over his scars and through the thin scattering of hair on his lower stomach. "And you won." He wouldn't be here if he hadn't, but it still sounds unbelievable.

"He did his fair share of damage, as you can see, but nothing fatal."

"That's too bad."

The look he gives me is only slightly amused. "You would have preferred the bear, huh?"

"I would have preferred ten bears to you."

Thorin smiles, but it's not a friendly one. I've fooled myself into thinking we were connecting on a human level until he stands from the couch and shoves down his sweats and boxers.

I look away the moment they clear his hips and close my eyes.

I've already seen his dick, so it feels silly, but it's all the rebellion I have left. When he lifts me from the couch, I suck in a breath. Begging won't help. I know that, but I still hear myself saying, "Please, Thorin. Do we have to do this now? I'm sore."

"All the more reason to get you used to fucking." He lays me down on the bear rug, and his gentleness confuses me. When he joins me, I burst into action and flip onto my stomach. I try to crawl away, but Thorin grabs my leg and drags me back.

"Fuck you!" I scream in his face when he succeeds in flipping me onto my back again. "I don't want to!"

"No?" He forces a hand between my thighs and uses it to palm me. "Then what's this, Aurelia?" Neither of us speaks as he slowly explores my pussy with the rough pads of his fingers. The friction is perfect and before long my thighs slowly fall open of their own accord. "Tell me why you're ruining my fucking rug if you don't want it," he whispers.

"That's not…it's not…"

"Yes?"

"It's not my fault, Thorin."

His blue gaze softens and then I feel his thumb stroke my engorged clit like a caress. "No. It's not, baby. It's mine."

"Please don't do this," I beg with tears in my eyes that will never fall. "This can't really be the kind of man you are."

My statement hits its mark, and he snatches his hand away like I struck him. For the length of a single breath, he actually looks like I got through. "What the fuck do you know about me, huh? You don't know shit."

"I know you want to hurt me. I know I never did anything to deserve the way you treat me. I know I don't want this."

"Jesus, Aurelia. Why can't you just shut the fuck up sometimes?" Thorin sits back, rubs his temples, and sighs. Despite his so-called stress, his hard-on never goes away. It stands tall and imposing, like a threat. "I don't want to hurt you. This doesn't have to be a bad experience for either of us. Just don't fight me, and it can be good for you too."

"No."

Thorin drops his hands and just stares at me.

It's just like a man to think wanting autonomy over my body makes me unreasonable.

"Yeah, well, you know what I think?" He grabs both of my thighs and forces them apart before climbing between them. I try to buck him off, but he's too heavy. Thorin has a hand over my mouth before I can scream again, but I do it anyway, right into his palm. "I think you do want it," he whispers roughly. I scream again behind his palm when he lines up his cock with my pussy. "I think it turns you on telling us no. I think if I fucked this little cunt right now, you'll scream for me and it won't be to stop."

I moan in horror when he presses forward and does exactly that.

Thorin forces his thick cock inside me while I shake my head and scream obscenities.

He doesn't go slow like Khalil, letting me get used to his length. Thorin plows all the way inside until it should be impossible for him to go any farther.

And then he removes his hand from my mouth, pushing inside until his balls rest against my ass.

He gets so deep, I yelp loud enough to wake the cabin.

Thorin leers down at me as he starts fucking me with short, brutal thrusts. "Does that feel good, wolf?" That is the third time he's called me that. What happened to *songbird*? What changed? My head rolls to the side as I moan and wrap my legs around his waist. "Yeah, you want it harder, don't you? Tell me you love it when I take what's mine."

"I'm not yours," I remind him with my eyes closed. "I *hate* you."

Thorin growls, and I tighten around his cock at the animalistic sound. "I hate you too," he returns without any of the venom. "You drive me fucking insane."

A moment later, I feel his lips on my shoulder, kissing and sucking and biting as he pounds in and out of me. My fingers slip through his blond hair and hold tight as I lift my shoulders off the rug enough to peer over his and watch the heady vision of his powerful body working and using me.

"Oh, God," I whisper as I watch. "Oh, *God*." I can't look away from the flexing muscles in his ass. *Yes. Yes. Oh, fuck, yes.*

Ruining my fun because he's a dick, Thorin flips me onto my stomach and yanks me onto my knees. He shoves back inside me hard enough to drive me forward until my chin is hovering over the bear's head whose carcass we're fucking on like some fucked-up threesome.

I think about my dream and how savage the guys looked wearing those masks.

And then I imagine how much more intense this coupling would be if Thorin were wearing one right now while I'm on all fours for him, and he's grunting and growling like my own twisted version of the Beast.

"Oh my God," I whine long and low when my hips finally start moving on their own. "Oh my God, I'm going to come."

My breasts sway when Thorin picks up the pace and rides me like he's testing if I'm truly indestructible.

It feels like we're *mating*.

The sound of our sweaty skin clapping echoes around the cabin, and I don't even care about being overheard. Seth and Khalil will know I enjoyed what Thorin is doing to me, just as I didn't totally hate last night with Khalil.

My fingers curl into the low pile of the rug when I start to come. I slap a hand over my mouth to muffle my scream, but it's no use hiding it from him.

I know he feels me coming when he makes a strangled sound in his throat.

Thorin takes hold of my hair while I come and yanks my head back so that his lips are next to my ear. "How many times, Aurelia? How often did you fantasize about having your little pussy ravaged? Once? Twice?"

What is he talking…like, a day?

If so, then *yes*. God, yes.

After a while, it became a part of me. I stopped noticing when it happened or even being bothered by it. It was my dirty little secret.

My dark desire.

It doesn't mean I don't hate them all the same—even if Seth, Khalil, and Thorin are giving me what I've never been brave enough to speak aloud, let alone ask for. I always thought it would be *my* choice if I ever gave in to it.

Lowering my hand only once I'm done coming, I close my eyes when he sinks balls deep again and empties them inside me. I can still feel him coming when he reaches down and starts rubbing my stomach. That uncomfortable feeling returns as I remember our earlier discussion.

"I like this look on you."

"What look?"

"Your belly swollen."

My fight-or-flight response kicks in before I can fully understand why, but when I try to crawl away from him, Thorin wraps both arms around my middle and holds me still.

Oh, God, he makes me take it.

Every drop.

"Thorin...you can't...*please.*"

Leaning forward, he sinks his teeth into my shoulder and continues filling me up.

When it's finally over, he collapses on the rug, but he takes me with him, tucking me against his side while he catches his breath. I'm forced to cuddle my monster while he enjoys his fucking afterglow.

I think I prefer Khalil's kindness of kicking me out of his room after he's done with me.

Ten minutes pass without either of us saying a word.

I don't like how comfortable I'm getting wrapped in his muscles and warmth, so I break it. "How many times have you thought about it?"

Thorin seems to know exactly what I'm asking. "Never. Not until you."

"So I'm special then," I retort dryly even as I feel my relief causing my body to finally accept his embrace. "Lucky me."

He gives me one of his exasperated sighs. "You asked, Aurelia." When I don't respond, he takes my chin and forces me to meet his gaze. "Come shower with me."

I cringe away from him. What he's demanding is out of the question. It's too intimate. I can't risk him blurring the truth of what we are to each other. I fuck them all and they keep me alive. Anything more is asking for trouble. "Why?"

Thorin's already standing and helping me up when he answers. "Because I said so, wolf."

"That bear you killed," I say as I grab Khalil's robe from the couch and pull it on. "What did you do with it? Did you...eat it?"

Thorin grabs his discarded clothes and starts for his bedroom. "No. You're standing on him."

I'm wearing one of Thorin's T-shirts and *nothing else* when I leave his room alone an hour later. I'm freshly showered and feeling like I own my body again. Thorin's still inside his room getting dressed for another day of making sure I'm never found.

At the same time, Seth is coming up the stairs from the basement, looking worse for wear. There are dark circles under his eyes, and his black hair is sticking up at different angles as if he's been gripping it.

Seth's eyes widen when he sees me, and then his gaze drops to my throat, and he pales.

I know what he sees—the purple bruises left from his hands around my neck. I guess I don't have to question if he remembers trying to kill me.

And then it dawns on me that in the last twenty-four hours, each of them have found a way to leave their mark on me—Thorin on my shoulder, Khalil on my breast, and Seth on my neck. All temporary, but unwanted, nonetheless.

"Sunshine…"

I walk past him without responding.

I don't want to hear whatever bullshit apology he wants to give for hurting me again. If Seth's looking for forgiveness, he's not going to get it. I tried to kill Khalil, but you won't catch me on my knees begging for absolution.

They all deserve to burn.

Maybe I do too.

I can feel Seth follow me into the kitchen, but I ignore his pleas for my attention. I just open the fridge and try to figure out how the hell I'm going to make my mountain men an edible meal without a single homemaking bone in my body so that we don't rinse and repeat the last two nights.

And when the hell did I start thinking of them as mine?

I don't own them. Not yet. But when I get out of here…

A hard chest colliding with my back interrupts my vengeful thoughts. Two strong hands follow, grabbing my waist and sliding up to help themselves to my tits.

"Mmm," Khalil hums against my neck before kissing it. "Good morning, Goldilocks. I missed you when I woke up."

"Then you shouldn't have kicked me out of your bed," I remind him, unenthused.

Grabbing the carton of eggs from the side door, I go to step back, and Khalil lets me. As soon as the fridge door is closed though, he shoves me up against it and starts grinding his morning wood against my ass.

"Khalil, I have to—"

"Forget breakfast, Goldilocks. Fuck me instead." Khalil groans as he shamelessly dry humps me against the fridge.

Instantly, I'm annoyed *and* horny again.

They punish me when I don't cook for them and then distract me when I try.

I'm beginning to think the housework is just a ruse to keep my mind off running, and *this* is all they truly wanted.

"Khalil, I *just* washed you off me, and Thorin's already beaten you to my pussy this morning. Twice. I'm all fucked out. Can you not?"

Khalil lifts his head to pull my ear between his teeth. "Fine, then I won't fuck your pussy," he whispers while taking his dick out of his sweats. "But you can still get me off."

I only have enough time to place the eggs on top of the fridge before Khalil grabs my hips and starts mimicking fucking me hard from behind. I want to say the friction does nothing for me, but God help me, it does. Even my hard nipples poking through the shirt and rubbing against the cold, hard surface is enough to make me consider reaching between my thighs and rubbing my clit.

"Ah fuck. You're starting to learn, aren't you, baby? You're…so… fucking…sexy," he growls between hard thrusts.

I've always known I was beautiful, but so are a lot of women.

I never knew how powerful and potent it was to be caught in the thralls of someone irresistible, though—not until I found this cabin and they found me. I know exactly what they're feeling because I feel it too. In my line of work, I'm surrounded by a lot of attractive men. I've just never been powerless to that attraction before—not like this.

"Give me a kiss," he demands.

I turn my head without hesitation and catch a glimpse of Seth watching us glumly from where he's sitting at the kitchen table before my lips lock with Khalil's. His movements grow more frantic, knocking the fridge against the wall and creating a whole scene as he gets closer to coming.

And then he does.

When he's done, he backs off, and the moment I shift, I feel where he came.

I make an angry noise when I touch the hem of Thorin's shirt and realize it's wet. "Khalil!"

"My bad," he says, not at all sounding like he means it. Shaking my head, I start to leave the kitchen, but he stops me with a hand on my wrist. "Where are you going?"

"To change. I can't feed the three of you covered in cum, Khalil. That's nasty."

"Here. Just take mine." He pulls the black tank he's wearing over his head and hands it to me before I can argue that it will only take me a couple of minutes to find my dress.

Reluctantly, I lift Thorin's shirt over my head, revealing my naked body just as Thorin walks into the kitchen. He's wearing the same yellow-and-black snowsuit I saw Khalil in yesterday while the top half dangles around his waist. This close, I can see the black-and-white logo clearly.

The Cold Peaks and Jackal County Search & Rescue.

The words are printed around an illustration of three snow-covered mountain peaks.

It feels like I'm going to vomit.

The scowl on Thorin's face makes me quickly cover the front of my body with his shirt until he turns his head and directs it at Khalil. Wresting Thorin's shirt from my hands, Khalil tosses it at Thorin, and a pissing match ensues while I quickly cover my body with Khalil's tank. It's long enough to cover my ass and pussy, but my breasts are practically spilling out of the sides since I'm busty.

It's obvious at this point that Khalil coming on me was a calculated move to get me out of Thorin's shirt and into his.

As if it matters.

"We don't have time for you to get your dick wet," Thorin says coldly. "We should already be at the camp."

Camp? There's a camp? A camp for me? And they're going?

"Well, maybe there would be time if you'd stop acting like she only belongs to you," Khalil gripes back. "Twice, Thorin? Seth hasn't even had his turn yet."

"Like you care about anyone's dick but your own," Thorin returns.

My cheeks flame as I listen to them talk about me like I'm not a real person.

"At least I didn't have to fuck her twice because I'm such a bad lay."

"Sure. That's why you didn't fuck her twice."

Catching the shade, Khalil growls. "It will be a cold day in hell before you have more stamina than me, Thayer."

Lifting two eggs from the carton, I rise onto my toes as high as I can since they're both tall as hell. I then use their heads to crack both eggs open and watch them freeze mid-argument when the yolk spills into their hair and down the sides of their scowling faces.

Seth forgets his pouting and starts howling, daring me to do it again.

"Hey, boneheads," I say scathingly. "I'm right here, and for the record, I belong to me. Now get the hell out of my kitchen before I change my mind about feeding you."

"Aurelia…"

Thorin doesn't get more than my name out before I fist my hands, squeeze my eyes closed, and yell as loud as I can, "*Geeeeeet ooooooout!*"

CHAPTER TWENTY

SETH | ZEKE

S unshine is mad at me." I lean against the island as Aurelia pours steaming coffee into three travel mugs. I'm close enough to touch her, but I don't. I can't bear to have her pull away from me like she did all during breakfast, which was actually not…that…bad.

"Yes, Seth. Sunshine is mad at you."

"Why?"

Aurelia sets down the coffeepot with a thud and whirls around with her eyes narrowed. "Are you serious?"

I chew my lip when I realize it was a dumb question. I'm too used to Thorin and Khalil, who brush off my violence and make excuses for me when Zeke's memories and mine take over.

"Is it because of last night?"

"You mean when I tried to help you, and you almost killed me?" She throws her hands on her hips, and I can't help but remember the way Khalil held them as he used her to get himself off. It was all I could do not to reach inside my snowsuit and stroke my own cock, but I didn't think Sunshine would appreciate that since she was pissed at me. "Yes, Seth. It's because of last night."

"I'm sorry."

"Save it." She gives me her back again and puts the lids on the tumblers.

I don't hang back this time, though. I step up behind her and wrap my arms around her waist.

She tenses but doesn't shrug me off.

Progress.

"Someday, I'll tell you about what happened to Zeke," I promise. "I'll tell you about him, and me, and Bane. I'll tell you what they did to us, but only when you're not mad at me so that you don't think I'm fessing up to make you feel sorry for me."

Aurelia tries at first to pretend she doesn't care, but then she's turning around in my arms and peeking up at me. "You said his name last night. Zeke. Who is he?"

I take her hands and place them on my face. "He's who you should see when you look at me. This is his body, Aurelia. I just live in it."

Her lips part to respond, but then she shakes her head. "I don't understand."

"Zeke and I share the same body, but we're not the same people. We don't just have different names. We have different memories, sometimes, and different mannerisms. We don't always like the same things either. His favorite color is black. I like purple. We even sound different."

I hold my breath, expecting her to freak out, but all she says is, "Purple? Wow. I wouldn't have guessed that."

"It looks fun," I explain with a shrug. "I like fun."

Finally, Aurelia grins at me, but it doesn't last. I can see the wheels turning in her head and her struggling to name the pieces she's putting together in her head. "So what you have is like…multiple personalities?"

"It's called dissociative identity disorder, but yes."

"Seth, that's crazy."

"Yes, exactly."

"No, I'm sorry." Her light brown becomes flushed. "I didn't mean it like that. I–I'm sorry. That was rude." She starts trembling in my arms, too afraid that I'll hurt her.

"Shh. It's okay." I turn my head and kiss her small hand that's still holding my face. "It sounds pretty fucking whacked to me. One day, I just woke up in this body with no idea of who I was, where I came from, or why I was being tortured. I had no memories. All I had was Ezekiel."

"Tortured?" she gasps.

I kiss her nose and say, "Later."

"So this is his body, and you…"

Aurelia leaves me to fill in the blanks. "Bane and I protect him."

"Bane?"

"You don't want to meet him," I warn. My grave tone makes her eyes widen. That guy even freaks me out, but I don't want to scare Sunshine, so I leave it at that. Aurelia's lucky it was me that Ezekiel woke up that day and not his guard dog.

"Is he scary?"

I nod, so she peers at me curiously.

"Scarier than you?"

I don't like hearing that she's scared of me, but I guess that's fair. "Oh, yeah."

Her voice is casual as she drops her hands from my face to my shoulders before sliding them down my chest. She touches me willingly for the first time, and maybe that's why I think nothing of it when she asks, "Are Thorin and Khalil afraid of him?"

"Yes."

"Hmm. So if you all share the same body, how do you protect Zeke?"

The swift change in subject confuses me for a moment, but I go with it. "I take his pain. Zeke is…fragile. He wasn't always, and it's not as bad as before Thorin and Khalil got him out, but he has a setback every once in a while."

"Out? Out of where?"

"The Seeds of the Undying. Zeke's father had another son. The brothers met when Zeke was nineteen. Isaac tracked Zeke down in Nevada and convinced him to visit his ranch in New Mexico and hang out for a while. That's how Isaac phrased it at the time, so Zeke went, but it was bullshit."

"It didn't go well?"

"No. It did not." I can feel the darkness and pain rising inside of me, but one look into Aurelia's trusting eyes as she lets me hold her, and I push it down.

"What happened?"

I nuzzle my nose in her neck and say, "Another time, remember?"

"Fine. It's just hard to believe that Thor and Khalil let Isaac take Zeke. They seem territorial. Protective," she admits reluctantly.

My lips pull back from my teeth in a silent snarl. "That's because they weren't there," I say with more than a decade's worth of resentment. "Thorin and Khalil left Zeke all alone to make better lives for themselves elsewhere—without him. I don't care much for Zeke's friends, but I have to give it to Thor and Khalil. They love him. Had they been there, they would have seen through Isaac's bullshit and protected him. Zeke was always too trusting, always going with the flow. It was irresponsible to go with Isaac."

"Is that why you hate Thor and Khalil? Because they weren't there for Zeke?"

"Yes."

"Seth, you know that's not fair, right?"

"Maybe."

"No, Seth. It's not their fault Zeke's brother was a monster, and it's not Zeke's fault his heart was open to love. It's what we do. We give ourselves over to love and hope we don't get hurt."

I bite my lip to keep from telling her that it feels exactly like what's happening between us, except I *know* I'll get hurt because she won't stop trying to leave. "I guess I'll have to take your word for it."

"You mentioned setbacks before. Like what?"

"Like you."

She looks shocked when she says, "*Me?*"

"Zeke was the one who found you that day. He was afraid you were here to hurt him, so he woke me."

"He *woke* you?"

"When one of us retreats, another alter takes over. Zeke is the only one who can wake up at will. We can keep him suppressed but not for long, and it's not easy."

"So what do you do in there while one of the others are out here?"

"We sleep."

"You're not aware of anything that's happening around you? Like at all?"

"Only what we choose to share with each other."

"Oh."

I dip my head and run my nose down her neck. I wonder if she knows that it was my soap she used in Thorin's shower today. She smells like me. "Don't worry, Sunshine. I'm going to tell him about you. I won't be able to resist. You're my girl."

"I'm not your girl."

"Oh." This crushing feeling settles in my chest at her rejection. I should be used to it by now, but I don't think I ever will. It fucking hurts. "I get it." It kills me to put some space between us, but I have to because it feels like I'm splitting into two pieces, and I still want nothing more than for Aurelia to claim them both. Is this what heartache feels like? "You like Thorin better."

"No."

"Khalil?"

"Definitely not."

Sighing, I rest my forehead against hers. "I don't understand, Sunshine. Help me. Please."

"Seth…" I lift my head, and Aurelia chews on her bottom lip while she looks up at me curiously. "How old was Zeke when you woke up for the first time?"

"Twenty-two."

"And you've never had a girlfriend?"

"No."

"Have you ever kissed a girl?"

I frown as I shake my head. "No, I…I guess not." Is that why she doesn't like me? Because I don't have experience? Ezekiel does. Maybe I could ask Thorin or Khalil. It would be humiliating, but for Sunshine—

"So you're a virgin?"

I drop my head and nod reluctantly. "Yeah."

"Seth."

I shake my head because I can't look her in the eye now that she knows, but Aurelia doesn't give up easily. She rises onto her toes, wrapping her arms around my neck, and she presses her sweet lips to my cheek over and over.

"Kiss me," she urges when I just stand there like a dope.

"Really?"

"Kiss me, Seth. It's okay."

She's barely finished the sentence before I press my lips against hers with a groan. The kiss starts off chaotic and uncoordinated, a dance of two people learning each other's rhythms. But it doesn't take us long to create our own.

"Like this, Sunshine?" I ask against her lips.

"Mm-hmm, yeah." Aurelia moans and presses herself hard against me. "Just like that, Seth."

Her lips are so soft. *She's* so soft.

I like kissing. But only with Sunshine. She's the only girl I want to share all my kisses with. I know it the moment we come up for air, and she has this sparkle in her eye as she smiles at me. I can't see ever wanting this with anyone else. I may have to kiss her all the time. What a bummer.

"Okay, Seth." Aurelia breathes heavily. "I'll be your girlfriend on one condition."

"Yeah?" I hold her closer. Now that I have her, I can't let her go. "What's that? I'll do anything."

We both jump like we were caught with our hand in the cookie jar when we hear Thorin's bedroom door slam closed. He must be done washing the egg out of his hair.

His heavy footsteps are heading this way, so Aurelia says quickly and quietly, "Don't let them hurt me."

She turns away from me just as Thorin enters the kitchen.

Khalil is right behind him.

They're both dressed in their snowsuits so we can spend another pointless day looking for our girl when we've got her right where we want her. Well, almost.

"Tell me you at least forgive me for last night," I demand. I can feel Thorin and Khalil watching us, but I pay them no mind as I turn Aurelia back around to face me. "I don't want to hurt you. I like you, Sunshine. A lot."

"Why?" Aurelia blurts out with a mixture of surprise and disbelief as if she doesn't think there's anything about her worth loving.

"Because you'll never stop fighting. You won't give up like I did."

She's frowning, and I wonder if I said the wrong thing until she blushes and tries to play it off by grabbing one of the coffee tumblers and handing it to me.

"Thank you, Sunshine." I lean down to kiss her but pause, just shy of touching her lips, to make sure it's okay. When she gives a small nod, I smile through the kiss before pulling away. "You take such good care of us."

She looks torn about the praise before settling on, "Thanks."

"Goldilocks," Khalil calls. She looks past me toward him, and I press a hand to her hip to let her know that I'm here. I won't let them hurt her.

She doesn't do more than flick her gaze toward me and back to Khalil. "Yes?"

"We'll be back for dinner early, and we'll be hungry. I prefer not to have a repeat of last night because you're out of chances. Stay inside and make yourself useful. Understand?"

By some fucking miracle, I stay where I am instead of flying across the kitchen to rip out his entrails and lay them at my girlfriend's feet.

Girlfriend.

Fuck, that feels good to say.

Aurelia George is my *girlfriend*. My first...and my only.

"Yes," Aurelia answers softly. She grabs the other two travel mugs and steps away from me to give them to Thorin and Khalil. "I understand."

CHAPTER TWENTY-ONE

AURELIA

I stalk my mountain men—or rather their footprints—across the small clearing and into the woods. Grabbing Harrison's coat, Cassie's scarf, my boots, and the hat and goggles Seth gave me from under the den's couch cushions where I'd stashed them cost me precious minutes, but the snow, for once, is my ally.

Following them out here is in direct opposition to my promise to behave and the more sensible plan of biding my time, shoring up my strength, and gathering supplies.

But that was before Thorin mentioned a camp.

Now that I know the men holding me captive are the very ones tasked with rescuing me, my gut tells me that I need to find that camp if I want to go home.

The guys have a head start on me and know where they're going. The sky is clear, but the wind has a temper today, so it's taking everything I have to keep up with them while staying hidden. After only a few minutes, I'm winded and chilled to the bones.

God, it's colder than I remember. I don't think I'll ever get used to it.

The wind blows the top layer of snow around, so their footprints become less and less visible the farther from the cabin I get. For a moment, I worry about finding my way back. And I scold myself for forgetting the reason I'm out here in the first place.

If I can find the camp, I won't be going back.

I'll be going *home*.

Back to my life and career if I still have one.

It's the only thought that keeps me going for the few miles it takes until I finally catch up to Thorin, Seth, and Khalil. I slow my steps when I spot them through the gap in the trees. They're standing near a set of snowmobiles at the edge of a valley.

The suits they're wearing provide better protection from the cold than the pair of Seth's sweats that I borrowed. He's the slimmest of the three, and with my wide hips, the fit is snug but perfect.

The three of them are huddled around, discussing something—probably me—while I sneak closer. The crunch of the snow seems loud, and I clutch the ice pick that I found hidden and forgotten behind some meat in their freezer a little tighter. If they spot me, I'm toast. They already warned me I was on my last chance. Seth promised to protect me from Thorin and Khalil, but I'd be naive to trust his word.

Near the edge of the forest, I duck behind one of the trees with a thicker trunk while they break apart to climb onto the snowmobiles.

Of course, they'd lied when they said the only way through the Cold Peaks was on foot. The valley at the base of the mountain range was vast and stretched for *miles* in each direction. Those snowmobiles would cut down their travel time tremendously, and it would surely take me hours—if not the whole day—to cross on foot.

I'll never catch up.

But maybe I can follow the tracks? It's risky. If I stay exposed for too long, I'll die. If I encounter any more of the predators in this hellhole, I'll die. If I get lost, I'll die. Thorin, Khalil, and Seth already said they won't come for me.

I'm still debating my next move when they lower their goggles, start the Ski-Doos, and take off. Rational thought flees the chat as I push away from the tree and start after them.

I run for less than a minute before I accept that I can't keep up. Another five spent stumbling more than running in the thin mountain air, and I'm gasping for breath. The snow is too dense, too thickly packed. It nearly reaches my shins, and each step forward costs me too much energy. My underused muscles are already sore from the exertion of keeping me upright.

Still, I keep going.

There's no way I can turn back now, no way I can go back to that cabin where they confuse and make me crave things I should hate. And the longer I spend lost in their orbit, the more I want to know what made them as alone and broken as me.

It's dangerous. It's unhealthy. It's…inevitable.

I don't stop when I reach the edge of the valley where they had been. I charge across the frozen plain, even as my lungs burn from exertion and the threat of getting lost rises with every other step.

This has to be the dumbest, most desperate thing I have ever done.

Even more reckless than fighting off a pack of wolves to save someone whose last name I can't even remember.

I'm not more than a few feet inside the valley when I lose sight of them. The wind, snow, and mist swirling in the air is even denser up ahead, and it quickly swallows them up. The sound of the Ski-Doo engines fades soon after, and I'm left with only my gasping breaths and my heart pounding in my ears.

Out of breath, I fall to my knees. A moment later, I tip my head back and scream my frustration for only the mountain and wildlife to hear.

Somewhere in the distance, a lone wolf howls back.

I don't know how long I kneel on the frozen ground before I drag myself up again. I wrap my arms around my shivering body and force my feet to keep pushing the rest of me forward.

I have to find that damn camp.

I have to get off this mountain before I lose myself to it and the men who claim it as fiercely as they've claimed me.

Khalil, Seth, and Thorin are already getting to me. I can feel it.

The thick fog shrouding the rest of the valley welcomes me into its deceptive fold, and soon, I can't tell which direction I'm going. When I turn back the way I think I came, all I see is more of the gray curtain. I retreat and retrace for what feels like hours, but it just feels like I'm going in circles. Where had the fucking sky gone?

At some point, it starts snowing again, and I hear Seth's voice in my head, followed by Khalil's and Thorin's.

"It's cleaner for us to let you perish from exposure or the impact of falling from a cliff because you can't see more than five feet in front of you," Seth informs me.

"It looked pretty clear outside to me."

"*Wait awhile,*" Khalil snaps.

"*The weather here can turn in an instant,*" Thorin adds.

In conclusion, RIP Aurelia.

At the time, I thought those assholes were being cruel when really they were trying to save me from myself without lifting a finger to *actually* save me.

The snowfall has been getting heavier for hours until I can barely see my numb hand right in front of my face. The temperature has been dropping steadily, and the winds are howling. It all feels very familiar. It feels like the storm that took down my plane.

I tell myself that if I found the cabin once, I can find it again.

It's not until I reach the edge of a frozen lake that I'm forced to face what's become more obvious by the hour.

I'm lost.

CHAPTER TWENTY-TWO

KHALIL

The camp is bustling with activity when the helicopter that picked us up from the exfil point drops us off at the edge of the encampment. All around us, the search team is rushing back and forth in and out of tents, either packing up or tying down equipment. It's too early to call off the search, at least for a couple more days. It's only first light, which we barely made because Aurelia is a distraction that's going to get us caught.

It doesn't matter how much I remind myself of the danger she poses, though.

We're not. Giving. Her back.

The world could be on the cusp of total ruin, and the only way to save it would be to let Aurelia George go, and I would still let it burn. I know my brothers feel the same.

If we're the hand, fuel, and match, she's the friction to set it all aflame.

"What's going on?" Thorin asks the moment we step into the command tent.

There are several tents around the camp for barracks, medical aid, supplies, armory, and food. I swear the older man scouring maps at the center of the largest one grows ten years older each day we don't find Aurelia. Sheriff Kelly is too kind not to care, as if it were his own daughter missing, and for the space of a heartbeat, I do feel guilty because we're the reason he's probably lying awake at night, kicking himself for not doing enough.

The blame lies with us and no one else, but for the first time, I realize it's everyone else who will shoulder it.

"We just got word there's a nasty squall line headed this way. I'm moving everyone into town until it passes."

Keeping in character, I ask, "What about the search?"

"We're going to have to call it off for a few days, son. It's too dangerous, and we don't need anyone else going missing or getting hurt."

"A few days? The princess won't last a few more days, Sheriff."

"And if she's dead," I add, "her body will be buried under too much snow to ever find."

"I know, boys. It's a tough break, but I'm also accountable for the men and women who volunteered. They all have families who want to see them home safely too." When we all just glower, Sheriff Kelly sighs. "Look, I'm sorry you came all this way for nothing. I tried to radio before you left, but no one answered."

Thorin and I share a glance, and I know we're thinking the same thing. We had our hands too full with Aurelia to check the damn radio.

"Don't sweat it, Sheriff. Our frozen nuts just have us a little grumpy."

Sheriff Kelly chuckles. "Well, it's the perfect reason to head on home then, boys. Hole up, stay warm, and find a way to pass the time. We're going to get hammered pretty hard, but if anyone can ride it out, it's you three."

I'm already nodding my agreement with that plan when I notice what looks like a pile of junk stacked on one side of the tent.

"What's this?"

"We dug those up near the crash sites and brought them here. It looks like luggage. Most of it's destroyed, but some of it's good. Figured America's sweetheart would want a little comfort when we find her."

Indeed.

But she'll have to earn it like everything else.

One of the deputies arrives with some emergency, and Sheriff Kelly excuses himself before leaving the tent.

Seth and I walk over to the salvage pile as soon as he's gone while Thorin keeps watch. It's taken our whole lives and nine years stuck in seclusion together to be in sync like this without even saying a word.

"Exactly how long was her uncle planning to keep her exiled?" I gripe ten minutes later while searching through yet another dented trunk full of clothes and shoes. "This is a lot of shit, and barely any of it's useful out here."

We're taking a huge chance that this stuff hasn't been inventoried yet, so we have to be careful not to take too much so the missing items won't be noticed.

"Don't know," Thorin says with his back to us. "But I think Seth was on to something. Her uncle probably wanted her out of his hair for a while."

"Or permanently," Seth mumbles as he studies Aurelia's flat iron like it's a foreign object.

"She'll want that," I tell him. He nods and stuffs it inside the large duffel bag we're using to carry her things back. I'm already picturing the look on her face when we show her. Although it's Aurelia. It's hard to predict how she'll react. She's as likely to chuck the flat iron at Seth's head as she is to show a little gratitude. "And lay off with the murder plots. You're just looking for a reason why she can't go back to him."

"Don't need a reason. I'm crazy, remember?"

"Seth, you're not crazy," I tell him. "You're...you."

"Thanks," he returns dryly.

"Call it love, call it wrong, call it a one-way ticket to hell," Thorin says. "We're not letting anyone take her from us without killing anyone who tries. Agreed?"

"Agreed."

I'm slower to respond as a smile takes over my face, and I shake my head in awe. No one at home would ever believe that I, Khalil Poverly, was settling down. "Fuck it. If you're not willing to shed a little blood for your woman, is she even yours? Yes. Hell yes. Agreed."

"So... Who's going to break it to Aurelia?" Thorin muses.

"Not it," Seth and I say at the same time.

Thorin glowers at us both.

Finding an unopened box of tampons, I toss it inside the now full duffel bag and zip it closed.

"What's this?" I look up to see Seth holding a blue, flat, round container. When he opens it, there are tiny pills inside—some white and some pink—in a circular pattern with dates under them. He sniffs them and asks, "Candy?"

"It's birth control."

"Birth control?"

"Yeah. You remember I told you how it works." Seth nods slowly. "Well,

Aurelia is supposed to take one of those every day so that she doesn't get pregnant when we come inside her."

"Leave it," Thorin orders tightly.

I raise my brows at him, but when he glares over his shoulder at me, I roll my eyes and take the pills from Seth before tossing them back inside the nearly emptied suitcase where we found her toiletries and makeup.

"But if Sunshine's taking those pills, it means she *doesn't* want to have a baby, right?" Seth asks as we leave the tent with the overstuffed duffel.

It's going to be tough as hell sneaking out of the camp with Aurelia's shit without being noticed.

"Yes, but Thorin wants to breed her."

"Why?"

"Because he's an idiot."

"I heard that."

I shrug as we keep to the edges of the camp, heading for home—for Aurelia. "He thinks she won't want to leave if she has our baby. And because the perv gets off on it."

"I can still hear you."

"Do you think it will work?" Seth asks curiously.

I rock my head from side to side. "It's not the dumbest idea he's ever had." Thorin sighs loudly.

"But babies complicate shit," I continue. "I think further dividing the attention of the girl we're still trying to bond with is a mistake. None of us have ever shared a woman before. We don't even know if it will work."

"Well, if you think it's such a bad idea, why did you leave the pills?" Thorin snaps.

"Because when you fuck up, I get to swoop in and make it better. You know what they say about a shoulder to cry on…" Crudely, I grab my dick. "Also, I'm not helping with late-night feedings and diaper changes. Fuck that. You'll be one hundred percent on your own." Winking when Thorin scowls at me, I pick up the pace. All this talk of Aurelia has me eager to get back to her.

Also… The sixth sense that mysteriously materialized with Aurelia's arrival has been buzzing since we reached the camp. I'm not sure what it means yet—if she's hurt, upset, or in trouble—but I'm dubbing it the Girlfriend Tingle.

Even though we leave the camp earlier than expected, we still don't make it home until early evening. The storm Sheriff Kelly warned us about arrived sooner than expected, so flying back to the north side of the valley where we left our Ski-Doos was out of the question. The trek back was hard, but it's nothing we haven't done a thousand times.

By the time we reach our clearing, the shitty visibility makes it hard to see even our cabin, a mere three hundred feet away. There's no glow from the windows to guide us from the fires that should be burning inside, so it's my second clue that something is wrong.

Aurelia didn't seem keen on defying us again when we left her this morning, but I wonder if she's a better actor than I thought as we step inside the cabin and don't see her waiting for us.

The fires Thorin lit before we left are mere embers, so we're once again returning home to a freezing cabin. Dropping Aurelia's duffel bag and our packs by the door, the three of us search the cabin to see if she's fallen asleep again. By the time Thorin walks inside his room and returns empty-handed seconds later, I'm praying she's just taking a nap. The three of us silently search the cabin from top to bottom before meeting back up in the living room.

Thorin has a torn look on his face while Seth paces and pulls at his hair.

If Aurelia doesn't walk through those doors in the next few minutes, he's going to lose his shit. We all are.

"You…" I gulp. "You think she ran?"

The vein in Thorin's neck bulges when he finally explodes. "Of course, she ran! We haven't given her a fucking reason to stay." He unzips his snowsuit, and I frown at the motion while he drops onto the couch. He frees a bottle of bourbon from under one of the couch cushions and takes a swig before leaning his head back to glower at the ceiling.

"What are you doing?"

"What does it look like? I'm drinking."

"It looks like you're on your ass sulking when we need to go find her, Thor."

"And why would we do that?"

"What do you mean why? Because she'll die!"

"I seem to recall you telling her that's exactly what would happen if she left, and she did it anyway." He lifts his head to give me a hard look. "Give me one good reason why we should go chasing that ungrateful bitch when she's made it clear she'd rather die than be with us?"

"Because she's *our* ungrateful bitch, Thor."

"Really?" He waves a hand around the cold, bleak cabin. Aurelia's brought so much life to it in just a few days, and she doesn't even know because we never told her. We've been merely existing before now. Most days, we couldn't be bothered to utter a word or climb out of bed if it wasn't to hunt or rescue some dumb teenagers who'd wandered a little too far and gotten themselves trapped or lost. "Do you see her here? Because I don't."

"Thor—"

"You two do what you want. Waste your time rescuing her so she can run again the moment our backs are turned. God-fucking-speed." He offers a sarcastic salute.

"You're a selfish dick, you know that? You're probably the reason she left. I heard how rough you were with her this morning. She told you *no*."

"Yeah? Well, she told you no, too, or did you forget? And I don't recall you trying to stop me, Khalil. You were too concerned with getting off to worry about her well-being, so I'd look in the mirror if I were you."

"Fuck you. We both know you've been the biggest asshole to her. You—"

Hearing something slam behind me, I whirl around to see the front door wide-open and banging against the wall. A gust cold enough to make my muscles lock up blows inside the cabin. The gale is strong enough to push my solid frame back a couple of steps, and Aurelia—our girl and reason for being—is out there in that, lost and alone.

"How did the door get open?"

I don't hear Thorin move until he's standing next to me with a pinched expression. "Seth."

Frowning, I look around for him, but the spot where he was pacing a hole in the floor is empty, and his pack is gone. I feel the blood drain from my face and hands when I realize he must have slipped out while Thorin and I were arguing.

"Jesus, he went after her alone."

Thorin sends the bourbon bottle sailing across the room, where it hits his bedroom door and shatters. "Goddammit!"

CHAPTER TWENTY-THREE

AURELIA

I can't feel…anything. I can't feel my face, fingers, or toes. All I can feel is the brutality of the mountain and the storm swirling around its peak. Giving up on finding my way back to the cabin, I've been trying to find shelter for hours, but I can't see a thing.

There's only a wall of white all around me.

I know after the first hour of being caught in the storm that it's worse than any of the others. The extra protection only prolongs my death, but it won't be enough to stop it.

I won't survive the night.

My body aches from the violent shivering while my steps and breathing slow. When I reach the same six-foot-slanted rock I'd passed an hour ago, my soul withers and my legs collapse under me.

It's hopeless.

I've been going in circles, and I can't entirely blame the low visibility for it. I've been wandering aimlessly because my heart can't decide on a direction—home or…home.

Pathetically, I leave myself lying face down in the snow so I can just die already. I know I probably shouldn't sleep when I'm one step from death's door, but my lids, ladened with frost and snow, are growing heavy, and I can't walk another step.

All I need is a few minutes.

Ironically, it's the same thing I said when I climbed into Khalil's bed that first day at the cabin and look where it had gotten me.

Whatever.

This is long overdue. It's not fair that I got to live when so many good people died—Cassie, Harrison, Tyler... If I wasn't convinced that I'm a terrible person, I sure as hell know it now. Dying cold and alone seems just.

It feels like my eyes have only just closed when I hear something that makes them pop back open. My head feels like it weighs a hundred pounds when I lift it and peer through cracked eyes.

I must be dead already. There's no one there.

"Aurelia!"

Satan, is that you?

"Aurelia!"

I'm coming, evil hell Daddy.

"AURELIA!"

Okay, don't get pushy.

It figures I'd trade three growly, demanding alphaholes for another.

"Aurelia!"

I groan when my heart jumps in my chest, and I realize I'm not dead. That voice... I know it. I never thought I'd hear it again, but there's no mistaking it. I'd know it anywhere.

"Aurelia!"

So, not evil hell Daddy, then.

Just one determined and loyal bodyguard. Tyler.

I gasp when I hear his voice again, leaving no room for doubt. How did he survive the avalanche? How did he find me?

"Aurelia, answer me!" He sounds farther away now as if he's turned to head a different way.

"Come back," I croak out as Rose did in *Titanic* after the ship sank and she *let Jack die*. It feels like I'm floating alone on a door in the middle of the cold, dark sea. Only, in this version, Jack isn't dead. He made it somehow, and he came back for me. "Tyler, I'm here!"

My voice isn't loud enough to rise above the wind, much less reach him wherever he is.

He must be close.

That knowledge is enough to make me stand, though it takes me a full minute to climb to my feet.

"Tyler!" I scream a little louder this time. "Tyler, wait! Ty—"

My shout is cut off, and I stop when I see something large and fast dart from the left up ahead. At first, I wonder if I'm hallucinating until I see it again, closer now and heading in the opposite direction.

"What the…"

A low rumbling sound has the frozen hairs on my nape and arms rising as I look behind me for the source.

All I see is the snow falling so heavily that it creates a shimmering curtain of nearly solid white.

I know I'm not alone, though. I can hear pattering in the snow, and it's coming from every direction. No matter which way I turn, I can't pin it down. Whatever it is that's stalking me, it's not alone.

I can barely keep calm when I catch another glimpse of something faster and larger than a dog running past in my peripheral vision. I just keep walking, head down, arms wrapped around myself, hoping that this new threat is just curious and goes away now that I'm up and moving. They probably spotted me lying in the snow and couldn't resist an easy meal in this storm.

"Tyler!" I call out again.

The only thing that answers back is a howl that expels all the air in my lungs. It's so cold I can see my breath curling in the air in front of me.

I hear more pattering, and even though my muscles tense, I somehow know not to run. Maybe I have my short time in the cabin to thank. Each time I ran from Khalil, Seth, and Thorin, they pursued me like any beast of prey. They pinned me down, and they sank their teeth in—often literally. My running activated their need to chase, and there's no reason to think it would be any different now.

So I keep walking with even, steady strides even though my heart is pounding and I'm terrified.

When I spot part of a branch lying in the snow, I risk stopping long enough to pick it up. It's almost as tall as me and looks sturdy enough, so I keep my gaze on a swivel as I slowly pull the ice pick from my pocket. It's not as big or sharp as the hunting knives the guys carry, but it's better than nothing.

I start to chip away at the broken end with the six-inch spike and have just managed to make a point—though not a very sharp one—when I hear my name again.

"Aurelia!"

I gasp, and my head snaps in that direction. "Tyler?"

"Aurelia, where are you?"

"Tyler, I'm over here!"

I quicken my steps and don't realize I'm running with my makeshift spear until I hear a snarl so vicious my steps slow abruptly until I'm standing still. A moment later, the storm seems to part, and something large and terrifying stalks from the snowy veil.

Black fur, four legs, sharp teeth, and glowing yellow eyes.

"Oh, shit."

Wolves.

A single breath shudders out of me before I turn back the way I came. When I do, I see another wolf with white fur and blue eyes blocking the path. The wolf's hackles raise the moment I turn, and it bares its teeth while folding its ears back.

Fear paralyzes me, so when I hear a snarl, my eyes are the only part of me that moves in the direction of the gray wolf closing in.

Teeth snapping draws my gaze to my right, to the final wolf with brown fur completing the kill circle.

My death will not be quick.

Cassie's wasn't.

I watched them tear her apart, and there was nothing I could do about it when I was armed with an *axe*. All I have now is a branch and little more than a butter knife the wolves can pick their teeth with after they're done with me.

I flinch when the white wolf bares its teeth. Remembering how one of the wolves that attacked Cassie came after me when I tried to save her, I grip the thick branch tighter. Its blue eyes seem to track the movement, and then it snarls again.

"Just fucking do it already," I say through gritted teeth while holding its gaze.

I don't expect the first attack to come from the side.

I barely pivot in time to raise my arms when the gray wolf tackles me to the ground. The branch I hold at its throat is the only thing keeping it from ripping out mine as it snaps and snarls at me from above. My teeth are bared, too, as I clench them in concentration and beg my muscles to hold.

The other wolves don't immediately attack once I'm pinned like they did to Cassie. They circle, barking and growling, but they don't go for the easy kill. I have a feeling the alpha sent the smallest one in to test me.

The powdered snow under the gray wolf's giant paws flies up from its claws as it scrapes the ground to get closer.

One of those paws finds my shoulder, and I scream.

Sharp claws dig in and shred through my flesh, and I pray that I black out from the pain so that I won't feel it when the rest comes.

But I don't.

Even when the pain is blinding and blood oozes from the wound, I stay woefully conscious.

And unlike me, the wolf shows no signs of tiring.

My arms are already trembling from the effort it takes to hold it off. If my predicament weren't so terrifying, I'd laugh at God's twisted sense of humor.

I survived a plane crash, three days in the wild, and six days with three feral mountain men just to be torn apart by wolves. I'd been spared those other times so that I might suffer the worst possible death.

Well, that tracks.

Even with my focus on staying alive, I can still hear Cassie's pleas. I can still see her pretty face twisted with pain and fear as they fed on her.

I failed her. Tears prick my eyes, but they don't fall. They never fall.

Cassie's dead when it should have been me.

If I hadn't been such a bitch to Tania, if I hadn't been so determined to destroy the life I hated so much, my uncle wouldn't have felt the need to exile me. None of this would have happened if I'd just done that stupid interview with Avery fucking Shaw, told my side, and moved on.

"Cassie, I'm so sorry. I'm sorry I didn't fight harder," I plead in vain.

She's gone just like the others.

My sobs cause my grip to loosen on the branch, and the maw of the wolf and its flesh-shredding teeth gain an inch.

As I stare death in the eye, a dark thought scales the stubborn wall my mind has built.

The glowing green eyes of the wolf are almost hypnotic as I think about how much easier it would be to let it kill me. *Coward.* Maybe this death will go quicker than I think. *It won't.* The longer I stare, the more numb I become, and when my hold loosens on the branch this time, it's not entirely unintentional.

One last memory pierces my thoughts, but this time, it rises from the icy moat built around my heart where I trapped it.

"I like you, Sunshine. A lot."

"Why?"

"Because you'll never stop fighting. You won't give up like I did."

You won't give up like I did.

You won't give up like I did.

You won't give up like I did.

You won't give up... I did.

The frozen surface of that icy moat cracks and blue flames explode from the fissure in my heart as I lift my head and shout at the gray wolf. "Fuck you!"

My injured shoulder burns when I push the branch tighter against its throat and heave my body up. I throw the wolf off me, and it skids several feet away as it scrambles to right itself. Reaching for the ice pick that fell when the first wolf attacked me, I have just managed to wrap my cold fingers around the handle when another wolf lunges forward.

I can't stop it from sinking its teeth into my arm, and I scream.

The bite of the alpha burns like acid as I tighten my grip around the ice pick before returning the favor. I plunge the short blade into the wolf's black fur, and it yelps but holds on to my arms. Tearing the weapon free, I stab it again, over and over, until the wolf unlocks its jaws and falls to the ground.

I forget about the other wolves as I stab their alpha over and over while it stares up at me through eyes that I realize are more golden than yellow. They feel like a mirror.

"You fucking piece of shit. You fucking bitch. You deserve this. You deserve to die. Die! Die! *Just dieeeee!*"

I hear a crack in the air that pierces the howling wind and echoes through the forest. My head snaps back, and I search the gray, clouded sky for lightning but see none.

"Aurelia!"

The third attack finally comes when a heavy weight collides with my back. The gray wolf and I are limb-locked as we roll across the snow. It's not until I hear a loud boom and the ground shudders underneath me that I notice the fallen tree.

It landed right where I was just kneeling.

I don't even notice the weight of the wolf on top of me falling away or that it doesn't attack until I hear it speak.

"Aurelia, what the fuck!"

Blinking, I turn my head toward the sound and see that it's not a wolf, but a man. One I never thought I'd see again.

"Tyler?"

He pauses and then says. "Aurelia, it's *me*…" He says his name, but I don't hear it over the wind.

Lifting my hand, I hold his dark cheek and smile. I barely notice that my shoulder and arm don't hurt anymore. "Tyler," I repeat softly. "You're alive."

He's really here.

My bodyguard doesn't respond as he shakes his head and hauls me to my feet. "Aurelia, listen to me. It's the cold. You've been exposed for too long. You're—"

A howl rents the air, and I gasp, my eyes widening as I look around for the three remaining wolves. I don't see them, but I know they're there.

Meeting Tyler's gaze, I utter one word. "*Run.*"

The memory of the last time I saw him—when he told *me* to run—enters my mind as I take off in the opposite direction with Tyler and the wolves hot on my heels. I remember in vivid detail the avalanche moving fast down the hill, the cliff that marks our dead end, and the ravine below as Tyler falls into it. I hadn't imagined that.

How is he here?

How did he find me?

It should be impossible that he's alive, much less okay, yet he's here.

"Aurelia!" he calls after me.

I don't stop.

Tyler catches up to me and takes my hand, pulling me along behind him. His hands are more callused than I remember. Why that detail sticks out at me when I'm literally running for my life is beyond me, but it feels important.

Tyler's longer legs make it hard not to fall behind, but when I look over my shoulder and see the brown, white, and gray wolves chasing after us, I keep up. The tree falling must have scared them off long enough for him to get to me, but now the wolves have grown bold again. They snap and snarl too close behind us as we race through the forest, and I'm worried for Tyler.

Somehow, I know they'll hurt him if they catch us.

Thorin, Seth, and Khalil—they'll kill him for trying to take me away.

"Just shoot them!" I scream. Why isn't he shooting them? There's a gun right there on his hip.

Tyler looks down at me and then stops. Before I can yell at him to keep going, he lifts me into his arms. "Hold on to me, Sunshine. I've got you."

Warmth spreads through me at the endearment, and it bids me to trust the man who uttered it. I wrap my arms around his neck and stare into his green eyes, which I always thought were brown. When I frown, Tyler's jaw tightens, and he begins running again.

We'll never outrun the mountain men nipping at our heels, so I sure as hell hope Tyler has a plan.

CHAPTER TWENTY-FOUR

AURELIA

S eth!" someone barks.

The voice is deep, angry, hoarse from shouting over the wind, and panicked, so why is it that simply hearing it so close by fills me with comfort?

I can hear the storm I got caught in raging around me. At some point, I must have rolled onto my back from my face down position in the snow. The gap in my memory is startling, though. While I still feel the frozen ground underneath me, the sheet keeping the wind and snow from reaching me while trapping my body heat is new.

But that's not right either.

The last thing I remember is...Tyler. He came for me. He found me. Wolves attacked me, I nearly got crushed by a tree, and then we were running—

Someone yells again before I can consider opening my eyes to look around, and recognizing the voice, I decide to keep them closed. How the hell did they find me?

"Seth, get that goddamn fire going!"

Thorin?

I thought he'd be the last person to come for me after swearing he wouldn't. I believed him.

"I'm fucking trying!" Seth shouts back over the wind. "Everything is wet! I can't get a spark!"

A flicking sound follows, and then Seth blows on something before viciously swearing. At the same time, I hear snow being dug nearby.

When I pry open my eyes the tiniest bit, the first thing I notice is that night has fallen. There's too much snow and wind to see the stars that are usually so vivid out here, but the nearly pitch-black sky leaves no room for doubt. What little of the moon pierces the blizzard is our only source of light.

That and the occasional golden glow sparking in my peripheral vision.

Letting my head fall to the side, I spot Seth kneeling over a teepee fire as he tries to light it, but even I can tell from here that the sticks, tinder, and dead leaves are soaked through. He tries anyway because our situation is too dire to give up.

"I think I have some dry kindling stashed in my pack," Khalil says as he continues to dig. Oh my God... They're going to bury me alive, aren't they? It seems more likely than Khalil, Thorin, and Seth risking their lives to find me. "Try that."

The snow crunches under Seth's booted feet as he rises and rushes over to Khalil's heavy-looking pack abandoned by my feet.

That's when I see them—two more imposing figures hunched over a few feet away. Thorin and Khalil are holding what looks like shovels as they work together, hurriedly scooping up snow and tossing it onto the mound that's nearly as tall as them and at least ten to twelve feet in diameter.

When did they find me?

How did they find me?

And where's Tyler?

I must move or make a sound because Seth's head snaps up, and he looks over at me.

The thought of what they might have done to Tyler has me passing out again, but I still hear the words Seth says before I do.

"We got you, Sunshine. We're here. Just hang on..."

I'm startled awake again when I hear the crunch of something being stabbed into the snow-covered ground near my head.

"The quinzee should be hard enough to hold now!" Thorin shouts. "Let's get her inside!"

A moment later, I'm lifted from the ground. The storm still hasn't abated, and when I crack my eyes open, I see the trees swaying hard and the gray storm clouds through the canopy.

It's still night.

And a testament to how fucked we are that Thorin, Khalil, and Seth decided it was safer to make camp and ride out the storm than try to make it back to the cabin.

How far did I wander?

The answer is not really as imperative as why I'd left the cabin in the first place. It wasn't survival. Only fear could have driven me to do something that stupid.

But when I left the cabin, I didn't flee in fear of them. I was terrified, yes, but not of them. It's why I had to leave.

The thermal blanket that looks like a foil tarp is now wrapped tightly around my body as Thorin carries me from the fire. Seth not only managed to light it, but he built a small enclosure to keep it from going out. He's crouching by it now, his lean frame shivering as he holds his hands close to the flames to warm them. I'd never noticed before how long and capable his fingers were until the glow of the fire touched them.

Why does that stick out to me at a time like this? Only a licensed therapist could tell.

Embedded in the snow next to him is the ice pick I stole.

Thorin and I only go a few feet before he says to Khalil, who's following us, "You go first, and then I'll hand her to you to pull inside."

Khalil does as Thorin says, and the moment he crouches and disappears, Thorin looks down at me like he's known all along I am awake. Like a coward, I quickly snap my eyes closed.

"You're a pain in my ass, wolf." When I just continue to play dead, I think I hear him chuckle, albeit reluctantly. "Sleep, Aurelia. We'll be home soon."

I shiver in his arms, and he clutches me tighter.

Thorin lowers me to the ground again when Khalil calls out, and then I feel Khalil's hands under my shoulders, dragging me across the snow. The last thing I see before I give in to Thorin's demand is the mouth of the hollowed-out snow mound before I'm pulled inside its dark interior.

"She was screaming and stabbing the ground when I found her," I hear Seth whisper when I come to again.

The storm seems calmer now, but that could change at any moment.

We're not out of the woods yet—literally.

"You think something attacked her?" Khalil asks right by my ear. I can hear the frown in his voice and his cold breath skating over my cheek. It must be his chest I'm lying on.

"Maybe...but she was alone."

Khalil's chest rises sharply, and then he and Thorin swear.

What? No. What is Seth talking about? There were wolves. Didn't he see them? What about my injuries?

They don't know I'm awake, so I keep as still as possible even though I want to check my arm and shoulder where the wolves bit and clawed me and then *scream* at Seth for making me sound like I made it all up. Had I?

But wait—he wasn't the one who found me.

It was—

"But that's not our biggest problem," Seth mumbles before I can finish the thought.

"What?" Thorin and Khalil both ask tightly.

"She kept calling me Tyler."

It's silent, and I wonder if they can hear my heart racing. Seth says I called him *Tyler*? No, that's not right. It felt so real. *He* felt so real. Tyler was alive. He made it. He—

"You mean the guy we found a week ago?" Thorin asks dryly.

I black out again.

CHAPTER TWENTY-FIVE

AURELIA

It's morning when I wake up again, and I'm warm. Burning is more accurate. I also don't hear the storm anymore. All I hear is the steady heartbeat beneath my ear. I could write a song to that chaotic rhythm.

"Morning, Sunshine."

When I lift my head, I see Seth's face staring down at me. He looks relieved and angry and hurt and…something else I don't want to name because it's too perilous. "It was you," I gasp as I curl my fingers into his thermal shirt. I feel his hard abs right below my fingers as my lips tremble with that same unnamed emotion. "You came for me."

Seth's cold lips brush my forehead. "I'll always come for you, Sunshine. I told Thanatos that you were mine, and he couldn't have you. Not without taking me too."

I'm speechless.

What do you say to a person you've only known a few days but who vows without one ounce of irony or whimsy that he'll follow you into death?

"Stalker."

Seth smiles at my response, but it's small and fleeting as he pulls me closer while I look around.

"Where're Thorin and Khalil? They were here, or did I hallucinate that too?"

"It wasn't a vision," he tells me as he rubs my back. "They're scouting for a way home."

"You mean they *don't know*?" I sit up, but without Seth's warmth, I'm immediately cold. I force myself to stay put and *not* use him as a human blanket even though I know he won't mind. I'm sitting on his lap while he continues to lie on his back, and I have a feeling it's the only reason he doesn't yank me back down with him.

"That storm did a lot of damage, Sunshine. It will be tough finding a safe path back, and they won't risk you until they're sure."

I stare at the opening of our little snow cave and the sunlight that makes the packed and hardened snow gleam. Khalil and Thorin *built* this for me—risked their own lives to keep me safe and alive until the storm passed. It's a full minute before I'm brave enough to ask, "Are they mad?"

"Livid, baby." Seth thinks about it and then says, "Actually, I think we're both in the doghouse. It'll be fine. We just need to get you home, and then you can start making it up to us."

My stomach sinks while my pussy tightens at the thought of it—two warring reactions that I'm careful not to give away.

"Maybe tie you to the bed so this doesn't happen again," Seth muses.

I chuckle nervously. "I can't tell if you're joking or not."

"I'm not."

"Oh."

"If it makes you feel better, they'll probably tie me up too, so at least we can keep each other company."

"Why?" When he doesn't answer, I take a stab in the dark. "Because you came after me?"

"Because I came after you without them."

That's when I remember Seth was alone when he found me, except I thought at the time that he was Tyler. Thorin and Khalil must have caught up with us after I passed out the first time.

"Well, maybe all the hot air they blow around when they return will warm us up." Seth laughs, but it sounds forced. My suspicions are confirmed when he sits up and lifts me off his lap to set me down on the sleeping bag next to his. *Okay...* His green eyes are piercing as he props his arms on his bent knees and studies me like he's figuring out what to make of me. "What..." Looking away, Seth drops his head to stare at the ground between his bent knees.

"Oh, God," I say when realization slams into me. "You're mad at me, too, aren't you?"

"Nah."

"Seth, don't lie to me." His face is pinched as if he's debating whether he wants to have it out with me or let me get away with putting us all in danger. "It's okay. You can tell me. I'm a big girl. I can take it."

"It's just…" He shoves his fingers through his dark hair, blows out a breath, and then stares at me through hurt eyes that weirdly make me want to die. "I don't get you, Sunshine. Even less than I did before. You agreed to be my girlfriend, and then you ran. What am I missing? Were you serious, or was it another lie?"

"I…"

Seth squints when I take entirely too long to answer. "Okay, I understand."

He gently pushes me aside and then tries to leave the snow cave. I should let him go, but for whatever reason, I grab his arm.

"Seth… You *kidnapped* me." He flinches, but I dig in. I won't let him run from this any more than they let me run from them. "And you've done nothing but treat me like a chew toy ever since. Don't you dare try to make me feel guilty for a little white lie."

"It wasn't a little white lie to *me*."

"And you trapping me is no small thing to me!"

"Stop fighting us, and we won't have to," he says tightly.

"And they say romance is dead. Besides, I thought you liked it when I fight back?"

"You know what the hell I mean, Aurelia. Fight us, but don't fight *us*. Just stop running. What the hell do you have to go back to anyway? There's nothing real waiting for you back home, and you know it."

Seth's words, while true, are a punch to the gut.

He hasn't known me long and already he's guessed that I've been nothing to no one for a very long time. There hasn't been anyone in my corner since my parents died. No one to truly miss me now that I'm "gone." I'm sure even my fans have already moved on.

Heat flames my cheeks and neck, and before I know it, my mouth is moving, and I can't stop the vitriol. Poison, is my weapon of choice whenever people get too close. "Wow. Thanks for the reminder."

It's my turn to crawl out of the cave and away from this discussion, and Seth doesn't stop me. Although he's slow to follow, he does follow.

I'm shivering almost immediately with my arms wrapped around myself in the early morning light, but I'm too stubborn to go back inside the shelter that looks like an igloo, so when he finally emerges and drapes Harrison's coat over my shoulders, I'm grateful.

I don't speak or look at him as I stick my arms in the sleeves—partly because I'm pissed at him for what he said, but mostly because I'm pissed at *me* for what *I* said.

"I'm sorry," I offer as soon I'm burrowed inside the warmth of the coat. It's the extent of the regret he'll get from me because even though he risked his life to save mine, he still holds it in the palm of his hand. I force myself to meet his gaze. "That was low even for me."

"I forgave you when you said it, Sunshine. Can you forgive me?"

"I'll think about it." Peeking up at him, I tuck my lips into my mouth to keep from laughing, but Seth has no problem letting his free.

"Oh, Sunshine. If you want me to stop being obsessed, you're going to have to start making this easy." Taking my arms as he pivots to stand in front of me, Seth pushes me against the side wall of the quinzee.

"Won't it collapse?" I ask with a gasp when I feel the cold against my back.

"No. Thorin and Khalil know what they're doing." It's all the explanation he offers before he leans down and kisses me.

"*Mhm, mhm*, Seth," I immediately protest. "Morning breath."

He chuckles but doesn't stop kissing me, and I realize very quickly that his morning breath isn't foul at all.

Oh, God.

He probably brushed last night or before I woke, and I'm the only one with yuck mouth.

Feeling self-conscious, I push him away. "Okay, that's enough."

Seth laughs, then walks over to his pack, which he'd dropped by the quinzee's opening. He rifles through it before handing me a brand-new toothbrush still wrapped in plastic, a canteen full of fresh water, and a travel-size toothpaste.

"Knock yourself out, baby."

I squeal and throw my arms around his neck. "Thank you! Thank you! Thank you! Best boyfriend ever!"

Seth steals another kiss, closemouthed—thank God—and then pushes me toward the cluster of trees between the fire and quinzee.

"I'm going to go take a piss," he announces. "Stay where I can see you."

I sketch a mocking salute. "Yes, sir!"

"Sunshine."

Fire pools in my belly at the rare commanding note in his tone. I think running last night changed something in Seth too. I think his hold on me just got a little tighter.

"Yes, Seth," I offer with a note of obedience that surprises even me. "I'll stay put."

"That's my good girl."

I turn away before he can see my reaction to the praise. *Sick, sick, sick, sick, sick, sick, sick.* By the time I'm done brushing my teeth, Thorin and Khalil have returned to the camp bearing two dead rabbits.

Khalil starts rebuilding the fire while Thorin lays out the rabbits on a large, flat rock.

I don't know why I feel nervous when I walk over to sit next to the fire with them, but I'm shivering again, and it has nothing to do with the cold.

"Good morning."

Utter silence greets me back.

I wait for one of them to respond, but they never do. They both pretend they didn't hear me as they continue to work.

"Look, I know you're mad at me, but Thorin mentioned a camp, and I thought I could follow you. I didn't mean to put you or myself in danger. I hope you understand why I had to try."

Thorin skins the smaller rabbit while staring at me like he wishes the creature were me and Khalil arranges some dry kindling he managed to find.

"Anyway, I just wanted to say thank you for finding me, I guess. I'd probably be dead if you hadn't."

They finally respond, and before they're done, I really wish they hadn't.

"You'd definitely be dead," Khalil says coolly.

"And for the record, we didn't come for you," Thorin adds. "We came for Seth. He just happened to find you before we could drag his ass back home and leave you to rot."

"Oh." My cheeks flame because I thought... I *assumed*... God. "Okay, um. Well...thanks anyway."

I stand, but my knees feel weak. I keep my chin high as I walk away from the campfire, and it takes all that I have to do so.

"Don't even think about leaving this camp, Aurelia."

I spin back around, my gaze narrowing on Thorin, who is already watching me. "Why do you care?"

"You don't want me to show you how much I care, so I advise you not fuck with me."

My hurt feelings make my eyes prickle while my voice sounds thick from the unshed tears when I speak. "Go to hell, Thorin."

I storm away just as a whistling Seth returns to camp. We pass each other as I head for the quinzee, but when he flashes me a flirty smile and reaches out for me, I dodge his touch and keep going.

I can feel Seth's confusion like an arrow in my back, and then I hear him bark at his friends. "What the hell did you guys do?"

I don't wait around for the answer before crawling back inside the quinzee.

How the hell all four of us fit inside of here last night, I'll never know. The three of them are huge, so they must have been sleeping practically on top of one of another. Three bedrolls are laid out, and I don't bother trying to figure out which belongs to who as I crawl inside the middle one and will myself back to sleep.

I knew they'd be mad, but I didn't expect them to be cruel—not after glimpsing how hard they worked to save me. How desperately.

They care. I know they do.

So why try to hide it?

Why push me away and make me feel like an unwanted nuisance?

Maybe because you're acting like one?

I fall asleep, and the guys leave me alone until breakfast is done, and Khalil snaps at me from outside the quinzee to wake the fuck up and fuel up for the journey. He makes it clear that since I want to be a brat, they will *not* be carrying me back. What the hell? I didn't even know that was an option.

Grumbling, I reluctantly crawl from the shelter, dragging the bedrolls with me. I have a bitch of time getting them rolled up tight to fit inside their already full packs, and none of the guys help me—not even Seth.

Thorin, Khalil, and Seth have a kind of Three Musketeers thing going on. When one of them is pissed, they're all pissed, and apparently, that rule extends to me.

Seth is probably just upset that I rejected his affection earlier, but *I've* decided that if one of them pisses me off, then they all can kiss my ass.

Thorin silently hands me a cloth filled with rabbit meat when I join them, and I eat while the three re-roll their sleeping mats before securing them with twine and stuffing them back in their packs.

"How long will it take to get back to the cabin?" I casually ask while chewing on the surprisingly juicy meat. Really, I'm just curious how far I'd made it yesterday—for when I try again later of course.

"We're only a few miles' hike from the base of our mountain."

I pause mid-chew as the blood drains from my face. "That's it?"

No… That can't be right. I wandered for hours. I was *lost*. I was as good as *dead*. There was no way my circumstances would have been that dire if I didn't at least make it a respectable distance. How could I have been that close to the cabin without ever finding it when I found it before without even looking for it?

The three of them look at each other before staring down at me.

Khalil is the first to speak. "You didn't accomplish anything other than nearly getting yourself killed, Aurelia."

"Maybe think about that the next time you run from us," Thorin says.

Seth speaks last. "Or better yet, don't run at all. We won't be so forgiving a second time."

CHAPTER TWENTY-SIX

THORIN

I s this really necessary?" Aurelia whines for the umpteenth time. "It itches."

The four of us are sitting around the fire in our living room, waiting for the storms we've been pinned under for days to pass. After rescuing Aurelia, we made it back to the cabin just in time for another squall to hit us hard. Only these cabin walls we'd built with our bare hands separate us from certain death while we have the perfect view of the storm-ridden wilds out of the panoramic window overlooking the Cold Peaks.

Khalil had wasted no time rigging an ankle monitor of sorts, using an avalanche beacon, which now adorns Aurelia's ankle. It's a bluff that he gambled she wouldn't call since the tracker only picks up the signal within two hundred feet. All she needs to know is that we can find her even faster if she runs again—which she will.

It's given us a little peace of mind that our pet won't get far, but Aurelia's been spitting venom ever since—even more than usual. Honestly, she's lucky it didn't occur to Khalil to make a shock collar instead. She's lucky I don't *suggest* it to him.

Khalil looks up from the small wooden block he's been carving for the last hour and gives her a hard look. "Are you going to run again?"

He's still salty from the black eye she gave him after he told her the monitor was for her. It had taken all three of us holding her down to get it on and a very descriptive warning of what would happen if she took it off. She can, of course, *if* she can find something strong enough to cut through the thick metal cuff.

"Probably."

214 · B.B. REID

"Then it's necessary."

"It *itches*."

"You said that already."

"That's because it really itches!"

"The cuff stays on, wolf."

Aurelia shifts her displeasure to me, giving Khalil a much-needed break from her complaining. "Classic misogyny," she says with a scoff. "You say it's because I'm a danger to myself, but I don't see you tagging Seth. He was out there too."

She has a point...

Hearing Aurelia throw him under the bus, Seth sits up and gapes at her. "What the fuck, Sunshine?"

"Shut up, Seth. You want to talk about betrayal? You let them do this to me."

My brows dip. What the hell is she talking about? Since when is Seth on *her* side?

"Hey, hey." Reaching down, Seth strokes her full bottom lip, and my cock hardens when Aurelia looks up at him like she's finally getting what she was after all along—not the cuff off as she claimed.

This.

Our attention.

We haven't been ignoring her like she thinks—Khalil with his carving, me with weapons maintenance, and Seth with his book. There isn't a single moment when we stop being aware of her, but keeping our hands busy has been our only way of keeping them off her so she could heal. Right now, Aurelia's the only one without anything to do since she finished cleaning this morning, and we're all still full from breakfast, which was marginally better than her recent attempts.

"We told you, Sunshine. It's for your own good. We're just trying to keep you safe."

The eager look clears, and Aurelia yanks her face away. "You cannot be serious."

"Fuck it," I say, setting down the crossbow since she won't shut the fuck up. It draws her gaze again, and I see her interest in the weapon. She's curious about it, and God help us all if she ever figures out how it works. "You want to know what your real issue is?"

"Thorin, don't," Khalil's pussy-whipped ass warns.

I ignore him. "You keep waiting for us to give you a good excuse why we're doing this. There is none. There never will be. We do it because we want you and because there's no one to stop us from taking what we want. As long as you keep trying to get away, we're going to keep tightening your leash until you give us no choice but to strangle you with it. This is your home now, wolf, and the three of us are where the rest of your life starts and ends. It's up to you how much of it you enjoy, but the tracker stays on until you convince us we don't need it."

Aurelia falls quiet, and I consider it progress.

A week and a half ago, she would have screamed obscenities and insults, but she's finally learning that nothing she says will suddenly turn us into good men. We've been nothing but honest about who we are and what we want from her. She just chooses not to listen.

Just as we chose to live in the wilds because redemption was the last thing we were looking for.

There's no saving us.

There's no saving Aurelia either.

Aurelia doesn't talk back, but not a minute later, she starts fucking with that damn tracker again, and even Seth looks exasperated with her. She yanks and tugs and grumbles her frustration when it doesn't budge. If she could bend that far, I have no doubt she'd chew her own leg free.

"Aurelia," Khalil says without looking up from the wolf he's carving into the left half of the block. "Go make me a sandwich."

Her head pops up, and she stops trying in vain to get the monitor off—to get free of us. Quietly, she stands and leaves the room. I go back to lubricating the crossbow rail, and Seth returns to his book the moment we hear her working on Khalil's sandwich in the kitchen.

"You know she's going to spit in it," I warn Khalil without looking up.

After blowing away some of the loose shavings from his carving, he says, "I know."

Five minutes later, I'm switching the crossbow out for one of the handguns when Aurelia returns with a plate and glass of milk.

"Mmm," he hums. "Look delicious, baby," he lies. "Thank you." Khalil takes the plate and glass and sets them on the coffee table before pulling her onto the recliner with him.

"What are you making?" she asks as I clear the chamber before taking the handgun apart.

Sneaking a peek at them, I see Khalil frowning down at the carving like it perplexes him. I'd guessed what it was the moment he started carving. "I don't know yet."

"Well, if you sell this one, can you please trade it for a decent conditioner? My hair can't take much more of this two-in-one nonsense you barbarians use. I may have to shave my head."

I pause at that.

Khalil's clearly been talking if she knows how we pay for most of our supplies. We sank all of our money into this place years ago and now save every penny of the wages we get from SAR missions in case we have to run again.

When our gazes meet over Aurelia's shoulder, Khalil shrugs, not even bothering to try to deny giving in to his inane need for pillow talk.

"I'll think about it," he says before going back to his carving.

It leaves Aurelia's mind to wander. "So, what do you guys do for fun around here?"

Seth grunts but doesn't look up from his fantasy book when he answers, "This."

Aurelia is back to looking horrified. "What, like every day?"

"Only when the weather is bad," I answer. "But yeah, pretty much."

"But this isn't fun. It's…it's inhumane. You don't even have Wi-Fi. Don't you get bored?"

"Yes, wolf. We get bored. Sometimes downright feral with cabin fever, but that's only been an issue of late. For the first year, we were too busy learning how to hunt and survive to be bored. And then we started building this cabin somewhere between the second and third year. I wish I could say it went flawlessly, but it didn't, and it ate up four more years. Learning every inch of this mountain forward, backward, and sideways took another three."

"Okay, well, that's eight years. You said you've been out here for nine. What did you do with the last year of your life? How did you pass the time?"

Seth is the one who answers, closing his book so that he can meet her gaze. "We thought about you."

Aurelia immediately stiffens. "But you said you didn't know who I was."

"We didn't. But we knew the kind of woman it would take to handle all three of us. We knew it would have to be someone just as monumentally and irrevocably fucked-up—whose darkness rivals our own." Picking up his book again and staring at the pages, Seth says with an ironic lift of his brows, "Got to say, Sunshine, you did *not* disappoint."

"If I'm so dark and screwed up, why do you call me that? I'm like the least pleasant person ever."

Seth sighs wistfully while his gaze moves across the page he isn't reading. "Because I've lived my entire life without seeing the sunrise, and then one day, there it was, sleeping in my brother's bed."

The last thing any of us expect is for Aurelia to crawl out of Khalil's lap and into Seth's.

Khalil is so pissed he drops his carving when she stands from the recliner and walks the short distance to the couch where Seth and I are sitting. I watch from under my lashes as Seth welcomes her with a grin, and then they kiss.

For a really long fucking time.

When they finally come up for air, Aurelia rests her head on his shoulder while Seth beams like she just reached inside her chest and offered him her beating heart. "Read to me."

Seth starts reading.

"So, she's definitely working Seth," Khalil whispers to me an hour later. Once I was done cleaning and sharpening the weapons, Khalil offered to help me carry them back down to the basement. Seth and Aurelia are still upstairs, and we can hear Seth reading animatedly to her.

"Of course she is."

She'd be dumb not to, and our girl is fucking amazing.

Out of the three of us, Seth's the softest with her. He actually *likes* her, while I enjoy using her mouth and pussy and nothing more. Well, maybe her ass too, but that will come later.

"Any thoughts on what we should do about it?"

"Nothing." I shrug as I store the crossbow inside and shut the locker doors before securing the chain around the handle and locking the padlock with the key dangling from twine around my neck. It's a fucking risk keeping our only protection locked up like this and not easily accessible, but Aurelia has given us no choice.

Our wolf is bloodthirsty, just like us.

"Nothing?" Khalil echoes.

"Seth may be a virgin, but he isn't dumb, Khalil. You see the way she lets him touch her. He's working her too."

Khalil hums like he hasn't considered that before. His senseless jealousy over Aurelia pretending to like Seth more has been clouding his head.

"All right then, so we do nothing." Khalil is just starting to relax when the sound of Aurelia's shrieking laughter floats down the stairs, and his hackles raise once more. "But I swear to God, Seth better fuck it up soon, or I might smother them both." In a flowery voice, he mocks with his arm outstretched, "*I didn't see the sunrise until you.* Who the fuck does he think he is? Yeats Junior?"

I smirk as I tuck the locker key back inside my shirt where it stays safely hidden from Aurelia. "Mad that the student has become the master or because you've lost your touch?"

"Can never happen," he returns smugly. "I'm Khalil motherfucking Poverly."

I groan as I start for the stairs. "Please don't tell me she's rubbing off on you already."

Aurelia has finally stopped obnoxiously reminding us of who she is—as if we could forget—and now Khalil's ass is taking a page from her book.

"I don't know what you're talking about," Khalil denies as he wraps his hands and then grabs his boxing gloves from the hook.

The sound of him warming up on one of the speed bags follows me up the stairs.

"And the dragon that everyone thought was a myth soared across the field, roaring its fury at being disturbed from its centuries-long slumber," Seth narrates.

"Oh no," Aurelia says.

"Mm-hmm," Seth hums his agreement. Rolling my eyes, I'm on my way to the kitchen to dig up lunch when I hear Seth ask, "Can you take one more?"

Pausing, I look back in time to see Aurelia give a nervous nod.

Seth smiles and pecks her shoulder.

A moment later, Aurelia tenses, her head tipping back as she moans his name softly. "Seth."

Forgetting my empty stomach, I sneak over to the living room as Seth continues to read aloud.

"Hardened warriors *screamed* in terror and trembled in fear at the sight of the terrifying dragon with black and gold scales. Many ran for their lives, but there was no escaping Mantonoth the Bane. Each who ran met a fiery end. The bravest became a feast for the hungry dragon."

"Oh, God." Aurelia starts writhing in his lap now. There's no way she finds the story that enthralling. "More, Seth."

I round the couch where they're sitting to see Aurelia with her peasant dress bunched around her waist, one leg slung over the couch arm, and three of Seth's fingers lodged deep in her pussy, and from the sounds that fill the space between her moans, she's *sopping*.

Aurelia's eyes flick toward me and quickly dart away upon realizing she and Seth aren't alone anymore, but she doesn't ask him to stop. Taking a seat in Khalil's recliner, where I'll have the best view, I get comfortable.

Seth ignores me as he continues to read and finger Aurelia's pussy. "The tyrant Fae king looked on helplessly as, one by one, his soldiers and army fell to the claws, teeth, and fire of his grandfather's greatest enemy. None were a match for Mantonoth the Bane."

I can see her puffy lower lips parting for him each time Seth tunnels his fingers inside. I can even see her arousal coating his fingers when he pulls out just to push them deep again.

As the tension in the story rises, so does Seth's pace until Aurelia is crying out for him.

His unintentional edging exacts its toll on our thorny little cum dumpster, and Aurelia bites into her bottom lip, the divot between her brows deepening as she squirms in agitation. "Seth…*please*."

I can see Seth's hand pause in uncertainty, and I give myself permission to stop biting my tongue and help him out.

"Her clit, Seth. She needs you to stimulate it so she can come," I remind him. The advice draws Aurelia's grateful gaze to me, and she doesn't look away even when Seth withdraws his fingers and beelines for the engorged nub.

She's still staring at me when Seth finds it, her muscles seizing as she comes with a sharp cry.

I stay where I am until Aurelia is relaxed and Seth is reading again, and then I force myself to stand. I can feel their curious gazes following me as I disappear inside my bedroom right off the living room.

I head straight for my nightstand, where I keep the lube.

Aurelia's already soaked, but a little extra insurance won't hurt for what I have in mind.

When I return to the living room, my gaze zeros in on Seth's hand, which is now idly rubbing the inside of her stretched thigh as he finishes the chapter.

"The once green meadow became an oasis of blood and body parts and death as Mantonoth exacted his revenge on mankind for the death of his beloved. His mate. Ollantia."

Seth closes the book and sets it aside.

"Did everyone die?" Aurelia asks sleepily.

"Of course. Gruesomely."

She sighs in contentment, then leans her head back and closes her eyes. "Good."

"Sorry about that," I say as I reach them. "Aurelia seemed so greedy for your fingers. I thought she might need a hand."

Seth tears his face and nose away from Aurelia's hair, where they were buried, and raises his brows in question. His gaze drops to the lube in my hand and then returns to me several times before understanding finally dawns in his green eyes.

He's always been fascinated with that particular kink. Now's as good a time as any since Aurelia's already come once and doesn't hate him at the moment. She's nice and pliable.

"Go slow," I warn when I toss the bottle next to him.

Seth nods as I take a seat on the coffee table and pray it holds my weight because I have to see this up close. "Sunshine."

Aurelia doesn't respond, and Seth has to nudge her ass awake because she dozed off that fast from coming so hard. Her thighs are still gapped open and I can see her pretty pussy glistening. I have to grip the table with both hands to stay where I am when Aurelia jerks awake. Her brown, sleepy gaze is unguarded for once as she blinks at me.

"Huh?"

The urge to tell her how beautiful she is gets stuck in my throat while Seth nuzzles her neck with a smile. "Wake up, gorgeous. We're not done with you yet. Thorin wants to see if you can take more. You can do that for him, can't you?"

She blinks sleepy eyes at Seth, and slowly, some of her vigilance returns when she notices the lube. "I think so."

Seth continues to rub her thigh with his free hand. "You're so good to us, Sunshine."

Aurelia doesn't respond, so he quickly helps her out of her dress before she can change her mind and then shifts them both so that they're lying on their sides. I grab the bottle of lube before they crush it and make a mess.

Once Seth has them arranged the way he likes, he props his head on his fist and stares down at Aurelia. "You okay, Sunshine?" Her eyes are closed when she nods. "Do you want me to stop?"

Her eyes pop open, and the surprise in them makes me drop my head for some reason.

"You mean you would?"

"Probably."

Aurelia snorts as she shifts onto her back to stare up at him. Her eyes even twinkle when she grins. "Liar."

"I'd seriously consider it?"

"*Liar.*"

I lift my head when Seth and Aurelia's teasing ends, and they fall quiet as she makes up her mind.

True to her unyielding nature, she makes us wait.

My skin prickles with anticipation when the seconds tick by without her answer. Seth doesn't seem all that worried, though, as he traces shapes—fucking *hearts*—on her stomach.

"No, I don't want to stop."

My breath rushes out of me, and I don't even care if they hear it.

"Are you okay with Thorin staying, or would you like him to get lost?"

My gaze shoots to Seth and narrows, but his focus is on Aurelia.

I can still hear Khalil taking his excess energy out on the punching bags downstairs. Maybe I'll join him if Aurelia says no because if I don't get off in some way that doesn't involve my hand, I...will...lose it.

She peeks at me but can't quite meet my gaze when she answers quicker this time. "He can stay." And then she just has to add, "Maybe he'll learn something."

The two of them snicker at my expense while I roll my eyes since we both know she's full of shit. Aurelia had no issues coming on my dick—more than once, so she can't even claim it was a fluke.

"Just get on with it," I say with a sigh.

Seth palms one of Aurelia's breasts as he leans down and kisses her with tongue and teeth and a hunger for her that can never be sated. Aurelia moans in his mouth as she squirms beneath, and my dick jerks in my jeans, watching them both.

"Before we begin," he says. "I need you to do something for me, Sunshine."

"What?"

He leans down and whispers something in her ear. I don't get that he's talking about me until her gaze nervously flicks toward me, and she grabs the hem of Seth's shirt for dear life.

"But he'll be *mean*."

"No, he won't." Seth lifts his gaze and glares meaningfully. "Will you, Thor?"

I have no idea what's happening or what the fuck I'm supposed to do, but I wave the white flag anyway.

At least for tonight.

"See? Thor wants to make you feel good too. Go ahead."

Aurelia casts me another unsure look before she climbs off the couch. I sit up straight when she comes to stand in front of me, and then she shocks the shit out of me when she kneels and reaches for my belt.

I sit there dumbfounded when she undoes the buckle and then the button on my jeans. All I can do is swallow the need to take control when she pulls the zipper down, and then I lift my hips so she can wrestle my jeans and boxers down my legs.

"Aurelia is going to use you," Seth finally explains when she stands and straddles me. My hands automatically find her wide hips to steady her, and that's when he adds, "But you're not going to touch her." *I'm going to kill him.* "I need her slick, Thor, so feel free to come inside her."

Jesus Christ.

I drop my hands, and Aurelia lines up my cock with her pussy and then sinks down the length like she's been doing it forever. She's so slick already, so she takes me in her snug pussy easily enough, and the moment I'm balls deep, I realize what an asshole Seth is.

I have to let her use me without touching her, and I don't know if I can.

"How does it feel, Sunshine?"

"It feels…" Her entire body trembles on top of me before she moans, "*Good.*"

My dick grows inside her as if wanting to make sure she feels me everywhere, and Aurelia whines.

"Perfect," Seth says as he sits up and takes his own dick out of his jeans to stroke it slowly. "I want you to fuck yourself open. Stretch that pussy nice and good for me, Sunshine."

"Why?"

"Because I said so."

"Okay."

They talk to each other as if I'm not here, and I can't bring myself to mind once Aurelia starts riding my cock.

The coffee table rocks under our combined weight, and I say another prayer that it holds because Khalil might kill us both and keep Aurelia for himself if we break another piece of furniture that he made.

Sweat forms on my brow from the effort it takes to keep my hands to myself. Aurelia's hands find my shoulders to hold on to when I lose a little bit of control and start thrusting my hips up to meet hers.

"Oh, God, yes."

"You like that, my wolf?"

"Yes, yes, fuck me, yes."

Aurelia looks like a queen while she uses me. I grit my teeth and look past her shoulder at Seth, who is watching us through a half-lidded gaze as he jerks his veiny cock to our rhythm. "Seth, goddammit. *Please.*"

"No touching," he groans. "She's mine."

I don't bother to remind him that she belongs to all of us since I know what he means. It's his turn with her, so he's in charge tonight.

Lowering onto my back, I tuck my hands behind my head and stare up at the vaulted ceiling while Aurelia rides me. It's the only possible way—short of being tied down—that I can play by their rules. The change in angle causes Aurelia to gasp, and then she loses her mind, snaking her hips back and forth while her nails dig into my abs.

"Ohmygod, ohmygod, ohmygod," she rushes out, making the words sound jumbled. "I'm going to come. Make me come…please?"

I'm still thrusting up, fucking her back, and giving everything I got because Aurelia George has to be the sexiest, most addicting woman I've ever met.

If she wants it, you better be damn sure I'll fucking *give it* to her.

Seth swears and rises from the couch, roughly grabbing her chin from behind just as I feel her pussy squeezing my cock and forcing my orgasm from me. His grunt and arm jackhammering his cock tells me he's coming to, spilling on her back while I come inside her with an equally animalistic sound.

When Seth recovers, he brushes her curls aside. "Did you enjoy that, Sunshine? Didn't I promise Thorin would be nice?"

Aurelia's eyes are half-closed when she gives a sated nod.

Her nipples are hard as fuck and pointed right at me. I start to sit up so I can give them the attention they need when Seth pulls her off my dick and bends her over the couch arm.

I already know what he's going to do before he even kicks his jeans away from his ankles.

"What about—"

"Another time," Seth cuts me off before lining his cock up with Aurelia's pussy. If he's miraculously hard so soon after coming like a fire hose, then I get why he changed his plans.

"Seth—" It's all the protest Aurelia can get out before he's easing into her and stealing her breath. "Seth, wait," she insists once she's caught it. Aurelia starts to struggle when he ignores her, fucking in and out of her pussy slowly.

"Jesus, look at you," he praises as he wraps a hand around her nape to hold her down. "You're so fucking beautiful, baby. You know that, don't you? You're so special to us. I'm glad you're my first. My only."

"Seth, really… I need a minute," she whines. "*Seeeeth.*"

I'm still feeling boneless from my orgasm, so I'm slow to rise from the coffee table. I'm pulling up my jeans when Khalil stomps up the stairs with a scowl.

He takes one look at Seth pummeling Aurelia's sweet pussy and walks over to whisper something in his ear. Whatever he says has Seth pausing to put one foot on the couch cushion. "Like this?"

Khalil claps him on the back. "Perfect."

Seth thrusts forward again, and Aurelia squeals while rising onto the tips of her toes to run from the deeper penetration. I'd bet anything that being ignored and used has her fucking drowning his cock right now—maybe even more than mine when she was in control.

Khalil catches me buckling up my belt and raises his brow. "You too?" When I shrug, he says, "Thanks for the party invite, jackasses."

"It was a spur-of-the-moment thing."

Though not entirely.

We've been leading Aurelia here ever since we got her back to the cabin. Khalil will have his turn next, and *then* we'll be square for the risk Aurelia put us all in when she ran.

The tracking monitor was only part of it.

After that, it was just a matter of waiting until she was fully healed because we might break what's ours, but we'll always piece her back together with the utmost care.

"At least he's finally getting his dick wet," Khalil mumbles as we fall into a trance, watching them.

"Yeah…"

Having already come, Seth lasts a lot longer than any virgin should.

Aurelia is now biting into the couch arm to muffle her screams while he fucks her so hard the couch scrapes across the hardwood floor.

They're damn near in the dining room when he finally comes with a hoarse shout. He pulls out of her and doesn't make it farther than two steps before he collapses on the couch next to her with his spent cock resting on his thigh.

Knowing it isn't over yet, Aurelia remains where she is, with cum seeping out of her as she dutifully waits for Khalil to take his pound of flesh.

He doesn't keep her waiting long.

Khalil walks over to the couch and gently wraps a hand around her nape. He pulls her up until she's standing with her back to his chest.

Aurelia's long lashes flutter as she fights to keep her eyes open while leaning into the warmth and comfort that he lends her. "Sleepy."

"I know, baby. Seth rode you good," Khalil states with a purr. "But it's my turn now. Are you going to deny me?"

Aurelia shakes her head and Khalil lifts her by the waist. He carries her into the dining room like a limp rag doll and deposits her on the edge of the table. Following, I lean against the island in the kitchen to watch. "You don't have to be awake for this, you know. Would you like that?" Aurelia doesn't speak as she leans forward to wrap her arms around his neck and rest her head on his shoulder. But she nods. Khalil swears like she just made all of his dreams come true, but he still holds himself off from acting on it. "I need to hear the words, Sleeping Beauty. Tell me you understand what I'm about to do to you."

"I'm going to fall asleep and you're going to fuck me," she slurs. Releasing him, she uses the last of her strength to lower her upper body onto the table all the while holding his gaze. "So fuck me, Khalil."

His body was strung tight like a drawn arrow before but with only four words she unleashed him. Finding her in his bed that first night awakened something in Khalil that was previously dormant. He roughly shoves her legs wide with one hand while dropping his shorts with the other. Khalil watches her intently while he strokes his cock, waiting for the moment when she loses the battle with consciousness. It happens with a final flutter of her lashes and the shift in her breathing as her body becomes completely lax on the table.

Khalil immediately enters her, his gaze almost reverent as he pushes inside. Aurelia's brows furrow from the intrusion but she doesn't wake. She gives him what he needs, wantonly feeding the frenzy and the fantasy.

Feeling like I'm intruding, I retreat to my room to wash my hands and dick.

Khalil's still fucking her when I return. Aurelia's still pretending she isn't aware of it all.

Seth has disappeared as well, and I can hear the downstairs shower running.

I walk past Khalil to get started on dinner since Aurelia will be in no shape to do it herself once he's through with her.

Khalil takes his sweet time, too, enjoying the way she looks with her eyes closed, her head tipped back, and her graceful neck exposed while her legs rest in the crooks of his elbows.

When Khalil grows closer to his nut, he picks up the pace, his thrusts becoming deeper and rougher—almost as if seeing how far she'll let him go before she gives up the pretense of being asleep.

The dining table rocks noisily from his thrusts, and still Aurelia acts blissfully unaware of it all.

Will she wish that it had been real in the morning?

"Aww, fuck fuck *fuck*," he barks when he finally comes with three hard shoves. Aurelia plays her role perfectly, making a small distressed sound like she might be coming to. Khalil reacts like he might go another round before thinking better of it. Swearing, he pulls out of her and yanks up his basketball shorts. "Damn," he suddenly mumbles as he stares between her legs. When his head turns toward the kitchen, our gazes meet. "Thor, you got to see this."

"What?" Abandoning the carrots Aurelia took from the root cellar this morning, I walk over to the table, something like worry twisting in my chest.

Did we go too far? Did we hurt her?

When I reach the table, Khalil makes room for me so I can see between her legs.

And just like that, I'm hard again when I see our collective cum seeping out of her pussy—Seth's, Khalil's, and mine.

I can even tell the difference.

Reaching out, I scoop our cum with two fingers and push our seed back inside her.

"I swear, this girl is going to destroy me. Her pussy is too fucking good. *She's* too fucking good. Fuck," Khalil grumbles as he watches me shove more of our cum between her lips. Aurelia, who was sneakily trying to squirm away from my fingers goes still at his words, and I grunt my agreement as I force the last of our seed inside her pussy.

Aurelia's hell-bent on being free of us, but she hasn't even caught on that all she has to do is fuck us to death. She really has brought out the worst in us. Her darkness feeds our own, and each day, it grows large enough to swallow us all whole.

Until then... We'll use her, make her ours, and keep her safe.

"Seth's still in the shower. Is it cool if I use your bathroom to get her cleaned up?"

"Fine by me."

Khalil lifts Aurelia like the precious cargo she is and carries her into my room while I return to the kitchen to finish butchering our goddamn dinner.

CHAPTER TWENTY-SEVEN

AURELIA

I feel like a new woman when I wake up in the middle of the night.

The feeling fades when I open my eyes and realize where I am—when I feel the heavy weight of a strong arm keeping me in place and my pussy twinges at the same time with a reminder of what happened after Seth finished reading to me.

I'm in Khalil's bed again, and he's lying on his back next to me with his eyes closed. One muscled arm is bent under his head while his other hand rests on his abs. His braids are secured under a do-rag, the black satin material dark against the stark white pillow. He doesn't have a shirt on, and I take a wild guess that he's naked below the waist too.

Finding Khalil sleeping in his own bed isn't what surprises me.

Waking up in Khalil's bed doesn't shock me one bit either.

The puff of air I feel blowing through my curls makes it even more obvious than the arm around me that Khalil and I aren't alone in his bed. I dare to peer over my shoulder, and Seth's face comes into view. It's his arm holding me close. His dark lashes sweep his cheeks as he sleeps soundly, but remembering what happened the last time he didn't, I gently push his hand off me.

Seth moans, and I flinch.

When he doesn't wake up and strangle me again, I breathe a sigh of relief and quietly pull the covers aside. Since I'm in the middle, the sheets are pulled off Khalil's waist where they're draped, revealing that he's wearing boxer shorts at least.

I wait a few seconds to see if the movement wakes him before sitting up.

Crawling to the foot of the bed without so much as jostling the mattress is tough, but I manage. I even get both feet on the cold floor and straighten.

But I don't get more than a step toward the door before a deep, rumbling voice says, "I didn't give you permission to leave my bed, Aurelia."

Not sleeping deeply enough, apparently.

Spinning around, I have a lie spilling off my tongue by the time I face him. "I have to ask your leave to use the bathroom now?"

Khalil peeks one eye open and uses it to look me up and down. "Sure," he says to be a dick.

Adopting my sweet tone—my America's-sweetheart voice—I ask, "Can I go pee, sir? Is that okay?"

My glower doesn't faze him as he stretches his long body before rolling onto his stomach. "You may." Teeth clenching, I start to leave the room when he adds, "And then come right back to bed."

Damn it!

His voice was muffled by the pillow, but I know pretending I didn't hear him won't work. No way out of it now, I leave to go pee, knowing he'll be listening for evidence that I am. After I'm done, I stare in the mirror and look for signs that they've ruined me beyond repair.

Other than the sweet ache between my legs, I feel no worse for wear, so I shut off the light and leave the bathroom. I guess I took too long because Khalil is sitting up and resting against the headboard when I walk back inside the bedroom. Seth is still asleep, and I absently rub my neck as I pray to God he stays that way.

"Thanks for the shirt," I say as I walk toward the bed and round the foot of it to stand on Khalil's side.

"No problem..." His voice trails off and Khalil looks at me strangely when I continue to stand by the bed rather than climb over him. "What the fuck are you doing, Aurelia?"

"Scoot over."

"Why?"

"Because I don't want to sleep next to him."

"*Why?*" When I don't respond, understanding dawns, and Khalil sighs before pointing at all the tiny light woven through the beautifully twisted canopy. "It's safe, Goldilocks. He's not going to hurt you."

"Look…" I huff. "Seth told me why he has nightmares, so I'm not holding what happened against him. I'm truly not." Resting a hand over my heart, I stare into Khalil's brown eyes and hope he can see the truth in mine. "But it makes no difference if Seth kills me accidentally or on purpose. I'll still be dead."

"He told you about Isaac?" Khalil sounds surprised.

"Not much, but enough."

Khalil doesn't respond. He just lifts me off my feet by my waist and dumps me on the bed next to him—between him and Seth. "Oh my God," I groan. "You guys are the biggest assholes! Does how I feel really not matter to any of you?"

I don't wait for an answer and start to crawl to the end of the bed. I'll take sleeping on the floor rather than with any of them at this point. God, they're such jerks!

I don't get far before Khalil wrestles me onto my back and between them again.

"Get off me!"

"How about you stop being such a worrisome pain in the ass and *look*."

I hear something metal rattle against wood. When I turn my head, I see Khalil holding the slack in a short, thick chain attached to the headboard with cuffs at the end and Seth's left hand dangling from it.

I gasp in horror. "You tied him up?"

Khalil narrows his gaze. "I'm starting to think you have what he has," he remarks, referring to Seth's DID.

"Screw you, okay? I don't like this. Untie him. I can go sleep on the couch. It's not a big deal."

"It is to me. I want you in my bed where you belong, Goldilocks. And do you think you're the first one of us Seth almost killed in his sleep? Why do you think the cuffs were already there?" I didn't notice them before, honestly. I was always so quick to leave Khalil's bed whenever I found myself in it. "And anyway, tying Seth up tonight was his idea. He wanted to hold you and be there when you woke up to make sure you were okay after taking all three of us. I offered to let you both sleep here and keep an eye on the situation, but Thorin wouldn't have it after what happened last time, so Seth let us cuff him."

I bite my tongue when I feel myself about to ask why Thorin isn't here too. The bed is large enough to fit all four of us but barely. We'd have to get real close and personal to make it work, and I don't think we're there yet. I'm flipping out over waking up and finding myself sandwiched between two of them. All three of my mountain men would have sent me into a spiral.

"Are you implying that there were times you cuffed Seth *without* his consent?"

Seeing an argument on the horizon, Khalil groans and rolls off me. He starts rubbing his eyes, pretending he's suddenly too exhausted to talk. Sitting up, I shock us both when I straddle his waist until his strong body is locked between my thighs. Khalil's hands automatically find my ass and start massaging. My body craves his touch, even if my heart and mind rebel against it.

Well, not so much my heart these days and only the untampered part of my brain that remembers I'm not here by choice.

Luckily, Khalil provides the perfect distraction.

"You don't understand what he was like before you, Goldilocks. Seth didn't only try to murder Thorin and me when he had a nightmare. He would do it just because he didn't like the shape of the clouds in the sky that day. He'd say they were suspicious."

"You're exaggerating."

"Actually, I'm sugarcoating it." Khalil turns his head and pushes aside the ends of his braids peeking from the bottom of the durag. I can see a long scar on his throat, starting from under his ear that I'd never noticed before.

"Seth did that?"

"He tried to cut my throat once because I said I missed boxing."

"Well, that makes sense," I mumble without thinking. I don't realize how odd it sounds until Khalil looks at me funny. "Seth told me he blamed you and Thorin for not being there for Zeke when Isaac tricked him. Saying you missed boxing must have triggered those impulses. He might have even thought you were planning to leave Zeke again."

"Yeah." Khalil stares off, and I can tell he's blaming himself too. "I figured that might be the reason he hates us."

"Khalil…" I grab his chin between my fingers and force his gaze to return to mine. "You do know it's not your fault, right?"

He hums noncommittally and then glances at Seth before shrugging. "It doesn't matter what I know or what's true. What matters is that Seth blames us, and there's nothing I can do to change what happened to Zeke—to both of them."

"You're right. There's nothing you can do about that, but there's plenty you can do to reassure him that you won't leave again."

Khalil smiles a little sarcastically, flashing straight, white teeth. "You mean like moving to the middle of nowhere and staying put for almost a decade?"

"Close. You're here because you think you *have* to be, not because you *want* to be. Don't you think Zeth knows that?"

"Who?"

"*Zeth*. Zeke and Seth," I explain when he continues to stare at me cluelessly.

Khalil's expression turns wary. "They're not the same person, Aurelia. You know that, right?"

"Of course. I'm shipping them."

He pauses. "You're what?"

"Damn, I forgot you've been up here forever. And let me tell you, you've missed a lot. But also…not a damn thing," I ramble nervously when Khalil just continues to stare up at me like I've grown two heads. This might not be the right household to joke about that. "Shipping is when you pair two people—usually romantically, but not always—together."

"And people do this because?"

"It's fun and cute, and we're lazy."

"All right." Khalil stares at me for a moment longer, and then he turns his head to stare at Seth like he's seeing his frenemy through new eyes. Khalil's eyes are calculating when his attention eventually returns to me. "So, you're saying Thorin and I should stop acting like a captive, and Seth will stop treating us like one?"

I'm already nodding, and it's not until Khalil grins that I realize I was set up. He looks triumphant and adorable as he playfully slaps my ass hard enough to make it wobble.

And now *I* want to murder him.

"Good *night*," I say tightly.

Sliding off Khalil's body, I return to my spot between them while Khalil turns on his side, giving me his back. After a few minutes, I'm still staring at the canopy, admiring the woven lights that make Zeth feel safe. The fact that Khalil cared enough to do this for his friend and brother has me regarding him differently, and I don't want to do that, so I finally give voice to the reason sleep evades me.

"What happened last night?" I ask, knowing Khalil is still awake. Even though he's clearly a light sleeper, he won't let himself fall back asleep until he's sure I am. "I don't remember anything after Seth…finished. Did I pass out? Did you…?" *Fuck me.*

Wanting to continue the fantasy outside of the act makes me feel all kinds of screwed up, but the familiar heat blooming in my belly begs me to keep going.

Khalil lifts his head to peer over his shoulder at me. At first, he looks confused since I had clearly been awake when he fucked me—barely, but aware nonetheless. And then he catches on "Do you really want to know?" he asks, playing along.

My gaze drops like I'm wounded. I stare at the blanket covering me, and I nod. "Yes."

"I fucked you."

"Oh."

"Do you have a problem with that?" he asks curiously.

A dry laugh that I don't have to fake punches out of me. "Would it make a difference if I did?"

"No."

"Then I'm not upset."

At some point, I realized the only choice my mountain men had left me was anger. I could choose to hate them for baring these darker parts of my soul or accept that I didn't hate it as much as I'd like to.

Currently, I'm teetering somewhere in the middle.

"Did you like it?" I don't know why I ask. I shouldn't care. He's a monster, and I'm one for trying so hard to understand him.

Khalil takes a while to answer. "It was cool."

And suddenly I'm wishing I hadn't played my role so fucking well. I couldn't see his expression with my eyes closed. Hell, I was barely conscious, but I remember how his fingers dug into my skin every time he sank himself deep inside me. I also remember him losing control.

Khalil was definitely downplaying it.

Maybe he feels weird about what we did too? He's kinkier than I thought, that's for sure.

My stomach growls, and it's hard to miss in the quiet room. I remember that I tapped out while they were fucking me and skipped dinner. Khalil sighs heavily, then leaves the bed and room without a word. He returns three minutes later with dinner and a glass of water.

"Who cooked?" I ask in surprise as I accept the plate of trout, wild rice, and carrots.

Khalil places my water on the nightstand. "Thor."

Taking a tentative bite of the trout I'd thawed and seasoned earlier, I'm pleasantly surprised by the burst of flavor.

Holy shit, I'm getting better.

"This isn't bad," I say when I notice how tender the trout is. It's pretty fucking easy to overcook fish, as I've learned the hard way. "Why doesn't Thorin do the cooking since he's clearly better at it than me?"

"Because it's unfair to ask him to hunt the food and cook it too. We do take turns, though."

"So you and Seth don't hunt with him?" I ask.

"We do occasionally, but we rarely catch anything. We mostly go to keep Thorin company."

"Hmm…"

Khalil notices the wheels turning in my head and says, "What?"

"Nothing." I scarf down the food until the plate is empty, but when I go to leave the bed and take it back upstairs, Khalil takes it from me and leaves the room.

This is new—being pampered and cared for by them.

I'm curled up next to Seth, timidly running my fingers through his dark hair by the time Khalil returns. I see him pause in the doorway, but he doesn't remark on my change of heart to snuggle with Seth as he goes to his side of the bed and climbs back in.

As soon as he does, Seth's breathing changes, and he awakens with a groan. I force myself to stay where I am, to not leave his arms when he might need me, and to not be afraid. I'm just starting to relax when he mumbles with his eyes closed, "Sunshine?"

My fingers reach out of their own accord to caress his stubbled jaw. "I'm here, Seth."

The chain rattles when he drops his cuffed hand. There's just enough slack for him to circle my waist with both arms and pull me closer.

I let him.

"You shouldn't have done that," I scold when I remember how it felt to have him inside me, taking and owning what's his. "Your first time should have been special. *I* would have made it special if you'd given me time." It takes me a moment to realize I'm pouting.

Seth tucks an errant curl behind my ear without even opening his eyes. It's the same one that's always falling down the center of my forehead and brushing my top lip. "It was special, Sunshine. It was with you." I'm quiet for a long time, so he peeks an eye open. "Was yours?"

I snort. "No."

Behind me, I hear Khalil grumble sleepily, "What's his name?"

"And would you like us to kill him slowly or quickly, Sunshine?"

I roll my eyes because, *really*? Hypocrites much? My first time wasn't good or memorable, but it was a hundred percent consensual, which is more than these two can say. "None of your business, creeps."

Eyes closed once more, Seth brushes his cold lips over my forehead. His chest gives such a deep rumble in contentment that my toes curl in the sheets as he says, "We're your creeps."

"What's this?" I ask as I hold the bottle of conditioner—*my* conditioner—that Thorin gave me after I made them breakfast and then waited on them while they ate, refilling the plates and mugs in my milkmaid costume like some kind of medieval tavern wench.

Some dark part of me I'm not yet ready to give credence to even liked it. It's been fucking me up ever since, so I was grateful when Thorin pulled me aside and unknowingly took my mind off it.

How the hell had they found my expensive conditioner in all of *that*? Thorin and I are standing by the floor-to-ceiling A-frame window that overlooks the upper deck and Cold Peaks. I still haven't found it in me to enjoy the view, though I pretend I can't get enough of it whenever I stand or sit here for minutes, sometimes hours at a time, looking for a search plane to flag down.

"It's your reward for last night."

I gape at it and then at him. "No, this isn't enough."

"Excuse me?"

I toss the conditioner, and it hits his chest before falling to the floor at our feet. "Need I remind you that I let all three of you fuck me last night? Rewarding me with the conditioner that I already own is not enough. I want more," I say, like the spoiled princess they already think I am.

But fuck 'em. I bet none of them have ever taken it up the ass thrice in one night.

"Like what, Aurelia?"

I don't even pretend to think about it as I cross my arms and pop my hip. "I want the loft."

Thorin looks stumped for a moment, and then he just looks annoyed.

God, he's such an asshole.

Out of three of them, he's the only one I'm having a hard time waving the white flag for. He's the only one who hasn't tried to make me feel like he actually wants me here.

In my peripheral vision, I can see Khalil's and Seth's eyes darting back and forth as they silently watch Thorin and me go at it from the living room…again.

We've been fighting nonstop ever since we made it back to the cabin almost a week ago. Thorin's pissed because I ran, and I'm pissed because I know if it were solely up to him, he would have let me die. And I still let him use me.

"For what?"

"To sleep? For a space to call my own? You all claim this is my home now, and I should get used to it, but there's nothing here that's mine."

Shrugging, he says, "So, take the couch. We have two."

"I want somewhere *private* to sleep and relax."

"No. You want someplace you think we can't get to you."

My shoulders drop as I say a little despondently, "I didn't fight any of you last night."

"You fought a little."

"Because I know you like it!"

Gripping my neck, Thorin drags me close, but he doesn't squeeze. He just wants to remind me that he *could*. He just wants an excuse to touch me, and dammit, I'm panting for it.

"You liked it too, Aurelia. Don't make the mistake of thinking you're different from us," he says in the low voice that I've come to know means sex is on his mind—hot, filthy, raw, animalistic *sex*.

My cheeks warm as I stomp down the urge to submit. My pussy will not be calling the shots this time, thank you.

With Seth, it feels like we're two horny teenagers who've just discovered our bodies. With Khalil, I'm the outmatched novice being turned inside out and wrung dry by someone with far more experience. But with Thorin... God, it feels like we're guided by carnal instinct alone. There's no other reason why we feel the need to pick a fight whenever one of us wants the other. It's foreplay that's just for us.

"Those are my terms, *Thorin*."

He shoves me away from him when he lets me go. "I'll think about it."

"Well, I'll *think* about letting you touch me the next time your dick is hard."

"As you love to remind us, wolf, what makes you think I'll care if you want it?"

That strange cord low in my belly that only they seem to reach tugs. "Go to hell."

"I'll fucking *run* there if it means I don't have to listen to your ungrateful ass."

"Ungrateful?" I shriek. "Ooh! What do I have to be grateful for? Huh? Tell me, Thorin. Please explain to me why coming inside me equates to a half-empty bottle of conditioner. Am I really worth so little to you?"

His blue eyes widen in shock as if I'd slapped him, but the reaction is gone as fast as it appeared. He shoves a hand through his blond hair, his jaw twitching as he looks away briefly before meeting my gaze again. "Fine. You want the loft? Take it," he says through clenched teeth. "But make no mistake. When we tell you to sleep in our beds, your ass better fucking run to it."

"Fine!"

"*Fine.*" Tugging me forward by my corset, Thorin kisses me hard enough to bruise my lips before pulling back and glaring down at me. "And just so we're clear, *never* imply that you mean nothing to me again. It's a fucking lie, and I won't tolerate it, wolf."

"If you want me to believe it, Thorin, it's not enough to say it. You have to *show* me. I want to feel it."

Thorin stares at me, his gaze no longer angry. I'm unsure when he let me go and left me standing there alone.

CHAPTER TWENTY-EIGHT

SETH | ZEKE

Spring is only a couple of weeks away, and despite Mother Nature's attempt to bury us one last time in snow and ice, her most willful flowers are already in bloom. Newly hatched butterflies, free from their chrysalis, flit around the snow, looking for flowers to pollinate.

"Seth... What the hell are you doing?" Khalil gripes when I stop for the third time.

Crouching by a bed of perennials, I study the yellow flowers peeking out of the snow. "What does it look like?" I toss back. "Picking flowers."

"For *what*?"

I smile as I gently finger one of the dew-dropped petals. "For Sunshine."

After selecting the best ones, I add them to the bunch I've already collected and stand. "You think Aurelia likes flowers?"

Khalil glances down at the colorful bunch clutched in my fist and then the flowers I just picked. "I think they're poisonous, Seth."

"Dude, you don't have to sell me on them. I already know they're perfect for our girl."

Khalil sighs and rubs at his brow. "Seth, we need to talk."

Raising the flowers, I sniff them and bask in the different smells. "About what?"

"Your attachment to Aurelia for starters?"

I sniff the flowers again and wonder how I'm going to get them back to her without ruining them. I've never given flowers to a girl before, and neither has Zeke. I've searched his memories backward and forward, but the most romantic gesture he's ever bothered to make to a girl is to remember her name. That part doesn't bother me so much because I know Sunshine is territorial, but this is our first time giving her flowers. They have to be perfect.

"What about it?"

"You need to slow down. We still don't know if she can be trusted, and Zeke is still an issue. You're going to split eventually, and he's still very fragile."

"Stop saying that," I snap unintentionally. "Zeke's stronger than you know."

"Sure, but what's going to happen when he's ready to wake up? Have you thought about that? Have you figured out what you're going to do if you have to choose between them?"

"What do you mean?"

"When Zeke wakes up, and he can't handle the fact that she's around, you know what we'll have to do, Seth."

"Thanatos?" Khalil nods solemnly instead of rolling his eyes like he usually does whenever I mention the god of death, and I feel the blood drain from my face. "No."

"Yes."

"No, fuck that. Zeke won't take her from me. He owes me that much. *I* took his pain! I did!"

"I know that," Khalil snaps, his face tightening a moment later with guilt and pity.

Khalil reaches out to try to put a comforting hand on my shoulder, but I move away. "How can you even say this after all that's happened? Aurelia's ours. She's one of us."

"She doesn't want to be."

I shake my head only to realize he's right. She doesn't. "We can change that."

"How, Seth?" He looks down at the flowers in my hand with scorn and then raises his brows. "It's a little late for hearts and flowers, don't you think?"

"No." Shrugging off my pack, I pull out the fantasy book I read to Sunshine last night and find the last page I read before slipping the stems inside so that the heads stick out the top like a bookmark. It's not foolproof. The petals might still be crushed, but it's the best I can do.

As I'm closing the book, the winter aconite catches my eye.

The even number of golden petals reminds me of Sunshine's hair, so I remove it from the bunch before closing the book and stuffing it back inside my pack.

Khalil and I start walking again while I stare at the flower in my hand.

Before I can stop myself, I'm plucking the first petal.

She loves me.

It floats away in the wind, but I don't watch it go.

She loves me not.

The second poisonous petal follows the first.

She loves me.

One by one, the petals fall until I reach the last.

She loves me not.

Frowning down at the empty pistil, I don't realize I've fallen behind until Khalil glances behind him and calls my name with a sigh. Throwing the flower stem down, I crush it under my heel as I catch up.

Aurelia may not love me yet, but that can change.

It has to.

Because I'm already in love with her.

"Seth," Khalil calls when he notices my despondency.

I swear, even the sky darkens, the gray clouds blocking some of the sun.

Sunshine, don't go…

"We always knew this was temporary," Khalil says, but I'm only half listening. "I know it doesn't seem like it, but there will be other girls. I can promise you that. We won't be on this mountain forever."

"I don't want anyone else, and neither do you." I turn my head to study his profile. Khalil's jaw is clenched as he stares straight ahead, refusing to meet my gaze. I'm right, and he knows it. He doesn't want to give her up either—not even for Zeke. "Maybe instead of telling me I need to move on, you and Thor should start owning how you feel."

Khalil's shocked gaze flies to me, and his mouth falls open like he wants to deny that he's not completely gone for Sunshine, but I beat him to it before he can utter one syllable of bullshit.

"The snow is going to melt soon," I remind him. "She could still leave. You won't be able to use the *weather* as an excuse forever."

"There are plenty of other things in these wilds that can kill her."

I shake my head. "She's passed every test. The mountain won't kill her." It's going to sound unbelievable coming from me, but over the years, we've gotten the sense that our mountain was sentient. It throws everything at you to either forge something it can wield or let nature take its course. It looks into the soul of anyone who trespasses and decides the trials you'll face. If any. No one's ever been tested more than Aurelia George. When Khalil doesn't respond, I add, "We still have time to make her want to stay, Khalil."

"Doubtful."

"God, you're a fucking pussy. I should have smothered you in your sleep when I had the chance."

Khalil stops dead in his tracks, so I wind up a few steps ahead of him. "When would you have had the chance?" he sputters incredulously.

"Oh, plenty of times." Spinning around, I close the gap between us despite the warning in his body language to keep my distance. Khalil's not the only apex predator, so I forge ahead. "And let me be clear. If I find even a single hair on Sunshine's head out of place, I'll show you just how unserious I was all those times I tried to kill you. I'll flip that fancy kill switch that Zeke doesn't think I know about and wake Bane."

"Cura, what the hell are you—"

"Chrysa—"

"Stop," he barks and then shoves me immediately. "What the fuck is your problem? How do you know about that?"

Raking Zeke's fingers through his hair when it falls free of the careful coif I prefer to his messy bed hair, I say coolly, "Don't worry about it. You just remember that I do, and never mention killing Sunshine again. How can you when you've seen how perfect she is for us?"

"Because she's a fucking loose end who's going to outlive her usefulness, and you're the dumb fuck who can't see that she's using you."

"She's just trying to survive. Any one of us would do the same."

"Don't be such a fucking simp, Seth. Aurelia's no damsel in distress. She's the evil queen you save the damsel from."

I step into his face and the deadly tension between us skyrockets. "She's also the only reason I tolerate you breathing her air. If Zeke wakes up, he won't be able to take care of her on his own. We might be using her, and she might be using me, but *I'm* using *you*."

Instead of looking worried that I've threatened his life twice in a matter of minutes, he smirks. "I guess you better back up off me then."

I hold his stare for a few seconds longer before I back out of his reach. Only then do I give him my back before continuing our trek to the rescue camp.

Not a minute after Thorin and Aurelia's weird yet sexually charged fight this morning, we got the call from Sheriff Kelly that it was safe to resume the search. It was either a genius move or a terrible one, leaving them alone together. I guess we'll see soon enough since I am more than a little eager to get out of the cold and home to my girl.

I quicken my steps, ready to get this pointless day of searching over with so I can see her again. After my argument with Khalil, I trust Thorin alone with Sunshine even less than before.

What if Thorin and Khalil already decided they were done with her? What if Thorin staying behind was a ploy to get me out of the way while he disposes of her?

What if he's hurting her right now?

My gut roils while my hands become fists. I'm ready to turn back and run all the way to Big Bear, the mountain peak where our cabin is, when rational thought sneaks up on my murderous rage.

No...

I saw the way he looked at her this morning. Thorin's not done with her yet. If anything, his obsession's grown. Aurelia's gotten under his skin and is clawing her way into his heart. I know it. Maybe Khalil knows it too, and that's why he's trying to reinforce this rift by convincing himself that all she is to us is a loose end.

Aurelia's safe at the moment, but for how much longer?

Khalil has a fucking point. Even if we convinced Sunshine to stay, when Zeke wakes up, it all comes crashing down on us. I won't be around to protect Aurelia, while Khalil and Thorin will be forced to choose between their best friend and the woman who hates us. Letting her go isn't an option either because she'll almost certainly be back to ruin us in return.

"You're supposed to be on our side," I hear Khalil call after me.

"News flash, I was *never* on your side. Zeke might think you care for him, but I don't. Friends don't leave."

Khalil sighs. "Seth…stop."

"Why?"

"Stop!"

Scowling, I slowly turn around to see what the fuck is so urgent and find Khalil no longer looking like he wants to murder me. He looks like he wants to hug me.

I can't decide which possibility makes me hate him more.

"What the fuck is it?"

"I'm sorry, okay? I'm sorry I wasn't there when you needed me. I'm sorry I didn't try harder to convince you to come on the road with me when I asked, and I'm so fucking sorry I let that much time pass without us speaking. If I hadn't…" He lets his sentence hang as he drops his head. His broad shoulders tremble, and I have the feeling he's holding on by a frayed thread. "If I hadn't, I would have known something was wrong. I could have gotten you out sooner. I'm sorry I took so long to remember my brother. I'm sorry I wasn't a better one to you."

Swallowing past the emotions knotted in my throat takes some effort. "Why are you telling me this? I'm not Zeke."

It's the only thing I can think to say because I can't let him off the hook that easily. All I know is my resentment. Burning hate is the only way I know how to connect with them at this point. That…and Aurelia. And Khalil just told me he'd take her from me, too, one day.

Fuck him.

"I know that," he says quickly. "I just…" Khalil's chest expands when he breathes in and out deeply. "I don't just think of you as being a part of Zeke. You are real, and I care about *you*, Seth. That makes you my brother, too, even if you don't feel the same."

He reaches for me, but I take a step back as my gaze narrows. "How do I know you're not just saying this so that I'll let you hurt Sunshine?"

"Because you were right, okay? I don't want to be rid of her."

"I knew it!" Forgetting the heavy topic of my imprisonment and daily torture, I grin triumphantly when the discussion returns to Sunshine. "You feel her too, don't you? She doesn't just have us by the cock and balls, Khalil." I tap the side of my head with my finger. "She's in here too, pressing against your skull."

Khalil gives me a dead look. "I think they call that a tumor, Seth."

"Oh, yes, I know." I continue to grin until it feels like my face will break. "Love. It's gloriously gory, isn't it?"

And Aurelia, our gorgeous little tumor, is quickly spreading and working her deadly magic on us all. I love her so fucking much.

Two down, one to go.

Thorin's a stubborn bastard, but Aurelia doesn't give up easily—not that she'll admit what she's doing to us. Aurelia's a ruthless queen who wants to burn the world. All she needs is us. Her loyal fire-breathing dragons who will protect and avenge her.

Someone should tell her.

No, that might scare her off.

Better to lie low and let her conquer us one by one.

It takes another hour for Khalil and me to reach the exfil point where we're choppered to the camp. Once our boots are on the ground, we track down Sheriff Kelly, who's speaking to one of the rangers. Spotting us, he ends his conversation and walks over.

"Appreciate you boys making it down so quickly. I know it was last minute." The sheriff's gaze bounces between Khalil and me before searching behind us and realizing it's just the two of us. "It looks like you're missing one," he observes slowly. "Where's Thorin?"

"Sorry, Sheriff. We got caught up in that squall last week, and Thor caught a nasty case of pneumonia," I say, delivering the excuse we rehearsed. "He stayed at home to finish recovering."

After Aurelia's failed escape attempt, we'd be morons to leave her alone again, so Thorin volunteered to stay behind and keep an eye on her. She's been on her best behavior ever since we saved her, and I'd like to think she's finally settling in, but I know it's more likely that she's feeling discouraged after almost dying.

Her feelings of defeat won't last, so Thor, Khalil, and I have been on guard all week, keeping her mind inside our cabin so that she stops thinking of the life she lost.

"Oh, hell," the sheriff says grimly. "I'm sorry to hear that. I'd normally turn you around to go look after him, but we've already lost too many vital days, so we need all hands on deck. What do you say I send my wife to check on him? Her homemade soup could heal anything. One sip will have him right as rain in no time."

"We appreciate that, Sheriff, but it's looking up. His fever is down, so he should be back on his feet in a couple of days."

"Good, good. That's great to hear." Despite his words, his expression becomes pinched. "Although, it makes what I'm about to ask difficult."

Khalil keeps a straight face. "Yeah? And what's that?"

"We need you two to stay at the camp for the next couple of days."

"Why?"

"Because this is it, boys." The sheriff removes his hat with a grave look on his weathered face. "We're searching every square inch of these mountains round-the-clock, and if we don't find Aurelia George in the next forty-eight hours, we're calling off the search. Permanently."

I nod my agreement. "You did everything you could, sir. This isn't your fault."

"Yeah, you might be right about that, son, but it won't keep me out of the bottle tonight." He starts to trudge off when he pauses and peers at us. The scrutiny would make lesser men squirm. "You know… She's the only one we haven't found. All the others, every single soul who was on that plane—dead or alive—has been found except her. We even gave what pieces were left of that poor girl we found near a wolf den back to her family. But Aurelia George? Nothing. Gone. Vanished into thin air. It makes you wonder, doesn't it?"

Khalil and I make eye contact, though we're careful to keep it brief. "About what?"

Sheriff Kelly's expression is stricken as he glances past us toward the imposing snowcapped peak that rises above the one we're standing on. "If the stories we've all heard about these wilds are true." When his kind but somber gaze returns to us, he says, "By the way, I know you said it's unlikely Aurelia made it that far, but the Westbrook kid finally woke up two days ago, and he's claiming she was with him when the avalanche hit." *Fuck, fuck, fuck.* "I wanted to give you a heads-up. We'll be focusing our search primarily on your mountain. Because it's a high-profile case, and we don't need those overbearing Americans pointing the finger at us—no offense—the CAF can't risk leaving any stone unturned." When Khalil frowns and parts his lips to argue, Kelly holds up a hand. "It's over my head, Poverly. I'm sorry. This isn't my call."

Khalil and I hold our breath as the sheriff walks away, and the moment he's out of earshot, we exhale harshly.

"So that's bad," I deadpan.

Swearing viciously, Khalil snatches our personal two-way from its clip and starts trying like hell to reach Thorin.

CHAPTER TWENTY-NINE

THORIN

G ood luck," Khalil says from the other end of the channel.

The irony isn't lost on me that my brothers will be roughing it and spinning lies for the next couple of days, but I'm the one in need of prayer.

"Yeah, you too."

Tossing aside the two-way radio, I pick up the axe and resume chopping wood outside the shed. It's unnecessary since we've got plenty, but I needed out of that cabin.

So much for fresh air.

Seth and Khalil just gave me the heads-up to stay inside and out of sight while the search team combed our mountain. We should have seen it coming, but we get tunnel vision when it comes to Aurelia.

She's the only one still missing, and Big Bear is the only place the team hasn't searched because of us. The military can't stare down the eyes of the world empty-handed and claim they gave it all they got, knowing more than a third of the Cold Peaks wasn't combed. It would leave too much room for speculation and questions of competency. It could even bring the entire search team itself into focus.

Making it all the easier for Isaac to find us.

Swearing, I leave the axe buried in the tree stump and rip off my gloves before grabbing the radio and heading inside.

I see Aurelia the moment I step through the front door.

She's standing in front of the panoramic window below the loft, staring out at the two smaller peaks and the valley between, but her eyes aren't on the miles and miles of brutal wilderness below our cliff.

They're cast to the sky like she's waiting on something.

Letting the front door slam behind me, I wait for her to act caught, but true to form, she doesn't give a damn that I know what she's up to. Her head just keeps swiveling back and forth. "Get away from the window."

"Why?"

Of course, she doesn't move and continues to stare out of the glass.

Aurelia's been doing that lately. At first, I thought it was because she enjoyed the view. It is pretty epic. But our devious captive doesn't strike me as someone who appreciates nature.

No, it's much more likely that she's plotting another escape.

After our fight this morning, we pretty much stayed out of each other's way, but it didn't last. I didn't make it an hour without eyes on her before I tracked her down and found her up in the small loft *singing*.

Her powerful voice held me arrested long enough for her to realize she had an audience, and then—as if it never happened—she stopped. Hoping she'd sing for me again, I offered to carry down the heavy boxes we'd stored up there and forgotten about. I even dragged up Khalil's thick bedroll and extra pillow from the basement for her to sleep on, but all I've gotten for my trouble is a cutting side-eye and her telling me to go away while she finished dusting. I sat on the couch watching her for a while before accepting that she wouldn't sing again while I was around, so I left to chop wood.

Instead of explaining that I don't want to risk her being spotted by a passing helicopter, I walk over to join her at the window. I wrap my arm around her waist, and she doesn't fight me, even when I lean down to mark up her neck with my stubble. "Because I said so, wolf. Let's go take a shower."

We're still pressed together when she lets me ease her away from the window.

"I can't do this. I can't do that. Why don't you just throw me in the dungeon and be done with it? Grab that." Aurelia points to the conditioner now resting on the coffee table, and I swipe the bottle as we pass.

"Kinky, but we don't have one."

"What about the root cellar? You could put a lock on the door and—"

Aurelia stops, and her expression becomes appalled when she realizes she is actually *giving* me ideas on how to lock her down.

I smile as we enter my bedroom, but it feels strained from the effort it takes not to give in to the dark impulse to do exactly that. "Don't tempt me, wolf."

Aurelia rolls her eyes half-heartedly and clears her throat. "You didn't have to babysit me," she claims once we're in my bathroom. "I'm not going to run."

My gaze flicks to hers as I reach for the thin bow tied between her breasts, and she stops breathing when I pull on the string. The small slit in her bodice parts a little while my hand drops to her brown corset with embroidered daffodils. "You've said that before, but I remember you running."

"Okay, I'm not going to run *again*."

Slowly, I loosen the laces on her corset until it falls to the floor, and her bodice parts even more, her nipples spilling out of her dress.

"I wish I could believe you, my wolf, but then you wouldn't *be* my wolf." Aurelia wraps her arms around her stomach like it's upsetting her all of a sudden and chews on her bottom lip. I pause in relieving Aurelia of her dress. "What's the matter?"

"Nothing," she says too quickly. "How did you learn to hunt?"

The swift change in subject stumps me for a second, but I play along. "A lot of trial and error. It was either learn or starve, and if it was just me, maybe I would have starved, but I had Khalil and Zeke and neither can hunt for shit."

"Can you teach me?" she blurts. I raise my brows, and it's the wrong reaction because Aurelia becomes flustered and tries to backpedal. "N-never mind. That was stupid."

"Why?"

She huffs. "I don't know why. I said forget it, okay?"

"Aurelia… *Why* do you think it's stupid to want to take care of yourself?" I clarify.

"Oh." She shrugs and then reaches for my jeans. I doubt she's even aware she's undressing me like this is normal for us as she talks. "I don't know. I guess because I haven't had to lift a finger for myself in…well, ever." I toe off my boots and step out of my jeans once they drop to the floor while Aurelia lifts my shirt over my head with my help. "My uncle has always taken care of me. I wouldn't know how if I tried."

"Yes, you would."

Aurelia skates by my statement like it will burn her if she gets too close, and I let her as I turn on the shower. Once the water is warm, we both climb in. She's not as nervous as the first time we showered together, but I can tell she's waiting for me to jump her like last time.

"So, what did you do before you came to be one with nature?" she asks to try to distract me.

Watching her step under the weak spray to wet her huge mound of curls, I answer while somewhat entranced. "Recon. Marines."

"Ooh." Her eyes bug playfully but then sobers when she remembers what I'm capable of. "Scary."

Laughter punches out of me unintentionally. "Not really. A lot of watching and waiting. I can't think of a more boring job."

Grabbing my shampoo, she squirts some in her small palm and then starts to lather her hair. "Is that why you don't do it anymore?"

"No. Zeke needed me more, and nothing was going to keep me away. Desertion wasn't an option, so I got myself discharged."

"How?"

"I punched out my CO." After an awkward silence, I say, "Don't worry. He had it coming."

"Wow. Extreme. You must love Zeke."

"He's my brother," I say simply.

Aurelia nods her understanding but looks sad for some reason. "I wish I had siblings."

"We're not related."

"No, I know. I just… I don't have friends either."

My head cocks to the side while my eyes narrow. She's got to be bullshitting me. "None?" She gives an abrupt shake of her head, and since I can't stand to watch her struggle to wash her hair any longer, I turn her around and take over. "How is that possible?"

Aurelia is an international icon with more power and money than one person should have. Surely, there have been people—even if their intentions were self-serving—who have gotten close.

"Other than the obvious?" she returns wryly.

I grunt as I work my fingers over her scalp and watch her lashes flutter. "You're not that bad, wolf. Have you met me?"

"You're not…that bad."

I laugh and use my grip on her hair to pull her against me until my dick is nestled against her plump ass. "Careful," I warn playfully.

"Are we seriously bonding over being terrible people?"

Grinning, I kiss her neck, and then I ask again as I work the shampoo through her hair, "So, why don't you have friends?"

"My uncle wouldn't let me."

My hands pause as something cold and angry rises in my chest. "The fuck are you talking about?"

Aurelia tenses, and I force myself to chill the fuck out. Marston George hasn't been the only villain in her life. The fact that I don't want her to be afraid of me should be enough for me to leave this shower right now, but I don't. Something changed after we got Aurelia back to the cabin, and I don't want to ruin it before I can figure out whatever the hell this is.

"Tell me what you mean," I demand a little gentler.

"It's not a big deal, really. Haven't you heard that it's lonely at the top?" Aurelia tries to mask her pain by chuckling through it, but only stony silence follows. "I, uh…I wanted to be a singer since I was nine," she explains. "When my dad died a few years later, my uncle became my guardian. He said I had to stay focused if I was serious about being a star. I had to make singing my whole world, so I did. Nothing came before it—not my mom, who was in rehab, or even school. I dropped out before I even got to high school, and my uncle hired a private tutor and called it homeschooling, but most of my days were spent building my voice and learning how to perform."

"What about others in the industry?"

"Oh, sure. There were people I met on my way to the top. My uncle even set me up to 'date' or befriend other high-profile celebrities whenever I had a new album or tour coming up, but none of it was ever real. And I learned the hard way how fast clapping can turn to stabbing. My uncle didn't have to convince me of shit after that. Life is the best teacher, right? Once I hit the big time and everyone knew me, the only thing that mattered was my image. My persona was so carefully curated and protected that I didn't even recognize myself anymore. How could I ask someone to like me for me if I didn't know who I was, you know?"

I nod but don't speak as I rinse the shampoo from her hair.

Aurelia is pensive for a few moments before she says, "The last meaningful relationship I had was with my bodyguard, Tyler. He was the closest thing I had to a friend, but I knew if I ever actually believed it, my uncle would catch wind, and I would never see him again."

Her voice softens when she says his name, and I stare at the top of her head as my hands continue their task. I barely keep the possession out of my tone when I ask, "And was Tyler more than just your bodyguard?"

"Huh?"

"You heard me."

And just like that the spell that made her pliable and forthcoming is broken. "Crying over spilled milk, Thorin? That's so unlike you," she mocks.

Shaking my head, I snatch up the conditioner and apply a generous amount to her hair. "Just answer the question, Aurelia."

"Why does it matter? He's *dead*." Choosing to step right over that, I don't bother to correct her assumption. I just turn her around to face me and hold her stare until she submits in the only way Aurelia can—purely fucking infuriatingly. "What can I say, Thorin? A girl has needs."

"He didn't meet them."

She looks taken aback at my confidence. "How would you know? You weren't there."

Wrapping both hands around her neck, I push her against the tiles and choke her until she's clawing at my hands and arms for air.

And then I give it to her.

I let her throat go and force her lips against mine before she can even draw a breath. I give her the air in my lungs until she's convinced she can't breathe without me. And then I kiss her until she's breathless again so that I can be the one to revive her.

One kiss and she forgets she wants to be saved. Instead, she's clawing and panting for *me*, not freedom.

Instead of fucking her senseless like she wants, I pull away, only far enough to see the brown in her irises, while shoving a hand between her thick thighs and cupping her warm pussy. "Because I know what you need, and the only ones depraved enough to feed that fantasy were right here waiting for you, Aurelia. That's how I fucking know."

She rolls her eyes but, for once, doesn't deny that she craves this. She probably even thinks she deserves it. Whether she does or not makes no difference to me. I would have kept her, anyway.

"Anyway, he's ex-military too. You'd probably have liked him."

I should have drowned his ass when I had the chance. "I guess we'll never know."

I don't want to talk about Tyler anymore. I don't even want her to remember him. I might want to string her uncle up by his ankles and then gut him like I would my dinner before I eat it, but he had one thing right.

Distracting Aurelia from herself is the best way to keep her in line.

My dick is brick-hard from that kiss, so I lift Aurelia off her feet and wrap her legs around my waist. Lining myself up with her entrance, I hesitate and I'm not even aware of the question on my lips until it falls off.

"Do you want it?"

Too late now to pretend I don't care.

Aurelia looks surprised but not more so than me when she nods. Her breath hitches when I enter her pussy slowly while staring into her eyes. I don't give her a chance to recover when our hips finally meet. I work to muddle that head of hers by fucking her hard against the tile wall.

"Don't mention him again," I warn against her soft lips as she mewls from the rough treatment. "I don't care if I'm not around to hear it." I'm grateful to Tyler for keeping Aurelia alive and leading her right to us, but that's as far as my gratitude extends. "Don't *fucking* say his name again. I won't share any part of you with anyone but my brothers. Understand?"

Digging her nails into my back, Aurelia nods with a pinched expression, and I don't even realize I'm easing up until her expression smooths and she softens in my arms. "Don't stop."

"Then kiss me."

Her head snaps forward, and Aurelia crushes her lips against mine with an eager moan while I fuck an orgasm out of us both. After she's caught her breath, I set her on her feet and keep one arm around her waist when she sways. Silently, I wash the conditioner out of her hair.

"Do you still hate me, wolf?"

I must be a glutton for punishment because what other answer could there be than yes? I don't know what I'll do if she does. Punish her for telling the truth? It's too cruel even for me.

Slowly, she shakes her head, as if she doesn't want to admit it. "Not as much at the moment. Keep it up."

Finished with her hair, I crush her against me as I hold her and feel her heart beating wildly against my abs. "You're just saying that because I made you come," I joke.

It's a piss-poor attempt to run from this.

Because it's foolish what we're doing. What we're *letting* happen. I'm not even trying to fight it anymore. Quiet as it's kept, Aurelia scares the shit out of me.

Teeth sinking into her bottom lip, her brown gaze becomes unfocused for several moments before it clears, and she shrugs. "Maybe."

We finish showering and I wrap a towel around her and then me. After, I leave the bathroom to get dressed while Aurelia stares at herself in the mirror. I find one of my shirts for her to wear, despite the clothes we salvaged from the camp, because I like seeing her in my shirts, and return to the bathroom. Aurelia's fussing with her hair now and cursing as she tries to part her tangled curls with her fingers.

"What's wrong?" I ask as I stand behind her.

Her gaze flicks to mine in the mirror before returning to her hair. "Nothing."

"Looks like something."

"You won't understand."

"Try me."

Sighing heavily, she drops her arms. "Okay. Well, I have to do something with my hair before I lose my mind, but I don't have any of the stuff I need."

"Like what?"

"A comb or brush for one?"

"What else?"

Turning around to face me, she folds her arms and runs down a list of products that make me wonder if she's secretly building a bomb instead. When she's done, I raise my brows. "Is that all?" I ask sarcastically.

"Forget it." Her nostrils flaring, she faces the mirror once more and goes back to trying to section her wet hair.

After the third or fourth wince, I can't take it anymore and leave the bathroom. I walk over to my bed, and after making sure the coast is clear,

I pull her duffel from under my bed. I'll have to find a better hiding place soon, but it's the least of my worries as the sound of Aurelia cursing hard enough to make a sailor blush reaches my ears.

The small case I'd found her conditioner in is sitting on top, so I find what she needs in no time. I hesitate only for a moment since the plan had been to use this shit as a bargaining chip before I remember an old adage.

Happy wife, happy life.

Kicking the rest of her shit under the bed again, I ease back into the bathroom with Aurelia's hair products. She ignores me when I walk in until I set the designer case on the counter, and her gaze flies to it before finding mine.

"What… How did you…?" She doesn't finish her sentence when she dives for the travel case and flips it open. A few of the bottles are busted, but most of them are intact. Aurelia doesn't seem to notice the mess as she squeals happily and then throws her arms around my neck and kisses me. "I don't even know how the hell you found this and just happened to have it, but I don't care. Thank you, Thorin."

I grab a handful of her ass—which is more than a *hand full*—and groan before stealing another kiss because I'm greedy like that. "That's right, wolf. Keep ignoring those pesky questions, and we'll get along just fine."

She sinks her teeth into my bottom lip until she draws blood.

My perfect, vicious thing.

Aurelia stays in the bathroom for hours.

When she finally emerges, the day is gone, and she looks exhausted but relieved. Light floods my bedroom from the bathroom when she opens the door and steps out wearing my T-shirt. The front of her hair is twisted to her scalp in small, neat rows, while the rest of her hair is in its usual unburdened mass, though the curls do look more vibrant than before. I'd always known she had beautiful hair but seeing it now has my fingers flexing, imagining her golden curls slipping through my fingers.

Aurelia doesn't notice me, doesn't even look my way.

I'm lying on my bed in the dark with my fingers linked behind my head. I'd been careful not to make a peep.

Shortly after leaving her alone, Aurelia started singing again.

She hadn't stopped—not once in all the time that she'd been locked inside my bathroom. When one song ended, she immediately started another, and I've been rooted to this spot ever since. Even when my hunger turned to pain, my back hurt, and I needed to piss like no other, I ignored the discomfort and stayed to listen to her sing about love and heartbreak and being true to yourself.

All things she knows nothing about, thanks to her uncle.

"So, when girls claim they can't go out because they have to wash their hair, it wasn't a lie after all?" I ask, startling her.

Aurelia yelps and jumps back with a hand on her heaving chest. "What the hell, Thorin? Could you be more creepy?"

"I could try." Tilting my head, I grin and end my slow perusal at her chest. "I know how much it excites you."

She glowers and ignores my statement. "Why are you in here?"

"It's my room."

"Shouldn't you be out raiding, plundering, and ravaging fair maidens?"

"Not today." Swinging my legs over the side of the bed, I stand and stretch, but it doesn't cure my restlessness.

Aurelia—despite her derision—gets me better than she should.

I've never been good at lying around the house and doing nothing. Cabin fever has already set in after being stuck inside for almost a week, and now it will be another two days before I can leave.

Fuck.

"So, is that your fantasy then?" I tease, hardening my expression as I approach. Aurelia nervously backs away with her hands up like I'm not stronger and faster than her. I bend and wrap my arms around her thighs just under her butt, and she yelps, her hands finding my shoulders when I lift and carry her out of the bedroom. "You want to be plundered and ravaged by a sexy Viking?"

"I didn't say you were sexy."

"You were thinking it."

"I didn't say you were a Viking either."

"You called me Ragnar when we first met."

Her eyes dart to the side. "And?"

"I happened to catch a couple episodes of *Vikings* before we left the States, and my memory is a little fuzzy, but I think I remember a certain humble blue-eyed, blond farmer turned ruthless raider who looks *nothing* like me."

"You're full of yourself, aren't you, Thorin…whatever your last name is."

"It's Thayer. And I could make you full of me, too. Just say the world, Aurelia." Since my face is level with her chest, I bite and kiss her breasts through my T-shirt as I walk, and her fingers curl on my shoulders when my voice drops a decibel. "I'll even chase if you want. I can throw you down on my furs and tear off your dress. You could scream for me, wolf. As loud as you can. I promise I won't stop."

"You're making fun of me."

My head lifts, and I stare into her eyes as I slowly set her on her feet inside the kitchen. "Aurelia, I know you're still trying to figure some shit out, but I can promise you that no one here is going to make fun of you for what you want. It's more likely that the three of us will come to blows to be the one to give it to you."

"Except if I want to leave, of course."

"Of course."

I don't want to ruin this tenuous peace we have, so I don't bother to suggest she might not want to leave—especially when I'm not sure how we even got here. One minute, we're fighting, and the next, we're stripping each other bare.

"I like your hair," I say as I brush her lip with my thumb. "Did I tell you that, wolf?"

She shakes her head while staring up at me with wide eyes. Her tongue darts out and licks the tip of my thumb, and my dick jerks in my sweats, wanting a piece of that action.

I sigh and drop my hand. "Get started on dinner. I'm going to chop some wood," I announce before heading for the front door.

Some distance seems necessary, but Aurelia has other plans.

She follows me out of the kitchen.

"Can I come?" The request stops me in my tracks. I look over my shoulder to see her looking hopeful, but I'm already shaking my head. "Why not?"

"Because you have to stay inside and out of sight for a couple of days."

"What's the big deal? I thought you said search and rescue wouldn't come this far?"

"I know what I said, wolf. It's just a precaution."

"Why?" she demands, looking seconds away from a panic attack. "You haven't had a problem with me going outside before. You said as I long as I stay within sight, it's fine. Why hide me now?"

I don't respond right away.

Two weeks ago, I would have taken great pleasure in pulling the rug out from under her, and while I still would if necessary, I can't with her looking at me like I'm the answer to her problems and not the reason for her distress.

When did I start wanting to be the former and not the latter?

Dropping my head, I rub at my temples. "Come on, baby. You know why."

Her sharp inhale is audible as tears well in her eyes but don't fall. It hasn't escaped my notice that even through all of this and what we've done to her, Aurelia never cried. Not once. "They're calling off the search?"

"Yes."

"When?"

"Two days."

"Two…" It's all that makes it out of her before she clutches her stomach and turns away from me. Aurelia doesn't say another word, and she doesn't come with me to chop wood. She leaves the kitchen in a daze and climbs the bookcase up to the loft before crawling inside Khalil's sleeping bag, where she stays for the rest of the night.

I end up making dinner for us, but she doesn't come down when I call for her. She hasn't eaten since this morning, and I know she must be starving.

I don't eat either because I can't stomach the food, so I try to check on Khalil and Seth, but they're unresponsive as well, which means it's not safe for them to talk. I glance up one last time at the loft before lying down on the couch.

Aurelia's silence is driving me up the wall.

I end up falling asleep, waiting for my wolf to snap out of it and come down, but she never does. When I wake before dawn, I peel myself from the couch, shower, and get dressed before grabbing what I need for the day.

Once I have my weapons and pack shouldered, I return to the living room.

"Aurelia."

No sound comes from the loft above me for a few seconds, and then I hear the sleeping bag rustle.

"Aurelia, I know you hear me."

"I hear you, but I'm trying not to," she grumbles sadly while sounding wide awake. Did she even sleep? "Go away."

So, we're back to this then.

I blow air out through my nostrils, but that's as far as I let my anger travel. I should have expected this, really. Aurelia may be acting like the perfect submissive, but she's never stopped charting a course for home.

I'm teetering between immense pride and grating frustration that she refuses to let us have our way. I'm pretty sure if Aurelia had fallen in line from the start, I would have grown bored after fucking her once and then thrown her off the deck like I imagined doing that first night.

It's just before dawn, so we don't have a lot of time to waste on her pity party.

"Get up, get dressed, and let's go," I order sternly.

"Why?"

It's her favorite fucking question.

"Because I said so," I reply, giving her my favorite fucking answer. She slowly sits up and peers out the tip of the A-frame window overlooking the peaks and the tip of the full moon peeking over the horizon before glaring down at me over her shoulder. She notices I'm fully dressed with the crossbow strapped to my back and my hunting rifle across my chest. "Let's go."

Aurelia scoots to the edge of the loft to climb down the bookcase, but I get there first and wrap my hands around her waist before lifting and setting her on her feet.

"Now, get dressed." I shove the warm clothes I pulled from the salvage we stole at her. If Aurelia recognizes the items when she takes them from me, she doesn't remark on it. It figures when I want her to ask questions and chew my ass out, she doesn't.

"Where are we going?"

"You asked me to teach you to hunt. We're going to hunt."

"I thought I had to stay inside."

"We won't be gone long, and we'll stay close to the cabin. It shouldn't be a problem so long as you do as I say and don't wander off."

"So, like normal then?"

"Exactly."

"Does this mean you'll show me how that works?" She points to the crossbow sticking over my shoulder.

"Why? So you can use it on me?"

"Maybe. Wouldn't you?"

"Be ready in ten or be left," I tell her so that she gets going.

Aurelia sticks her nose in the air when she walks past me and takes her stubborn ass down to the basement instead of using my bathroom, knowing the slight will irk me.

When she returns with the coat that belongs to another man, I grab the sleeve before she can pull it on, and we play tug-of-war with it until I manage to wrestle it from her without hurting her. Aurelia talks shit while I add it to the pile of firewood, but instead of pissing me off, I feel myself fighting back a smile.

It's never been my intention to break her past the point of repair—at least not since we decided she was one of us.

She falls silent when I return and hand her the winter coat Khalil grabbed from her luggage. It's puffy and white with a fur-lined hood and has yet another designer label I don't recognize, but it actually looks useful, unlike those boots she arrived in. She slips the coat on with a perplexed look on her face before tugging on the hat and gloves Seth gave her. I watch her hesitate a moment when she grabs the blue-and-purple-striped scarf.

"Something wrong?"

"This was Cassie's."

I search my memory for the name. "Your assistant?"

Aurelia nods. "Wolves got her the first day. I tried to help her, but I…" Her chin quivers as she tries to fight off the crushing guilt that I know she must feel. "I was useless. She died anyway. If it wasn't for Tyler finding me when he did, I'd be dead too."

And now I understand the hesitation. "Put it on," I tell her.

"No." She tries to step around me, but I grab the scarf and drape it around her neck. "Stop it, Thorin."

"Torturing yourself won't make you a hero," I say as I wind it around her neck. "It just makes you obnoxious and repetitive." Tugging on the tails, I yank her into me. "Take the fucking scarf and stay warm. Cassie would want you to have it."

"She hated me."

"And you hated her, I'm sure, but you still put yourself in grave danger to try to save her. Let Cassie help you now."

She's introspective for a few moments before smirking a little cruelly. It perplexes me at first sight until she says, "It's funny… You know who said the same thing?"

Fucking Tyler Westbrook.

"Let's go," I order before my jealousy puts us right back at square one.

As we start for the door, I pause to grab the compound bow and quiver I left on the couch. Aurelia's brown eyes widen, but she stays still as I slip the empty quiver over her shoulder and hand her the vertical bow. At first, she holds it awkwardly with both hands like an offering, but when I cross my arms to wait her out, she rolls her eyes and holds it down by her side.

"Rule number one of weapon training…" Turning, I start for the cabin's front door. As I pass the oval mirror on the entry wall, I catch sight of her arms raised as she aims the unloaded crossbow at my back with a narrowed gaze. "Never point it at anything you're not prepared to fucking kill, Aurelia."

She lowers the bow.

CHAPTER THIRTY

AURELIA

T horin has targets set up in a clearing not far from the cabin with an old campfire and a fallen log in the center, and I immediately recognize why he agreed to our ill-advised outing. Because the clearing is small, we're still mostly shrouded by the forest's canopy and unlikely to be spotted by a passing helicopter.

Tree slices, six inches thick and two feet in diameter, have been sprayed with red rings on the smooth face and a smaller black circle in the center for the bullseye. The targets are held on tripods made of sturdy-looking branches, and I count as many as twelve hidden among the trees. The closest is only fifty meters away, and the farthest is about three hundred meters.

I'm still gawking at the targets, feeling more than a little intimidated when Thorin distracts me from my thoughts by pointing out a hollow tree to my right.

"This is where Bruce used to live."

"Bruce?"

That's when Thorin tells me we're in the den of the surly bear who nearly disemboweled him and who currently adorns their living room floor.

"So, you moved into his territory, and when he tried to protect his home, you killed him?"

"No. We *left* his territory—or, at least, thought we did." Pointing to his torso, he says, "I found out the hard way when Bruce tracked us down miles away that bears are highly territorial and don't easily forgive a threat. The three of us had no idea what we were doing when we decided to live off the grid, so I'll bear the responsibility. No pun intended." When I just glare,

Thorin sighs, his breath a white cloud billowing in the cold air. "The bear gave me no choice, Aurelia. It was him or me. Do you believe me?"

Remembering the wolf I killed and the second one I injured with the axe from the plane while they fed on Cassie's entrails, I nod. It hadn't mattered to me that she stumbled upon their den while looking for other survivors. Cassie and those wolves died because of my mistake. I had no business judging Thorin. "I do."

"Good."

"Did you have to turn him into a rug, though? That's kind of mean."

Thorin shrugs as he sheds the long, heavy overcoat he's wearing as if it's not negative two hundred degrees out here. "So was trying to eat me. Besides, Bruce was already dead. I didn't think he'd mind." When I purse my lips in disapproval, he sighs. "You look at him and see a decoration, but to me he's a reminder that in order to survive out here, we needed to become apex predators ourselves. We needed to be as untamable as these wilds we call home."

"Well, you clearly succeeded."

Looking up from his pack that he's crouched over, he gives me an amused look. "Apparently not, wolf."

My cheeks are suddenly warm, so I'm grateful for the oversize hood that currently hides them from view. "Are you going to teach me to hunt, Thorin Thayer, or are you just going to flirt with me?"

"I'm an excellent multitasker." Rising from his crouch, he walks over to me while strapping some kind of hip quiver full of arrows to his leg. He then takes the bow that's lighter than it looks from my hand. "This weapon is called a compound bow. When I first saw you, you were filthy, bruised, and broken. It's the vertical cousin of the crossbow. And I still thought you were the most stunning creature I'd ever seen. There are some key differences between the two bows though. Your voice is like a fist around my heart, tugging and squeezing until all I want to do is rip my heart out of my chest and give it you. The compound requires more skill and strength to kill effectively. I know I don't deserve it, but I hope one day you'll sing for me. It's also slightly more accurate than the crossbow, but only if you know what you're doing. I've never known anyone like you, Aurelia George. I hope you stay."

"Stop that," I scold without any of the command needed to let him know I mean it. I'm palming my cheeks under my gloved hands because... God, they are so warm. Warmer than they should be out here. I feel Thorin's "flirting," which feels more like a declaration of love, all the way down to places he shouldn't be able to reach. My heart speeds up and slows down like it's searching out his and trying to match its rhythm. "You might be great at multitasking, but I'm not. I can't focus when you say things like that to me."

Thorin doesn't look cocky or smug at knowing he got to me. A contemplative expression crosses his face as he studies mine. I don't know what he sees that makes him inhale deeply, but he lets me off the look.

"Let's get started."

"I'm not a good student," I warn Thorin because I'm already regretting asking him to teach me to hunt.

"We'll see," he returns, and my eyes widen as he starts showing me all of the parts of the compound bow—the limbs, arrow shelf, grip, bowstring...

Ughhhh!

Et cetera.

Once Thorin's done listing and pointing out all the components, he makes me repeat them. We continue doing this for ten minutes in the freezing cold, despite my whining and complaining until I finally get them all right.

Only then does he pluck an arrow from the quiver and show me how to load it onto the shelf. His movements are smooth and confident, but when it comes time for me to mimic them, I fumble with the arrow until it slips from my fingers. The yellow arrow is bright against the white snow as I stare down at it.

"Are you going to pick it up?" Thorin quizzes with an impatient sigh.

"I'm thinking about it."

"Pick it up, Aurelia."

"Fine."

Five minutes later, I still can't get the damn arrow on the shelf without fumbling or dropping it. How does Thorin make it look so easy?

"Practice," he tells me after I ask him. "And so will you."

Ugh.

I'm not expecting him to step behind me—so close that I feel the heat from his chest warming my back and his lips moving against my cheek when he leans forward to see over my shoulder. "These fingers have always been so graceful," he purrs as he takes my hand holding the arrow. "All you need to know now is where to place them." I hold my breath as Thorin moves my fingers up along the hunting arrow until I reach the fletching. "Index and thumb only. It's not a cock, Aurelia. You don't need to fist the arrow like one." Thorin's husky laugh when I elbow him in the abs sends heat rushing down the slope of my neck and my heaving chest until my nipples harden under the heavy layers of clothing. "Good girl," he praises when I follow his instructions. "Now load the fucking arrow, wolf. Make me proud."

Holding my breath while he tightens his hold on my waist, I place the arrow on the rest, and two steps later, I have it fucking nocked.

"Holy shit," I exclaim as I stare down at the bow. "I'm a badass. I'll take my secret assassin card now. The Huntress has nothing on me."

Thorin blows out a breath and chuckles. "Talk like that around Zeke, and he'll come in his pants."

My smile drops as I look over my shoulder to meet Thorin's blue eyes. "Zeke? Don't you mean Seth?"

He shakes his head. "No. Zeke is into comics and crime documentaries. Seth likes fantasy and romance."

I turn my attention toward the bow in my hand again when I ask, "But he's never met me. How do you know he'll even like me?"

Thorin takes an unsettling amount of time to answer before sighing heavily. "I won't lie to you, wolf. It'll be rough when he wakes up. He'll need time to get used to you, but I think—"

"Don't make promises you can't keep, Thorin. What if he doesn't come around? You'll have to choose between us."

Thorin gave up his entire life to keep his friend and brother safe. I'd be a fool to think he'd choose me.

If Zeke can't accept me, I'm worse than fucked. I'm dead.

My fate rests in the hands of a man who is not entirely whole, a man I've never even met, and a man who has every reason to fear me.

And his name is Ezekiel Cura.

"Tell me, Thorin. Tell me right now that if Zeke wakes up and wants me gone, you'll choose me. Better yet, tell me that you'll let me go rather than kill me when he can't."

"Aurelia, I…I can't."

"I know. I wouldn't have believed you if you had. A monster I can live with, Thorin. A liar, I cannot."

I take one step away, and Thorin fists the back of my coat and yanks me backward until we're connected again.

"Why does it have to be this way at all, Aurelia? What if there's a way?"

"There isn't."

"We can make one," he says almost desperately.

"You're many things, Thorin, but you're not selfish. If Zeke needs me gone, that's the way it will be, and we both know why you can't just let me go." Peering over my shoulder, I stare into his frustrated blue eyes as I repeat his words from the night Khalil took me. "The fallacy is thinking that the choice was ever really yours." I feel his grip loosen, and I shrug. "Zeke will give you no choice, and neither will I. He is your friend. I'm a warm hole and a loose end. There was never going to be any other outcome but this one."

Thorin's breathing quickens as the same wildness he had in his eyes the night he found me returns. I'm slipping through his fingers, and he can feel it. What wild animal won't attack when its food is threatened?

Oddly, I don't feel dread when I pull away from him, nor do I fear that he will hurt me, but his reaction still surprises me.

The feral look eases into an unreadable one as he shrugs. "Then I guess I'll have to take a page from the book of Aurelia. When my back is against the wall and I have no choices left, fight like hell anyway and talk shit while doing it."

He doesn't give me time to figure out how to respond to that before taking the bow from me and continuing with his tutoring as if nothing happened.

"Keeping your shoulders level and your arm as straight as the arrow you're pretending to fire, I want you to pull on the string, hold for five seconds, and release." He unloads the arrow and quickly demonstrates before handing the bow back to me.

"I thought you were going to teach me how to hunt."

"I will." He waits until I raise the bow before adding, "First, you need the fundamentals. You need to learn how to use and respect the weapon you'll hunt with."

"Oh, fuck me. You're about to *Karate Kid* me, aren't you?"

"Yes, I am. Draw."

Holding the bow as he showed me, I impatiently wait while Thorin takes his sweet time studying my form. A bead of sweat has already formed on my brow from the strength it takes to keep the taut bowstring fully drawn. I don't know which is tighter—the tension in the string or the one between Thorin and me as he corrects my form. He kicks my feet apart to widen my stance, and I have to grit my teeth to concentrate. When his hands move from my arms to my shoulders to my belly and down to my waist, I give up with a gasp and relax my trembling arms.

Thorin doesn't look the least bit surprised.

"We need to work on building the muscles in your arms, or you'll never be able to hit anything useful. Again."

I lift the bow to try again. "If the crossbow is more powerful and easier to shoot," I struggle to get out as I keep the bowstring drawn, "how come you're starting me off with this?"

"Because I earned the right to be a lazy hunter. Release."

"Oh, thank God." Relaxing my arm with a heavy exhale, I grumble when Thorin corrects my form again before telling me to draw.

A few hours later, I'm questioning why I asked Thorin to teach me to hunt. Was I really that bored? I did need a break from being the perfect hostage in *The Cabin in the Woods*, and learning how to kill shit was fun, but fuck, I'd forgotten how cold it was up here.

I stopped feeling my nipples hours ago.

"Do you really hate your mom?" I ask Thorin out of the blue when we finally take a break from aiming drills.

I'm sitting next to him on a fallen log, watching him raid his pack for our lunch. We're sitting so close together that our thighs touch, and I tell myself it's just for warmth as I scoot a little closer until our hips touch too. As for my prying, I'm not sure why I want to know other than reminding myself who I'm dealing with.

But wouldn't that mean I already have my mind made up about who Thorin is? Is that fair when I'm asking him to bare part of his soul?

"She wasn't really much of a mom to me, but no, wolf. I don't hate her. She loved me when it suited her, so I guess it wasn't all bad."

"I'm sorry."

He shrugs but avoids eye contact. "Don't be. She isn't."

"How do you know?"

"The last words my mother said to me before she died was that she should have traded me for a better score when she had the chance."

"She didn't mean it, Thorin. She was sick. The drugs—"

"She was three years sober when she said it, wolf."

"Oh."

"As I said, it wasn't all bad. For a very brief moment in time, I had a somewhat decent childhood. It lasted until she started missing the high the drugs gave her, but I didn't know how to help her, and I couldn't see past my anger of losing her to them."

I wait for Thorin to finish pulling out a large thermos and two tin cups before I ask, "How did you know when she started again?"

As he divides the stew into the cups, he says, "She was mean for a while before she started hating her life a little less, and then she was nothing."

"I guess we have that in common," I whisper as I stare into the flickering flames and think about my mother, who also struggled with drug addiction.

But unlike Thorin, it didn't ruin my childhood.

No, I was blindsided by it when my father died, and my mother relapsed overnight after being clean for over a decade.

"We have many things in common, wolf. Care to share?"

He hands me one of the tin cups full of stew, and I use the excuse of taking a sip to buy myself time before answering. I'm pleasantly surprised at the temperature of the stew. It warms my blood almost immediately.

"I wasn't enough for my mom either," I finally say.

Thorin doesn't remark or refute it like I tried to, and I'm grateful for it as we eat in silence. Maybe he understands me more than I want to admit.

"When did you make stew?" I ask when it dawns on me that it couldn't have been this morning.

I'd lain awake most of the night, staring out the window the loft shares with the living room, crying inside like a winner. I'd even woken up an hour before Thorin to do more brooding and *not* crying.

It's not that I particularly aspire to be some weepy girl who is easily driven to tears and hysterics, but to never cry? It's just not normal. I can't even pinpoint when it even began.

"Last night, after you went to bed."

"Oh. Right." Remembering how my uncle despised it whenever I pouted or felt any emotion that kept me from putting on a perfect performance, on and off the stage, I feel panic welling up in my chest. "I, uh, I'm sorry about that, Thorin. It won't happen again," I swear.

I'm watching Thorin's face, so I see the moment his brows dip in confusion, and he stops mid-chew to glance down at me. I'm practically in his lap with how close I've burrowed into his side for his body heat—and okay, yes, the security too—so I can see the minute shift in his striking blue eyes. He wasn't angry before, even when we spoke of his mom, but whatever I said chased away the smidgen of warmth I'd found as the chill in his eyes grows colder.

"Let me guess," he says with a curl of his lips. "Your uncle?"

"He didn't like it when I complained," I explain, knowing it doesn't even scratch the surface. Even now, far out of his reach, I'm still following my uncle's rules. I'm still afraid of him.

I read a thousand responses across Thorin's visage before he settles on the one I don't see coming.

"Come here."

"Thorin, if I come any closer, I'll be in your lap."

"Then *get in my lap*." I almost forget to look unhappy about it when I stand and take a seat on his hard thigh. Once I'm settled, he says, "Baby, never forget. Even wolves howl at the moon."

I stare down at my stew as his words sink in. "I don't cry, Thorin. Ever."

"I know."

It should surprise me that Thorin's noticed that, too, but it doesn't. There isn't much about me he doesn't seem to already have a vested interest in. "I don't think I even know how anymore."

"I'm not particularly keen on seeing you cry, but it does worry me that you think you can't."

"I know I can't."

"Maybe you just haven't had the right motivation."

I lift a brow. "Are you saying you want to make me cry, Thorin?"

"We could try a few things guaranteed to make you weep," he suggests in a low voice that makes my toes curl, "but I have a feeling it won't be your eyes." Suddenly, it feels like I can't catch my breath, so I pinch my inner thigh to snap myself out of this Thorin haze I've fallen in. "Have I kissed you today, Aurelia George?"

"No. You know, I was wondering about that. I was thinking, 'What is Thorin Thayer's problem? All day, I put on the best performance of my life, playing the clueless female and letting him mansplain all the things to me, and still no kiss? What gives?"

"Perhaps if you use that mouth for something other than being a smart-ass, it would have occurred to you to kiss me."

"Meh."

The grin he flashes is slightly feral before he helps himself to a tight fistful of my curls. "Very well then."

His lips are poised right above mine when the sudden crackling of the radio startles us both. The garbled voices speaking back and forth interrupt the moment and keep us both frozen like deer in headlights.

"Fuck."

"What?"

Thorin doesn't answer me as he tosses the rest of his stew into the snow before snatching mine out of my hand and doing the same. "I'll have to take a raincheck on that kiss, baby."

Grabbing my waist, he lifts me off his lap and onto my feet before standing himself and throwing everything back into his pack.

I just stand there in bewilderment and watch him scramble uncharacteristically to erase our presence from the clearing before grabbing both bows and his pack from the ground.

"Come on." He wraps his hand around my arm as if he's expecting me to fight him.

We're standing so close now that I have to tilt my head back to meet his panicked gaze. "What's the matter?"

For a moment, Thorin doesn't look as if he'll answer. And then he says tightly, "One of the search teams is nearby. Four or five miles at most if the radio is picking up their signal. The clearer it gets, the closer they are, and they're closing in fast." The muscles in his jaw jump. "I have no way of knowing which direction they're coming from. They could be anywhere."

We could walk right into them on our way back to the cabin.

"Oh," I say quietly despite my heart pounding in my chest now. Can Thorin hear it?

His grip on me tightens as if he knows what I'm thinking. "Let's go, Aurelia."

"So we're going back to the cabin?" I ask lamely because, of course, we are. I'm stalling.

I think.

Thorin gives me a sharp look before releasing my arm and taking my hand, "We're going *home*, wolf."

He doesn't start walking or even force me to. For a few costly seconds, the two of us just stand there silently communicating with our eyes as the voices on the radio become more distinct.

This isn't Thorin's and my usual battle of wills. It's a negotiation that ends with a promise. I'm the first to move, turning my hand in his to link our fingers. He squeezes mine in response.

"Let's go home," I finally say.

It takes us longer to get back to the cabin because Thorin has to cover our tracks as we go, and with his gaze snapping my way every few seconds to make sure I don't run off screaming the moment his back is turned, it eats up even more time.

He doesn't stop watching me closely until I finally pick up a fallen spruce bough halfway to the cabin. I feel his eyes on me as I help erase my footprints from the snow, but I don't dare look his way under the guise of focusing on sweeping the needlelike leaves across the snow.

We're less than a mile from the cabin when Thorin's eyes leave me to search the trees for any sign of movement. His head has been on a constant swivel since leaving the practice range. I don't have much time—thirty seconds at most—so I make every second count as I unwind Cassie's scarf from around my neck.

Thorin is looking behind him now, in the direction we're traveling, when I let my fingers unfurl. Cassie's scarf slips from my hand, but before it can hit the ground, a wind picks up the lightweight material and carries it off.

Watching it disappear around a copse of spruces just as Thorin looks in that direction, I say a silent prayer that it makes its way back to her.

The cabin is unusually quiet without Khalil's and Seth's endless racket, and I find myself missing it when I step out of the downstairs bathroom hours later. Freshly showered, the loft and Khalil's sleeping bag beckon me, so I start up the basement stairs with exhaustion weighing down my bones as I climb.

The wide green and brown gingham twilly from my costume is the only hope I have of keeping my twists protected and curls pinned, so I'm tying that around my head when I reach the first floor and find Thorin crouched in front of the woodstove.

He's shirtless and wearing flannel pajama pants that match the flannel shirt I'm wearing. The same one I woke up in after I was unconscious and at their mercy for days. The reminder doesn't fill me with dread like it used to—not after witnessing the care they spent putting me back together. I don't even feel it when Thorin glances over his shoulder and stands when he sees me.

"You're wearing my shirt," he remarks.

"You're not getting it back," I say immediately. "It's mine now."

Thorin's teeth flash when he smiles and laughs at me for laying claim to his shirt. "I wouldn't have it any other way, wolf."

Lifting the material to my face, I sniff the collar and frown at the scent of detergent and nothing else. "I may let you borrow it from time to time, though. It's better when it smells like you."

Thorin rolls his eyes playfully, but I suspect it's to distract me from the fact that he's actually blushing. "How generous of you. You're too kind." His gaze lands on the loft and lingers before returning to me. When his lips part, I know what he's going to ask before he speaks.

The surprise comes when I answer the request before he can make it. "Yes."

I can see the tension leaving his shoulders even as the divot between his brows deepens. "You're sure?" He glances at the loft again, comes to some conclusion, and sighs. "It's okay if you don't want to, Aurelia. I won't force you."

Moving away from the stairs, I feel as if I'm under a microscope as I walk over to stand in front of Thorin. "I want to."

My assurance only makes him more wary and confused. "Why?"

"Because you care if I do. Come on." I take his hand, which is so much rougher and bigger than mine, and lead him into his bedroom.

We're forced to part when we reach the foot of his bed, and Thorin tells me to take the side closer to the woodstove in the corner. I walk that way, but Thorin doesn't seem keen on letting me go. Our fingers linger until the very last moment, and I round the bed. I can already feel how much warmer it is on this side of the room. Through one of the windows next to the bed, I can see the full moon glowing above the second-highest peak. I walk over to it while Thorin climbs into his bed. From the corner of my eye, I can see him sitting against the headboard...watching me.

"If this is Big Bear and the mountain I crashed on is Little Bear, what is that one called?" I point to the mountain in question. "Mama Bear?"

"Close," Thorin answers, and when I look away from the window, I see his amused smirk. "She is Maia."

"Maia?" I frown. "Why Maia?"

"Don't know." He shrugs as he ties his long, blond hair into a topknot. "Never asked."

I hum disapprovingly and take one last look at the mountain Maia before I walk over to Thorin's bed. I hesitate for a moment, long enough to glance at the open door before my gaze flies to Thorin's in surprise.

This isn't my first time sleeping in Thorin's bed.

Last time, he boarded the door shut so no one could get in or out. I was completely at his mercy. I can still see holes and nails in the frame from when he ripped the planks out the next morning and freed me without a word.

He hadn't even fucked me.

We'd just lain uncomfortably on opposite sides of his cold, hard bed until morning. It was brutal.

"You can leave at any time, wolf."

With that promise, I don't linger a second longer. I climb into his bed and quickly settle under the covers. His mattress is still harder than I like but is warmer than I remember. It's also smaller than Khalil's, so there's not much space left between us as we stare at each other in the dark with the help of the dimmed lamp on his nightstand.

"Good shower?"

"Mm-hmm. Yup." It's awkward for several moments as we lie on opposite sides of the bed. Timidly, I scoot toward the middle. "You?"

"It was okay," he says. Thorin reaches out and pulls me the rest of the way until the front of our bodies are flush and his arm can curve around me. "Water pressure's still shit. I need to remind Khalil about helping me check the pipes and pressure tank." Thorin dips his head to run his nose down my neck. "You smell like him, songbird."

"I used his soap," I admit as I peer up at him. "You think he'll mind?"

Thorin shakes his head on the pillow we're now sharing. "Not even a little. What's ours is yours, songbird."

"As long as I'm willing to spread my legs for it," I remind him dryly but without resentment.

Thorin nudges my chin and tips my head back for better access to my eyes when he asks, "Would you like to end our arrangement?"

I stumble over an answer before I settle on one that makes sense rather than the lie or the truth because they both scare me. "Seth and Khalil would never agree."

"Yes, they would."

"How do you know?"

"Because I know. Now, stop beating around the bush and tell me what you want, wolf."

"No, okay? No. I don't want to end our arrangement," I grumble.

Thorin searches my gaze and then kisses the pout from my lips before his lips travel to my ear. "Glad we got that straightened out," he whispers smugly.

God, I hate him.

Not really.

A little.

Ugh.

I can't even decide anymore if I hate the prick or not.

"It also reminds me that you owe me for all the hair products that have now taken over my bathroom."

I'm suddenly unable to catch my breath. I'm fucking panting for whatever it is he'll make me do. Only Thorin, Khalil, and Seth have the power to touch this part of me that craves this. "Okay."

"Turn over and present your pussy for fucking."

"What? Now?"

"Of course."

"What will you do?"

"Do you care?"

I swallow hard as my stomach dips. "No."

"Then turn. The fuck. Over." He punctuates each command with a kiss on a different part of my body until I'm aching for what comes next.

I turn over onto my stomach, and it causes the flannel to ride up, exposing the bottom curve of my ass to Thorin's gaze.

"Where are your panties, baby?"

"I didn't wear any in case you wanted to…in case you wanted me," I say shyly.

Thorin slips his hand under the hem of his shirt and sweeps his thumbs over the swell of my bottom. "You're perfect. Have I told you that, songbird?" He doesn't wait for an answer before demanding, "On your knees."

I do as he says until my ass is in the air and my pussy is exposed to the room. I can feel the heat from the stove and Thorin's gaze, and God, it makes me weep.

The bed shifts, and I feel him between my thighs.

"Khalil is going to kill me for this," Thorin mumbles cryptically. "He wanted to be the first." There is a pointed pause, and I grow impatient to the point of fisting the sheets to keep from snapping at him to hurry. Thorin notices and growls. "Fuck it. I can't wait anymore."

I wait for him to enter me without any thought as to what "first" he might be alluding to.

The last thing I expect to feel is Thorin's mouth on me.

He's lying on his back as he kisses his way up my inner thigh. It forces him to lift his head and then his shoulders off the bed by the time he reaches the crease between my upper thigh and lower lips.

"Thorin?"

I feel him biting into my thigh when I squirm. "Hold still, songbird. I'm going to eat this gorgeous cunt."

Thorin kisses my thigh one last time, but his intent still doesn't sink in until I feel his tongue flick my clit. I jump in surprise, arching away from his mouth, and Thorin slaps my ass in reprimand. "Do that again, and I'll tie you down."

I moan miserably, but I do not move again while Thorin tortures me with his mouth and tongue. I'm not sure I can ever get used to the sensation, but before long, I stop running from it.

Thorin rests his head on the bed again and drags me down with him by my hips until I'm sitting on his face. I panic a little at the idea of smothering him, and Thorin seems to read my mind, tightening his hold to keep me where I am.

"Jesus, Thorin."

I have no choice but to hold on to the headboard while he works his tongue through my pussy without mercy. Each time I'm close to coming, Thorin shifts his attention away from my clit, and the edging starts all over again.

Suddenly, the room is too warm, too stifling.

Eyes barely open, I move my hands to Thorin's flannel and quickly slip the buttons free until the panels part, and I can breathe again. The shirt slips from my shoulders and catches on my elbows, exposing me even more for Thorin's gaze as he watches me from below.

My nipples are hard against my palms as I cup my breasts and ride his face. When I come, it is with a splintered and delirious cry.

Thorin doesn't give me time to recover.

He dumps me onto my back unceremoniously, shoves down his pajama pants just enough to free his swollen cock, and makes quick work of fucking me into the mattress.

My heels dig into the muscled globes of his ass while he gives it to me with short, brutal strokes that make me scream and come again before he spills inside of me.

When Thorin doesn't immediately roll away but instead stays inside of me until his cock is flaccid, my suspicions are raised.

"I know...what you're doing," I accuse through attempts to catch my breath. He's lying next to me now, doing the same. "You're trying...to get me...pregnant."

"Congratulations, Aurelia. You're the last to know."

I narrow my gaze at his nonchalance. "It won't work." Thorin lifts his head to peer down at me with a curious look, but instead of telling him I know why he's trying to breed me, I say, "I'm on birth control."

"Oh, yeah? How long has it been since you've taken the pill?"

"Who says it's the pill I'm taking?"

He gives me an eerie look that tells me to cut the bullshit. It sends a chill down my spine that he once again knows more about me than he should.

"Well, I still won't allow it," I declare impetuously. "Consider my body a hostile environment, asshole. No sperm shall pass."

"Good. I think my sperm likes a challenge."

I punch the bed and glare at him. "Why are you all of a sudden impossible to piss off?" I yell.

Thorin laughs, then pulls me down to lie on his chest with a quick kiss on my forehead. "Blame yourself for making me this fucking happy, wolf."

My lips part, but no words come out.

He's happy? Why? Does he know something I don't?

I'm too afraid to know the answer, so I don't ask him, and we don't speak again for several moments.

I'm actually close to falling asleep when I mumble against his chest, "Can I ask you something?"

"I know what you're going to ask, and no, you don't snore… You do talk in your sleep, though."

I sit up with a gasp, and my hands brace against his hard chest. "I do not."

He grunts in disagreement but does not say more.

Rolling my eyes, I lie back down, and Thorin makes sure I'm curled back onto his chest. "That was not what I wanted to ask, you jerk."

"Ask your question, Aurelia."

"Actually, it's about that. What you call me. Sometimes, it's wolf, and sometimes, it's songbird. Why?" It's unusual to have more than one pet name for a person, isn't it?

"First, tell me why you think, and I'll tell you if you're right."

I roll my eyes, but then my mind sifts through all the times he called me wolf and songbird.

The former always seems to be when I'm being combative, protective, strong-willed, or even playful. He calls me songbird when I've either pleased, tamed, or surprised him. And he seems to reserve my name, Aurelia, for whenever I've exasperated or annoyed him.

"Wolf is for how you make me feel. Songbird is for how I make you feel."

"You will always be both to me, not one or the other," he confirms. "You are fierce, and you are gentle. You are spoiled, and you are selfless. You are terrifying, and you are fucking beautiful, Aurelia George. A dream and a nightmare. My songbird and my wolf. No matter what I call you, Aurelia, you are mine. I lay claim to every part of you."

My heart thumps against my chest while the rest of me is frozen. I don't blink or make a sound as I replay his words in my fried mind.

All of me.

He wants all of me.

Not just the palatable parts.

Does Thorin even know what he just offered me? Total and unyielding acceptance, which I've always dreamed of but never got, no matter how many people screamed my name or claimed to love me.

"Now, go to sleep," he orders. "We'll train some more in the morning."

Thorin, apparently done talking for the night, reaches over and shuts off the lamp, plunging the room into total darkness before he can see just what his words have done to me.

CHAPTER THIRTY-ONE

KHALIL

The search is over.

I'm so fucking relieved I don't even notice the tired ache in my muscles as Seth and I climb from the helicopter. It takes off immediately as we start the short trek down to the edge of the valley, where we left the Ski-Doos.

It's dusk by the time we arrive, and—minds on the same thing, the same want—Seth and I waste no time hopping on and speeding across the frozen valley. The ride is over in twenty minutes, but it feels like a lifetime until we reach the base of our mountain.

"Do you think Sunshine misses us?" Seth asks the moment we shut off the snowmobiles.

My gaze flicks to him. He's been talking about Aurelia nonstop from the moment it was safe to do so. "I doubt it, Seth. She hates us, remember? I don't think two days is enough time for her to forget that."

Who knows what kind of mood she's in after being stuck with Thorin? Who knows what kind of mood *he's* in after being stuck with her?

It doesn't slow my steps as we hike up to the cabin.

Seth practically runs there. He's already bounding up the steps to the front door by the time I reach the clearing.

He leaves the front door open, so I walk right through once I reach the cabin. I can hear him calling for Aurelia, but I don't see him, so he must be in the basement.

I start for Thorin's room when I spot the note left on the console table by the door. Seth must have missed it in his haste, so I read it.

Gone hunting. Don't wait up.
- Thor

Aurelia's with me.

I read the last line that was written like an afterthought several times and wonder if I've stepped into one of those multiverses Zeke is always going on about.

"Sunshine!" Seth yells as he rushes up the stairs. "Sunshine, we're home."

"She's not here," I tell him tightly. Handing him the note, I push past him rather than wait for what he has to say about it and go downstairs.

As much as I want to track them both down and shake them for being so reckless, I haven't showered in two days, and I'm crawling out of my skin.

I stop by the laundry room to grab a fresh towel and swear when I see there are none left. They're all soiled and piled up in the corner, along with the rest of the laundry. "This fucking girl."

Backing out, I strip off my clothes as I go into the bathroom directly across and shower anyway. When I'm done, I walk my naked ass out, dripping water, and find Seth pouting on the couch. He looks up and over at me, his eyes bugging when they land involuntarily on my dick.

"Dude!" He slaps his arm over his eyes. "A little warning when you're swinging that thing around?"

"You've seen it before, Seth."

"Not. Without. Warning."

Rolling my eyes, I walk into my room and search my drawers for clean clothes, only to realize I'm out of everything. Boxers included. I can't even find a clean pair of socks.

Sighing, I shove the last drawer closed and yank the sheet from my bed, wrapping it around my waist before walking back into the den. Seth avoids eye contact of any kind this time while I make my way to the stairs.

Thorin and I are closer in size, so I head into his room to raid his clothes and find a pair of cargo pants, socks, and a thermal.

For some reason, I peek inside Thorin's bathroom—maybe to see if he's hogging all the towels away—but all I see is…

Girl shit—bottles and jars upon bottles and jars of hair products, littering the sink and the ledge above it.

"Who's gone soft now?" I say to no one.

I grab one of the many hair ties on the sink and pull my braids up before leaving the bathroom. The kitchen is my next stop. After raiding the fridge, I find soup and make myself a bowl. I can hear the tub's water running downstairs as I eat, and when I'm done, I clean up after myself and go back downstairs to do the laundry.

Seth sings "High School" the entire time he bathes.

It's one of Aurelia's songs that he learned while we were at the camp, and I know why he took to it. Aurelia sings about all the things she missed chasing a dream, and Seth—in his own way—can relate. He never had a childhood or any of the normal experiences that Thor, Zeke, and I had. It's not the first time I've considered that each of us might have more in common with Aurelia than sex.

I'm wrapping up the laundry by the time Seth finishes his soak, and I'm still fucking restless. I've been trying to put Thorin and Aurelia, and what they might be doing other than hunting, out of my head by keeping my hands and mind busy, but it's not working.

Seth disappears inside his destroyed bedroom to get dressed, and when he returns, he's not dressed to relax.

What a coincidence. Neither am I.

"Going somewhere?"

"I'm going to go find Sunshine, and you're coming."

"Oh, am I?"

"Cut the bullshit, Khalil. You know you want to see her."

I roll my eyes but don't object when Seth grabs my sleeve and pulls me out of the laundry room. I follow him upstairs, and together, we gear up and leave the cabin. We haven't been home in two days, and it still feels that way because our home is out there somewhere—hopefully getting along.

Seth and I search Thor's usual hunting grounds but come up empty on each one. As we get farther away from the cabin, I tell myself that Thorin wouldn't be this stupid. The next spot we search is a large meadow near the lake that separates the Cold Peaks from the road to Hearth.

I sure as fuck hope Thorin wasn't reckless enough to take Aurelia this close to civilization. The search is over, but we're not in the clear yet. The Cold Peaks are still crawling with SAR while they break down the camps.

Seth and I argue about it the entire trek there.

I argue that Thor knows better.

Seth argues that Aurelia can be persuasive and can melt the mind with those soul-sucking eyes.

Madness.

We've all gone mad.

We're nearing the meadow when the avalanche tracker in my pocket starts beeping. It startles the shit out of me because I didn't remember bringing it. I must have grabbed it without realizing it, hoping to pick up Aurelia and Thorin's trail with it once we got close enough.

Two hundred feet.

She's close.

Hearing the steady beep, Seth stops, too, and cocks his head. "Sunshine?"

"I don't see them, but they're close."

Pulling out the tracker, I turn this way and that, taking a few steps every time I switch directions until the number on the screen starts to count down.

Coming to a stop once it tells me I'm within a hundred feet, I turn my head this way and that, but I still don't see her.

Before I can switch directions again, something rustles nearby. A moment later, I spot the bushy tail of a white rabbit as it darts from the bushes up ahead and runs toward the meadow. It barely makes it ten feet before the whistling sound, like something cleaving the air, reaches my ears just before the *shunk* sound of something sharp piercing its hide.

The rabbit falls over and slides a few feet across the snow.

Before I can investigate, another rabbit—this one gray—is startled from the same bush. It runs in the opposite direction—toward me instead of away—and as it passes, I hear that whistling sound again. This time, the arrow lands in the snow two inches from my foot.

My foot.

My goddamn foot.

"Hey!" I scream at the top of my lungs. "You better fucking watch it!"

Hearing a soft giggle followed by a deeper chuckle, I turn toward the offending sound and see Thorin and Aurelia walking toward us.

Thorin is holding his crossbow, and I immediately know it was he who shot the first rabbit, but what perplexes me is Aurelia. She stands next to him with another arrow notched in the compound hunting bow while she aims it right at me.

"You fucking missed!"

"No, she didn't!" Thorin shouts back.

Not finding a damn thing funny, my lip curls as I say sarcastically, "Oh, so you're suddenly an expert shot now? After two days?"

"Actually, it's the first shot she's made in two days," Thorin dryly corrects. "Aurelia needed the proper motivation, so I bet her she couldn't land the arrow within a foot without hitting you."

"What did she win if she made it?" Seth asks. He's bouncing on his toes with a gleam in his eyes. A little chaos and anarchy always get him excited, and Aurelia never stops finding ways to stir up both.

"I got to see Khalil cry like a bitch!" Aurelia calls out.

She's getting closer but not fast enough, so I decide to meet them halfway. In a weird twist, Aurelia lowers the bow as I stalk toward her, and she doesn't do a thing to stop me when I cup her nape and pull her into me. She comes without a fight, and I take the crossbow from her, handing it to Thorin without taking my eyes off her.

"You shouldn't have missed."

"I *didn't*. But out of curiosity, why?"

"Because I'm going to kiss you, Goldilocks."

Before she can object, I give in to the need that drove me to leave the cabin and find her. I devour her mouth and swallow her moans while driving her backward until her spine hits the tree. She gasps from the impact, but the pain only fuels her. Aurelia slides her hands under my coat and shirt and pays the pain back by dragging her nails down my abs. I grunt, but I don't stop. If anything, I kiss her harder.

"Mmm...okay, that's enough," she says, turning her head away while breathing hard.

I let her have that, but I keep her pressed against the tree as I make out with her neck. "Tell me you missed me."

"I thought about you once or twice."

My head pops up, and I glare down at her. "Quit playing with me, Aurelia."

"All right. I thought about you three whole times."

"What are you doing out here?" I whisper. I can hear Seth and Thorin doing the same with each other a few feet away.

"Hunting."

"And whose idea was that?"

"Mine."

Peeking over my shoulder, I make sure Thorin and Seth are still occupied, and then I grab Aurelia's throat and whisper, "Are you trying to run again, Aurelia?"

She stares up at me, her dauntless gaze shifting back and forth. It feels like she's staring into my soul. If she's looking for anything good, she won't find it. "Harder."

Shock ripples through me, and my grip loosens. It can't be. I must have heard her wrong. She's too goddamn good to be true. "Say that again," I demand.

"If you want to scare me, choke me harder, Khalil. You had no problem hurting me before. Don't pussy out on me now."

My fingers flex around her neck with indecision, and then I make one. I tighten my hold until her eyes flare and she bites into her bottom lip. *Fuck, she's perfect.* "Is this hard enough for you?" I ask while squeezing a little harder.

Her face turns red and then purple the longer I cut off her air supply.

Still, she doesn't fight me or beg me to stop.

Instead, her hand finds the waistband of my pants, and she yanks me closer, nodding only when she feels my hard dick pressed against her stomach. Shoving my free hand down her thick knitted tights, I slip two fingers inside and slowly fuck her wet pussy while staring into her eyes.

"Goddammit, Goldilocks. Tell me you weren't trying to run from us again." Finally, she jerks her head left and then right. I curl my fingers, and she makes a strangled sound that I cut off before Thorin and Seth can hear because this moment is just for us. "Are you lying to me?" She whimpers and shakes her head again, and then her lashes lower as she begins to lose consciousness. I can't help but think about the night I fucked her on the kitchen table, how much I want to do it again, and if she will let me. "Are you going to come for me?"

Her nod is weak, but her pussy tightens around me like a vise, and I know she's close. I grind the heel of my palm against her clit and let go of her throat.

Aurelia inhales, and then she lets out a wail as she comes, making a mess of my hand and her tights.

Seth pauses mid-word, and I can hear my brothers trying to be quiet as they sneak over, but I can't look away from our girl.

Fucking beautiful.

So softly I almost don't hear it, Aurelia pants as she says, "I did miss you, Khalil."

I kiss her again as I play with her pussy. I'm still kissing her when Seth whimpers like a sad puppy. Aurelia breaks the kiss and looks over at him while stroking my overgrown beard. "What's the matter, Seth?"

"Khalil's your favorite."

Aurelia snorts. "No, he's not. Thor is."

I snatch my hand from her tights like I've been burned. "What the hell? I made you come!"

"So? I can do that myself." Aurelia holds my gaze as she adjusts her tights. "Thor is giving me something useful. You want to be my favorite? Impress me."

"Yeah, we'll see how useless I am when you need to get off. Cabin rule number seven—keep those pretty fingers away from our pussy, Aurelia."

Her miffed gaze flicks to me. "We're not *in* the cabin."

"You heard what I said."

I shove away from the tree and stalk away before I strangle her ass for real. Thorin comes after me while Seth stays with Aurelia. I hear her tell him that she has to use the ladies' bush, and he cackles like her corny joke is hysterical. I don't even realize I'm fighting a smile until I hear Thorin cough to hold back a laugh.

The moment we're out of sight, I turn and hit Thorin in the jaw. Since he was expecting it, he's quick to parry, and the next thing I know, we're fucking each other up until there's blood in the snow, and we can barely stand. After he sends a vicious knee to my gut, I roll several feet away and try to keep from coughing up my stomach.

Thorin groans in pain as he crawls to his feet while holding his shoulder. "You…" He pants. "Done?"

I don't answer until I catch my breath and stand. "The fuck are you doing bringing her all the way out here, huh? Does she know how close she is?"

"No. Do you think I'm an idiot?"

"Yes!"

"Fuck you, Khalil. Aurelia doesn't know shit, but she will if you keep bitching about it."

"Don't kid yourself and *don't* underestimate her. Aurelia pays attention. You might as well have drawn her a fucking map. Anybody could walk by. Did you think about that?"

"Of course I did. I also promised her that I would kill anyone who tried to help her, and I'd make her watch." His jaw, which is already turning red, clenches as he steps toward me. "Do you think we've given her any reason to doubt my word?"

"Do you really think Aurelia cares about anyone but herself?" Thorin doesn't respond, but he doesn't have to. I'm right. Per fucking usual. "You shouldn't have brought her out here."

"It's done. Now tell me about the search."

I blow out a breath, and now that I've seen Aurelia, touched her, and heard her voice, the exhaustion returns, and I think about the return journey.

Hell, I don't know if I can make it.

"CAF called off the search with a promise to revisit if new evidence arrives. Something like spotting a girl that looks awfully like our superstar way out in the middle of nowhere, looking like she doesn't fucking belong."

"Lay off, all right? No one's around but us."

"You don't *know* that."

"No one's taking your toy from you, Khalil. Relax. Let her have some fun."

"Oh, so you're Prince Charming now?"

"You really want to do this, Khalil?"

"I want to know how you could be so selfish! I explicitly told you two to stay inside. Are you trying to get us caught?"

"I was *trying* to find a way to make life easier for all of us."

I pause my pacing. "So you were trying to get caught." The only possible way to un-fuck ourselves and regain a little peace is to let Goldilocks go, and that's not happening. Ever.

"No, you idiot. I was trying to make Aurelia happy."

"What the fuck does she need to be happy for? We're not! It's called solidarity."

"Weren't you the same one who said Aurelia's the answer?"

"And I still believe that."

"Then what the fuck is your problem, Khalil?"

"I don't want to lose her!" My shout echoes through the forest, and a flock of squawking ravens burst from the canopy while Thorin stares at me like I've lost my mind.

My heart maybe, but not my mind. My thoughts have never been more clear.

Shit, what the fuck am I saying? "I—"

"Khalil." Thorin shakes his head. "It's okay. I know. I feel it too. We won't lose her, brother. Whatever it takes."

The words my heart is bursting to echo evaporate when I hear Seth's desperate shout from far away. "Sunshine! Sunshine, where are you?"

Thorin and I don't spare each other more than a confused glance that turns into panic before we take off after them. When we reach the last place we saw them, Seth appears out of breath and looking ready for war. He pays us no mind as he picks up Thorin's abandoned crossbow and takes off back the way he came without even sparing us so much as a glance.

"Seth. Seth, stop!" He does, but I can tell he doesn't like it. His entire body is vibrating with the need to follow Aurelia wherever she's gone. "Tell us what's going on," I demand. "Where's Aurelia?"

"She was taken."

"Taken?" Thorin echoes. "By who?"

"Don't know, don't care. Now, are you going to keep wasting time, or are we going to go kill some shit before they get away?"

Thorin and I make eye contact, and then he grabs Aurelia's hunting bow.

"Lead the way."

CHAPTER THIRTY-TWO

AURELIA

I don't need a bodyguard to pee, Seth."

"What about a really kinky but devastatingly handsome voyeur who *wants* to watch you pee?"

"Hard pass."

Seth whimpers like a sad puppy but doesn't follow me, thankfully. To be safe, I walk for a while until I'm sure I'm alone.

I really do have to pee.

I'm sure they think I'm trying to run again, so I know I don't have long before they come looking.

After relieving myself, I stand and pull up my tights.

I take one step toward the meadow where my mountain men are waiting—and likely fighting over me—when I hear it.

A twig snapping.

My head snaps in the direction of the sound, and I turn toward it when I see something moving up ahead. I'm prepared to scream in case it's a wolf or bear and hope that Seth hears me, but it's neither.

Instead, it's a White man in his mid-twenties, of average height and with a ginger beard, who steps from the tree line. He's busy removing a cigarette from the pack, so he hasn't spotted me yet.

I wrestle with indecision in the seconds before he does.

Hide or hail?

There's a tree I can take cover behind until he leaves, but this may be my last chance of getting home.

The question is, can I trust him?

The last time I went looking for a hero, I found three villains instead. Better the devils I know, right?

My heart thunders and my head swims in confusion when I back away toward the tree, but I don't get the chance to hide because my would-be savior looks up before I can. His eyes flare with surprise over seeing another person, and my stomach sinks. For a long moment, we just stare at each other across the hundred feet or so that separate us. And then I do something I'll never forgive myself for.

I turn to run.

"Hey!"

A tortured sound escapes me, and I run faster. I can hear him chasing me, and even though I know I can't outrun him, I still try.

"Hey, wait! I just want to know if you have a light!"

I open my mouth to scream for Seth when I trip over a log and fall. The snow doesn't cushion my fall and knocks the wind out of me instead, giving the stranger time to catch up to me before I can climb to my feet. When he tries to help me up, I smack his hand away and scramble to put distance between us again, but a tree blocks my path.

The stranger doesn't advance, but I keep a wary eye on him anyway as I stand slowly.

"Holy shit," he says once he gets a good look at me. "*Holy shit*. I know you! You're that missing girl." He takes a step forward, and I flinch. Fortunately, he gets the message and keeps his distance. "Uh…Aurora, right?"

I search his gaze, and maybe I'm the dumbest bitch on Earth for falling for it, but I've also been living with monsters—fucking them and catering to their every whim. I think that makes me an expert on the subject, so when I see nothing sinister staring back at me, I relax enough to say, "Aurelia."

"Yeah, sorry." He removes the hood of his yellow winter jacket, revealing the mop of ginger curls underneath as he tucks his unlit cigarette behind his ear. "Aurelia. Nice to meet you." He places a hand on his chest and smiles. "I'm Pete."

"Hi, Pete."

"This is so wild!" Pete grins, and it's so genuine that I can't help but return a small yet nervous smile. He's in danger, and he doesn't even know it. I wasn't just running to save myself from another potential monster. I was running to save him in case he's good and kind and innocent. "You know everyone's looking for you, right?" he asks, breaking my thoughts. "And here you are. I found you. *Alive*. I've never met a celebrity before."

"We're overrated," I tell him.

"Do you think I can have your autograph? My sister is a huge fan."

"Sure. Got a pen?"

"Oh, crap." He blushes so cutely at his folly. "No, not here."

"Maybe next time, then." I turn to go. The faster I get away from him, the safer we'll both be. "See ya, Pete."

I hold my breath, praying he doesn't try to stop me. Instead, he does something even more foolish.

He follows me.

"So, uh… What are you doing out here? Are you lost?"

"Very."

Pete nods, and I can see him stealing glances. I can feel his confusion and the questions he must have. I know what he's thinking.

I look pretty damn good for a girl who's been missing for seventeen days.

The world around me slows at the reminder.

Seventeen days…

Is that all it's been?

"Well, listen. We have a camp not far from here and a van. We can take you to town. Easy peasy."

I stop walking and turn to face him. "We?"

"Yeah, some buddies of mine. We came out here for a little hunting, drinking, and R&R. Never thought I'd find America's sweetheart. Dude, I'm going to get so laid after this."

While Pete yammers on about how his brother won't get to think he's better than him anymore, I weigh my options like I have all the time in the world.

I've already been gone too long.

It's a testament of Seth's misguided trust and infatuation that he hasn't already come looking for me.

"Okay, Pete. I accept your help, but how about I skip the ride and use your phone?" Nice smile or not, I'm not risking falling prey to another asshole.

"You could try, but there's no signal out here. We're totally off-grid."

Goddammit!

I'm still debating my options when a voice that is not that far away and closing in fast warns me that I'm out of time.

"Sunshine!" The blood in my veins goes cold. "Sunshine, where are you?"

Pete frowns. "Who's that?"

I look up at him, and my breath shudders out of me, billowing in the stark cold. "Run."

"What?"

"No time to explain." I take Pete's hand, and we start running in the direction I saw him come from.

"You mind telling me what the hell is going on?" he shouts.

Before I can answer, I hear Seth call for me again. "Sunshine!"

Looking over my shoulder, the alarm bells in my head start clanging wildly in time with my racing heart when I see Seth burst through the trees at the edge of the meadow. I know the moment he spots us. His surprise to see I'm not alone stops him in his tracks, but I know it won't last.

"Don't talk, just run!" I order Pete.

We run for a few minutes before Pete says, "This way."

Too spent to argue, I follow him while stealing glances behind us every few seconds. Seth isn't following us anymore, but I know better than to believe that makes us safe. After running until we're both gasping for breath, we finally reach Pete's camp at the edge of the frozen lake. Little Bear looks so much closer from here, and I nearly fall to my knees when I recall Thorin's words from the night I found them.

"You made a mistake coming this far south. You were closer to town where you crashed."

On Little Bear.

I crashed on Little Bear, and it is *right there*.

Just across the frozen lake.

But in which direction is Hearth? Definitely not south, so I can rule it out with absolute certainty.

"Pete, you're back! How was your shit?"

I finally notice the three guys lounging around, shooting the shit, and drinking next to a van, just as Pete said. They drunkenly greet the return of their friend and then cheer even louder when they notice me and get the wrong impression.

"Pete! Ronnie found the weed," a pudgy guy with brown hair and smudged glasses says. "Does your friend smoke?"

Pete, apparently forgetting all about the fact that we were just chased through the woods, looks down at me and asks, "What do you say, Aurelia? Want to get high?"

"No. I want to go to town like you promised me. We need to go *now*."

"Chill. You're among friends." Pete ambles toward the campfire his friends are huddled around and pops a squat on a log. "Come sit, Aurelia. Guys, check it out. You know the celebrity that was in that plane crash a couple of weeks ago? It's her! It's Aurelia George."

All four heads fly toward me, and they gawk.

"No way! Hey, my girlfriend and I love your music," the short one with huge dimples and a mop of copper curls gushes. "We listen to it all the time. My name is Sam, by the way."

"Oh, right," Pete says, remembering his manners as if this is a social call, not a rescue mission. "These are my compadres. Ronnie, Sam, and Jonah."

"Hi, Aurelia." Pete's stoner friends all say and wave at the same time.

I ignore them. "Pete, you promised me a ride to town. Remember? I'd like to go now."

He shrugs and accepts the joint Ronnie hands him. "What's your rush, Aurelia? Stay and party for a while."

"What's my rush? You did see the guy chasing us, didn't you?"

"No." He blinks slowly. "What guy?"

Oh God, what have I done?

They don't stand a chance against my mountain men.

Huffing, I walk closer to the fire. "That doesn't matter. All you need to know is that he's dangerous, and he's not alone. We *have* to go."

"Okay, okay, we will," Pete promises as he hits the weed and pats the empty seat next to him. "Just let me smoke a few rounds first. I drive better high."

I debate simply leaving to find my way back to Thorin, Seth, and Khalil and hope they're in a forgiving mood. I look at the blue panel van and the first faces I've seen outside of my captors in two weeks, and I know that I can't.

I'm so close.

I was just beginning to accept my fate, and then Pete showed up. It can't be a coincidence, right?

It's now or never.

Sam, who is sitting closest to the old van, pours a cup of cocoa from his thermos. When he hands it to me, I start to turn it down when a plan that can only leave one more stain on my soul forms in my head.

There's music coming from the van's speakers, and thanks to the maxed-out volume, I even recognize the song that begins to play. It's Sleep Token's "Take Me Back to Eden."

The keys must still be inside.

Stepping over the sprawled stoners, I take the cup from Sam but stay on my feet as I sip at the warm cocoa, and I scan the woods for movement over the rim. The stoners are laughing and pointing at the two squirrels fucking not far away, and I have to resist looking over my shoulder at the van and giving myself away—not to Pete and his friends but to my mountain men watching.

I can't see them, but I can feel them.

They haven't attacked yet, and I don't have to wonder why. They're giving me one last chance to save these clueless but well-meaning campers.

Come back to them, and they'll be spared.

Run, and they die.

Both options are a lie.

Pete and his friends are dead either way. They've seen me. They know I'm alive. They could tell someone.

There's a chance I'm wrong, and Thorin, Khalil, and Seth haven't found us yet. If Seth went back for his brothers, it would have bought us some time, but not much.

Seth saw me with Pete.

I know what will happen if Thorin, Khalil, and Seth find me with Pete and his friends. I also know it will be so much worse when they come and I'm not here.

Once I'm done with the hot cocoa, I hand the empty cup back to Sam, who gives me a weird grin that I choose to ignore. "Pete."

He doesn't look up as he sloppily stacks chocolate bars and marshmallows on a graham cracker. "Yeah, babe?"

"Are you going to take me to town or not?"

"Yeah, sure. In a minute."

"You don't have a minute." My gaze lifts to the tree line again, and I swear the shadows move. "*Pete.*" My attention returns to the friendly stoner, and his gaze is slightly annoyed when his head finally lifts, but I don't care. I'm trying to save his life. "I'm going to go now. Are you coming?"

"Don't go. We're making s'mores."

"I have to, and so do you."

His brows dip with confusion. "Why?"

"Because you'll die if we don't."

Pete sobers as he gives me a weird look, but I don't shy away from the scrutiny. I hold his gaze as I move back toward the van. The others fall quiet while Pete's head swivels back and forth between me and his friends. He's looking at me now like I'm the scary thing in the woods they need protection from, and maybe I am.

It scares me how comfortable I got in my cage.

It scares me that a small part of me is even willing to climb back inside.

It scares me that I feel safer in my cage than I do now when the ones who put me there are also the reason I'm afraid.

"Whoa!" Ronnie shouts, standing up for his friend. "You don't have to be such a bitch."

The only sound is the crackling fire as I reach the driver's door. Ignoring him, I turn and grab the handle, ripping open the door and climbing inside. "Thanks for nothing, gentlemen."

I slam the door just as Jonah shouts, "Hey, she's stealing your van!"

The first bass solo in the song drowns out the rest of their shouts as I wrap my hand around the key and turn it. The van rumbles to life, but I don't get a chance to throw it into drive.

My dumb ass forgot to lock the door first.

It's yanked back open with an angry screech of metal, and Sam grabs me by my hair, dragging me right back out and throwing me on the frozen ground.

"And by the way, your music sucks!" he spews. "My girlfriend likes Tania better anyway."

That fucking does it.

Forgetting that I'm the one in the wrong here, I lift my leg and drive my foot into his kneecap. Sam howls in pain as he bends over to grab his smarting knee just as an arrow flies over his head where his face was not a second ago.

At first, I can't believe what I'm seeing. It happened too fast to be sure, but there's no mistaking the familiar green arrow embedded in the side of the blue van.

Hearing the *thunk* and following my gaze, Sam forgets all about his knee when he looks over his shoulder and sees the arrow lodged into the side of his van. "What the hell? My van!"

"Shit," the curse falls from my lips in a stunned whisper, and then I snap out of it, yelling, "Run!"

Flipping over, I try to scramble to my feet, but I'm tackled to the ground by Jonah. It knocks the wind out of me long enough for him to turn me onto my back again, grab my wrists, and pin me down.

"Where do you think you're going?"

"They're here!" I scream inexplicably as I wrestle to get from under him. "We need to leave!"

Jonah blinks at me through his glasses like I've lost my mind, and then he sneers. "Nice try, thief. There's no one out here but us."

"Get off me!" When all he does is nudge my thighs apart and wedge himself between them, I scream. It's not until Jonah attempts to stuff a meaty paw down my tights, and I scream again, that I realize why I'm screaming or, rather, *who* I'm screaming for.

My mountain men.

"Yeah, you're not going anywhere, princess. You—"

I hear the familiar whistling sound of another arrow cleaving the air and then a wet, sickening crunch as it finds its target this time.

My struggles stop as I stare up at Jonah in horror.

His grip on my wrists loosens, and then his astonished gaze lowers. He tries to speak when he sees the bright green arrow piercing his chest and the red bloom slowly spreading, but only a hoarse, hollow gasp escapes.

"Hey, Jonah," Ronnie calls out. "You all right, man?"

Only a gurgling sound answers back, and then Jonah's eyes roll back before he collapses.

"Oh, shit!"

I push their friend off me while Pete and Ronnie panic. Sam is the only one whose shock won't let him make a sound. He's also the only one standing between me and freedom.

This time, I don't hesitate.

I make the cold and calculated move of trying to push past him for the van, and just as I predicted, he reacts and backhands me hard enough that I go flying.

By the time I blink the stars away and look up, Sam's clutching his bleeding throat. This time, the arrow sticking out of his neck is yellow from the compound bow. *My* bow. Our gazes lock as he chokes on his own blood, and then he falls to his knees first before face-planting in the snow. I cringe when the arrow is shoved deeper from the impact and punches through the back of his neck with another sickening crunch. Shaking it off, I step over Sam's body to get to the van now that he's no longer in my way.

I can feel bad about what I've done later.

"Yo, what the fuck!" Ronnie screams as I climb into the front seat.

"Sam!" Pete cries in vain. His friend doesn't answer. Sam's eyes are still open but unseeing as his crimson blood stains the snow red. "I think…I think he's dead!"

Ronnie panics and tries to run for cover, but another yellow arrow to the leg keeps him from getting far. He collapses to the ground with a scream for help, but the only thing that answers is four more arrows, both green and yellow, when he tries to crawl away. After far too long, trying to cling to life, Ronnie eventually slumps in the snow with a haunting death rattle.

"Aurelia," Pete calls for me, and I tear my gaze away from the steering wheel to meet his through the dirty window. "What's happening?" His hands are shoved in his red hair and he's crying. He's the only one still alive, and it's because Seth, Thorin, and Khalil want it that way. They'll want him to suffer in order to punish me.

I'm not even aware of my hands leaving the steering wheel and moving to the door handle until I'm already standing on the other side and moving over to Pete. I'm careful not to look at all of the blood and bodies staining the once white snow.

When I reach out for Pete, he flinches and backs away from me, and I don't yet understand that *I'm* the unknown thing he's afraid of until he speaks. "Please don't hurt me. I'm sorry, okay? We just wanted to have a little fun. You wouldn't have even remembered anything!"

What? "Pete…" I try once more to reason with him—to save his life. "We don't have time for this. We need to *go.*"

His eyes fly over my shoulder without a word, and I know then it's already too late.

I feel his presence like an angry cloud looming over my head before he even speaks.

"*Wolf.*"

Hearing Thorin's voice, I squeeze my eyes closed. I can feel the other two there as well, adding to Thorin's fury with their crackling energy and endless deluge. If Thorin is the cloud, then Khalil is the lightning and Seth the rain that makes up this storm I've caused.

The three of them try to close around me, to cut me off from Pete, so I turn to face Thorin, Khalil, and Seth before they can, using my body to protect Pete's. My gaze bounces between my three captors because I can't decide which one is my best chance to reason with.

Seth looks like a rabid dog.

Khalil keeps trying to edge around me to grab Pete.

And Thorin still hasn't lowered the compound bow.

"Don't hurt him. Please. It's my fault."

"Of course it's your fucking fault," Khalil snaps. "We warned you." Grabbing my neck, he yanks me away from Pete and shoves me into Seth's waiting arms.

"Please! Don't hurt him!" I turn to Seth when Khalil and Thorin ignore me. They're closing in on poor Pete, who's trembling like a kitten staring down two pissed-off mountain lions. "It's not Pete's fault. He was just trying to help me."

"Pete, huh?" Seth's eyes seem greener than ever.

"Are you fucking serious?" I gape when I realize he's actually jealous of me simply saying another man's name.

"Are *you* serious?" Seth yells back in a rare show of anger. "*Him?*" He flings a disdainful hand toward Pete and then takes my arms in both hands.

I almost can't believe my ears when he shakes me and says, "How could you hold his hand, Sunshine? How?"

I should have known Seth was the last person capable of reason.

Hearing the first punch land, I plant my hands on Seth's heaving chest and shove him away. He lets me but only enough to turn around so I can see what's happening, and then he wraps his arms around my waist like we're lovers taking in a beautiful view instead of a murder scene.

"Be a good girl, and we'll make it quick, Sunshine."

"Like hell we will," Thorin barks. "Khalil." Khalil stops pummeling Pete long enough to look over his shoulder at Thorin, who unsheathes his big, scary hunting knife and tosses it into the snow next to them. "Take his fucking hands for touching our girl."

"What?" I scream and renew my struggle. Seth curses and tightens his hold when I nearly get free. "Are you insane? You can't do this!"

"Yes, the fuck we can," Thorin says while staring at Pete. "You have a lesson to learn, and since we're not willing to give up any part of you, Pete here will rescue you after all."

"I'm sorry! Please. I won't try to run again. I swear! Just leave him alone!"

"You know the harder you fight for him, the worse we'll make it, Sunshine." When I kick Seth in the shin, he grunts and then huffs out a frustrated breath. "Fuck it. I'll do it. Give me the knife." Tossing me down in the snow, Seth stalks over and picks up the knife.

Pete manages to land a punch that loosens Khalil's hold on him, so Thorin steps forward and aims the crossbow before he can even think about getting away.

This is real.

This is happening.

They're really going to torture and kill an innocent man and all because they won't hurt me.

So many people dead because of me.

Tyler. Cassie. Harrison. Susan. Ronnie. Jonah. Sam. And soon, Pete.

And those are just the names I know. There are also the pilots and the rest of my security team whose names I never learned. How much longer will the list get? How much blood do I need spilled before I'm satisfied?

No.

It ends here.

I have to *do* something.

Their focus is on Pete right now as Seth decides which hand he wants to cut off first. The psycho is actually reciting, "Eeny meeny miny moe." When the knife lands on Pete's left hand and Seth frowns his displeasure before choosing the right one, I know it's because it's the hand I grabbed when I ran from the meadow and from him.

"Are you watching, Sunshine?"

Hell no. I already feel like I'm going to pass out, and they haven't even begun. My eyes are heavy, and I feel so sleepy, but I can't. The only way to save Pete from being mutilated is to take their focus off him, so I burst to my feet and start for the lake. Even though running is what started this and is the last thing I should do, it's the only way.

"Aurelia!"

I ignore Thorin calling after me, as well as the temptation of the van. There's no time.

Besides, this isn't about getting away. I'll never outrun them. I just have to distract them long enough for Pete to save himself.

If he can.

I make it to the shore of the frozen lake, and even though the edges of my vision are darkening and my bones feel heavy for some reason, I keep going. I stumble my way onto the ice and ignore the terrifying sound of the subzero water moving beneath the surface. God, I hope the ice is still thick. Spring is just around the corner and the snow has already begun to melt.

"Aurelia! Aurelia, don't! It's not safe!"

They're the ones who aren't safe.

Somehow, I'd forgotten that, and I can't even recall when it happened. I just stopped fearing them and started craving their darkness, but this... this is too much.

The sounds the lake makes under my feet terrify me, but I don't stop. I don't look behind me either to see which of them is chasing me. Hopefully, all of them are, and Pete got away.

I'm nearing the middle of the lake when a new sound reaches my ears that has me slowing against my will. The splintering and rumbling continue, getting louder as it reaches me. My stomach tightens and my ears ring from how hard my heart is pounding.

Don't look down.

Don't look down.

I'm too afraid of what I'll see. Instead, I slowly turn and meet blue eyes. "Thorin…"

His gaze is on the ice beneath my feet, and I swear I see him pale. "Songbird, don't look down."

"The ice."

"I know, baby. Don't move."

A few feet behind Thorin, I see Khalil frozen in place, and then a few feet behind him is Seth.

I knew at least one of them would come after me, maybe two, but I was wrong.

They all came for me.

Pete is a distant memory.

The ice cracks again as if it can sense that I'm swooning over cold-blooded murderers and is deciding whether I'm too stupid to live.

Then again… The only safe way is back to them, so maybe the lake is on their side.

"Thorin, I'm scared."

Not just of the cracking ice, but the fracturing happening inside of *me*. What am I to do when I'm being pulled in opposite directions and without a compass to guide me? I don't want to be a prisoner, but even now, even after seeing them murder four innocent people out of *jealousy*—God, help me, I still want them.

Something is seriously wrong with me, but the thing is… I'm pretty sure I don't care anymore.

"I won't let you fall," Thorin promises.

"I'm so tired."

"I know, baby. They drugged you."

Even my shivering bones seem to pause. "What?"

"The one who gave you the cup." *Sam.* "I was watching him through the scope. He slipped you something, Aurelia. It's what's making you sleepy. My guess is you have another five to seven minutes before you're out cold."

"W-why would they do that?"

"Take one guess," he answers tightly. When I don't respond, he speaks again. "I wasn't going to let anything happen to you, wolf."

"I don't care what they were going to do. You didn't have to kill them, Thorin. That was *extreme*. You have to know that."

"The only thing I know is that I'll cross any lines to keep you safe."

"If they deserved to die, so do you, you hypocrite!"

"I didn't say we saved you because we're good. We saved you because you're ours, Aurelia."

Thorin takes a step forward, and I take one back.

The thin ice between us cracks a little more.

"What's the fucking holdup?" Khalil yells. "Stop fucking chitchatting! The ice is going to give!"

"Aurelia, we don't have time for this," Thorin says as gently as he can. I can still hear his irritation, though. And something else. Something foreign. He's...scared.

If I fall, I die. Probably.

Well, so what? I should have died in that crash. I should have died when I fought to save an assistant I cared nothing about. I should have died so many times in the three days I searched for salvation and found my penance instead.

Thorin, Seth, and Khalil aren't the only ones who deserve to die. I do too. Yet here we are, defying death at every turn.

"I think it's the perfect time, Thorin. You want me off this ice, and I say we need to get a few things straight."

Thorin reacts in a way I don't expect, but I guess I get? He tips his head back and yells his frustration at the sky. Out of the three of them, I probably test his patience the most. When his gaze falls on me again, it's carefully blank, and then he gestures for me to proceed like we're two war generals negotiating a ceasefire across a table.

"I don't want to be your prisoner anymore." His jaw tightens, and I can see him fighting not to tell me what I already know. "I know you won't let me go. I know. I'll stop fighting you. I won't run. But I want something in return."

"And what is that?"

"No more punishments, no more indentured servitude, and I want this tracker *off*."

The ice rumbles another warning, but I hold my ground—so to speak.

It won't hold for much longer.

"What's she saying?" Seth calls out.

"How the fuck should I know!" Khalil yells back.

Thorin ignores his brothers, his gaze remaining locked with mine. "And you?" he finally asks when the splinter in the ice spreads and reaches the tips of his boots. We'll probably both go down at this point, but he doesn't seem concerned as he says, "Can we still have our wolf?"

"I said I won't run."

"That's not what I mean, and you know it, Aurelia." Thorin steps toward me, and the ice breaks where he just was. Water rises from the small hole, but he keeps inching toward me until he's within grabbing distance. "You want more, and so do we. Just your body isn't cutting it anymore. You've given us a taste of the real forbidden fruit, wolf. Mind, heart, and soul. It's the only way I can sell it to them." He jerks his head toward Khalil and Seth. "And it's the only way you can sell it to *me*."

"You haven't earned that."

"Give us the chance to."

"You haven't earned that either."

He quirks a blond brow. "Are we negotiating or not, songbird?" When I hold my stubborn silence, Thorin gives in with a sigh. "Aurelia...please, baby. The ice."

"So leave. Save yourself."

"Not without you."

I bark a dry laugh and blink away the exhaustion creeping in. "So much for 'run, and we'll let you die,'" I mock with a slur. "You hurt me, Thorin. And don't tell me I liked it or that you're sorry, or I'll let this lake take me before I let you have *any* part of me."

Thorin falls to his knees, and I don't expect that.

Behind him, I can see that Khalil and Seth more clearly now. They've managed to gain a few feet. They're edging to opposite sides—away from the splintering ice so that they can be in position to grab us both.

"Then let it have me instead," Thorin says quietly so Seth and Khalil don't overhear.

My gaze snaps back to him. "What?"

"You said we deserved death. Promise me you'll take care of them, and I'll make it right. I'll fall through the ice and you'll never see me again."

"Thorin, that is…that is *not* what I meant."

He holds up his hands in supplication. "I don't know what else to do, songbird. Tell me how to make it right, and I will."

"You can't."

His blue eyes shutter. "Then take two steps to the right and let me go."

"*No.*"

It's then I realize my weight is the only thing keeping him from going under. I hadn't even noticed the crack spreading around us, creating our own little island while the water laps the surface. It makes sense now why Khalil and Seth separated. They're hoping to grab us both at the same time. But if one of them is too slow…

I eye Khalil as he reaches me and then Seth as he reaches Thorin.

Khalil is faster. They must have known that.

It means Khalil and Seth chose me over their own brother, and Thorin chose me over himself.

When my blurry gaze returns to Thorin, my tormented heart punches against my chest, and the mob of unspoken words that I've been too cowardly, stubborn, and prideful to speak burst free.

"I—"

I'm too late.

My side of the frozen island gives, and I fall through the ice so fast I don't make a sound.

The freezing temperature of the lake immediately sinks into my bones and cuts off my shout. The drugs in my system have finally kicked in, relaxing my muscles so that I can't fight my way back to them. It's as if the mountain gave me one last chance to accept the Eden it had offered me before deciding to devour me instead.

While the water pulls me down, and the darkness awaits me at the bottom, my eyes remain locked on the surface and the last of the sun's rays, illuminating the hole I fell through. I fight past the heaviness to keep them open, and when the light suddenly blinks out, I assume that I've lost.

Allowing myself one last gift before I'm lost forever, I picture their faces one last time—Thorin, Khalil, and Seth. I imagine them surrounding me like they always seem to until all I feel is them. The cold becomes a distant memory while the drugs keep me docile. It keeps me from fighting the water pulling me down.

Keeping the image of my three mountain men firmly in mind, my eyes finally start to close when the sunlight at the surface suddenly returns, and I see him.

He cuts through the current-less water like it's…well, water.

Our gazes find each other through the endless dark, and he swims faster. I can't swim, but somehow, I use the last of my strength to reach out a hand to him. I'm losing my fight with consciousness almost as fast as I'm losing the air in my lungs, but I hold on.

I cling to life until I feel our fingers graze, and then I keep holding on when Thorin links them together. He uses that tenuous connection to pull me closer and locks his arms around me before pushing us both back toward the surface.

Who could love a monster?

As it turns out, I can.

I can love, crave, and forgive three of them because they're *my* monsters.

I'm claiming them.

It's what I was going to say before I fell through the lake, and now it looks like I'll get my chance.

"Fuck, he got her!" Khalil shouts the moment Thorin and I break through the surface.

Khalil pulls me out of the lake while Seth helps Thorin, and then the two of them hover while Thorin catches his breath, and I expel the water from my lungs.

It's not a pretty sight.

The moment I'm done, Thorin uses the last of his energy to pull me on top of him and scans my face for proof that I'm really alive before dropping his head back with a heavy sigh and staring at the sky.

I rest my cheek on his chest and just listen to his heart as it beats wildly under my ear.

Why am I still conscious?

Worst roofie ever.

"I–I–I'm s-s-s-s-o c-c-cooooold."

It's all Seth needs to hear.

He lifts me off Thorin's chest and into his arms, and I burrow into his warmth. Khalil gives Thorin a hand up, and then the four of us *carefully* get the fuck off the ice before we press our luck.

I swear this damn mountain might be sentient.

Each encounter with death feels like a trial, and each time I pass, it doesn't just make me stronger. It brings me closer to the men who insist on keeping me.

Khalil shakes his head as we go and steals glances at me until I've had enough and grumble, "W-w-what?"

This cold is not only making me grouchy, it makes me want to die.

"You've got nine lives, Goldilocks."

I snort as I lay my head on Seth's shoulder. "D-d-death c-c-can't k-kill me. I'm-m-m Aure-Aurelia Geo-Geo-George."

Thorin sighs his exasperation.

Seth throws back his head and howls like a wolf.

Khalil leans over to kiss my frozen cheek. "And don't you fucking forget it, Goldilocks."

CHAPTER THIRTY-THREE

SETH | ZEKE

S unshine?" Aurelia's deathly still and too fucking quiet by the time we reach the edge of the lake. I'd been praying that Thanatos hadn't come to steal her anyway. "Sunshine, can you hear me?"

"Mmm, Seth, no," she whines with her eyes closed. "Sleepy."

"I know, baby, but you've got to stay awake. At least until we get you warm."

Khalil rushes past me and starts getting a tent set up near the fire. It's probably not a good idea to make camp at the scene of a crime, but we can't risk the longer trek back to the meadow, and we still need to dispose of the bodies.

Pete's included.

Realizing we're back at the camp, Aurelia's head lifts, and I know she's searching for him. I tuck her head back against my shoulder before she can spot Pete lying in a pool of his own blood with his throat slashed. I know she ran to save him, and I don't want her to be sad that she failed. His death was quick, rather than the slow one we planned, but I know asking Sunshine to see the bright side in that will likely send her right back out onto that lake.

"Can you stand?" I ask once we're by the fire.

She nods, and I carefully set her on her feet before lowering the zipper on her coat and pushing it off her shoulders. Khalil shoos Thorin away when he tries to help with the tent, so Thorin comes over and pops a squat on the log while I undress our girl.

"You too, Thorin. Clothes off," I order when he rocks the log from how hard he's shaking.

He'd already shed his coat before going into the lake after Sunshine, so he fists his wet thermal and lifts it over his head without a word. Thorin isn't much of a talker, but he's unusually quiet even for him, and my mind shifts to the reason why before I can stop it.

Something happened between him and Aurelia on that ice, and whatever it was, Aurelia now clings to me instead of pushing me away. I could kiss Thorin if I thought he'd go for it.

One thing at a time.

The talk they had, not the kissing.

Khalil has the tent set up by the time I'm done getting Aurelia's clothes off. Even drugged and hypothermic, it doesn't take our princess long to notice that she's naked out in the open. I can only imagine how this would look if someone were to happen by and see dead bodies everywhere, a naked and drugged-out girl, and the three of us like rabid guard dogs protecting their bone.

"Heyyyy… Where did my clothes go?" she sluggishly asks as I walk her back toward the tent with my arms around her waist.

"I took them."

"Whyyyyy?"

"Because they're wet, you're cold, and I'm going to warm you up."

"Mmm, I know how you can warm me up," she teases uncharacteristically.

"Yeah?" I can't help but smile down at her. It's too bad my cock is soft-serve after almost losing her again.

There will be no fucking tonight.

I get Aurelia inside the tent and into one of the bedrolls Khalil has laid out. Thorin follows, and I try not to be jealous when he climbs inside with her but no luck.

I'm jealous as hell but not murderously so, like when I saw Aurelia grab Pete's hand.

I can hear Khalil outside the tent moving the bodies, so I make sure Aurelia and Thorin are both tucked in tight before kissing Aurelia's forehead. I fuck with Thorin by trying to do the same, and he scowls at me while mushing my face away.

"I'll be right back, Sunshine. You two stay put."

Leaving the tent, I find Khalil standing at the back of the van with the doors thrown wide open. He's already done hiding the bodies inside, but he has a weird look on his face, and then he mutters, "This shit looks like something out of a serial killer documentary."

"What is it? What did you find?"

His head snaps toward me, and then Khalil rushes to close the van doors. "Seth, I want you to promise me something," he says once they're secure and he's standing in front of them, making it clear I'd have to get through him to see whatever the hell freaked him out.

"Yeah? What's that?" I only half listen as I look around to see that the bodies are gone, and the blood's been covered up with fresh snow just in case anyone happens to pass by. It's sloppy and risky, but it will have to do until we can figure out a way to cover our tracks properly.

"Do not under any circumstances look inside this van."

That gets my attention. Unfortunately for him, it also piques my curiosity. "Why? Because of the bodies?"

"No. Just trust me."

It's an automatic response for me to say that I don't trust him, but for whatever reason, the words don't come.

I...do...trust him.

And it's all because of Aurelia.

She makes everything better. It doesn't hurt as much inside Zeke's head because all I can think about is her, and I don't hate Thorin and Khalil anymore. Well, at least not enough to kill them. Anyone who knows better than to let precious treasure like Sunshine get away can't be *too* bad.

"Or you can stop treating me like a child and tell me. I can handle it, Khalil."

"And if you can't? Aurelia is ten feet away, Seth. Bane could—"

"Bane won't be a problem, so stop stalling and tell me what's in the van."

Khalil debates it before sighing heavily and saying, "Honestly, I can't decide what creeps me out the most, but you should know there's a cage." Khalil watches me carefully while my skin prickles with unease. "I'm guessing it's where they kept them."

"Who?"

Khalil glances at the van again and pales. "The girls that came before Aurelia."

I'm guessing the ones who weren't as lucky to have a few monsters of their own on a leash.

Pete would have put Sunshine in that cage.

Pete would have done things to her that I don't have to imagine. Because once upon a time, in a different place and a different cage, I was the one in the cage.

And yet, Aurelia held Pete's hand without a thought and not mine.

My gaze drifts to the van again and the cage inside. It's where Isaac kept us when he wasn't taking Zeke apart piece by piece. The cage was no bigger than a large dog's—no room to stand, sit, or stretch my legs in. It got so uncomfortable at times that I longed for the sharp edge of Isaac's knife or his favorite—the volts of electricity when he tried to fry me from the inside out.

"Seth... You with me, buddy?"

I hear Khalil, but he sounds far away.

I'm not on our mountain anymore.

I'm on that cold metal table. I can feel the leather straps holding me down, biting into my torn, flayed, and charred skin. I can taste the blood, tears, and vomit in my mouth. I can hear Isaac telling me what an honor it is to be chosen as a sacrifice. I can see his face, a carbon copy of Zeke's father, and those soulless eyes staring down at me from under the single light that swings back and forth above like a pendulum.

You were born to die.

You were born to die.

You were born to die.

I was born to die.

I'd forgotten how dark it is here.

I'm back in the cage, and the bars are closing in on me. I push against them, and I'm back on the table. I scream from the pain of Isaac's knife, and I'm in the cage again. The cycle never ends—the pain, mutilation, and torture.

Wishing I were dead...

And it won't...not until we give in to Isaac.

Zeke has to die so that Isaac can live forever.

It's Zeke's penance for their father having an outside child with Zeke's mother, and immortality is the gift Thanatos offers Isaac in exchange for Zeke's sacrifice.

"Seth!" Khalil snaps. "Goddammit. I told you that you couldn't handle it!"

"Sunshine," I gasp. "I need Sunshine."

It's so so dark here.

If I don't see Aurelia in the next ten seconds, I can't promise I won't drown Zeke in the lake to *make it stop.*

Dropping to the ground, I curl Zeke's body in on itself because I can't convince my brain that we're not in that cage. The scars and burns on his arms, chest, and legs bite like they've split open again and we're bleeding.

I used to be able to handle the pain. It used to be all I knew, but then Sunshine…

"All right, Seth. Come on. I'll take you to her."

I can't move, so Khalil tries to take my arm, but I jerk away and bare my teeth before he can touch me. All I see is Isaac's hand holding the knife. Khalil's brown eyes flash with hurt, and I know all he can see is Zeke—his best friend—too broken to trust him. The sting of my rejection fades, and his tone is patient when he speaks.

"I won't hurt Zeke," he promises patiently and then pauses. "I won't hurt you either, Seth. I got you. I got you both."

I know.

I don't tell him that, though. Every time I try, the words get stuck in my throat.

He left Zeke all alone.

I can't trust him. What if he leaves again? Zeke doesn't need him. He has Bane and me.

I don't need him either.

I don't.

I don't, I don't, I don't.

Exhaling harshly, I shove past Khalil and leave him standing there in that disappointing silence as I enter the tent.

Aurelia's already sleeping off the drugs with Thorin curled around her front, so I strip off my shirt and lie down next to her to lend her my body heat. The jostling must stir her awake because her eyes open when I take her from Thorin and turn her to face me.

"Seth?" she asks groggily.

I bury Zeke's nose in her hair and ignore him pushing and clawing to take control. He's ready to wake up, but I'm not ready yet. I know he's curious about her, but it will be in vain.

I won't let him remember.

I know I promised Aurelia that I'd tell him about her, but I can't. She's mine. All mine.

"I'm here, Sunshine."

"What's wrong?" Her question is barely more than a sleepy rumble, but I still understand her.

Just like she apparently understands me.

"Nothing."

Her eyes blink open and slowly clear at whatever she sees in mine. "You sad, Seth?"

I hold her a little tighter and sigh when her peaches-and-daffodils scent hit me. "It's better now."

Khalil still hasn't come inside the tent, and I know it's because he's keeping watch. We're exposed out here, and me losing my shit a few minutes ago only reminded him of the threat of Isaac finding us.

If he's even still looking.

I'm starting to wonder at the real reason why we've never tried to know for sure. It wouldn't be hard, but the others swear it's too risky.

It's quiet in the tent, so I assume Aurelia's gone back to sleep until she does the last thing I ever thought possible.

She starts to sing.

I don't recognize the song, but then again, I don't recognize most songs. I don't really listen to the words anyway—something about love, memories, photographs, waiting, and coming home. It doesn't matter. She could be singing about toast, and I'd be completely gone for it. It's her voice that holds me.

It rises as the song's tempo picks up, and the tent flaps part as Khalil ducks inside. I don't look away from Aurelia, but I can only imagine the look on his face mirrors mine.

She's incredible.

A handful of verses later, the song is over.

"Oh, sure. Sing for him," Thorin grouchily says as he turns over in his sleeping bag and gives us his back.

Aurelia blushes and elbows him, but he's already sleeping again.

"Is that one of yours?" I ask.

She smiles lazily without opening her eyes. "'Photograph.' Ed Sheeran."

"You should sing us one of yours one day," Khalil low-key begs.

"Don't count on it. They're terrible."

"I'll love anything that's yours, Sunshine."

She shakes her head and sighs. "They're not mine. They never were. They belong to the countless songwriters my uncle trusted more than me to make a hit."

"Words are words. It was you that made them beautiful," Khalil says. "It was you. All you. All along. Every time. It was how you used those words to make people feel."

"Feel what?"

"Anything. Everything."

"Yeah, no offense to ol' Ed, but I doubt I'd like that song half as much if he were the one singing to me."

"Remind me to make you eat those words one day. He's pretty good."

"Nah. You're better," I say confidently. She still eyes us skeptically, so I start singing what I remember of my new favorite song—the Aurelia George version.

Aurelia squeals after only a few choppy notes and slaps her hands over my mouth. "Stop! You're butchering it."

I grin while kissing her cold palms, and I'm still smiling when she slowly drops them like she's afraid I'll start singing again. I waggle my brows. "See?"

"Okay, I get your point. Just don't ever do that again. Stick to dancing, Seth."

"Oh, yeah? You like the way I move, do you?" I suggestively press my hips against hers, and damn it, my dick twitches to life when she presses back against me like she's game for a quickie.

"Cut it out. Both of you," Khalil scolds. "She's not out of the woods yet. She needs to rest."

"Actually, I could use a little more body heat."

The tent is intensely quiet for a few seconds, and when Khalil's dumb ass doesn't catch on to what Aurelia is asking, my irritated gaze travels to him.

He seems to be caught in a trance, staring at Aurelia, but he must feel me watching him because his gaze shifts to me, and I buck my eyes.

His brows shoot up, and then he bolts into action, crawling from where he was lounging with his back against the tent's pole near the opening. His bloodstained shirt is already gone, and his skin is clean again as if he washed up in the lake.

When Thorin rolled over, he left a spot open that was just big enough for Khalil to fit. He slots right in, and I try to remember not to act jealous and possessive when he takes Aurelia in his arms, and she rolls right over to him.

Like the handsy asshole he is, Khalil starts rubbing on her ass even though he just told me to keep my hands to myself.

Rolling onto my back, I stare up at the ceiling. It's not dark yet, but it will be soon. Khalil's already set up a few chem lights around the tent so that I don't wake up in the dark and lose my shit again.

"Seth?" Aurelia asks. I can tell by her groggy tone that she's finally falling asleep after only a few minutes of Khalil massaging her butt.

Noted.

"Yeah, babe?"

"Are you okay now?" she asks in a tone that isn't mockingly sweet like she's taunted us with before. It's genuine.

Rolling over until I'm pressed against her backside, Khalil hisses and yanks his hand away when I inadvertently trap it between Aurelia's ass and my cock. Ignoring him, I kiss her bare arm. "Perfect," I answer just as earnestly.

"What happened?"

"Cages trigger him," Khalil answers because he knows I won't.

I can't.

My gaze travels from Aurelia to Khalil in silent thanks.

Aurelia stiffens at the answer, and when she speaks, I rub my eyes tiredly because fuck me, she's sounding wide awake again. None of us are going to sleep until we're sure she's out cold, and I'm tired as fuck. "Where did you find a cage?"

"Inside the van. I'm guessing it was for you."

Her head lifts from Khalil's arm where it had been resting, and she frowns. "Why would they have a cage for me? They couldn't have known we'd cross paths."

"Judging by the filthy blood and semen-stained mattress I also found inside, you weren't the first girl they drugged."

"And they live on this mountain?"

I can hear the fear in her voice, so I roll over to mold myself against her back before pressing a kiss to her shoulder.

"No. We're the only ones who live on this mountain, Sunshine."

"They're drifters," Khalil answers. "They were just passing through."

"Oh. Okay."

"By the way, we're never getting a dog," Thorin grumbles out of the fucking blue.

"I'm confused," Khalil snaps. "Are you sleeping or just being a dick pretending to?"

Thorin makes over-the-top snoring noises.

Aurelia's the only one who laughs, but I do crack a strained smile while Khalil rolls his eyes.

"Dick," he grumbles.

"Been a long time since we've snuggled for warmth, eh, Thor?"

"Shut up."

Aurelia giggles again. "You three are awfully close. Have you ever—"

"No," we all say at the same time.

"Well, there was that one time Thor lost a bet to Khalil." Which I only know because Zeke told me.

Aurelia gasps and sits up. "No way!"

"Yeah, well, sorry to disappoint you, but forget it," Thor snaps. "We're not talking about this. And as far as I'm concerned, it never happened. End of discussion."

"Wow," Aurelia dryly teases as she lies back down. "Touchy."

"It was a hand job," I blab. "Thor gave. Khalil received."

"Seth!" Thorin and Khalil bark.

I roll my eyes. "Big deal."

"How the hell do you know that anyway? Zeke was awake when it happened."

"He told me."

"Of all the things he could have shared, *that* was most important?"

"I don't write the reports, Khalil. I just read them."

"So, what was the bet?" Aurelia asks curiously.

"I bet him that I could hit a bull's-eye from a thousand feet away."

"All those years spent hunting for our food, and Khalil can't hit shit but put a hand job on the table, and suddenly he's Chris Kyle."

Snorting, I roll over onto my back and tuck my hands under my head. "Khalil reciprocated," I say.

He reaches over our girl and punches me hard as fuck in the stomach. I groan and curse as I roll over away from Aurelia and fold into the fetal position.

"So, I take that to mean it's not something you're interested in repeating?"

"Sorry, Goldilocks. It wasn't for me."

"Yeah, whatever. You liked it," Thorin taunts.

Khalil ignores him. "Anyway. We have you now. I don't have to settle for rough palms and no eye contact over there." He tosses a thumb toward Thorin, who flips him off.

"What about you, Seth?"

I let my eyes drift closed as I get comfortable again. "Pass."

"How do you know if you've never tried it?"

"Aurelia, baby, gorgeous, light of my life… Go the fuck to sleep."

My eyes are closed, but I can hear her pouting when she grumbles, "Fine."

I can tell it's morning by how unbearably goddamn cold it is.

When Thorin and Khalil rescued Zeke from Isaac's cult, and I got to experience life outside of constant torture and endless pain, I compiled a list of my favorite things and everything that I can't live without, even if the world ended tomorrow—Meat Lovers pizza, rap music, frappé, cute kittens, fantasy novels, Christmas, and cotton candy.

Lame, I know.

But waking up with Sunshine in my arms?

Top of the fucking list.

She rolled away from Khalil and back to me at some point, and the weight of her warm body pressed against mine was better than any soft pillow or warm blanket. I drift off again to the smell of her golden curls in my nose, and I'm not sure how long I'm asleep before I feel her pulling away again. It's probably Thorin or Khalil, and I'm too tired to fight them for her, so I let her go and fall asleep again.

"Where are you going?" I hear Khalil ask the next time I'm jarred awake.

"Nature calls," Aurelia answers.

Hearing the rustle of the sleeping bag, I peek my eyes open to see Aurelia slipping on my shirt that stops just under her butt. Khalil follows her out of the tent, and Aurelia doesn't argue like she did when I tried to escort her yesterday. She's either still exhausted or knows there's no point after her run-in with the drifters.

"Ooh! Ooh! It's cold! It's cold!" she squeals as soon as her bare feet touch the frozen ground. I can see her tits bouncing and her mostly naked ass, hopping around outside the tent.

Thorin jerks awake from all the noise she's making and sits up to snatch the crossbow resting against the tent wall next to him. "What is it? What's happened?"

"Nothing." Sitting up, I crack my back from sleeping on the uncomfortable ground and whisper, "Just Aurelia being dramatic."

Overhearing, she yells, "Shut up, Seth!"

Khalil lifts and carries Sunshine over to the fire, where I left her clothes out to dry. He sets her on the log, and she folds her legs against her chest while she watches Khalil shake out her boots.

Thorin stands, and I can see that his cock is hard when he walks out of the tent with the crossbow. The moment his bare foot touches the ground, he swears viciously.

"See?" Sunshine shouts.

Rolling my eyes, I'm tempted to go back to sleep, but I don't want to without Sunshine. And since no one *else* seems to care how fucking early it is, I get up and leave the tent too.

My gaze unwillingly travels to the blue van with the cage and dead bodies piled inside, but I look away just as quickly and focus on Aurelia. She's already watching me and holds out her hand with a small smile.

I pretend my stomach isn't doing somersaults as I take it, and the trembling in my hands immediately stops as I let her pull me to her. Sitting on the log next to her, I lean over, and she lets me kiss her good morning.

Aurelia even slips me her tongue and doesn't bitch about morning breath this time.

It once again reminds me that something huge happened on that lake, and I'm not sure how much longer I can wait patiently until Thorin and Aurelia clue Khalil and me in.

Once Khalil's done checking to make sure her clothes are dried completely, he helps her into them, and then they walk toward the trees, where they disappear from sight.

Thorin finishes getting dressed and stalks after them to relieve himself too.

I stare at the flickering fire and ignore my bladder as I count the seconds until Sunshine returns.

I make it to five before I say fuck it and follow them.

Aurelia and Khalil are only a few steps ahead of us. When she turns her head to see Thorin and me following, she says wryly, "Wow. An armed escort just to tinkle. I must be the luckiest bitch in the world."

"You should be used to it," Thorin returns. "Didn't you have bodyguards?"

"Yes, but *they* went away when I told them to."

Thorin hums but doesn't respond any more than that. He just tosses his arm over her shoulder when he catches up and whispers something in her ear before kissing her forehead.

Whatever it is makes her blush hard as fuck.

Aurelia finds a suitable bush for her needs after five fucking minutes of searching and then makes us turn around and cover our ears while she goes.

We return to camp after we've all gone, and Thorin whips up some instant coffee once we're all around the fire again. As usual, we all sip quietly and pretend it's good.

Well, all of us except for one.

"This has to be the worst coffee I've ever tasted," Aurelia remarks after taking a single sip.

"Yeah, it tastes like sand, but it warms you up."

"So, any reason we're hanging around instead of going home? It's bad enough we spent the night where a mass murder occurred. Don't you think we're pressing our luck?"

"Mass murder? That's a stretch."

Sunshine's incredulous gaze rises to meet mine. "You killed four people for no reason. How is that not a mass murder?"

"We had a reason," Thorin says, unbothered.

"A very good reason," Khalil adds.

"Besides, killing rarely makes sense to anyone but the person or people doing it."

"You sound obsessed. All of you."

"With you?" Khalil flirts. "Definitely."

Seeing that she's getting nowhere with this bullshit argument, Aurelia drops it with a roll of her eyes. She can feign sympathy all she wants, but I don't see her shedding tears for the drifters.

Aurelia doesn't care as much as she should that we killed them, and *that's* what bothers her most. We've seen her bloodthirsty need for vengeance firsthand, so Aurelia can't even claim she wouldn't have done the same had she known what they intended.

And we wouldn't believe her if she tried.

Sunshine pouts for a solid five minutes before I grab her hand and pull her down into my lap. Aurelia straddles me without a fight, and when she smiles softly at me, I'm struck with this intense longing to keep her there.

"I want to eat your ass so fucking bad," I say to her before I even realize it's on my mind.

On the other side of the fire, Thorin pauses sharpening his knife, and Khalil spits out his coffee and starts coughing.

Aurelia's eyes flare with want, and then she smirks as she rubs my chest. "Sure you're ready for that, virgin? It's not for everyone."

Lifting my face, I rub the tip of my nose with hers. "Are you forgetting that you deflowered me, Sunshine? Trust me. I'm ready."

"Hmm…"

"Don't even think about it," Thorin's cockblocking ass commands when he realizes Aurelia is considering it. "As much as we'd all love to see that, we don't have time for it. We need to clear these bodies out and clean the scene."

"Party pooper." I tap Aurelia's butt, and she climbs off my lap so I can stand and stretch. "So, what's the plan?"

Thorin thinks about it for a moment and then asks, "We still have that lye lying around?"

"Sure. I think so. What about the van?"

Khalil shrugs. "We wipe it down and do our job. We call it in. Let Sheriff Kelly see what those sick fucks were up to. It puts the heat on them and off us. He'll assume they ditched it and disappeared on their own."

I nod my agreement and then steal a peek at Aurelia to see where her head is with all of this.

She's gazing at nothing, and I doubt she's heard a word we said.

Edging a little closer, I place a hand on her hip. "You okay, Sunshine?"

"I'm hungry."

It's quiet for a moment, and then Khalil blinks and shakes his head. "Okay. New plan. We feed our girl, and *then* we dispose of the bodies."

Smiling, Aurelia sidles up to Khalil and wraps her arms around his neck. He grins down at her, and Thorin sighs heavily like he knows what she's about to say.

"I've changed my mind," she whispers to Khalil. "You're my fave."

I smirk when they start slobbering each other down while Thorin glowers at them. Jealous asshole. "Cheer up, Thor. I offered to eat her ass, and I'm still not her favorite."

Thorin and Khalil taught me a lot about the opposite sex but forgot to mention how fucking confusing they are.

As soon as Aurelia breaks her kiss with Khalil, Thorin seizes her hand and tugs her into him hard enough that she collides with his chest. Shoving his hand in her hair, he wraps his other arm around her waist. "Why do you continue to test me, wolf?"

"Because you like it, Thorin."

Sunshine rises onto the tips of her toes and pecks his lips once before pulling away. He lets her but tracks her every step as she walks away from him.

Eyeing the compound hunting bow, Aurelia lifts it from the ground. "What do you guys say I catch us breakfast this time?"

"We'll never eat," Thorin quips.

Aurelia's gaze cuts toward him, and then she goes for her pack that—judging by how fucking heavy it looks—Thorin must have put together for her. Aurelia says nothing as she grabs a handful of yellow arrows sticking out of the flap and leaves the camp.

"Where the hell are you going?" Thorin shouts after her.

Turning around to face us while walking backward toward the trees, she yells back, "To catch some rabbits, you asshole!"

Cursing, Thorin snatches up his crossbow from where it is resting next to their packs before following after her.

"You'd think the two days they spent alone fucking and hunting would have helped them get along," Khalil remarks.

"I'm pretty sure being at each other's throats is how they flirt, Khalil."

He grunts, and then his brows rise as he watches Thorin stomp after Aurelia. "Yeah, I think you might be right."

My gaze flicks toward the van, and I say, "But just in case, you should go with them. Make sure they both come back in one piece."

Khalil thinks about it for a moment and then sets aside the canteen he was drinking out of. "Right again." He stands and takes one step before pausing to peer at me carefully. "You good here, Seth?"

I make a show of sitting down and getting comfortable. "Of course."

Khalil hesitates a moment longer before making a decision and holding out his fist for a pound as he goes.

I give him what he wants and then watch over my shoulder as Khalil stalks through the trees where Aurelia and Thorin disappeared moments before. I wait a little longer to make sure they're gone, and after a full minute passes, I suck in all the air my lungs can handle and exhale as I stand from the log.

Inching over to the van, I don't give myself time to back out when I reach it.

The moment I yank open the rear doors, the stench of death and rotting bodies hits me before I even notice the cage. Khalil stacked them on top of the filthy twin mattress that's stuffed between the cage and the cabin. The one I killed for stabbing Aurelia stares back at me through unseeing blue eyes.

Finally, I let my gaze travel to the black bars of the cage and the cramped space between them.

It's the same size as the one Isaac kept Zeke in.

Seeing no lock, I curl my hands around the bars on the door and pull. When it creaks open, I take one last look over my shoulder for Aurelia, Thorin, or Khalil, and then I climb back inside my cage.

My nose starts bleeding the moment the cage door closes behind me, but I wipe it away and ignore what it means.

I have to do this.

For Sunshine. For me.

For Ezekiel, Thorin, and Khalil too.

I thumb the scar from an old puncture wound in the center of Zeke's right palm, and like nerves that connect, the one on my neck throbs. Those scars are from the few that Isaac didn't cause, yet are the ones that hurt the most.

I have to prove to myself that I'm not a danger to them.

God, it smells awful in this van.

I lean my head against the bars and take small breaths only.

Death is a friend. Pain is my enemy.

No.

I feel my hands quake with the need to reach for the knife hidden in my boot. If Thorin or Khalil knew I had it, they'd tie me up and tell me it was for my own good.

Maybe.

But I wouldn't believe them.

Isaac may not have succeeded in converting Zeke—in convincing him to sacrifice himself for his brother's immortality—but he did succeed in making Zeke want to die.

Zeke's pain is so great that it bleeds over to me, and when the worst of it hits, I have no choice but to do what I was born for. Outside of Isaac's compound, there's no physical pain to take for him, only the one that torments his mind and soul.

I've tried to end it for Zeke many times, but Khalil and Thorin are always there, getting in the way. And when I nearly succeeded the last time, Bane stopped me.

Meddlesome fuckers.

That's all past me now. I won't let Isaac win, and not because it doesn't hurt anymore. It will always hurt. Pain lingers on the edges of our minds, waiting to strike the moment we remember it's there.

Sunshine makes it better. With every smile and every touch, the shadows retreat a little further.

Maybe I should let Zeke meet her. Maybe I should let him see.

But not yet.

I'm not ready for her to look at this face we share and see anyone but me. And maybe that's selfish, but I don't care.

Somehow, I fall asleep among the rotting corpses. Perhaps because I once felt kindred with them. A walking, talking, rotting corpse.

I'm still dozing when I hear the others returning.

Khalil murmurs something, and then Aurelia says more clearly, "Green doesn't look good on you, Khalil. Don't hate."

"Ain't nobody hating. I'm just saying that it was a lucky shot."

"Anyway." I imagine Sunshine rolling her eyes. "Where's Seth?"

My cheeks flush when I realize I'm still in the cage. I hadn't meant to fall asleep or let them find me like this. I'd planned to be lounging by the campfire, waiting for their return with a smile in place, like this cage hadn't nearly set me back nine years.

"I don't know. He was here when I left."

"Look, there's his pack. Seth!" Thorin calls for me.

I don't answer because I don't want them to find me in here. Those two fuckers will never let it go, and Sunshine...

No, I can't let her see me like this.

As if she hears my thoughts, she yells for me. "Seth!"

"Seth, you here?"

"Check the tent," Thorin orders.

A few seconds pass, then Aurelia says, "He's not in there."

"Where would he have gone?"

"I don't know. Seth!"

"Shit," Khalil swears. "You don't think—"

Thorin growls, "Isaac."

Shit. This is really getting out of hand, isn't it? I still don't leave the cage.

"How the fuck could they have found us?"

"I don't know. Start looking for tracks. We weren't gone that long. If we leave now, we can catch up."

"I'm coming with you," Sunshine says.

"Like hell you are," Khalil snaps.

"Like hell you are," she mocks. "I'm coming."

"This isn't a game. We're not hunting rabbits. Isaac is dangerous, Aurelia. We know what we're walking into. You don't."

"Don't give me that bullshit, Thorin. Am I one of you or not?"

"Why the hell are we wasting time arguing?" Khalil snaps. "We need to go get Seth!"

Seth.

Not Ezekiel.

I rub my chest and try not to be so easily won over.

"Why are you yelling at me? Seth doesn't even like you like that."

"Really, wolf?"

"Fine. I'll go get him." I hear snow crunching as if Aurelia is indeed leaving the camp.

"You don't even know where the hell you're going!"

"Are you coming or not?"

I raise my brows higher and higher as I listen to them bicker and turn on each other at the very thought of me being gone.

"Can we stop and think first, Aurelia?"

"No! They're getting away."

"And what is your plan of attack, hmm?"

In a voice so cold it sends chills down my spine and raises goose bumps everywhere else, Aurelia answers, "Attack."

"You were just crying over us doing the same when we thought you were taken."

"That was yesterday. Why are you always bringing up old shit, Thorin?"

"It was literally two hours ago when you called us mass murderers."

Unable to hold in my laughter anymore, I push open the cage door and crawl from the van. Luckily, the three of them are so busy arguing with one another that they don't notice me right away.

"This is so fucking stupid," Khalil says.

"I agree." Aurelia, Khalil, and Thorin whirl to face me at the sound of my voice. "I'm right here."

"Seth?" Khalil asks when he notices my hunched posture from the cage and the melancholy I haven't completely bounced back from.

"It's me," I admit reluctantly.

That wariness fades when I see his relief, and I wonder, is it because Isaac doesn't have me or that I'm not Zeke?

Aurelia rushes forward and throws herself at me. I catch her and kiss her forehead repeatedly while she stares up at me with too many questions in her eyes.

"Where were you?" Khalil demands.

"I was here."

"*Where?*"

"Here. Let's just leave it at that." Khalil doesn't look happy about it, but he thankfully drops it. "So, what's for breakfast?"

Thorin lifts the huge snake he's holding, and I make a face. Not my favorite game, but it will do.

"Damn, you caught that, Sunshine?"

She nods proudly. "Yup! Khalil scared it out of its hole, and I shot it on the first try."

"Mm-hmm. Wow."

Thorin is raising his canteen to his lips when my questioning gaze meets his over Aurelia's head. He pauses, his lips pursing as he gives a subtle shake of his head.

I cough to suppress my laugh.

I'd seen him sneaking a couple of arrows out of Aurelia's pack when he grabbed his crossbow earlier, so I figured it was more likely that he made the shot and hyped our girl up by letting Aurelia take the credit.

Thorin sips his water but chokes on it when Aurelia rests her head against my chest and says, "I saw that, Thorin."

He swiftly changes the subject. "All right. We have bodies to bury, team. Let's eat so we can get this over with."

CHAPTER THIRTY-FOUR

KHALIL

"Hand me that foot, would you, Sunshine?"

Aurelia gags as she lifts Pete's severed right foot from the black tarp and offers it to Seth. "I think I'm going to be sick."

Holding the head of the man who tried to take what was ours, I finally succeed in pulling out a particularly stubborn upper molar with pliers, and then my gaze flicks toward Aurelia. "I told you to wait in the tent."

"You also tried to leave me at the cabin when we picked up the supplies, and my answer is the same, Khalil." Her bravado falters when Thorin tosses a torso onto the tarp, adding it to the growing pile of limbs. "I just don't understand how this happened," she says quietly. "Pete seemed so nice."

"There's no such thing as a nice guy," Thorin remarks as he stands and wipes the blood from his hands with the cloth hanging from his back pocket. "There are only wolves and wolves in sheep's clothing."

"My dad was nice," Aurelia counters proudly.

"Oh, yeah?" Thorin laughs dryly. "Tell me about him. What did he do for a living?"

Her brows dip. "He drove trucks."

"And before that?"

"Sold drugs," she mumbles reluctantly. "But—"

"You don't need to defend him to me, wolf. He loved you, and you loved him. That's all that matters. What he did to survive and to provide doesn't mean he wasn't a good man. He just wasn't a nice guy."

"And they're different?"

"Very."

For some reason, Aurelia looks at me. Maybe she thinks I'm less jaded than Thorin because she asks, "What do you think, Khalil? Do you agree with Thorin that nice guys don't exist?"

I don't respond right away.

I'm stuck thinking about my own dad, who I haven't seen or spoken to in nine years other than the occasional letter so that he doesn't think I'm dead—sans return address, of course.

My dad is a religious man, a family man, and a workaholic. He's quick to smile, works every day at the construction company he built from nothing, pays his taxes and tithes on time, takes care of my mom, took care of me, and is a respected member of the community.

Does that mean he doesn't have skeletons in his closet?

I can't bring myself to say no and believe it.

Before Zeke disappeared, before the three of us ran to this corner of nowhere, before Aurelia, I never saw myself doing any of the things I've done. There's still a chance we'll leave this mountain one day. I could get married, have kids, start sitting at a desk at some dead-end job, and be on a first-name basis with my neighbors. And no one, except my brothers, will ever know the atrocities we committed before that.

I once thought I was a nice guy—a normal guy.

Ripping the last molar out of Jonah's mouth, I toss his decomposing head onto the pile and watch it roll, feeling nothing but a bone-deep satisfaction that I kept my woman safe.

Apparently I'm not a nice guy.

"I think if there are, they won't stay that way for long."

"Hmm. I'm afraid to ask. Seth?"

My gaze travels to him in time to see him shudder. "I've never met a nice guy."

"What about me?" Aurelia asks. "Do you think I'm nice?"

"I think you're perfect."

Aurelia glowers at his attempted evasion. "That doesn't answer my question."

Seth steps down from the log where he had been twirling Sam's head on his finger like a basketball. "Is that what you want, Sunshine? To be a good girl?"

She doesn't even have to think about it. "No. God, no. Tried that. Hated it."

"Ah. You want to be bad."

Aurelia bites into her lip and gives the smallest nod.

Seth crouches in front of her where she sits cross-legged on the blanket he laid out for her as if we're at a picnic. "I picked flowers for you, you know."

"Really?" Her brown eyes brighten. "Where are they?"

"They died."

"Oh." Aurelia looks faintly amused as she stares back at Seth. "Well, it's the thought that counts, I guess."

"This is better." Seth holds out the head he's still holding.

Aurelia's brows shoot up. "You're giving me a severed head?"

"I was thinking that once all the skin falls off, we can turn it into a vase. To hold all the flowers I promise to pick for you again."

Thorin and I make eye contact when Aurelia's gaze softens, and she nervously takes the head from him. "Seth... I love it."

"Aurelia, you can't keep the head," I tell her.

"Why not?"

"Because it's evidence?"

"But, Khalil—"

"I said no, baby."

Seth leans over and whispers something to her that I can't hear, and Aurelia giggles. When her eyes find mine before flicking away when she sees me watching, I know those bitches are talking about me.

I'm still staring at her when Aurelia hands the head back to Seth and stands. I don't look away as she walks over to me and places her hand on my right shoulder.

My hands are covered in blood, so I don't touch her, but God, I want to.

Instead, I hold very still and let her do what she wants to me. Aurelia moves to stand behind me, and then her other hand finds my left shoulder and starts massaging.

"You're tense, Khalil. Did I do something?"

"No."

"*Can* I do something?"

Fuck it.

Reaching behind me, I pull Aurelia back around to my front, where I can see her. "You can start by telling me what the hell happened on that ice. What changed, Aurelia?"

Thorin pauses from loading the body parts into the steel vat that we plan to turn into a pressurized cooker, using lye to dissolve the bodies. It won't be pretty. There's any number of things that could cause the sheriff to suspect foul play, but there's nothing to link us back to the drifters, so it won't matter.

But if the cops find even one hair of Aurelia's, we're fucked.

"What do you mean?"

Thorin, not as willing to be coy, answers, "Aurelia and I made a deal."

"What kind of deal?"

"I agreed to stay and be yours on the condition that I'm no longer a prisoner."

"Okay…"

"That means the tracker comes off, and the punishments stop."

"How do we know you won't run?"

"You don't. You just have to trust me."

"Trust you…"

"Like I'm trusting you not to make me regret it."

"And if we say yes?" Holding her hips, I lean forward and kiss her belly. "That means you're ours, Goldilocks—no bullshit, no tricks, and no take backs. You're in this one hundred percent until the day you die and every day after because just try to stop us from following you. All of you, Goldilocks. We want everything."

Aurelia and Thorin exchange a look, and then he smirks. "Told you."

"Yes, Khalil," Aurelia says softly. She places bloodstained hands on my cheeks and then leans forward to kiss me. "I'm yours."

Unable to resist, I pull her into my lap. "Are you sure you're ready for that?"

"Do you really care if I am?"

A nice guy would.

But I'm not a nice guy.

"Seth, bring me the tool bag." While Seth gets the tools, I stand and let Aurelia take my place on the log. When he brings it over, I remove the smallest screwdriver from the bag and unscrew the metal cuff.

It falls into the snow with a thud, and I hold Aurelia's gaze as I massage the tender flesh around her ankle. I remember what I said to her after I put it on the first time.

"Does it hurt?"

"Yes."

"Good."

I remember the conflicted look in her eyes when the tracker was locked in place, and she realized she could run but couldn't hide from us—when she knew she was trapped. She wanted it but resented the feeling.

There's only one emotion present now.

"You want something, Aurelia. Do you want to tell me, or do you want me to take it?"

"I said that I am yours, Khalil. You can do whatever you want to me. I won't fight you."

"Not even a little?"

Warmed by the fire, she's not wearing her coat, so I can see her nipples harden through her shirt. "Well, maybe a little."

She smiles, but I don't return it because it feels like I'm being pulled in two directions—the need to take her up on her offer and the need to protect her from me. From all of us. She's mine now, so it comes as no surprise that the latter proves the stronger urge.

"In that case, you're going to need a safe word," I say. And then I direct my next statement to everyone. "No more playing without one."

Thorin and Seth both meet my gaze and nod their agreement.

"Okay…" Despite her agreement, Aurelia frowns in confusion. I can see the question she doesn't want to let herself ask.

Jesus. She has no fucking idea what I mean.

"The way we play comes with risks," I explain. "It can be dangerous. For you and for us. If you get scared or reach your limit and want to stop, a safe word ensures that happens."

"It helps to pick a word you wouldn't normally use in a sentence," Thorin says.

Understanding dawns in Aurelia's wide eyes. "Okay. Umm…" She looks around. "Tree," she says and then immediately winces.

I bit into my bottom lip to keep from laughing. "Try again, baby."

Her eyes travel over my shoulder once more, and she wrinkles her nose. "Eyeball?"

My hands travel over her thick and soft thighs. "Maybe something less gory."

She's quiet for a few moments. "Crucible," she says and though her chosen safe word clearly carries more than one purpose, I nod.

"Perfect. Thorin?" I ask without looking away from Aurelia.

"Cashew," he says since he hates them.

"Seth?"

"Umbra."

I barely keep from rolling my eyes. "And mine will be double Dutch," I announce as I stand and help Aurelia to her feet. I pinch her chin between my thumb and forefinger and tilt her head back to meet my eyes. "Don't forget yours, Goldilocks. We're trusting you to use it whenever you need it. No other word will stop us. Understand?"

"Yes."

I hear Thorin sliding the lid of the vat into place, and I look over my shoulder to see the tarp has been cleared. Seth is folding it up while Thorin secures the barrel.

"We done here?" I've never been so eager to get home before.

"Yeah." Thorin glances up at the gray sky, and I do too. "But it's going to rain soon. We should stay another night."

"I never want to see another dead body again," Aurelia says when we enter the tent with Seth a few hours later. She drops down on Thorin's sleeping bag with a groan since he decided to do some reconnaissance before bed instead of joining us.

It's taken us all day to dispose of the drifters and clean the scene, and now we're all exhausted, cold, and moody as hell.

"Now that you're one of us, you might see a few more."

I smile when she glares at me, but the scowl slowly fades after a few seconds when I pull my hair from the tie.

I took my braids out when we bathed earlier, using water from the frozen lake, so my curly hair is now wet and loose around my shoulders. Aurelia eyes me like I'm a piece of meat, which makes me want to drop to my knees and worship her. It's been a long time since a woman has looked at me like that, and I never particularly noticed it then as much as I do when it's Aurelia.

"What?"

"Nothing. I was just wondering… Who braids your hair?"

"I do. And Thorin when I can convince him." When she raises her brows in surprise, I laugh and answer the question before she can ask it. "We don't even have a TV, Goldilocks. We've had a lot of time on our hands over the last decade, and we get bored a lot. I taught myself, and then I taught Thorin. It was just another way to pass the time."

"What about Zeke?"

"He tried, but could never sit still long enough to learn."

"I see," she answers simply and then goes back to ogling my hair. "I could braid it for you sometime. If you want."

"I want," I answer quickly.

Aurelia leans back on her elbows as she fights a smile and loses. It's small but flirty and spreads the longer we stare at one another. Seth crawls onto the bedroll next to her and places a hand on her naked thigh since all she's wearing is one of my spare shirts.

"Khalil's got a nice body, doesn't he, Sunshine?"

"Yeah," she says with an appreciative sigh. Her gaze becomes unfocused again but never leaves my body, even as Seth traces shapes higher and higher on her thigh.

"Look at those abs," Seth coos when his hand disappears up the shirt's hem. Aurelia sucks in a breath while staring at my stomach, and I know he's touching her pussy. "I bet you want to see more…" Her gaze shifts to meet Seth's, and a divot between her brows appears, but I can't see what he's doing to her under that fucking shirt. "Don't you?"

"Yes."

"I've got a better idea," I say as I drop to my knees on the sleeping mats in front of them. "Lift your shirt and spread your legs."

Aurelia hesitates when her nerves overcome her and even tries to change the subject. "W-where's Th-Thorin?"

"He went to make sure you're safe," Seth answers. "Now, do as Khalil says."

Gaze dropping, she reaches for the hem and lifts it slowly. She peers up at me with a guilty expression when it clears her pussy, and I can finally see two of Seth's fingers already lodged deep inside.

"Is this what you wanted to see?" Seth asks me.

"Hell yeah."

"You see how sexy you are?" he asks Aurelia as he casually tunnels his fingers in and out. I fall into a trance as I watch his fingers sink inside and her lower lips part for him. Her pussy is so wet that if I closed my eyes, I would still know every time he pushed them deep and withdrew to do it again. "Khalil's drooling, baby. He wants to taste you more than anything." When she parts her legs even more at the thought of my mouth on her, Seth adds a third finger, and she whimpers. "One day soon, I'm going to give you all five. Would you like that?"

"All f-f-five?" Aurelia stutters. "You mean…" At Seth's grave nod, Aurelia snaps her legs closed, and I pry them right back open. Her panicked gaze bounces between us before settling on the person who caused her distress. "Seth Cura, I will not under any circumstances allow you to *fist* me."

Seth hums his amusement at her refusal while I distract Aurelia by lifting my shirt over her head. She wears our clothes so damn well that I never want to see her in anything else. Well, except for that costume that makes her look like a dirty milkmaid. Jesus, she even has the jugs for it.

Her breasts are bared for us now, and Seth wastes no time wrapping his lips around her nipple. He traps it between his teeth, and Aurelia jerks when he pulls her nipple taut, stretching it out until her mouth falls open.

"Oh, fuck. Seth."

She shoves her fingers in his hair and grips the strands tight, but her gaze flies to me when I lie down on my stomach between her thighs and yank her wide hips closer to me. Sensing what I'm after, Seth removes his hand from between her legs to palm her other tit with his wet fingers.

Aurelia looks nervous all of a sudden. "Khalil?"

"Tell me again that you're really ours," I demand.

Seth frees her nipple from his teeth to stare down at her while he waits for her answer too. Aurelia swallows, and I worry for a moment that she's going to take it all back. Or that I was dreaming earlier when she said it.

"I'm yours."

My tongue darts out, and I lick her clit. "No more running?"

"I'm yours," she repeats with a desperate lilt, and I flick her clit a second time. "You sure?"

The last thing I expect is for her to release Seth's hair and grab mine with a vicious pull that brings my mouth closer to her sex. "Do not tease me, Khalil."

Damn.

"Give it to her," Seth urges as he pries her fingers from my hair and moves behind her. "She's earned it."

Yes, she has.

Palming the back of her thighs, I fold her legs in half until her ass and pussy are upturned, and then I dive in with a growl.

"Khalil, fuck," Aurelia yelps at the first swipe of my tongue. "Ohmygod, ohmygod, ohmygod…"

Knowing that she's been aching for it all day, I don't ease her into it.

No more teasing.

No more fucking waiting.

I swirl my tongue through her arousal while I rip open my pants and pull my dick out for some relief. When my mouth returns to her clit, her thighs tense, and her head drops back on Seth's abs.

"Nah. Watch him eat that pussy."

Peering up, I see Seth gripping her hair, keeping her head up and lust-drunk gaze on me as I devour her cunt. She's still fighting it, and since I can't have that, I sit up, lifting Aurelia's hips as I go until her body is suspended in the air like a bridge between Seth and me. Her head rests on Seth's shoulder now while her legs drape mine.

Only then do I ease my tongue inside her pussy, and as I expected, her body convulses, and she tries to stop me from tongue fucking that pussy but can't.

She's completely at our mercy.

With Seth's help holding her up and her legs wrapped around my neck, I'm even able to stroke my dick while I worship our girl. She's so fucking sweet. Her scent fills my nose until it becomes impossible for me to want her more than I do now.

The sounds she makes as I feast on her pushes me too close to the edge, and just as I'm about to fall, she comes with the sharpest cry, and I let go of my dick to keep her secure and safe while she loses herself to the feeling.

I'm still kissing and licking and taking everything she gives me when she finally settles.

Carefully, I set Aurelia's limp body on the sleeping bag and gesture for Seth to join me. There's a quizzical furrow on his brow as he crawls down the sleeping bag and sprawls on his side next to me.

"Goldilocks," I call once he's in place. She's already half asleep but becomes more alert when I say, "We're going to go again."

"What?" She snaps her legs closed. "No. I can't. I—"

"Seth needs to learn."

"But—"

"Are we going to have to tie you down?"

Shivering at my firm tone, there's a sparkle of excitement in her eyes when she shakes her head and relaxes.

"Open that pussy up for Seth, sweetheart."

Aurelia does what I ask and hooks her arms under her knees before pulling her legs wide. Her lower lips spread like flower petals, and Seth swears.

"God, it's so pretty."

"Yes, it is, and it's yours to eat, Seth."

Sensitive after her orgasm, Aurelia jerks when Seth steals his first taste. His eyes bug in alarm, and then he looks up at me to see if he did something wrong.

"She'll get over it. Keep going."

"Okay."

"Hold your fucking legs open," I bark when I notice Aurelia trying to ease them closed.

"You're torturing me," she whines.

"Legs open, mouth shut," I amend. "Go ahead, Seth."

He licks her pussy again, and Aurelia's body trembles, but she doesn't complain. Her eyes are closed, and her head is turned away as she holds her thighs open for Seth and lets him have his way. He takes his time exploring her while I palm the back of Seth's head as he feasts on her, directing him where to go and controlling how much pressure he applies.

"Like this?"

"Yeah, you're doing so good, Seth. You see all that cream leaking out of our girl's pussy?" He nods. "That's for you. Lick it up."

Seth is a quick learner, so I let go of his head, and he groans before putting his whole face in it. Stroking my dick, I watch him lap at her pussy without mercy. Whenever I feel my balls tighten, I slow my strokes, keeping myself on the brink, but I don't let myself come.

Finally, Aurelia breaks her stubborn silence, wailing so loud a wolf howls in the distance, and I nearly blow my load like an amateur.

"Oh, God, yes. Seth!" I smirk when he attacks her clit, and she starts throwing that pussy at him. "Right there, right there, right there. Fuck!" Aurelia's back bows, and she comes again while Seth continues to kiss her pussy. When her lush body relaxes, and her beautiful brown skin is coated in a sheen of sweat, Aurelia raises a languid hand and pushes Seth's head away. "Seth, baby, please," she pleads breathlessly.

He sits up and stares down at her like she's too good to be true.

I know the feeling.

Rising to my knees and moving behind him, I undo Seth's pants before reaching inside and pulling his dick out. He's already hard, but I give it a couple of quick tugs before guiding him to our girl's swollen pussy. Seth flexes his hips once he's in place and sinks inside her with a groan that vibrates through his body and mine.

"Jesus, she's so fucking tight."

"I know."

And to think, she's all ours…

To ruin as we will.

"Fuck her good, brother," I whisper to him so she can't hear. "I want her spent and so high on orgasms she can't think straight."

"Yeah?"

"Yeah." I move my hand so Seth can get balls deep, and then I reclaim my dick.

I can't stop thinking about the night I fucked her while she pretended to be asleep. I never thought it'd be my kink, but here I am, dying to do it again.

I watch over Seth's shoulder as he does as I ask and rides her hard. He pounds that pretty pussy to a lovely red pulp, but any sound Aurelia makes is trapped under the hand Seth has around her throat. He pins her to the tent's floor and makes her take it while she holds on to his hips and asks for more.

"God, you…fuck it so…good, baby," Seth babbles. "Wish I could…take you with me…when I…sleep. Just you and me, Sunshine. Would you like that? Huh? We could make each other feel so…fucking…good."

Aurelia mewls, her heavy breasts bouncing and swaying from the rough movements. I fall into a trance as I watch the two of them. I'm still watching them when Seth's thrusting hips stutter to a stop, and he comes with a hoarse shout.

He doesn't move until he's done unloading his cum, and then he drops onto his bedroll beside her to catch his breath. Since Seth came so quickly, Aurelia is still awake, though barely.

It bodes well that she's not tapping out early like before. With three cocks to service, Aurelia needs to be able to take more than she can handle.

Got to get that pussy used to us.

Shoulder to shoulder, Aurelia and Seth share a lazy kiss while he reaches over to play with her pussy.

I'm a patient man, so I move to lie on her other side, but Seth has other plans.

"Go sit on Khalil's cock. I want you to keep it warm while you suck me off."

Jesus.

Before I can reach for her—because fuck yes to that plan—Aurelia crawls on top of me, and we share a passionate kiss with no end in sight, even when our lips are swollen and raw.

With her mouth still fused to mine, she reaches for the hard, hot length trapped between us and begins stroking my dick as she asks, "You're going to fuck me when I pass out, aren't you?"

"Yes."

She moans brokenly, and I can feel her leaking all over me as I turn her around to face Seth. He's standing over us now, soft cock in hand as he lazily strokes it back to hard.

Aurelia places her hand on my abs as she lifts her hips and guides me to her. Looking over her shoulder, Aurelia holds my gaze as she slowly sinks down on me. My toes immediately curl, feeling her warm, tight walls hug me like a glove. I can feel Seth there, too, easing the way.

Her lashes lower when her pussy flutters around me, and then she moans. "Oh, God, Khalil. Yes."

"Goldi—" I grunt, my head falling back when she stuffs more of me inside her little cunt. "Fuck."

Aurelia stops just shy of taking all of me, and then her focus leaves me as she turns back to Seth and reaches for him.

Seth swats her hand away from his cock and says, "All the way down."

"But—"

"Aurelia."

They have a staring contest, and when Seth quirks a brow, I feel my dick being swallowed by more of her warmth.

Aurelia makes a startled sound because I'm fucking hung, and then Seth says, "Good fucking girl. How does that dick feel?"

"He's so hard."

My dick twitches inside her pussy, because, yeah, I am.

"That's for you, Sunshine. Do you know what you do to us?"

Aurelia shakes her head.

"You make us wish we could go back in time…find you sooner," I answer. "Nine years without you, Goldilocks."

"That's three thousand three hundred and fifty-five days too long," Seth says. He's a fucking whiz at math, so he probably added it down to the day we left, accounting for leap years and all.

Had we met Aurelia even a moment sooner, we would have dragged her along with us to this corner of nowhere. She would have been our captive no matter how we met.

"Well, you have me now, so don't fuck it up," she warns as she begins to bounce on my dick. The movement causes her tits to jiggle, so she holds them up with both palms.

Seth's gaze snaps to them and heats. I can see the moment he shifts gears.

Spitting in his palm, Seth strokes himself, getting his long cock nice and wet before he slips right in, slotting his long, veiny cock between her gorgeous tits. Aurelia moans from Seth fucking her tits and starts riding me faster. Seth's eyes glow with excitement as he stares down at her. She's literally his every fantasy come true. She's all of ours and more perfect than even we could have imagined.

"Stick out your tongue, beautiful."

Aurelia does as he asks, and the bulbous head of his cock slides across the tip of her flattened tongue on his next upstroke. Aurelia doesn't make a sound, but I can feel her reaction the moment she tastes the salty tip. Her pussy strangles my dick so hard that we both become paralyzed from it.

"Shit, fuck, shit, fuck, shit, fuck." Squeezing my eyes closed, I try to ride through it without coming because I have my own fantasy that I am still waiting to make a reality.

When Seth groans, I open my eyes again to the sight of Aurelia's head bobbing up and down as she sucks him off now. I'm content to watch them for a little while, but then something green and acidic rises in my chest, and I skim a hand over her plump ass.

"Goldilocks."

It's all that needs to be said.

Her wide hips start moving again as she deepthroats Seth, and just like that, I'm placated. I'm a demanding, jealous bastard, but Aurelia has proven time and again more than capable of managing us.

She's a little too fucking good at it, but right now, control is the last thing I care about.

Seth is no better.

I can see the three words he's practically itching to say, but his next breath punches out of him. Aurelia releases his cock, and she must hold out her tongue for him to deposit his load because I can see his arm furiously pumping as he comes.

The moment Seth's done, he stumbles back a couple of steps. His legs are no longer capable of holding him up, and he falls on his ass.

Rising to my knees and bringing Aurelia with me, I wrap my arm around her waist to keep me inside her and grab her chin. Turning her face around, I tongue her down before she can swallow, and just as I suspected, it makes her ravenous.

She sobs into my mouth and starts bouncing on my dick again.

Our knees dig into the sleeping bag as I return her eager thrusts. Across from us, Seth is sprawled out with his softening cock lying on his thigh. He watches us swap his salty cum through lowered lids, his glistening abs contracting as he tries to catch his breath.

"You're a fucking slut for our cocks, aren't you, Aurelia?"

Her inhale is sharp, and then she's nodding rapidly. "Oh, God, yes," she admits on a gasp. "Yes. Don't stop. Don't stop. Don't stop."

"Are you our whore?" I ask her. When she nods, I decide that's not good enough. I stop fucking her and tighten my arm around her waist so that she can't use me either. My voice is thicker with my complete obsession for her as I ask, "Are you my girl, Goldilocks?"

"Yes, Khalil." She turns her head to nuzzle her face against mine as the rain relentlessly patters the tent. "I'm your girl."

"For how long?"

"Always."

"And forever?"

When she nods with her eyes closed, I know she's close to giving me what I want. I start fucking her again. And harder this time. I screw another orgasm out of Aurelia, and she passes out in my arms before the last wave passes.

Feeling my balls tighten, I kiss her sweaty shoulder before bending her over. Her soft cheek rests on the bedroll while I lift her hips a little. When she's in the perfect position for fucking, I pull out before slowly easing back inside.

I fuck her with a few shallow pumps to make sure she's well and truly out of it, and then I snap my hips and see stars the moment my balls touch her pussy.

Throwing my head back, I mindlessly pound in and out of her.

I'm rough.

Maybe too rough, and that's what makes it so perfect.

I fuck her however the hell I want. She'll be a little sore in the morning, but I'll take care of that too. I'll always take care of her needs.

Unfortunately, I've been edging myself the entire time Seth and Aurelia played, so I don't last.

The tent opens just as I'm dumping my load inside her unprotected pussy, and when I look over my shoulder, I see Thorin stalking inside. He's soaking wet from the rain, and it looks like the walk hasn't done shit to his mood or pent-up energy.

Finished coming, I roll over onto my back and leave Aurelia where she is. Face down, ass up.

My hand pets her flank appreciatively while Thorin's gaze beelines to her pussy, his blue eyes flaring with heat when he notices mine and Seth's cum seeping out.

"Don't waste it," he snaps.

Rolling my eyes, I reach over and plug her cunt with two fingers to keep our seed from spilling out.

Kinky, paranoid fucker wants her knocked up badly.

It doesn't matter to Thorin who gets it done. He wants her barefoot and pregnant and completely at our beck and call.

Aurelia still has no idea.

She doesn't know the half of what she's signed up for, but she thinks she does, and it almost makes me feel sorry for her. We're all too much of a selfish bastard to warn her.

"How was your walk?" Seth asks as he crawls into one of the sleeping bags.

Thorin quickly sheds his wet clothes. "Almost froze my nuts off."

"Lucky you. We've got the perfect place to warm your cock." Seth reaches over and draws Aurelia into his arms. He kisses her forehead and then shifts her around until she's facing him. Lifting her leg in invitation, he props it on his hip. The position leaves her pussy exposed. Room enough for Thorin to slot his cock right in.

Thorin doesn't look away as he sheds the last of his clothes.

His dick is already half hard when he climbs onto the sleeping bag behind her while I move to lie at our girl's feet. Anything comes through that tent, and they'll have to get through me to get to her.

Thorin isn't put off by our mingled cum.

He swipes the head of his dick back and forth through the mess we made, and the sound of our desires is obscene in the quiet tent. Finally, when he's fully hard, he lines up his cock with Aurelia's warm hole and eases inside. Aurelia's lips part with a gasp, and her fingers dig into Seth's arm as Thorin sinks himself to the hilt.

He must hit a spot too deep because Aurelia wakes with a start. "Hmm… wha…?"

"Shh," Seth immediately soothes. "It's just Thorin, Sunshine. Open up for him."

"Thorin?"

"I'm here, wolf. Go back to sleep."

Aurelia sighs in contentment and then blinks tired eyes as they peer through the darkness before finding me lying at her feet.

"Was I good?"

Aw, fuck me. "Yeah, baby." Crawling the short distance over to her, I kiss her deeply while she still tastes like Seth. "Thank you for being so perfect. Now, do as Thorin says."

Aurelia drops her head back on the mat and relaxes. "Okay."

And that's how we all fall asleep—Seth holding onto his Sunshine for dear life, Thorin nestled deep inside his wolf, and me guarding my Goldilocks against anything and anyone that might ruin this piece of happiness we've stolen for ourselves.

Our second chance.

CHAPTER THIRTY-FIVE

AURELIA

The sun hasn't finished rising yet, so the frost and fog on the kitchen window block most of my view of the wilds.

A curl is stuck to my sweat-slicked cheek as my fingers sink into the dough I let sit out all night. The counter and my hands are covered in flour with a homestead recipe book open next to me as I attempt to make homemade artisan bread from scratch.

Like my last three attempts, it's not going well—mostly because I've been distracted from the start.

The culprit swirls his hot, wet tongue between my legs, and the hold my teeth have on my bottom lip gives. A low moan slips free, but it seems loud inside the quiet cabin.

It's still early in the morning. I thought I'd have an hour to myself—long enough to finish the bread at least—before one of them woke to harass and molest me.

It's hard to feel put out about it when I'm moments from coming.

As if he knows and wants to extend my torture, Seth lifts his head while his fingers continue to work in and out of my cunt.

"How's that, Sunshine?"

"Amazing," I answer, panting. "Until you stopped."

Chuckling, his warm breath skates over my pussy and sends a tingle down to my toes. Seth groans like a man starving when I wiggle my ass in demand, and then he goes back to making good on the least frightening wish he made at the lake.

With Seth fingering my pussy at the same time he's eating my ass, I double over the counter and flour and dough and come with a string of expletives and pleas spilling out of my mouth.

I stay where I am while I wait for my legs to stop shaking, and so does Seth—on his knees behind me—while he sinks his teeth into the plump curves of my ass. I know that when I survey my body later, I'll see the tokens each of them left behind—Seth's teeth marks, Khalil's handprints, and the scrapes from Thorin's stubble between my thighs.

Straightening, I turn to face Seth as he rises to his feet.

"Do you have it?" I ask as soon as he's towering over me.

"Open."

Parting my lips, I stick out my tongue, and Seth uses the same fingers he had stuffed inside my cunt to carefully place a tiny pink pill on my tongue. He draws his hand back at the same time I hear someone heading this way, so I swallow it immediately.

"Thank you. Best boyfriend ever."

Seth's eyes sparkle like I knew they would. "Don't mention it."

This has been our secret routine since the day we returned to the cabin a week ago. My mountain men agreed to no more punishments, but I should have known they'd have a workaround. They wouldn't punish me for being bad, but they were dead set on making me work for the rewards.

When Seth dangled my birth control in front of me under the guise of curiosity, I couldn't believe it. I also had the feeling Thorin and Khalil weren't aware that he had it since he waited until they went to meet with the sheriff about the drifters.

I told Seth I would do anything for the pills, so he made me put my money where my mouth is—literally.

The first pill was in exchange for a blow job that ended with a money shot. I traded letting him massage my feet for the second pill, which I hadn't minded at all. I have no idea if the pills will be effective after missing so many days, but for my peace of mind, I have to believe they will.

"I'm going to go shower," he says before kissing my cheek and giving my ass, which he just had his face between, a squeeze.

He passes Khalil on the way out of the kitchen, and I brace myself for more demands. My mountain men aren't just feral. They're insatiable.

Khalil notices me through sleepy eyes and prowls over to cradle my face in both hands before giving me a kiss. "Morning, Goldilocks."

God, his voice, still rough and heavy from sleep—not to mention his unbound and unkempt hair hanging around his broad shoulders—pools liquid heat inside my belly.

"Morning."

"What are you doing up so early?"

"Making bread. Being a good housewife."

Still holding my face, his arresting brown eyes peer over my shoulder at the messy counter. "You know you don't have to do this stuff anymore. No more indentured servitude, remember?"

"I know. I wanted to."

And because I realized just how easy it is to get bored out here without Wi-Fi, phones, or even a television. I *need* something to do, or I might break my promise and run for the nearest exit. Besides, I don't mind as much now that they're not making me.

The idea of taking care of my men when it's *my* choice doesn't feel icky or make me murderous.

I...like it.

I'm still really fucking bad at it, but I haven't forgotten they kidnapped me, so...oh well.

Khalil's face suddenly splits into a grin, revealing the most dazzling smile. "You're bored, aren't you?"

"*So* bored."

Khalil laughs, and I decide the sound is even better than his morning voice. "Well, you have the right idea. It helps to pick a project to pass the time. The more time-consuming, the better."

"Like what?"

Khalil frowns at my question, and I'm sure it's because I look as lost as I feel. "Is there something you've wanted to try in your spare time?"

"I didn't have spare time," I answer simply.

His frown deepens even more. "Never?"

I shake my head and intend to leave it at that, but somehow end up spilling my guts. "When there weren't songwriting or recording sessions, there were rehearsals, tours, performances, photoshoots, business meetings, interviews, and appearances. To tell you the embarrassing truth, those three days in the wilds were the closest I've ever come to a vacation. So no, I've never thought about what I might want to do for myself if I had the time because I haven't had a single moment that was just for me in a very long time. My uncle was immovably rigid in how I spent my days, and he had no qualms about reminding me that if I didn't stay on top, the world would forget about me. I wasn't irreplaceable to anyone. And you know what?"

"What?" Khalil inquires quietly. "Tell me. I got you."

His thumb stroking my cheek does something impossible to the turmoil inside me, something I never expected to ever happen. It chases it away, if only for this moment. I know that everything will be okay if I finally break my silence and that what's left of my world won't disappear from under my feet or that my uncle can't get to me because Khalil won't let him.

I believe him.

I…trust him.

"It worked. Uncle Mars kept me so isolated that my fans were all I had. I couldn't let them forget about me, so I did whatever he wanted. I dressed up, I sang the songs, I played the part, and told myself it didn't matter if I liked me because *they* loved me."

And when they stopped, all I had left was my self-loathing.

Khalil searches my gaze, and the jumping muscle in his cheek tells me he's clenching his teeth—*hard*. "I know you, Aurelia. You didn't take your uncle's shit lying down. What happened when you refused?"

"I know what you're thinking, Khalil, but he never hurt me. I was always in the public eye, so he couldn't risk the bruises. Uncle Marston was very good at making me feel incredibly fucking worthless, though. I was no one if I wasn't Aurelia George, the girl with the golden voice, and he made sure I never forgot it."

"What. Did. He. Do?"

"Besides the mind games? Uh, let's see. Sleep deprivation was one of his favorites because it meant he still got his way. Uncle Mars would keep my schedule jam-packed so that I would only get an hour or two of sleep if I was lucky. That would sometimes last for weeks. Extreme diet restriction thanks to some horse-faced bitch who went viral tweeting that I would be prettier if I lost weight. That started a weeklong discourse about body image, and yours truly got to be the focal point of *both* sides of the argument. But hey, the first time Uncle Mars nearly starved me to death, I lost thirty pounds, and everyone congratulated me on this newer, smaller me."

And whenever I was particularly defiant, or Uncle Mars was particularly cruel, he'd make me overeat just so he could later force his fingers down my throat so I would barf it all back up. It's what sparked the rumors of me being bulimic several years ago, thanks to one of my many ex-assistants. I almost got canceled for that, too, so my uncle leaked rumors of a new album in the works to distract them, and it worked.

"He did these things to you...for telling him no?"

"Anything could set him off. If I lost an endorsement or botched an interview or canceled a show because I got the flu... You get the picture."

"Yeah," Khalil says tightly. "I get the picture."

"The diabolical part of it all was that my uncle used singing, the only thing I was allowed to have, to hurt me. He took the one thing that made me whole and used it to break me."

"He didn't break you," Khalil denies with absolute certainty.

"No? I seem pretty fucking messed up to me."

"No matter what *we* threw at you, there hasn't been a single moment when you haven't pushed back. No, baby. He didn't break you, but I won't tell you the scars aren't there."

I wouldn't believe him if he tried. I can feel them just beneath my skin, waiting to show themselves through cruel words or sneers.

"Aren't you going to tell me I'm wiser, more beautiful, and stronger for them? Or any of the platitudes people use to dismiss the pain of others?"

"No. You are all of those things, and it has nothing to do with your bitch-ass uncle. If anything, he did what he could to take them away from you, but it didn't work. That's why I'm going to kill him."

"Khalil... You can't say things like that."

"Why?"

"Because you don't mean it."

"Don't I?"

"You'd have to more than just care about me, Khalil. You'd have to—" I stop myself before I can make a fool of myself.

"Say it," Khalil urges. There's a burning in his eyes that scares the shit out of me, and if I'm not careful, it will catch. "I'd have to what?"

You'd have to love me.

Because I'm a coward, I don't say it aloud. I drop my head with a shake so that I don't have to watch that fire bank from my denial. Khalil, thankfully, doesn't push further.

"You're irreplaceable to *me*, Aurelia." My head snaps up with a gasp. "That's why I meant it."

"You mean, if someone prettier, thinner, and more cooperative than me dropped out of the sky, you wouldn't trade me in for a newer, less troublesome model?"

Khalil scoffs like the notion of wanting anyone other than me is preposterous. "Definitely not."

"You sure? She might actually know how to cook."

"When we contemplated the girl who would be perfect for all of us, her culinary skills never came up. You're stuck with us, Goldilocks."

"Lucky me."

"Smart-ass." Khalil pinches my butt and then massages the spot. "When you figure out what you want to do, let one of us know so we can get you whatever you need. Understand?"

When I nod, he steals a chaste kiss that is anything but when I feel it between my thighs. I love Khalil's kisses, even though they make me feel out of my depth. Actually, I'm pretty sure it's why I love them. They make me feel so light on my feet, I fear I'll float away, so I cling to him as hard as I can, like he's my lifeline.

"Good. I can't wait to taste your bread." Why the fuck does that sound dirty as hell? I shiver and hope he doesn't notice that mere words have me behaving like a bitch in heat. "Need help?"

"With what exactly?"

Oh my God. Am I...flirting? It feels natural to do so, as natural as resisting this intense connection stirring.

Khalil's eyes flare as he picks up the ball I just threw in his court. His hand drops to my waist, and I feel his thumb sweeping my belly through Seth's T-shirt. "Whatever you need, Goldilocks. Did Seth not treat that precious pussy right?"

"What makes you think we did anything?"

"His face...and yours."

Thorin appears in the kitchen, his sleepy gaze becoming sharper the moment he notices Khalil and I locked together. I know that if I sucked Khalil's dick right now, I'll want Thorin's too, and then Seth will return from his shower and...

The bread will never get baked.

Deciding to turn off the horny switch, I spin back toward my ball of dough, but I can still feel Khalil hovering.

"I'm fine," I tell him. "Go stick your hand down your boxers and do whatever useless boyfriends do while I take care of everything."

"Boyfriend," Khalil says in a kind of confusing growl-purr combination that makes my toes curl against the cold floor. "I like it, Aurelia."

"Me too," Thorin chimes in with an equally sexy rumble.

Me three.

I feel Khalil kiss my neck, and Thorin takes his place a moment later. I don't even have to think about it when I turn my head to meet his lips over my shoulder. Thorin's hair is down, and I can't help but reach up to run my fingers through the silk while he feeds me his tongue. He can't help but touch me either, sneaking his hand under Seth's shirt and palming my bare tit. The cabin is quiet again except for our heavy breaths as we make out and the birds chirping just outside the window.

Birds...

Holy shit.

Spring must truly be around the corner.

It means the snow will melt, and the mountain pass will open. But... How did Pete and his friends make it up here if it wasn't already?

"How did you sleep, songbird?"

"Like a baby," I lie breathlessly.

After a week of sleeping in either Thorin's bed or Khalil's with him and Seth, I'd insisted on sleeping in my loft last night once the three of them were done with me so that I could get up early without waking one of them.

"Yeah?" Thorin, unconvinced that I slept better in a sleeping bag on the floor than wrapped up in one of them, waits for a better answer.

"Okay, fine! It was cold."

Thorin's chuckle is quiet, and then he kisses my nape before whispering in my ear, "Next time you need warming up, you know where to find me, wolf."

Thorin leaves, and not a moment too soon. My nipples are already hard, aching points against the cotton of Seth's T-shirt, and if Thorin had ordered me to my knees, I wouldn't have refused him.

An hour later, a happy squeal leaves my lips when I lift the roasting pan and see the perfectly golden dome underneath. All of my other attempts left me with an overcooked lump sunken in the middle, but I'd finally perfected the temperature.

Removing the bread from the trivets on the stovetop, I set the baking pan on a separate rack to cool while I carry the platters of eggs, bacon, and fried apples to the table, where my mountain men are already seated.

"I don't get you three," I say with a huff as I place their breakfast in front of them. "You have power. Why not make life easier and get modern appliances too? Maybe a real stove? Or a TV?"

"We thought about it," Khalil says from the head of the table. He snatches a strip of bacon from the platter as soon as it touches the table. "It's the reason we went solar."

"And?"

"We didn't do it," he says around a mouthful of bacon.

"Yes, I can see that. Care to share why?"

The three of them are quiet while they help themselves to the food that—even if I do say so myself—looks at least edible today. They still haven't answered by the time I take my seat between Khalil and Thorin and across from Seth.

I'm wrestling between pressing the issue and shrugging it off when Seth says, "They were afraid of getting too comfortable."

"And it's a pain in the ass getting shit up the mountain," Thorin grumbles.

"Oh, speaking of which, you're out of eggs, flour, salt, and yeast."

Thorin pauses, filling his plate with a lift of his brow. "You mean all the things you used to make that bread?"

"No." I roll my eyes and pretend I don't feel their scrutiny. All three of them are watching me closely right now. "You don't need eggs for bread."

"Hmm."

"Guess you're going to have to make a store run."

"Guess so," Seth answers tightly.

Before I can examine Seth's souring mood, Khalil places the plate he's filled with food in front of me. I watch a little dumbfounded as he wordlessly grabs the pitcher of water and pours me a glass.

"I—thank you." Our gazes meet, and I look away like a coward. My attention shifts to my plate that's piled with more food than I can eat.

"Thanks for making breakfast," Khalil returns smoothly despite my need to make shit awkward for no reason. "It looks good."

I scoff. "You don't have to lie."

See? There I go again. Awkward.

Khalil nudges my foot under the table, and my gaze flies up to meet his. "I wasn't."

I feel my cheeks warm, but this time, I don't look away. I go for inappropriate humor instead. "I'm impressed, Poverly. We're a long way from grunting and growling, and *you woman, we men, make food.*"

"I do not sound like that."

"You all sound *exactly* like that."

Thorin grunts in amusement or annoyance. It's hard to tell, but it proves my point, and that's all I care about. I keep my smug gaze on Khalil, who sucks his teeth and scowls at Thorin.

"My God. I could write a book," I muse aloud. "Are bodice rippers still a thing?"

"You're awfully chatty this morning," Thorin retorts.

My head swings his way. "Are you telling me to shut up, Thayer?"

"And piss you off? No, my wolf. I know better."

Just to really annoy them, I start testing out potential titles. "*Winter's Burn. This Twisted Eden. The Villains' Surrender.* Ooh, I like that one. *The Captive Who Loved Them.* What do you think, Seth?"

My eyes fall on him, expecting to see him still glowering at his empty plate for some unknown reason, but he's staring at me now through wide eyes with his mouth open.

It's not until I see Thorin and Khalil wearing similar expressions that I realize my blunder.

I said I fucking loved them. At the very least, I alluded to it. Is that how

I feel? No, it can't be. They're ruthless, and I'm soulless. We're a match made in hell, but woefully incapable of love.

"A-a-actually, I think I will shut up now."

"Why would you do that?" Khalil purrs as he sits back in his seat with an arrogant twist of his lips. "You were just getting to the part where you apparently love us?"

I stare down at my plate. "Can we just forget I said that?"

"No, I don't think we can," Seth answers smugly.

"And *I* don't think our story classifies as romance, do you? Maybe a case study for Stockholm syndrome, but that's the best I can do."

It's quiet for a moment, and then Thorin asks, "Are you saying you want to be romanced, wolf?"

I shrug as I scoop up a forkful of eggs. "It would be nice. So far, Seth's been doing all of the heavy lifting."

Seth grins at that while Thorin and Khalil both drop their forks as if I'd slapped them.

"Are you fucking kidding me, wolf? I dove into a frozen lake for you," Thorin protests.

"You did," I acknowledge as I bite my bacon in half. "Why do you think I haven't been spitting in your food lately?"

Thorin rolls his eyes as if that doesn't surprise him in the least.

We eat in silence, but I can tell the three of them are thinking about what I said. I'm thinking too, but not about that. Suddenly, it comes to me.

"I know what I want to do now," I tell Khalil. The others perk up at that, their gazes swinging to Khalil and back to me.

"Yeah?" Khalil asks. His mood has soured ever since I told him he needs to step it up. "What's that?"

"Gardening."

"Come again?"

"I want to start a garden."

"We have a garden," Thorin retorts grumpily.

"But you haven't grown anything, so I thought I could give it a try. Wouldn't it be easier to stock up for winter if you grew your own produce right here?"

"Maybe."

"So what's the problem?"

"There's no problem," Khalil says firmly. "Thorin's just being a prick."

"Oh, so like usual then?" That earns me a scowl from him, and I blow him a kiss in return.

"We'll have to go into town for the supplies," Thorin reminds Khalil.

The three of them exchange a meaningful look, and my stomach sinks a moment later when it hits me with the force of a sledgehammer—the reason for their hesitation.

They still don't trust me.

Here I am, giving them everything like a fool when they're still holding back.

My eyes prickle, and the room spins faster and faster until I inhale a deep, steadying breath. "You know what?" I shakily say as I rise from the table. "Forget it. Fuck the garden. I…I don't know what I was thinking."

"Sunshine—"

"I said forget it, Seth."

I feel all three of their eyes on me as I hurry from the dining room.

I can't let them see.

I can't let them have another part of me they don't deserve.

These tears that I know won't spill but have never come so dangerously close to doing so before now. They don't deserve a single one.

I haven't been out on the lower deck since my first night when Thorin marooned me for not wanting to give it up. At the time, it was just another stage set for my death that I somehow escaped yet again.

Right now, it's my sanctuary.

My legs are threaded through the wooden rails while my bare feet dangle over the unforgiving wilds below. It's a clear day full of vivid colors, but I don't see any of it. My forehead rests against one of the bars, and my hand clutches my turning stomach as I take rapid, deep breaths and tell myself this is better.

It would have never worked between us anyway.

I'm too fucked-up to truly love anyone.

And they… Well, it's clear they are capable of caring deeply for someone other than themselves. Their bond makes me envious sometimes.

But our biggest obstacle isn't them or even me.

It's Ezekiel.

None of us can truly know what will happen when he wakes up.

We are reckless, making promises before that eventuality occurs.

"Damn, girl. I've been looking for your ass everywhere," Khalil fusses, breaking through my chaotic and confusing thoughts.

I didn't even hear the deck door open or him sneaking up on me. I lift my head and pray my face keeps my secrets as he drops his powerful body down next to me while facing the opposite way.

Our gazes meet, and he places a possessive hand on my naked thigh. I'm still only wearing Seth's T-shirt, which is heavy with his natural scent of juniper and leather. Goose bumps spread in every direction from our point of contact, even as my heart cracks inside my chest. I tell myself it's the breeze from being up so high.

Khalil may want me, but he doesn't trust me.

"It was only a matter of time before we fucked up, but it seems I gave us too much credit in thinking it wouldn't be this soon."

"What do you want, Khalil?"

"I wanted to check on my girl." I laugh at that as I stare out at the Cold Peaks without really seeing them. "And to say I'm sorry."

"For what?" I ask casually—as if my fractured heart isn't already trying to fuse itself back together. I hold it at bay.

"It's been my pleasure to make you feel many things—desire, anger, hatred…happiness." At that last word, I finally let myself look at him. "But I never dreamed of making you sad, Aurelia."

"I'm not sad."

"No?"

"I'm…annoyed."

Khalil's hand leaves my thigh to tuck an errant curl behind my ear. His thumb somehow sweeps my jaw as he whispers, "We're very annoying."

My lips twist when I feel myself wanting to smile. "I won't argue with you there, Poverly."

"That's a first."

"Don't push it." My nostrils flare, and Khalil drops his head against the railing with a sigh.

"Trust is earned, Aurelia. Every time you promised us you wouldn't run, you ran."

"I know that," I snap and feel my cheeks and neck warm at the reminder.

Khalil's brown eyes soften a moment later. "Do you?"

I feel myself softening against my will too. "Yes, Khalil." Freeing my legs from between the rails, I stand, and so does Khalil. "Maybe I overreacted. I think I'm getting my period."

My period…

It's due in a few days, and I'm suddenly terrified that it might not come at all.

One problem at a time.

"Let me stop you right there. You didn't. We hurt you, and the last thing we want is for you to invalidate or downplay your feelings. Not for us or anyone." When he reaches for me, I go to him. "All we ask is that you give us the chance to fix it. Don't run away."

"And how will you fix this? Even if you did trust me, I can't leave this mountain, Khalil. Someone will recognize me."

"Trust is earned," Khalil repeats as he reaches inside his heavy winter coat. It's the first time I notice he's fully dressed. "But it's unfair of us to withhold it forever without giving you the chance to claim it."

He pulls out a wooden object that's flat with curved edges with two downturned oval holes for eyes near the center, a long snout for the nose and mouth, and two triangular tips for the ears. I recognize the carving he's been working on for over a week—since the night Seth lost his virginity, and Khalil and I both discovered we're a lot more depraved than we realized.

"What is that?"

"I wasn't sure at first when I started, but it was your face I saw the entire time I was carving it."

I glance down at what I now realize is a mask and then back at him with a raised brow. "I look like a wolf?"

Khalil's smile is sly as he hands me the mask. "I don't know. Put it on, and I'll tell you."

I hesitate long enough for my heart to skip a beat, and then I curl my fingers around the wooden mask. "It won't be comfortable," Khalil warns me before I can lift it toward my face.

"I think I'll manage."

He looks nervous as I fit it over my face, and the world immediately narrows around me. All I see is Khalil as I stare back at him through the eye holes in the mask.

"Can you—"

Khalil is already reaching for the ties, securing them in a knot behind my head. He then turns me around to face him and checks the fit.

"Never take the mask off, and don't speak to anyone," he commands.

My stomach fills with nervous butterflies. "Are we really going into town?"

I was resigned to never leaving this mountain again.

"Yes. If anyone asks, your name is Aurora. You're my cousin visiting from the States."

It's all the instruction I'm given before he takes my hand and leads me over to the deck door.

"So, where are you from?" I ask curiously.

Khalil glances at me over his shoulder as we enter the house. "Six Forks, Nevada."

"Hmm…never heard of it."

CHAPTER THIRTY-SIX

THORIN

I want to drive," Aurelia announces when we finish topping off the snowmobiles with the gas cans.

She's bundled from head to toe in gear to protect her from the cold and hide her identity. Thanks to the balaclava, there isn't so much as a single golden curl visible, but it doesn't help untwist the knot in my stomach. The only part of her visible to us is her brown eyes, but even Aurelia has been careful to keep her thoughts guarded. She knows we're watching and waiting to see if she's playing us.

God, what the hell are we doing?

We knew she was working Seth, but maybe she's working us too. One look at the devastation on her face this morning, and I knew I'd give whatever to make sure I never saw it there again.

We're at the base of our mountain, preparing for the fifty-mile journey to the small town of Hearth, and it's all I can do not to drag her ass back to our cabin and tie her to my bed. I don't care what happens to me if we get caught, but Aurelia being taken away from us... I'll die before I let that happen.

Khalil crooks his finger since his ride is the only one equipped for two passengers, and Aurelia walks over to stand next to him.

"Do you know how to drive one of these?"

"No." She chews on her bottom lip while we wait for her to confess whatever she obviously doesn't want us to know. "I don't know how to drive anything. I don't even have my license."

Khalil is the only one of us who grew up in a stable, loving home, so his brows shoot up in surprise. "Your uncle never taught you how to drive?"

"That would be a no."

Clenching my teeth to keep my thoughts to myself, I silently watch Khalil give her a quick tutorial. "Throttle. Brake. Never press them both at the same time. When turning, shift your body in the direction you want the bike to go. Keep your feet on the running boards at all times. In the event you fall off, this clip will disable the ignition," he says as he fastens the cord and clip attached to the key to her belt loop.

As I've been doing regularly since she dressed in a pair of my Ski Bibs for the trip to town, my gaze travels to Aurelia's plump ass while her back is turned, and I feel most of my anger melting away as I imagine making her ride me in reverse later.

"That's it?" she asks.

"Pretty much. Hop on." Khalil slides a yellow helmet over her head since she isn't wearing the mask right now before sliding a red one over his own. He then scoots back into the second seat, and Aurelia takes the driver's seat. I watch her gloved hands nervously curl around the handles, and then our eyes meet through the open visor of her helmet.

"Stay behind and don't stray."

Once she nods, I look to my right at Seth, who is already straddling his Ski-Doo and wearing his green helmet. Our gazes meet, and he jerks his chin, silently acknowledging my unspoken order.

Only then do I slide my blue helmet on with a heavy exhale.

This isn't just a huge mistake. It's a necessary one on all counts. We get to show Aurelia that we're willing to trust her. And she gets to prove to us that we can.

I turn the key in the ignition and take off without warning. If I don't now, I never will. I've realized it's much easier to keep Aurelia prisoner and deal with her hate than make her want to stay and hope we'll be enough.

One makes me a coward, and the other...

I'm not sure what the other makes me, but I'm not so selfish that I can completely disregard a possible future in which Aurelia is happy too.

One glance over my shoulder shows her keeping up. Seth is hot on her tail, and while I can't see Aurelia's face, instinctively, I know she's smiling.

We're halfway through the valley when I decide she's got the hang of it, so I pick up a little speed. Moments later, I hear her voice through the speakers.

"Whooooo! This is amazing!"

"That's okay," Seth deadpans. I can hear the smile in his voice. "I didn't need eardrums."

"Oh, shit!" Aurelia screeches even louder, making the three of us groan. "You can hear me?"

"Bluetooth, baby. We can all hear you," Khalil answers.

"Thorin, go faster!" Aurelia immediately demands.

"You sure you're ready for that?" Instead of an answer, I hear her engine accelerate. Aurelia breaks formation and speeds past me with Khalil holding on for dear life and Seth cheering her on. "You don't even know where you're going!" I shout when I recover from my shock.

"Then you better keep up!"

I feel a grin split my face at the same time I hit the throttle. The four of us race across the frozen valley. Aurelia's got all of that deadweight—a.k.a. Khalil—slowing her down, so I barely have to max out my speed to catch up to her. Seth is not far behind, but I can tell he's not really trying for some reason.

I don't give it much thought as I continue to gain on Aurelia. I'm still inching closer when Khalil suddenly twists in the rear seat and throws something. Whatever it is, I barely have time to duck the missile before it can hit me between the eyes. Instead, the orange sails over my shoulder and bounces off my snowmobile's reflector, *cracks it*, and then hits the ground.

"Why the fuck are you throwing shit at me?" I bark.

"Mario Kart, asshole!" Khalil throws another fucking orange.

It finds its mark this time, hitting my right shoulder so hard that I lose my grip on the accelerator and some of my speed. Growling, I press on the gas to catch up again, dodging all the over-ripened oranges that Khalil just happened to bring with him.

I'm starting to suspect this race was their plan all along—Aurelia's, Khalil's, and maybe Seth's too. They probably plotted to fuck with me, knowing I have a competitive nature.

Khalil finally runs out of oranges about five hundred feet away from the forest line that marks the end of the valley, so I decide to make my move, shifting to the left side of Aurelia's Ski-Doo and increasing my speed. Despite Khalil's frustrated encouragement, Aurelia is still too nervous to max out her speed, so I'm confident I have the easy win in the bag.

My front bumper is inching closer to Aurelia's rear when something slams into me from the right side. I swear viciously, feeling like my brain is bouncing around in my skull as I veer off track and lose speed as quickly as I'd gained it. Aurelia bursts forward, but I'm too busy reaching for the gun on my hip to worry about the race. When I aim in the direction of the impact, I expect to find a hungry bear staring down my sights—nothing else could have hit me with that much force—but all I see is one-hundred and eighty pounds of dead meat.

I can't see his face, but I know he's proud of himself.

"Seth, what the hell?" I bark as I consider shooting him anyway.

"Team Sunshine, bitch!" To Aurelia, he shouts, "Go, baby, go!"

Fucking pussy-whipped, purse-holding traitors.

Aurelia hits the throttle and soars across the finish line while Seth flips me off and follows her. Khalil is cheering the loudest as the three of them stop near the gap in the tree line to celebrate with their cheating asses. I hear Aurelia giggling through the Bluetooth as Khalil and Seth high-five each other over their stolen win.

I'm purposely quiet as I take my time catching up.

They can't see the grin I'm wearing or feel the way my heart is aching at the picture laid out before me. I can't recall the last time I saw my brothers this carefree and alive. And Aurelia… She's in rare form today too—open, unresistant, and laughing—and I wonder if we're being gifted a glimpse of what could be or taunted with a fool's dream.

One perfect girl for three very different men.

Aurelia, Seth, and Khalil don't have a clue what I'm feeling, so the three of them are quiet and guarded by the time I cruise across the finish line to join them. And I don't feel the least bit bad about it. Pretending to ruin the mood is my petty revenge for being teamed up on.

Cutting the engine, I school my expression before removing my helmet, and Aurelia does the same. She's still beaming and beautifully flushed from the thrill of the race, but when she notices me watching, her smile dims a little, and she lifts her chin in a clear challenge. "Well?"

I just barely hold back my grin. "Well, what?"

"Are you going to be a sore loser, Thorin Thayer?"

Leaning forward to rest my forearms on the handlebars, I hear Khalil and

Seth snickering and give them unimpressed looks before meeting Aurelia's gaze once more. "Of course not, my wolf. Congratulations on your victory."

Aurelia looks gut punched before she looks away. We both know I'm not talking about the race.

Aurelia's got us wrapped around her finger, and not one of us is interested in untangling ourselves. It's only Aurelia who seems to shut down whenever we bring up the fact that she obviously feels something more than just reluctant lust for us.

She agreed to stay and give us everything, including her heart, yet... she's not.

Not yet, at least.

I tell myself I can be patient. We haven't had the best start. We haven't earned *her* trust yet. But even after all my Marine training, patience has never been a virtue of mine. I want to possess every inch of this woman— her darkest desires, voluptuous body, rare smiles, teeth and wit, and soul... however it comes.

She stares toward the trail leading to Hearth when she asks, "So, are we hiking the rest of the way?"

"Fuck no," Khalil grumbles after popping off his helmet. "We wouldn't reach town until well after nightfall, and then we'll be too tired to show you around."

I cut Khalil a sharp look, which he pointedly ignores.

Aurelia keeps her expression perfectly sedate, leaving us to wonder if she's calculating the distance between the valley and Hearth. There's an odometer on the snowmobile, so if she pays attention, she'll know exactly how close the town is soon enough.

Suddenly, the hidden cloth I'd brought—the one I hoped I wouldn't need—is burning a hole in my pocket.

We're pretty remote out here, but not so much that we're completely cut off from civilization. The townspeople of Hearth are just all too happy to ignore our presence since they're used to these mountains being uninhab-ited anyway. Sheriff Kelly visits occasionally, but even he knows we want to be left alone, so he keeps his visits to a minimum. It was hard dodging his many questions when he first discovered us hiding out here, and for a while, we were subjected to his overbearing scrutiny. But then we proved useful when we helped him find some missing honeymooners a few years ago. The sheriff's been our only link to the main world ever since.

"We'll ride the Ski-Doos down to the main road where our truck is waiting," Seth informs her.

"Oh. Okay."

"Aurelia," I call as I swing my leg over the snowmobile and stand. The hard snow crunches under my boots as I walk the short distance over to her.

"Yes?" Her head swings my way, and she frowns when I remove her green and brown gingham headband from my pocket. At night, she uses it to tie her hair up, so it was easy to find on my nightstand.

"I'll need to blindfold you, baby."

Her entire body tenses. "Why?"

"You know why." Aurelia's pouty mouth opens to argue, but I beat her to it. "Your chance to prove we can trust you will come once we reach town. Until then, we're not taking any chances."

Her lips snap closed, and she glowers at me. I can tell she has an attitude but doesn't fight me as I step forward to cover her pretty brown eyes. Once the headband is tied behind her head, I lean down to brush her lips with mine to soften her a little, but she doesn't kiss me back. She turns away from my touch while her chest heaves from her heavy breaths, and I imagine if she were a dragon, smoke would be expelled from her flaring nostrils. She might even turn me into a pile of ash if she could, and I don't blame her.

I shake off the sting of her rejection as I help her stand from the snowmobile so that Khalil can take her place in the driver's seat, but I'm still thinking about it the entire way down to the main road.

CHAPTER THIRTY-SEVEN

AURELIA

Thorin rushes me the moment I climb unsteadily off the snowmobile. I'm still wearing the blindfold, but I know it's him because of the heady scent of cardamom that's even stronger now with one of my senses blocked.

And because I could feel his eyes on me the whole way down.

Blindfolded, I had no sense of time.

How long did it take us to reach the main road? An hour? Maybe less? I wouldn't be surprised if those fuckers went around in circles or took the scenic route to throw me off even more.

Before I can figure it out, I'm pushed against what I'm assuming is the truck they spoke of as Thorin quickly crowds me. My helmet is ripped off my head, but he leaves the blindfold on as Thorin says, "I know what you're doing, wolf, and it won't work."

It's an effort to keep my tone level when I respond. "What am I doing, Thorin?"

"You're trying to make me feel bad for blindfolding you."

I don't even have to fake my derisive snort. "Trying to make you regret behaving like a controlling, domineering asshole is like trying to make fire feel bad for burning me. I don't waste my time with trivial pursuits, Thayer."

I hear a low whistle and a stifled laugh come from somewhere close, and then car doors opening and closing. I'm guessing Seth and Khalil got in the truck to give us some privacy.

"Kiss me."

"No."

"Why not?"

"You know why," I answer, returning his words from earlier.

I don't flinch when Thorin wraps his hand around my throat. He doesn't squeeze as he lifts me onto my toes, but the threat is evident as it sends a nervous thrill down my spine while my panties become damp. I feel his warm breath skating my mouth a second before his lips do—just as he did at the top of the trail. When I ignore the request a second time, still refusing to kiss him, he slams his fists on the roof of the truck and shoves away from me with a frustrated growl.

The truck roars to life behind me, and then I hear what sounds like gravel under his boots as Thorin retreats and opens the truck door.

"Keep the blindfold on and get in the truck."

I mock salute and reach my arms out to feel where the door might be, but then Thorin sighs and guides me inside with a hand on my lower back.

There's a steady rush of heat from the vents as it works to warm up the truck. I feel Thorin climb inside next to me before shutting the door and the four of us inside.

"So who's driving?" I ask to quell the nervous toil inside my belly.

Their individual scents quickly mingle and take over the small space, just as they do back at the cabin. It's almost eerie how much it calms me.

"I am," Khalil announces.

"I don't know how to drive either, Sunshine," Seth confesses.

I reach out a hand toward where I think the front passenger seat is and fumble around until I feel the powerful muscles of Seth's shoulder under my palm, and then I squeeze.

It's quiet for a moment longer, and then Khalil asks, "Would you like to learn?"

As it turns out, Seth is a *very* confident driver.

A little too damn confident if you ask me, Thorin, Khalil, the other drivers on the road who rage-honked as we sped by, about fifty traffic laws, and from the sounds of the angry bleating I heard…a goat?

Each time Seth sped around a curve, I swear I could hear Thorin and Khalil's sphincters tightening along with my own. Khalil had stopped bothering to give him instructions less than five minutes in, and the three of us have been holding onto the "oh shit" handlebars ever since.

It takes us roughly twenty minutes to reach the town limits from the bottom of the trail, even with Seth's speeding. I know the moment we arrive because Seth slams on the brakes, which is probably the first time he's bothered to use them.

My heart is beating so fast that, at first, I don't notice Thorin reaching behind me to untie the blindfold. It falls into my lap, and I'm suddenly staring through the front windshield that's still defrosting. Seth is fiddling with the radio as he waits for a group of small children wearing safety vests and holding hands to finish crossing the street with their teachers. Once the last child is safely on the sidewalk, he takes off again but sticks to the speed limit as we cruise the street with stores on either side.

The buildings are mostly brick with different kinds of awnings. The dirty snow that had been paved from the street is now piled up at the edge of the sidewalks that have also been cleared. Even the sidewalks themselves are charming. The colorful bricks are wet from the earlier rain that must have fallen, while the puddles that gathered reflect the roofs of the buildings and black lampposts. Dividing the street as a median are leafless trees sporting fresh buds with spring just days away, and I wonder what color they'll be. For some reason, I imagine pink cherry blossoms and wonder what they mean.

The town is bigger than I imagined but still much smaller than I'm used to. We pass a bakery, pizza parlor, hair salon, pharmacy, hardware store, and post office before Seth finds an open parking spot. We haven't yet reached the intersection dividing the street and remaining businesses, so I know there's more to explore—assuming I get to.

Khalil looks over his shoulder at me the moment I unbuckle my seat belt. "Tell me the rules, Goldilocks."

I sigh but list them off. "Don't talk to anyone, don't wander off, and keep the mask on."

"Good girl."

I hide my reaction to the praise under the guise of slipping on the wolf mask. Thorin helps me secure it and then slips the oversized hood of my winter coat on.

I'm completely disguised.

"You don't think the mask will freak people out?"

"We already freak people out," Thorin answers but doesn't elaborate.

The three of them climb out of the truck, and I linger for the space of a single deep inhale before I join them.

The town is…loud.

There aren't even close to as many people as I'm used to seeing in LA. However, after nearly a month in the wilds, I've grown accustomed to the quiet. I almost prefer it.

Because of that longing for home, I look back the way we came—at the three snowcapped crowns of the Cold Peaks looming in the distance, waiting for our return. *Home.*

Khalil slips his arm around me before I lose myself to that conflicting feeling, and the four of us travel down the sidewalk. We garner some looks as we walk by other pedestrians, but perplexingly, it's not my mask that causes most of them.

It's them.

My mountain men.

Thorin, Khalil, and Seth stand out like three tall, menacing, sexy sore thumbs.

I, Aurelia George, for the first time in over a decade, am a fucking nonfactor. Of course, they don't know it's me under the disguise, but I have a feeling it wouldn't make much of a difference if they did. This feeling of being invisible is strange but freeing.

Seth looks back at me as he leads the way. Khalil is next to me while Thorin guards our backs. "Got your list, baby?"

"Right here." I pull out the list I quickly scribbled together before we left the cabin and wave it in the air.

The house stuff is easy, but I have no idea what I need to start a garden. Khalil says they already have most of the supplies from his previous attempts. All I have to do is decide what kind of garden I want and purchase the seeds.

I'm downright giddy at the thought of doing something of my choice besides singing, but I don't let it show. Three weeks is not nearly enough time to exorcise my uncle completely, so I'm still very much afraid of him finding a way to snatch this small slice of happiness from me too.

"The market is this way—"

"We need to make a pit stop," Thorin interrupts Khalil.

Seth, Khalil, and I stop walking.

"Where?"

"Here." Thorin grabs my hand and pulls me inside the store we're standing in front of before I can see what it is.

I'm thrust inside a store that reminds me of an REI, only a fraction of the size, dim lighting, and the overbearing smell of weed.

"Welcome to Ran—" Coughing interrupts the greeting, and my gaze follows the sound to the counter where an Asian kid around eighteen years old is pounding his chest while smoke expels from his mouth with each cough. He's wearing a black polo with the store's logo on the front and a beanie pulled low over his head. "Dall's," he finishes. "Call me J.R." Another cough follows. "Randall is my father."

"Hi, J.R.!"

My mountain men shoot me dirty looks, and I realize a second later that I've already broken the first rule.

But you know what's even weirder than the mask?

Not speaking when spoken to.

Being a bitch will draw even more attention than the mask and have me sticking to people's memories like glue.

Thorin tugs on my wrist, leading me through all the racks of clothing, ski equipment, and camping gear to the back wall where the shoes are. In front of the mirror dividing the wall of shoes are two plaid ottomans that have seen better days.

"Sit."

I take a seat and look around. "What are we doing here?"

"You need new boots. Something better for the terrain. I'm tired of watching you split your feet open with those pitiful excuses for boots you're wearing."

"I'll have you know these are *Dior*."

"Well, then you should have left them at the D-oor."

"Oh my God." I snort and slap my hands over the mask where my mouth would be. Thorin pauses his perusal of the hiking boots to look back at me quizzically, and I drop my hands to tease him. "Did Thorin Thayer, full-time grump, and part-time asshole, make a joke?"

He rolls his eyes and turns back to the boots with a ghost of a smile. "I joke."

"You do not."

Khalil sits on the second ottoman and tugs my right foot into his lap. I try not to gape as he works the laces free and tugs off my boot.

"What size shoe do you wear, songbird?"

"Seven," Khalil and I say at the same time.

"And how do you know that?" Khalil just gives me a look like it's a dumb question and removes my other boot. "Oh, God," I say, coming to my own conclusion. "Don't tell me you have a foot fetish too. I honestly don't think I can handle another kink between you three."

"Seth doesn't have any kinks."

That's Khalil's response.

"He told me he wants to put his hand inside of me. His *hand*. As in all five fingers and his palm too. How is that not a kink?"

"You can handle it," Khalil says with absolute certainty.

"I cannot and will not."

Khalil hums noncommittally, but I still hear the unspoken "we'll see" underneath it. Thorin finally chooses a boot for me to try, handing it to Khalil before he walks off. I peer over my shoulder to watch him prowl over to the counter where Seth is leaning and speaking low with J.R.

"Take a picture. It will last longer," Khalil teases.

I snap my head back toward Khalil, who is slipping the hiking boot onto my right foot. "Huh?"

Khalil finishes tying the lace and taps my leg. "Wipe that drool from your lip and tell me how that feels."

Like a cloud, I think as I stand and pace the short aisle between the wall of shoes and the seating area. "I like a boot."

Khalil peers up at me, caressing his bottom lip with his forefinger as he studies me, and I fall into a trance watching that finger sweep his lip.

Have I mentioned how fucking sexy Khalil Poverly is?

If we'd met in high school or college, I never would have stood a chance with him. I was rather lame before my uncle pulled me out of school. I had no swag or confidence and only textbooks for friends. Girls like me were never noticed by boys like him.

"You really can't help but be a bitch, can you?"

I surprise us both when I drape my arms on his shoulders and straddle his lap with a coy smile. Khalil's muscular thighs under my ass is better than any cushioned ottoman. "Not really, no."

I rub his shoulders in apology, and Khalil tilts his head to kiss my neck. My lashes flutter when his kisses grow more heated until he's sucking and biting on my neck too. It makes me wet, thinking of him leaving his mark like he owns me. It makes me insatiable, knowing he does.

Before long, I'm swirling my hips and grinding on his growing erection and wishing we were alone because I really want his dick in my mouth right now.

The spell is broken too soon, though, when Khalil lifts his head suddenly. I can feel the abused skin of the spot he was marking throbbing when he mumbles, "Shit."

"What's the matter?"

"J.R.'s watching us."

"So?"

"So judging by his wide eyes and the fact that he just turned red as a tomato, I'm thinking either Seth or Thorin already told him you were my cousin."

I fly out of Khalil's lap even though it's already much too late to put the awkward back in the bag.

I'd forgotten about our cover story.

"Oh, oh my God," I mumble. Meanwhile, Khalil clutches his stomach as he bends over from laughing so hard. I punch his shoulder as hard as I can. "It's not funny, you jerk! He's going to think we're weirdos!"

No longer laughing, Khalil snorts while I chew a hole in my lip. "It's a little funny." When I glare, he sobers and rolls his eyes. "You do realize we're not *actually* cousins, right?"

"Why couldn't you have just made a story about me being an ex-girlfriend or something?"

"Yeah, that would have been better."

"You're...not...helping," I grind out.

Khalil sucks his teeth and stands, and I fight the urge to take a step back. Even after all this time, the height difference is jarring. Add on all the muscle he's packing and the fact that he's quite literally capable of murder, and yeah, I still get a little nervous.

And to make matters worse, my pussy likes that I feel intimidated.

"Fuck him. Come on," Khalil orders.

Keeping the hiking boot on and swiping up my own useless one from the floor, I reluctantly let Khalil lead me over to the counter. Thankfully, J.R. isn't there when we walk over. Thorin isn't either, and I spot him over by the sleeping bags, holding a basket already overfilled with items. After a quick perusal, he selects one and rejoins us at the counter.

"Is all of this for me?" I ask as I look over all of the gear. There's a rope, a compass, a map, a watch, a first aid kit, a head lamp, an honest-to God hatchet, a foldable spade like the ones they used to build the quinzee, a fire starter, a canteen, a sleeping bag, a tent, and a bunch of other shit I don't know how to use.

"Yup."

"Why?"

"So if you change your mind and run again, you can at least keep yourself alive long enough for us to come and get you."

I have no idea how to respond to that, but I find myself searching for words anyway. "I—"

"Whoa!" J.R. says, returning with a shoebox containing the other half of my new boots. "Did Halloween come early?"

I hear a click and see Seth with his folding knife out and poised under the kid's throat before I can tell him to kiss my ass.

"Okay, okay. No harm. Jeez." A pause, and then, "So, what's the deal? Is she disfigured or something?"

"Yes, J.R.," I quickly answer despite his insistence on talking around me instead of to me. Thorin sighs like he's finally resigned to me never doing what I'm told. Maybe. But also, I don't want this kid's blood on my hands. Seth *will* cut him. "I'm horribly, horribly scarred, and if you look me in the eye, I'm afraid you'll turn to stone. Ah!"

I lunge like I'm going to attack. Thorin, Khalil, and Seth howl when J.R. jumps back and throws his arms over his eyes.

"No! Don't turn me into stone! Please!"

"She's fucking with you, J.R.," Khalil says. "Ring us up, and stop smoking so much weed."

"Really?" He still has trouble meeting my gaze, but I'll give him a D-minus for effort when he finally does. He seems nice. Gullible as fuck. But nice.

I flash him a razor-sharp smile that he can't even see. "Maybe."

There must be something in my tone though because his eyes widen, and he quickly gives us our total, throws our shit inside two reusable bags once Khalil pays, and flees through the door behind him marked "Employees Only."

Seth grins at me. "I think you scared him off, Sunshine."

"And he didn't even say goodbye." I fake a pout.

I feel hands on my waist, and then I'm being lifted and turned before I'm sat on the counter. Khalil pulls off my remaining leather boot and slips on the hiking one.

"Thorin chose well. These are good," he tells me as he ties the lace.

I'm barely listening as I admire his hair and my handiwork. Rather than his usual plaits, I'd given him two fishbone braids that stop past his shoulders and emphasize his sharp cheekbones rather than hide them. It's almost a shame he chose a profession that could have ruined that pretty face instead of utilizing it because Khalil Poverly could have been a model. Or maybe a porn star because that dick and that body…chef's kiss.

"They're cushioned for long hikes and will keep your feet dry and warm in the winter and cool in the summer."

"Yeah, I guess they're cute," I say, admiring the unique tan color with bright purple laces. They stop right above my ankle like my old ones, except they don't chafe. They even come with a detachable zippered pouch on the side. Yay!

Seth chuckles while Khalil flicks me an exasperated look.

Thorin takes my designer calfskin boots, which were part of a limited-edition collection, and…throws them in the trash.

"Hey! I paid two grand for those!" The three of them blink at me like I've lost my mind, and I cross my arms. "I don't appreciate the judgment. I'm a billionaire, remember? I could spend my money on a bunch of dumb shit and still never run out of money."

Thorin swears and fishes my boots back out of the trash. He throws them into the box that the hiking boots came in while Khalil helps me down from the counter.

Seth grabs the bags from the counter, and I almost forget that I'm mad at Thorin when he takes my hand this time. I don't pull away, though; I let him lead me out of Randall's. I look around once the four of us are standing on the sidewalk again.

"So where to now?"

"Fuck," Khalil breathes.

I swing my head his way and find him looking off in the opposite direction. "What?"

"What the hell is he doing here?" Thorin barks under his breath rather than answer me. "He's supposed to be at the lake today."

"Who?" I ask again while looking around in confusion.

"He hasn't spotted us yet," Seth reasons. "We could still—"

"Boys!" A hulking man with a thick salt-and-pepper mustache and a warm smile interrupts. The gray uniform he's wearing makes me think he's a postal worker since it's the post office he just stepped out of, but it doesn't explain why my big, bad mountain men are shitting a fucking brick all of a sudden. "You didn't tell me you were coming down for supplies today. You're a bit early, aren't you?"

The man approaches, and when he stops barely a foot away, I finally spot the shiny gold badge on his right chest and read the seven black letters emblazoned on the metal.

Sheriff.

My stomach bottoms out.

I guess that explains why Khalil, Seth, and Thorin are ready to take me and haul ass in the opposite direction.

The sheriff finally notices they're not alone, and his eyes widen when they land on me. "Where are my manners? I'm so sorry. I didn't see you there, young lady. I'm Sheriff Kelly. Pleased to meet you."

I…don't say a fucking word.

I couldn't if I wanted to. It feels like I'm being strangled with the threat of what Thorin, Seth, and Khalil will do to this man if I do.

The sheriff's bushy brows turn down in confusion, and he chuckles awkwardly. "I s'pose the pleasure's all mine?"

Scream!

Tell him who you are!

Throw yourself at his feet and beg him to rescue you!

I don't do any of those things. I'm pretty sure I press a little closer to my guys. I feel a hand come to rest on my lower back, but I'm too nervous to look and see who it belongs to.

"Sorry. This is my cousin, Aurora," Khalil explains. "We were pretty close growing up, so she decided to visit me for a few weeks, but she gets shy around strangers."

"Oh. Well, you've come to the right place to get away from folks. Not too many around here. And these three aren't very social either, so you'll fit right in, though I'm sure you know that already."

His kind eyes roam my face, and I see the faint pinch in his brows when he notices my mask. Unlike J.R., the sheriff's too polite to ask about it.

"I guess that explains why you're a couple of weeks early for supplies?"

"Yup," Seth says simply.

Out of three, he's the only one who isn't tense. In fact, he looks downright bored. But no, that's not right. Seth gets excited when trouble is brewing, which means he's pretending right now.

Holy shit… This is bad.

We could fool the townspeople, but I'm guessing the sheriff is too shrewd.

"Well, welcome to Hearth, Aurora. We're glad to have you with us, and I hope you enjoy your stay."

With a tip of his hat, the sheriff walks off.

The moment he's out of hearing distance, Khalil takes my arm. "We got to go."

"Wait. What about the seeds and other stuff we need?"

"One of us will return for the rest in a couple of days," he answers tightly.

Without me, he means.

As we approach the dark gray, heavy-duty truck, I take one look around the quaint town. There's a fat chance I'll ever see it again, so I look my fill, stumbling over my feet as Khalil pulls me along.

Seth reaches the truck first and opens my door for me. He kisses the top of my head in apology before rounding the truck bed and climbing in on his side.

And just like that our outing is over. I barely got to see anything.

I go to follow my guys inside the truck when I feel eyes on me and pause. Looking around, I spot the culprit three cars down.

It's the sheriff.

He's standing next to his cruiser, watching me with a contemplative look on his face, and I don't look away.

I can't.

I hold his gaze through the mask, and time slows as we stare at one another. The town, the truck, and even my guys fade away as the sheriff attempts to unmask with me his eyes, and I teeter between wanting him to and wishing he'd go away and forget he ever saw me.

Judging by the suspicion rapidly growing in his gaze, I know there's little chance of that.

A horn blows nearby and snaps us out of it.

The sheriff lifts a hand and waves like he's greeting a neighbor instead of the missing woman whose face has undoubtedly been plastered all over every news channel in the world.

Lifting my hand, I force a smile before remembering he can't see it and awkwardly wave back.

I don't exhale until I'm safely inside the truck.

Thorin, who's in the driver's seat this time, starts the engine while Seth blindfolds me. I feel the truck making a U-turn, and then he speeds all the way back to the trail where the snowmobiles are parked.

The mood by the time we return to the cabin is dark as hell.

Thorin puts my bags down and then goes back outside to blow steam chopping wood.

Khalil goes down to the basement, where he trains well into the night.

Seth goes to lock himself inside his destroyed bedroom, and I have a feeling it's to keep himself in rather than keep us out.

Sensing that it won't end well for me if I poke the bears, I quietly perform my duties. I put everything away, mop the wooden floors, organize the kitchen cabinets, and make their dinner, which goes untouched. There's safety in reminding my mountain men why they're keeping me alive. Afterward, I shower, grab a gardening book from the shelf to study, and crawl into my loft to hide until morning.

Hopefully, they'll be in a better mood.

As much as I try, I can't get how the sheriff looked at me out of my head. Once the basement quiets and Thorin comes inside, only to go straight into his room, I allow myself to admit what Thorin, Khalil, and Seth must have already figured out.

The sheriff knows.

CHAPTER THIRTY-EIGHT

AURELIA

ONE MONTH LATER...

A ureliaaaaa!"

Birds burst from the canopy at the roar, and a whimper tears from my lips. Knowing who that pissed-off voice belongs to, I pick up my speed despite my body begging for a reprieve.

I've already been running for miles.

My heart pounds so fast that each beat feels more like a stab, and with each passing minute, it becomes impossible to catch my breath. But I keep putting one foot in front of the other. I can't risk slowing because I know the men chasing me won't. If they catch me, they'll keep their promise and punish me for running.

The pack on my back is heavy, and I'd move so much faster without it, but I can't risk leaving it.

I wish I could say the last month has been bliss, but no.

It's been weeks of waiting for Sheriff Kelly to come. That first morning after, Thorin and Khalil nearly came to blows over the decision of whether to take me and run.

Of course, Thorin was for it. Khalil wasn't so willing to give up their home for the slight chance that the sheriff didn't believe them.

And... He was right.

The sheriff never came.

I figured it would take him a few days to piece it together, but after the first week passed and then the second without him darkening our doorstep, I began to wonder if I imagined that moment between us.

Only the mood of my mountain men this past month confirmed that I hadn't. And then one night, when I was brave enough to ask about that day in town, Khalil revealed a little of their history with the sheriff, and I finally understood why the man hadn't come.

There might have been a second when the thought crossed the sheriff's mind about my true identity, but in the end, he didn't *want* to believe that the men he regarded as sons could do something like this right under his nose. It's the same willful ignorance many parents show, who know their kids are obnoxious little shits but pretend they're perfect angels instead.

Sheriff Kelly's choice not to follow his gut was the first time I understood that I was truly on my own. And now I needed to do something about where that left me.

Thorin, Khalil, and even Seth have been surly, paranoid, broody, overly possessive, and un-bear-a-ble.

Needless to say, I couldn't take it anymore.

The moment I stopped feeling their eyes on me for even a second, I ran. That brief head start is the only reason they haven't caught me yet.

I run for another half a mile before I can't take another step. I'm in much better shape than I was two months ago, thanks to Khalil and sheer fucking boredom, but I'm still gasping for air while the stitch in my side pulls tighter.

I stop next to a broken tree. The top half sweeps the ground that's free of snow now that it's spring. The last frost ended a week ago, and the flowers are already in bloom. The area looks familiar, but I'm too tired to care why. My curls are plastered to my forehead, and sweat stings my eyes as I catch my breath. Why hadn't I gone for one of the snowmobiles?

You know why.

Maybe…just maybe… I want them to catch me.

I'm a masochist like that.

A sound nearby catches my ear, and my head snaps in that direction.

Gotta move.

I groan miserably and push away from the tree I'm leaning against, but then the sleeve of my costume dress that I just mended a few days ago snags on a branch of the broken tree. I impatiently try to wrestle it free and feel the threads tear open once more.

"Damn it," I whisper.

Once I'm free, I take one step away from the tree, but a twig snaps underneath my foot, and I freeze.

"Did you hear that?" I hear Seth ask.

"I think she went this way."

Fuck, fuck, fuck!

They're closer than I thought.

I stumble forward in the opposite direction, picking up speed until I'm running again, woefully aware that each clumsy step only gives away my position. They're not trying to be quiet either, and why should they? They're faster than me, and there are three of them.

The knowledge forces me to slow down again until I'm sneaking between the trees. I spot a deer about a hundred feet away, watching me as it chews grass.

An idea forms.

Khalil, Seth, and Thorin are closing in fast, and I know it's only a matter of time before they find me.

Picking up a sizable rock, I sneak closer until I'm within throwing distance, and then I chuck the rock at the deer. It takes off when the stone hits the ground, so I tiptoe in the opposite direction.

"She's over here!"

Thinking it's me, I hear my guys giving chase after the deer. I even spot Seth leading the pack about thirty feet away.

I use the cover of their footfalls to sprint the other way, but they realize they've been played much too soon. I can hear them gaining on me again until one of them stumbles and groans like they're in pain. Against my better judgment, I pause.

That sounded like Khalil.

"Will you stop fucking around?" Thorin gripes. "We need to find her."

"Fuck you, Thayer. I stubbed my goddamn toe." I roll my eyes at the drama queen while Seth laughs like a maniac. "It's not fucking funny," Khalil snaps. "That shit hurts."

Seth laughs even harder, and then I hear a fist connecting with flesh, followed by the sound of them fighting. Instead of using the distraction of their own testosterone to put a little more distance between us, I let a laugh slip, and I don't have to wonder if they heard me.

"You better run fast, little wolf, because we're coming for you!" Thorin roars.

Shit.

I really am too stupid to live.

The bushes next to me began rustling, making a fuck ton of noise before two rabbits burst free and run for cover in another.

And now I know why this area seems so familiar.

The meadow.

I actually made it all the way to Thorin's farthest hunting ground.

Thorin must succeed in breaking up the fight because I hear the three of them running again. I spot the same rabbits darting from the bushes again, and I know where they're heading. For some fucking reason, I think it's a good idea to follow them like I'm a rabbit being hunted.

As I suspected, my furry friends make a mad dash for the meadow, where they disappear in the surprisingly tall grass. I slow just inside the edge of the meadow and gawk, my hands brushing the wild grass and occasional flower as I venture deeper.

Thorin hadn't exaggerated the beauty of the meadow. It's a sea of white, pink, and purple flowers, while the blue, orange, and yellow butterflies flitting over them only add to the variegated display.

"Aurelia!"

The pissed-off sound of my name ends with a terrified gasp from me.

No more than thirty feet away, Thorin emerges from the forest line to my right, and I drop onto my belly and start crawling before he can spot me.

"I fucking saw you, you piece of shit!"

Fuck. I belly crawl faster. I can still lose him in the grass. I can—

"There you are."

Gasping, I peer up and scream when I see Khalil standing over me. I hadn't even seen or heard him enter the meadow. They must have split up at some point.

Divide and conquer.

"No!" I spring to my feet so I can run, but I don't get more than a step before I feel his hand wrap around my hair. A second later, I'm being yanked back so fiercely it's a wonder my neck doesn't break.

I hit the ground hard enough to daze me for a few seconds.

Long enough for Khalil to drop down on top of me, take my dress in both hands and rip it down the middle. My breasts spill from the confines, and his angry gaze snaps to them.

Realizing I can't overpower him, I go for begging instead. "No. Please—"

"Safe word?"

I answer him by sending my fist soaring in a beautiful fucking cross punch, and it connects with Khalil's jaw, snapping his head sideways. My knuckles scream on impact, but I ignore the pain as I twist onto my side to escape.

He's not alone though, so I don't get far.

Seth appears—seemingly out of thin air—and I find myself cornered and captured once again. Relieving me of my pack, he forces me on my back for Khalil once again, and even though my nipples pebble from their rough handling, I still fight with everything in me to get away.

"Don't fucking touch me!"

Ignoring me, Seth grabs my wrists before I can give him the same treatment I offered Khalil. His hold is so harsh the fragile bones twinge, and I cry out from the pain.

Seth isn't moved.

His face could be carved from rock for all the emotion he gives. Simmering deep beneath the anger, though, is want. I know right then that Khalil won't be the only one ravaging my pussy once he's done.

Khalil uses his knees to shove my thighs apart to make room for himself, and it's only then that I notice his jeans are lowered over his ass, and his dick is out. He's still watching my bare breasts when he spits into his palm and begins stroking his hard cock while on his knees.

My stomach tightens as I watch him grow, the angry purple head already leaking pre-cum. I start struggling anew when he leans forward to settle between my thighs. I'm not wearing panties, so there's nothing left to stop him.

"Khalil, wait. I don't want to." Ignoring me, he rubs the tip of his cock back and forth through my slick. "I said I don't want to. Stop! Please! I'm sorry I ran. I—"

"Sorry?" he echoes coldly as he presses forward, my unprotected pussy flaring helplessly around the broad head of his cock. It feels like a threat. "How sorry are you, Goldilocks?"

"I'm *so* sorry. I don't know what I was thinking."

"No?" I don't realize Thorin's found us until he speaks. When I look up, I find him standing over the three of us like a vengeful god. "Because I think you knew exactly what you were doing, songbird." I start to tell him where he can stick his thoughts, but he drops to the ground next to us and presses his hand over my mouth. "Give her what she wants."

Khalil's hips meanly punch forward, and he doesn't stop until his balls are pressed against my ass. My eyes roll back inside my head as I release a tortured groan under Thorin's palm.

I can feel all three of their eyes on me as Khalil ruthlessly fucks me into the ground, crushing the wild grass and freshly bloomed flowers. Newly hatched butterflies fly over us while a few Peeping Tom bunnies watch the debauchery from nearby.

If some hikers or campers were to walk by, they'd have no idea what was happening within the shelter of the meadow. The knowledge makes me fight a little harder, the heels of my boots digging into the ground as I try to buck Khalil off me. He responds with hard shoves that are even more disarming than Seth's hold or Thorin's hand. Without fail, Khalil reaches that sensitive spot deep inside of me that he pounds over and over like one of his speed bags. I can feel my own orgasm beginning to crest when he finally buries himself one last time, throws back his head, and paints my contracting walls with cum.

"Goddamn, this bitch's pussy is lethal." Khalil swirls his hips one last time before pulling out of me and rolling away. I'm lying frozen on the ground, staring up at the sky with my thighs gapped open, and the hem of my dress rucked over my hips when he says, "You got to try it, Seth."

"Yeah?" Seth lets go of my wrists to take his turn, but I take them all by surprise when I burst into action, sitting up before he can and dislodging Thorin's hand.

I manage to crawl away a few feet, but a heavy weight lands on my back when Seth tackles me from behind, sending my half-naked front to the ground.

"Stop it!"

He responds by yanking my ass into the air, forcing me onto my hands and knees. I try to crawl away again, and he snatches me back before slapping my ass so hard my ears ring.

"Please, *please* don't fuck me."

"Or what?" Lining up his cock, Seth shoves inside of me.

Khalil's cum eases the way, but I still feel every inch of Seth's rage once he settles deep inside me. I don't think he's ever been this hard.

This time Thorin isn't quieting my cries, so they are free to revel in them as Seth fucks into me like an animal from behind. He ignores my continued pleas for him to stop while holding onto my hair in one hand like reins while his other clutches my hip to keep me still for him.

The liberties they take with my body without any remorse shouldn't feel this good, and yet here I am, clawing the ground and trying not to throw my ass back to meet Seth's thrusts. I can feel the soft grass digging into my knees and the flowers brushing my hard nipples as my tits sway back and forth, and it only confuses me more.

Even the rough, guttural sounds Seth makes pushes me closer and closer to that ever-looming edge. Luckily, Seth comes before I do, and then he shoves me away like I mean nothing to him as he stands.

Two down, one more to go. Exhaustion clings to me already. A bitch really needs to work on her stamina.

Collapsing onto my side, I don't even attempt to escape when Thorin folds himself against my back. He wraps a hand around my throat anyway because he knows that could change, and I close my eyes as he lifts my leg and enters me slowly. I can feel him watching my face as he takes his sweet fucking time. I can feel the other two watching us from where they lounge on the ground, enjoying their afterglow.

When I crack my eyes open, I see Khalil and Seth's eyes pinned to where Thorin and I are joined. Each time Thorin pushes in deep enough that I feel his balls, Seth stops breathing, while Khalil's chest rises and falls a little faster. When Thorin retreats, they watch the way my lower lips part and how their combined cum coats his length, easing the way for him when he plunges back inside of me.

I gasp when the tip lodges against that fleshy spot inside of me at the same time Khalil reaches over. The moment the rough pads of his fingers touch my clit, I erupt on Thorin's cock with a strangled cry.

Thorin doesn't make a sound when he comes, but I feel his cum joining Seth and Khalil's, so I turn my head toward him and find him watching me like he's afraid I'll disappear if he stops for even one moment.

I did kind of do exactly that this morning, so it's not an irrational fear.

A few minutes later, we're all still lying in the meadow, resting silently while birds chirp from their nests in the trees nearby and butterflies flit overhead, and I find myself tracing their flight patterns to stay awake. Every so often, I hear the soft thud of rabbits moving around the meadow.

After ten minutes, I hear Khalil or Seth shift in the grass nearby. Also hearing it, Thorin's head pops up from his doze, and he groans when he lifts my hand to check the watch on my arm and realizes that we've been here too long.

Feeling him finally free his soft cock from inside me, I peer over my shoulder and meet his warm, blue gaze.

"How was that, my wolf?"

Slowly, I let my smile free like a secret I'd been holding onto for too long and roll onto my back as I give a languid stretch. "That was perfect."

Leaning forward, Thorin bites my bottom lip before licking the abused spot and kissing me. "We got to go."

It's spring, which means more visitors in the Cold Peaks—hikers and campers will come out in droves, especially to visit the nearby lake. I hadn't meant to make Thorin, Khalil, and Seth chase me this far from the cabin, but I can't bring myself to regret it now.

They needed this as much as I did.

A chance to re-stake their claim and prove to themselves that they'll catch me no matter what, so I can fucking breathe again without the weight of their suspicion and insecurities.

The four of us right our clothing quietly since none of us actually took the time to undress, and then Khalil grabs and shoulders my pack before we start back for the cabin.

"Did you really have to throw her down so hard?" Thorin gripes at Khalil, and we both groan.

Have I mentioned the pissing matches between the three of them have been nonstop? Before, they were a united front against me, and now that I'm theirs, they've moved to staking their individual claims.

Since I know why Thorin is complaining, I respond before Khalil can. "I'm not pregnant, Thor. Give it a rest."

"You've been here two months, and you haven't had your period."

"Have you forgotten all the shit that's happened in that time? There are any number of reasons why it didn't come," I snap.

"You mean like letting us come inside you whenever we want?"

I ignore that, and Khalil and Seth start walking a little faster to get away from us. This isn't the first time Thorin and I have had this argument. "Besides, I've only missed one. It doesn't mean anything."

"Okay," he says smugly.

"It *doesn't*."

"*Okay*."

I growl at him and start walking faster to get away from him, but my legs have other plans, wobbling like Jell-O since they worked me over good, and I stumble around like a fawn that's just learned to walk.

I can feel Thorin eyeing me. "You okay?"

"Fine."

"I can carry you."

"I said I'm fine."

He catches up to me in one and a half steps and swoops me up in his arms. "Then indulge me, songbird," he whispers.

Giving up the pretense of not wanting to be doted on like the lost and stolen princess I am, I rest my head on his shoulder and close my eyes. "Fine."

"Ahhh!!!" My scream after we reach our clearing and approach the cabin has my mountain men on high alert as they stop to draw their weapons and look around for the threat.

"What? What is it?" Khalil asks with murderous fury etched all over his face.

Grinning, I bounce on my toes as I point toward the small plot off to the side. It's been shoveled clear of snow to make way for the fresh soil that's already been turned over and raked into four neat lines.

When my guys stare at me over their shoulders like I've lost my mind, I push through the circle they made around me and run over to the garden. Falling to my knees outside the four wooden planks that protect the garden, I squeal again when I see the little green leaves sticking out of the ground in the middle. I studied those books for days, insisting I wasn't ready before Khalil dragged my ass out of the cabin and shoved a spade in my hand.

Two weeks later, after much self-doubt, I'm staring at those long, thin first leaves no more than an inch long, thanking photosynthesis for doing its job.

I hear footsteps behind me as my mountain men join me, and then Khalil makes a sound of surprise when he sees it.

"Holy shit. You did it," Khalil praises.

"Damn. That's some fine-looking green, Sunshine."

"Congratulations, songbird."

Khalil crouches next to me and reaches out a curious brown hand toward those precious green leaves, and I panic, slapping it away. "No, don't touch it!"

He snatches his hand back and cuts his gaze toward me. "*Ow.*"

My cheeks warm in response. I did kind of overreact. "Sorry."

My gaze returns to that fragile, feeble sign of life, and I squeal even louder this time.

All three of my guys wince and groan.

"All right, I'm going in the house before I lose my hearing," Thorin grumbles before stomping away.

Khalil stands and flees as well, but Seth lingers. "Coming, Sunshine?"

I tear my gaze away from the leaves to look up at him. "In a minute. I—" A gasp leaves me, and I shoot to my feet. "Seth…your nose."

He blinks in surprise and then touches his nose. When he pulls his hand back to inspect his fingers, he doesn't react to the blood on them, and it sends my worry through the roof.

It's happened before.

"What's going on?"

"Nothing." He quickly turns away from me, but I chase after him. My hand on his arm stops him even though he can break free anytime.

"That's not nothing, Seth. Why is your nose bleeding?"

He still won't meet my gaze as he shrugs. "No reason. It does that sometimes."

My hands start shaking. "Stop lying to me and tell me why."

Instead of explaining, I watch him visibly shut down, and it's such a strange reaction coming from him. Seth is the most open and honest person I know. He wears his heart on his sleeve, and it's one of the things I love most about him. With Seth, I never have to doubt how he's feeling or what he feels for me. "Does it matter?"

"Yes."

Huffing, he starts walking again, so I run to cut him off. Seth swears as he stops in his tracks. "Sunshine—"

I launch myself at him and throw my arms around his neck. When his hands automatically find my lower back, I feel tears rise up, and for the first time, I think they might actually fall.

"Seth... Don't do this. Please. Don't leave me with this worry and no answers. It's cruel, and that's not you. Talk to me. Let me help you."

It's just a nosebleed, so I'm probably overreacting, but Seth's determination to hide and lie about it tells me I'm not.

He sighs, and I feel him shake his head, not in rejection of my plea, but as if he thinks he's failed me somehow. "I didn't want you to worry, Sunshine."

"Well, it's too late for that!" I cry a little hysterically.

I feel his hand caressing my back soothingly. "Everything's going to be okay."

"How can I believe you when you're keeping secrets from me?"

Seth skims his lips over my forehead and, likely realizing I won't let it go, says, "My nose is bleeding because of Zeke."

"Zeke?" I echo. Lifting my head from his shoulder to see his face, I search Seth's gaze. "Why would he do this to himself? And to you?"

"Because he wants to wake up, and I..." Seth clams up again.

My racing mind fills in the blanks. "You've been holding him back." I stagger back a step when he nods. "Seth, why? If this is hurting you—"

"Because I'm selfish," he answers, releasing a shuddering breath as he nuzzles my face. "And because I'll do anything to keep you safe."

"You think he'll hurt me?" Seth shakes his head and again leaves me to fill in the blanks. When I do, the knot in my stomach tightens even more.

"You think Thorin and Khalil will." He shrugs, which means yes. "Seth, that's not fair. Thorin and Khalil said they'll talk to Zeke. It will take some time, but they swear Zeke will come around—"

"He won't," Seth says with a finality that makes my heart fall into my stomach.

"How can you be so sure?"

"Other than the obvious?" he says with uncharacteristic sarcasm. The obvious being that Seth literally lives inside Zeke's head. Who better to know the man than his alternate persona? "I'm sure because Ezekiel fell in love once. Did I tell you that?"

"What? No. No, you haven't."

"There was this girl at Isaac's compound. Tatum Brantford. Before shit got bad and Zeke still believed he was there to get to know his older brother, he met her. She was the daughter of one of Isaac's most devout followers. After Zeke fell in love with her, Tatum's father was appointed Isaac's secretary, and her family reaped the rewards of his newly elevated position."

"Just because they fell in love?"

"Because Tatum's the reason Zeke stayed. Isaac couldn't just kill Zeke. It had to be a sacrifice. Zeke had to die by his own hand, or the ritual to make Isaac 'immortal' would never work."

"You mean Isaac was conning people into killing themselves?"

"It's much easier if the sacrifices are already suicidal, but Zeke wasn't, and Isaac knew that. He needed time to break Zeke."

"And when brainwashing didn't work, Isaac turned to torture," I guess.

Seth nods, and his eyes become hollow and haunted as the memories resurface. "When Zeke's instincts were telling him to run, when people went missing, and he began to suspect the Seeds of the Undying and his brother were responsible, Zeke stayed for Tatum. She told him she couldn't leave her family, and he stayed because he loved her."

"She honeypotted him?"

"*Yes.*" Sadness for a man I'd technically never met clings to my heart as I wait for Seth to deliver the final blow. I know it's coming, and he doesn't keep me waiting for long. "Tatum made Zeke fall for her and then used his love to hurt him. So no, Sunshine. Zeke won't ever come around because he won't trust you. I was the one awake when Thorin and Khalil found him. I saw their guilt and felt their rage, and those feelings never really left them, so I can tell you with absolute certainty that there is nothing on this earth—not even you—that will make Thorin and Khalil abandon their brother a second time."

Seth kisses my forehead and walks away. He leaves me standing alone while this new life I'd stolen for myself slowly crumbles around me.

CHAPTER THIRTY-NINE

AURELIA

Seth is back to normal in no time—as if the nosebleed and what he told me yesterday had never happened.

Well, that makes one of us.

It makes me wonder how long he's been suffering the nosebleeds alone and watching the clock winding down if he's able to recover so quickly.

On top of that, Thorin and Khalil have noticed that I've been withdrawn. At first, they were simply confused and then extra attentive, but after that didn't work, and I continued to insist that everything was fine, they became frustrated with me.

I mean more than usual.

The four of us are sitting out on the upper deck enjoying the warm spring afternoon. At first, it was just me, but apparently, the three of them have entered the clingy stage of this new, weird space we're in because everywhere I go, they follow.

I mean more than usual.

"Seth," I say as I run my fingers through his lengthy, black hair. His head is in my lap as he lies between my legs on the lounger while I read him one of his favorite stories.

He jerks awake and stretches like a jungle cat before yawning and speaking in a groggy voice, "Yeah?"

"I think it's time for a haircut. You've gone from dashing debonair to surfer duuuude."

I'm smiling at my own joke until Seth stiffens, and my smile falls. I swear

I see Khalil and Thorin still as well. Seth sits up, and there's no mistaking the panicked look in his eyes.

"Uhh…" I look to Khalil and Thorin for help, but Khalil is making the sign of the cross, and Thorin looks ready to toss himself over the railing. "Did I say something wrong?"

"Seth doesn't like haircuts," Khalil tells me.

"We only cut it when Zeke is awake," Thorin adds.

"Oh." Closing the book and swinging my legs over the side of the lounger, I stand and shrug. "Well, in that case, never mind. I'm sure I'll learn to love this look too."

And let's be honest. My panties are dropping for Seth either way.

I thrust my fingers into his hair one last time, letting the long, silky strands slip through my fingers, and then I leave them on the deck to go back inside the house, sliding the glass door closed behind me.

It's laundry day, so I go from room to room, collecting the dirty clothes and towels strung all over the place since—let's face it—I'm a terrible maid. I then carry it all downstairs to the basement to get started.

I'm halfway through the first load while singing the final chorus from my favorite track on my first album when I hear shouting and something crashing. Dropping Seth's wet shirt back inside the sink, I rush upstairs and find myself in the middle of absolute pandemonium.

The kitchen table has been shoved into the side door.

One of the chairs is overturned.

There's a dent in one of the few walls that have drywall.

The antler chandelier above the kitchen table is rocking back and forth.

And there is blood…everywhere.

Khalil is slumped on the floor and leaning against the wall with a dent in it. Thorin is bent over and panting hard with one hand resting on the back of the couch and the other holding his bleeding side. I follow his murderous glare to Seth, who is sitting on the floor by the table with his forearms resting on his knees and small scissors dripping blood clutched in his hand.

"What the hell happened in here?" I scream.

Thorin's gaze flicks to me and then back to Seth. "He cut me."

"Okay. Why?"

"Because I tried to cut his hair for him."

"Why would you do that? I thought you said Seth hated haircuts," I immediately scold.

This time Thorin aims that daggerish glare at me. "If you want to blame someone, blame yourself. He wanted to please you and wouldn't shut up about it until one of us agreed to cut his hair, and *I* got stabbed for it."

"I thought you said he cut you."

Thorin closes his eyes. "Aurelia, I swear to God."

My gaze moves to Khalil, and I lift a brow. "And you?"

Khalil tosses an indignant hand toward Seth. "He fucking flipped out when I tried to stop him from killing Thor."

Finally, I allow my gaze to return to Seth. His blank gaze is fixed on the floor, and I'm not even sure he knows I'm here.

I take one step toward him when Khalil finally gets off his ass faster than any human should be able to move. "Don't even think about it," he warns, coming to stand between Seth and me. "Not when he's like this."

"Seth won't hurt me."

"I'm not taking that chance."

"It's not your decision." It's a testament to how bad Khalil's hurting that I'm able to duck around him and kneel in front of Seth. "Hey…" I lay my hand on his arm when he doesn't react. "Seth, can you hear me?" He peeks up at me and then looks away like he's ashamed before nodding. "What happened? Why did you attack Khalil and Thorin?"

"I didn't mean to."

My heart cracks in two. "I know you didn't. Thorin and Khalil know it too."

Behind me, Thorin snorts. I glare at him over my shoulder in time to see him rolling his eyes. Or maybe he's about to pass out.

Jesus, how much blood did he lose? It's everywhere.

I turn my focus back to Seth. Thorin may be injured, but Seth's the one who needs me most—needs *us* most—and I know Thorin and Khalil agree because they don't complain or leave to take care of their wounds. Thorin will risk bleeding out, and Khalil, who's clutching his head, will risk a concussion to make sure Seth is okay.

I haven't told them this and maybe never will, but their determination to care for each other—no matter the cost to themselves—is one of the things I love about them most. It's one of the reasons I agreed to stay.

"Goldilocks." I look at Khalil, and he nods to Seth's hand—the one holding the scissors—and I pick up on the unspoken order.

"Seth, can I have the scissors?" I hold out my hand for him to place them in, but he clutches the scissors tighter.

"I don't want to hurt you," he explains.

"You won't. Give me the scissors."

"If you have them, I will. I won't be able to help it, Sunshine."

I drop my hand with a sigh. "Why do you think that, Seth?"

"It's the memories of what Isaac did to him on that table," Thorin answers when Seth remains stubbornly silent. "He doesn't like anyone coming at him with sharp objects."

Hence, why Seth doesn't like haircuts…

God, I'm going to need a list so something like this doesn't ever happen again. I'm already cursing my big mouth. It fucking burns me that Seth thinks he has to go to such measures to please me.

"Seth, listen to me." He lifts his head, his green eyes filled with worry and shame. "Grow your hair down to your fucking knees. Dye it pink. Cut it all off. I don't give a shit. But never, ever put yourself through this again. I do not care what you look like, you fool. I love *you*." Seth's eyes widen, but I hold his gaze steady as I hold out my hand. Yes, I know what I just said, and I fucking meant it. "Now give me the damn scissors."

He holds out the shears, and I make sure to wrap my hand around the blades, risking cutting my hand open so that he doesn't see them when I take the scissors from him.

I feel Khalil hovering behind me, so I hand him the scissors without taking my eyes off Seth. The moment Khalil moves away to hide those fucking things, Seth reaches out and pulls me into his lap.

"You love me," he says while nuzzling my face with his.

"Yes, Seth." I tilt my head back and smile when he kisses my neck. "I love you."

"Oh, sure," Khalil drawls when he returns. "You get cut, and I get thrown into a wall, but Seth is the one who gets coddled."

Thorin grunts his agreement, and when I look over my shoulder, I see him swaying on his feet when he tries to straighten.

"Thorin!" Shooting to my feet, I rush over to him. I reach him just as he collapses back against the couch. "Khalil, help me."

Khalil curses and nudges me aside so that he can help Thorin around the couch. Thorin is passed out by the time Khalil lays him down, and my worry skyrockets. I'm actually wringing my fucking hands.

"Fuck," Khalil grumbles when he peels back Thorin's T-shirt to inspect the wound. "Seth got him good. Help me get this off."

I help by lifting Thorin's head and arms while Khalil frees him from the confines of the shirt. "What now?"

"We need the first aid kit. It's downstairs."

I go to stand when I hear Seth speak. "Here."

Looking up, I see he's already holding Thorin's med kit when I hadn't even noticed he'd left the room. Khalil takes it from him and thanks him.

"Shouldn't we take Thorin to the hospital?" I ask when Khalil begins rifling through the medical supplies.

"Not if I can help it. It's really not that bad. Thorin is just being dramatic to get you to fuss over him like you were doing Seth."

I start to tell Khalil how ridiculous that sounds when I catch Thorin peeking an eye open before quickly closing it when he sees me watching him.

"Are you freaking kidding me?" I yell as I stand.

Thorin sighs and looks pretty proud of himself when he opens his eyes now that his ruse has ended. "Can you blame me?"

"Yes!"

"Don't mind him, Sunshine. He's just jealous."

Thorin lifts his chin. "Damn straight."

I grab one of the throw pillows from the couch and hit him in the face with it. "I can't believe you."

I go to storm away when Thorin reaches out and catches my hand, aggravating his wound further in the process. Khalil barks at him to stay still, but Thorin keeps his blue eyes on me. "I'm sorry for making you worry, wolf. Stay with me. Please."

I debate it for a few seconds, torturing him even more than Khalil is as he cleans the wound before I go to kneel by Thorin's shoulder. I notice he's sweating profusely, so I tell Seth to bring me some cool water and a cloth. When he returns, I play nursemaid, dabbing Thorin's forehead with the cool cloth while Khalil patches him up.

Seth busies himself cleaning up the mess he made, and half an hour later, we're all too exhausted from this day to participate any further. Khalil orders Thorin to stay off his feet for the rest of the day so as to not tear open his stitches. Thorin asks me to keep him company, and Seth insists on coming too.

And that is the story of how the four of us end up in Khalil's bed since his is the only one big enough to fit the four of us.

I won't lie and say it isn't awkward at first.

It's not that the three of them aren't used to sharing a bed, but it's the first time they've shared it with a woman. Seth made sure to let me know that I was the first when he read the question in my eyes and the brewing jealousy behind it—and all before I could say a word.

"Well, since we don't have a TV, I guess we're going to have to entertain ourselves," I announce once I'm settled between Thorin and Seth while Khalil lays between my legs—much like Seth was out on the deck earlier. "Not sex," I clarify when the three of them start eyeing me like I'm dinner and dessert.

"All right then," Khalil drawls. "What do you suggest?"

"We could play a board game."

"That's not a good idea unless you want a repeat of earlier. Thorin is a sore loser."

"Cards?"

"We lost those years ago."

"Okay…" I ponder for a few moments before an idea pops into my head. "Tell me something you miss from your old life. Something you can't get out here."

"Two months ago, I would have said pussy, but now that we've got the best and she lets us do whatever we want, I'll have to change my answer to…my parents."

"It's sweet that you miss your mom and dad, but I'm not sure how I feel about you referring to my vagina as a separate entity, Khalil Poverly."

"Even though she's nicer to us than you?"

"What can I say? I'm a jealous bitch, and you're skirting dangerously close to never speaking to her again."

Khalil chuckles and turns his head to bite the inside of my thigh. He doesn't bother to soothe the spot after because he knows I like the pain, but his thumb sweeping my knee a few inches down speaks volumes as well.

"What about you?" I ask Thorin.

He has to think about the answer, and I'm not surprised. Living in a remote cabin in some far-off corner of the world is the exact kind of life I'd picture Thorin leading. Of the three, he's probably the most comfortable here, but I also know he'd go wherever Khalil and Zeth are. "Takeout," he finally answers, and I nod. It makes perfect sense considering he does all the hunting. That has to get taxing after a while.

"Seth?"

"Movies. No! Music." He makes a face like I'm pulling his teeth. "Movies and music?"

"It's okay, Seth. You can miss both."

"Well, in that case, can I add video games to my list right under my parents?" Khalil asks.

I gently massage his temples with my thumbs just in case his head still hurts. "Sure."

"What about you?" Thorin asks.

I don't even have to think about it. "Hot tubs."

"Hot tubs?"

"Yeah, I have one in my house. If this was an interview, I'd say it was my favorite place to dream up my next hit song, but that's bullshit. The truth is, the hot tub is where I get sloshed."

"Nice," Seth answers.

"You guys should really consider getting one. Maybe out there on one of the decks overlooking the wilds." I smile a little to myself as I imagine. "Yeah, that would be perfect."

"We have one," Khalil answers.

"Really?" I frown. As big as the cabin is, I'm pretty sure it would be hard to miss. Between the three of them, they must have fucked me in every room, against every possible wall, and on every surface by now. "Well, where is this magical, hidden hot tub? I haven't seen it."

"We'll show you tomorrow."

"Ooookaaaay."

"What else would you like to know, Sunshine?"

"Hmm." I tap my chin as I think about it. "Ooh! I know. The three of you could tell me about all the girls you used to date."

"Actually, I think I saw those playing cards somewhere the other day," Khalil says, faking like he's getting up to look for them.

"Nice try, Poverly." I grab his shoulder and shove him back down. "Now, you first."

He groans and swipes both hands down his face in agitation. "What do you want to know, Goldilocks?"

Thinking about what Seth divulged to me yesterday, I ask, "Have you ever been in love?" In my peripheral vision, I see Seth stiffen as if he's read my mind.

"Not really," Khalil answers lightly. "Love? Nah. Lust? Hell yeah."

"Well, who have you been *in lust* with?"

"You'll have to be more specific," he deadpans.

"Who was the one girl you wanted so fiercely that it consumed your every waking thought?"

"You."

I roll my eyes even as I feel myself fighting a blush. "*Before* me, Khalil."

He blows out an annoyed breath while I wait for the answer I'm not sure I want to know. It's completely unfair of me to ask, but it's too late to put the curiosity back in the bag. Khalil is already answering.

"Mrs. Wallace, my ninth grade algebra teacher. She was about sixty years old and wore church heels and bifocals, but man, she could deviate the fuck out of some formulas."

Thorin and Seth snicker.

"I hate you all."

"Goldilocks…" Khalil turns over and yanks me down the bed until I'm staring up at the twisted canopy, and he's hovering over me with both hands planted on either side of my head. My hands automatically find his hard pecs, sliding down to his six-pack and feeling his warm skin underneath my palms because I can't resist touching him. I know Khalil loves it when I do. "Who gives a fuck about the girls who came before? As far as I'm concerned, they don't exist anymore. There is no before you because there's only you. Our story starts and ends with you and me." A throat clears before Khalil rolls his eyes. "And Thorin and Seth too."

I slide my foot down Khalil's huge calf muscles, teasing him as I grin up at him. "Good answer, Poverly."

Since I'm wearing one of his flannels again—which I'd purposely left open—and only a thin pair of panties underneath, Khalil lowers his head and licks my sternum right over the spot where my heart beats. My nipples harden on contact, and I can't quite catch my breath after that. "And what about you? You still haven't told us if you fucked your bodyguard yet."

Feeling like all the air has been sucked out of the room, my foot drops back onto the bed at the reminder of Tyler. "What does it matter?" I ask, voice strangled. "He's dead."

"Exactly my thoughts," Thorin says.

When I turn my head his way, I see that he's glaring at Khalil. They exchange a look I can't decipher, and then Khalil rolls off me with a heavy sigh to settle between Seth and me.

I figure Thorin is just pissed at Khalil for upsetting me, which he didn't, not really. It's my own fault for bringing up the topic of old flames.

Not that Tyler was an old flame.

He—it's complicated.

It takes me a few minutes to recover—to push Tyler way down where I'm safe from ever thinking about him again. The guilt is just too crippling to bear without coming to a standstill. In these wilds, where anything could kill me if I let my guard down, it's too dangerous to risk.

Tyler, Cassie, and all the others are dead because of me, and here I am, trying to move on and steal a slice of happiness for myself as if I deserve any of it.

I should have done the Avery Shaw interview a year ago.

I should have lied to Tania after she told me that I was her idol. I should have smiled prettily and told her that she absolutely has what it takes to be the next me. Instead, I looked into the starry eyes of a dreamer and eclipsed it with the cold, hard truth.

She could never be me.

Because what it took to be me was my soul, and Tania was still new enough to save hers. I didn't care about that, though, if I'm being sincere. I'm not going to put on a false cape and claim I was only trying to rescue Tania when I spewed my venom.

The truth is, I hated her.

For being everything I never got the chance to be and then rubbing it in my face, I fucking despised her.

And if I'd lied, Tyler and the others would still be alive, and I'd never have met Thorin, Khalil, and Seth. The knowledge only fills me with even more turmoil because I can no longer imagine my existence without my mountain men being a part of it, nor do I want to.

I'd suffer a thousand falls from grace and fiery plane crashes just to find them again and again.

The knowledge and acceptance that I will always be the villain splits me open, leaving me vulnerable as I stare at the twisted branches and fairy lights. The guys are still talking among themselves. Meanwhile, it becomes hard for me to breathe, so I sit up with a gasp. I can feel their eyes snap to me when Seth stops mid-sentence. I can feel the soft bedspread underneath me as my fingers dig into it to keep me from floating away.

A moment later, it feels as if the room itself is shrinking until I realize it's Thorin, Khalil, and Seth pushing in and closing around me, letting me know they are there. I'm safe to process whatever the fuck is happening to me.

After the tearing, stretching, and crumbling are done, after I shed this skin that has never been mine, I become trapped in this new shell that's hard in places and soft in others—that is both full of color and uncomfortably transparent.

I still panic, even while knowing somehow that it's only temporary.

I try to put a name to it, but it escapes me. It hovers on the tip of my tongue and raises the hairs on my nape whenever I try to force it out—as if simply uttering the word when my mountain men can hear invites danger itself.

Is this what Seth, Zeke, and Bane feel whenever one of them splits?

"What is it?" Seth asks while placing a careful hand on my shoulder.

I barely hold back my flinch when I feel the strength in those fingers, but Seth snatching back his hand tells me he knows. I don't have to wonder if I hurt his feelings, but since I can't explain why my entire body feels like it might detonate at any second without spiraling further, I say nothing.

Pushing past my mountain men, I crawl to the foot of the bed and climb off. None of them speaks until I reach the door.

"Where are you going?" Thorin asks. There's a worried pinch to his brows when I look over my shoulder at them.

"I changed my mind," I say, watching blue, brown, and green eyes shutter when they mistake my meaning. "I don't think I'm going to need that nap."

I flee before they can convince me to stay, closing the door to Khalil's bedroom behind me as I go.

Gasping for air, I stumble up the stairs to the first floor and over to the front door until I'm out of the cabin. I don't stop running until I'm off the front porch and falling to my knees in the dirt path that's been hidden under snow all winter.

It's not until I've caught my breath that I realize the path, still partially covered in snow, diverges in two directions. The thinner trail leads straight ahead out of the clearing, and the second, wider path leads around the house toward the cliff, which continues past the gap in the trees that I'm only now noticing.

What...the fuck?

CHAPTER FORTY

KHALIL

W here are we going? And why can't it wait until a more godly hour?"
Aurelia huffs, partly from exertion and partly from annoyance at
being up this early.

"Because where we're going and what we'll do once we get there is not
for God's eyes and ears," I respond.

My cryptic answer only earns me a scowl from Aurelia.

We haven't been forthcoming after dragging her out of bed because our
destination is a secret. We don't have many chances to surprise her out here,
so as usual, we're forcing her to indulge us.

At our altitude and being early spring, it's still a little chilly in the
mornings, but it won't last, which is why we left the moment it was safe to
give us time to reach Maia. We're at the base of her now, making our way up
the trail in a single file line.

I chose to walk behind Aurelia so that I could stare at the bottom curve of
her plump ass hanging out of her denim shorts. I could kiss Seth for finding
them when we scavenged her stuff because the view is better than anything
these wilds could offer. I can tell she's not wearing panties either from the
way her ass jiggles, even within the tight confines of her shorts.

I tilt my head to get a better angle and trip over a fucking rock. My
stumble draws Aurelia's knowing gaze over her shoulder. "Now that's what
you get. Pervert."

She wiggles her ass teasingly, and I groan as I reach down to squeeze my
dick. I've never wanted anyone as much as I do Aurelia fucking George.

I'm damn near rabid and pitching a noticeable tent by the time we reach the cliffside halfway up the mountain. The travertine terrace overlooking the rushing river underneath has a stunning view of Big Bear to our left and Little Bear to our right and all the wilds in between. It never gets old, but Aurelia doesn't notice it.

She takes one look at the shallow pools of water with steam rising from the depths and gasps. "Is that what I think it is?" She squeals when I nod and leans over to see more of the hot springs.

"I know it's not whatever fancy hot tub you have back home, but it will more than do the trick, I promise."

"And look," Seth adds while reaching into his pack and pulling out two bottles of cheap wine and champagne. Aurelia had snuck them both onto the supply list before our last run to Hearth. Seth holds them both up now with a grin.

Goldilocks giggles when she sees them. "Seth, I think it's a little early for wine and champagne."

"Oh. Really?"

She snorts. "No."

Seth howls and starts thrusting his hips, making Aurelia laugh even harder.

It's not until Thorin, Seth, and I remove our clothes, revealing our swimming shorts underneath, that Aurelia sobers.

"Wait, I don't have a bathing suit."

My grin spreads even wider. "*We know.*"

Propping her hand on her wide hips, she turns to face me. "You expect me to get in there naked? What if someone comes?"

"I wouldn't worry about that. I'm sure Seth will scare them off." On cue, Seth starts barking and growling.

Aurelia still doesn't appear convinced even while looking at the shallow pools of water longingly.

"It's still early in the season, baby. Most of the Cold Peaks are still impassable and will be for another month or two. No one's coming."

"The three of *you* got up and down this past month. Twice."

"That's because *we* know what we're doing."

"And Pete?"

"That idiot was desperate and stupid enough to risk it. You know that."

More accurately, Pete and his boys were wanted for trafficking two counties over and had chosen the wrong mountain to hide out on. End of story.

"Fine." The three of us don't even pretend we're not watching her strip until she's naked. Aurelia looks around nervously like she's expecting a tourist to pop up the moment she's vulnerable. She has one arm covering her breasts and her other hand covering her pretty pussy, and that just won't do.

The unusual sight of her so insecure has me walking over to her. I stand behind her until my erection is nestled against her ass, and I bring my lips to her ear. "Do you really think we'd let anyone lay eyes on what's ours?" I whisper.

I'm already grabbing her wrists by the time she shakes her head. "No."

She still resists as I force her arms down by her side, but I easily overpower her until her perfect body is once more bared to the forested canopy on the other side of the river. We're high enough on Maia that we can see the top of the trees. "Khalil…"

She falls silent when I cup her breasts in my palms, massaging the heavy globes while I thumb her nipples. "Look at these perfect fucking tits," I praise. "And you're all ours. We got you, Goldilocks. You know that, don't you? You're safe with us, baby."

Thorin steps into the first shallow pool, which happens to be the largest, and offers his hand to her. Aurelia takes it, and he helps her down into the hot pool.

Steam immediately curls around them both while Seth and I follow them into the pool.

"Fuck, yes. This feels amazing," I hear Aurelia moan. The steam immediately veils them, but I can still see her body relaxing as she leans into Thor.

Seth comes up on her from behind while Thorin is plastered to her front, and I watch the former run his hands down her arms and over the goose bumps already covering her skin from the sharp contrast of the cool air and hot water.

Content to watch her with them for now, I hang back and take a seat on the uneven lip of the pool. Thorin is kissing one side of her neck while Seth is devouring the other, and I'm growing harder by the minute watching them consume her.

Without any direction, Aurelia reaches back and slips her hand inside Seth's shorts, and I know the moment she wraps her hand around him because he releases a shuddering breath and bites into her shoulder.

The pain of his teeth sinking into her skin only inflames her need, so she frees him from his shorts while jerking him off and kissing Thorin like they're long-lost lovers.

There's a moment when I think Aurelia might pull away and end this before it even really starts, and that's when Thorin cradles a hand against her belly. She stiffens, so Thorin quickly shifts gears and slips his hand between her thighs as if the moment never happened.

Aurelia softens once more and moans into his mouth while he toys with her clit. She starts jerking Seth faster while he matches her rhythm, thrusting his hips into her hand.

"Sunshine, baby, I'm going to come," Seth warns her hoarsely.

Aurelia uses her hold on him to tug him closer to her until the underside of his cock rests between her ass. And that's where he comes, his warm seed spurting onto her lower back and marking her as his.

The moment Seth quiets, Thorin ends his kiss with Aurelia, grabs the back of her thighs, and lifts her from the pool. Neither of them speaks a word as he lowers her down on his cock, but Aurelia isn't able to keep quiet for long as he drills in and out of her. Thorin's gaze is intense as he watches her take him, and if I had to describe what he was feeling, it would be nothing less than obsession. Aurelia looks like a goddess being worshipped by his cock.

"Thorin…please…"

"What's the matter? You want to come, songbird?"

"Yeah."

Thorin carries her across the pool before setting her down on her feet in front of me. When he spins her around, and she sees me, Aurelia tries to climb in my lap and mount me like a bitch in heat. "Khalil, make me come. Please?"

Thorin yanks her ass back with a possessive growl, and she growls back as he bends her over. Aurelia's head ends up hovering over my lap, so I grab a fistful of her hair while finally freeing my dick from the confines of my shorts.

"Is this what you want, baby?" I tap her perfect, pouty lips with my thick dick before working the shaft until pre-cum spills out of the slit. The pearly drop coats her bottom lip, so I use the tip to spread it across the seam of her pretty lips. "You want me in your mouth?"

Aurelia nods and holds my gaze while she licks my cum from her lips. I know the moment Thorin enters her again because that divot between her brows appears, and her mouth parts like she's full already when Thorin still has a few inches left to give our girl.

A plaintive moan slips from her lips when his pelvis finally meets her ass.

I carefully gag her with nine more inches until her nostrils flare against my thighs once I hit the back of her throat.

Groaning, I lean against the wall of rock, sediment, and mud behind me, and I keep her there for a while—long past her need to breathe. Aurelia sinks her nails into me while Thorin pounds her pussy, but I still don't let her up for air.

We're using her, and I can tell by Thorin's grunts and strangled curses that it drives our girl wild. I can only imagine what her tight little pussy is doing to him. It's the only thing that rivals her hot, wet mouth wrapped around me.

When I finally pull her off me, copious amounts of saliva and pre-cum cling to her mouth and chin while she coughs and gags and sucks in huge breaths.

"Had enough, Goldilocks?"

"No," she replies in a raspy voice.

"No?" My thumb sweeps her swollen bottom lip. "You want some more?"

"Yes. Yes, *please*."

Rather than give her what she's begging for, I tug at her lip. "Even though Thorin wants to breed you?"

"I Ic—" She hiccups when he goes too deep. "He does?"

"Of course. Tap my wrist three times, and I'll make him stop, Goldilocks. You understand?"

Aurelia looks torn but then she nods, and I finally break, feeding her my dick with the press of my hand on the back of her head. Once Aurelia's head is greedily bobbing up and down in my lap, I look around for Seth and spot him crouched over by our packs, fucking around with the champagne bottle. I refocus on our girl and trying not to come yet.

When I pull Aurelia off my dick again, she sucks in another huge breath and then turns her head over her shoulder. I know she's watching the way Thorin's scarred abs flex, and his blond hair hangs around his face and shoulders as he fucks her. It's almost as mesmerizing as the sight of her round ass jiggling from the impact. The sound of their slick skin slapping each time they come together mixes with the bubbling water of the pools while the steam continues to rise up, obscuring the three of us locked together.

"Thorin? I kn-know you're gonna...c-come...soooon. Can you *p-pleeee-ase* pull ooooout?"

Thorin's only answer is to flick his determined blue gaze up at me.

I grant the unspoken request, silencing Aurelia again when I grab her curls and force her face back toward me. Rather than tap my wrists like I instructed, she presses her lips firmly together, but I win our battle of wills when I reach down and tug on one of her nipples until she cries out from the pain.

I guide my dick back between her open lips with a groan.

Aurelia's sounds of protest are muffled but no less emphatic as she attempts to appeal to our softer side—as if such a thing exists. If Thorin wants her barefoot and pregnant, that's the way it will be. Only one thing will stop him, but Aurelia doesn't reach for it. She doesn't flee toward safety. She follows him into darkness.

I don't see her hand moving between her legs until Thorin makes a sound caught between pleasure and surprise, and I realize she's fondling his balls to make him come sooner.

"Goddamn, songbird." With possession and lust twisting his features, Thorin lifts his leg to rest his foot on the lip of the pool next to me, fucking her pussy from a deeper angle while I muffle her cries with my cock.

The three of us come together, but it feels too soon because I already need more. The sounds of our pleasure mix with the pop of a cork and the spray of the chilled champagne Seth managed to get open.

The moment Thorin empties his balls, he pulls out of her and swims away in the shallow pool while an exhausted Aurelia crawls into my lap with a pussy full of Thorin's cum and a belly full of mine. She rests her head on my shoulder and nuzzles my neck while I rub her back, avoiding the area where Seth's cum is drying. Staring up at the sky our star fell from, I wonder how the fuck we got to be so lucky.

It has been, without a doubt, a perfect fucking morning.

It takes us longer to get back to the cabin after we leave the hot springs since Aurelia is drunk and fucked out after the three of us decided to go a second round before we left.

We just manage to get her into Thorin's bed before she passes out with a mumbled good night despite it being the afternoon. Once she's out, the three of us lounge around Thorin's bed, content to watch her sleep for a while like the obsessive creeps she accused us of being.

"We shouldn't have let her drink today," Thorin says as he holds her.

I cringe from the other side of the bed when I realize the risk we'd taken today, but fuck it. Aurelia needed it, and we'd sworn to take care of her—to never make her want for anything or regret for even a moment choosing us. I eye Thorin over Aurelia. "You really think she's pregnant?"

He shakes his head as his eyes trace the delicate lines of her face. "I don't know. That's why we need to get her to take that fucking test. Until then, we're flying blind."

Rubbing my beard, I watch Aurelia's chest rise and fall, and I swear my own breathing slows to match her rhythm. "Aurelia's stubborn."

"Aurelia's not in charge," Thorin reminds me. "She's taking that fucking test."

"And if she is knocked up? She won't be happy about it. You know that, right?"

Thorin shrugs like an asshole. "Too fucking bad. She'll get over it."

"I think a baby will be cool," Seth decides from the foot of the bed where he's lying on his side, picking the threads in the bedspread. "Maybe one that looks like Sunshine."

My gaze flicks to him. "They require a lot of attention, Seth. A baby will take up all of her time."

"Oh. Well, then, never mind."

When my attention returns to Thorin, I catch him rubbing her belly like he tried to do at the hot springs before she shut down. "And you need to figure out if you really want a baby or if you're just hell-bent on trapping her, Thor. Really consider it and decide—preferably before one of us does actually knock her up, and it's too fucking late to take it back."

He glowers at me but doesn't argue because he knows I'm fucking right. Aurelia doesn't deserve to be saddled with that baggage because he's insecure.

"She wants us, Thor. She wants to stay. She's keeping us. You don't need to make it so that she can't ever change her mind. You just need to trust her. Do you?"

Thor stares down at Aurelia sleeping in his arms, and when he finally answers, his voice is thick with all of the things left unsaid between them. "Yes."

"Good." I exhale my relief as I stretch, feeling my own exhaustion creeping in. "Then chill the fuck out, bro. She'll give us a baby when she's ready. It should be her choice anyway."

I don't realize I've fallen asleep until I'm jarred awake a few hours later by a relentless pounding. At first, I think it's my brain knocking against my skull since I couldn't seem to turn it off even while asleep. When I lift my aching head and look around the room, I realize it's just Thorin, Seth, and me in the bed.

Aurelia's gone.

Seth wakes up next when the knocking continues, and then Thor.

"What the fuck is that?" Thorin asks in a groggy tone.

"I think someone's at the door," Seth answers as he rubs his eyes.

I stand from the bed, wondering if Aurelia stepped outside for a moment and got locked out, but when I step out of Thorin's room, I see her standing a few feet from the front door. She has a towel wrapped around her while her wet, curly hair hangs around her shoulders in perfect golden ringlets. Her dark roots are already starting to show, and in a few more months, her hair will be more brown than gold.

She must have been in the shower when whoever the fuck is on the other side of our door interrupted.

Aurelia's watching it now with a weird expression—like she doesn't quite know what to do, seeing as she obviously can't answer it.

"Goldilocks."

"It's the sheriff," she says. "I spotted him through the window. I thought he'd go away if no one answered, but he just keeps knocking." Finally, she looks at me when I say nothing. "He's not alone, Khalil."

"Fuck."

"Do you think he's here for me?"

"I don't know, baby."

"What are we going to do?"

"About what?" Thorin asks as he and Seth step out of his room. He frowns at the door when the knocking persists, and then his expression becomes blank when he remembers that only one person comes this far up. "Is that who I think it is?"

"Sheriff Kelly," I confirm.

"Boys, you home?" the sheriff calls out. "Open up!"

"I don't know about you guys, but I don't think we should open it."

Aurelia nods while tightening her robe. "I have to agree with Seth. Answering it seems like a bad idea."

"We don't have a choice," I tell them. My gaze travels to Thorin and then Seth, who both look like they are mentally preparing for war. "We need to see what he wants."

"We know what he wants," Thorin grinds out.

"Yeah, but why now?" I reason. We're all whispering since we're standing less than ten feet from the door. "Why not a month ago?"

"Change of heart?" Seth guesses.

"No," I say, following my gut. "It's something else. If the sheriff really believed we'd taken Aurelia, he would have come for her weeks ago."

Thorin holds my gaze as he tilts his head toward Seth in silent question. *Isaac?*

Could be, I communicate silently.

"I can hear you," Seth snaps. "And a door wouldn't stop Isaac if Thanatos has come for me."

"I realize now is not the time to ask," Aurelia whispers, "but who the hell is Thanatos? He sounds suspiciously made up." She narrows her eyes at Thorin and me as if she thinks we're the ones who planted that bullshit in his head.

"He's Death," Seth unhelpfully explains.

Aurelia just stares at him.

"In short?" Thorin blows out a breath and shakes his head like he can't believe what he's about to say. "Thanatos is a god from Greek mythology. It's said he appears when it's your time to go and carries you off to the underworld," Thorin adds.

"Okay. Sure." The face Aurelia makes says she thinks we're all nuts.

"Thanatos is how Seth understands death," I tell Aurelia. "No matter what happens, Seth knows everything will be okay if the winged god doesn't come."

She blinks at me, and then her mouth forms an O in understanding as she turns to peer at Seth through new eyes before nodding. "All right, so if it's not Ezekiel's brother, then who else would send a death squad to our door?" We're quiet long enough for Aurelia to catch on and look at each of us in confusion. "What? Why are you looking at me like that?"

I smile a little to myself as I say, "Nothing."

Maybe it was a slip of the tongue, or maybe Aurelia does think of our cabin as her home too. Either way, the three of us are too chickenshit to find out for sure.

It isn't as easy for Seth to hide his feelings, though, not with his chest puffed out like that. Aurelia referring to Isaac as *Zeke's* brother just assured Seth that he's as real to Aurelia as Thorin and me.

What Aurelia just gave us without even realizing it is so far from fucking nothing, but now is not the time to let it distract us.

But later…

Let's just say I'll be feasting tonight.

"You guys are weird," she says with a nervous giggle.

Thorin clears his throat and turns us back to the topic at hand. "If it was a SAR mission, Kelly would have radioed first."

"He probably tried, but we were out all morning, and we didn't take our radios," I remind Thorin.

Thorin opens his mouth to argue, but Aurelia beats him to it. "All of this conjecture isn't useful when there is a way to know for sure," she reasons. "Just answer the door."

"Yeah, you'd like that, wouldn't you?" Thorin snaps.

I palm my face.

Leave it to that grumpy, paranoid prick to send us flying back three steps when we just gained one.

Taken aback by the misplaced malice that must feel like an unexpected backhand slap, Aurelia whirls on Thorin with her hands on her hips. "Excuse me?"

He eyes her. "You heard me."

"Yeah, I did, but I'm not sure what your problem is, Thayer, so either spit it the fuck out or back the hell off."

His conflicted gaze travels to me over her head, and I know he's replaying our talk earlier while Aurelia was asleep. When I shake my head, he scrubs a hand down his face, wisely choosing to keep silent instead of letting those doubts resurface.

"Thorin's just crabby, Sunshine. He didn't mean it." Seth pulls her into him, and she lets him while keeping her hurt eyes on Thor, who refuses to meet her gaze.

"Seth," I say, coming to a decision. "Take Aurelia downstairs while I let the sheriff in."

"No need," Aurelia pettily replies. "I can see myself out." She pulls away from Seth, and as she passes me, I catch her arm.

"Do not make a sound, Goldilocks. I mean it. Not a fucking peep."

I brace for her to curse me out, too, but then she nods and tosses one last dirty look at Thorin before disappearing down the stairs into the basement.

The three of us wait, collectively wincing when we hear my bedroom door slam closed. If we've learned nothing else about our girl, it's that when Aurelia is pissed off, the three of us feel the effects for days. I move for the front door and open it just as the sheriff turns away to leave.

If Kelly showing up here unannounced wasn't enough to raise our alarms, seeing the eight armed men, who are *not* his deputies, standing behind him like statues definitely flips our collective switch into defense mode.

It takes me a second longer to realize it's not just Zeke we're hell-bent on protecting.

It's Aurelia too.

The grim-faced men are all dressed in black tactical gear, and I can tell right away that they are professionals.

"Ah! You are home. I was beginning to worry these old ears were failing me." The sheriff chuckles, but none of us return it as we size up the men behind him and wait to see why the fuck he brought them here. The sheriff picks up on the tension and says, "I'm aware you don't welcome visitors, but this is important, and it couldn't wait. Can we come in?"

"*You* can."

The less experienced mercenaries shift nervously when I reveal the gun tucked inside my waist while the other half meet my stare head-on.

None of this makes sense. Mercenaries aren't Isaac's style. Why pay a premium for professionals when he has brainwashed sheep to die for him for free?

We did our fair share of damage to his flock when we rescued "Zeth," but this still feels extreme. And if it wasn't for our unwelcome guests, I'd laugh at how quickly Aurelia's name for Ezekiel and his most troublesome alter had caught on. I can even guess what she's calling Zeke and Bane in that fascinating mind of hers.

"You can put that away, son. It won't be necessary. These men are part of a private security firm and came a long way to *speak* with you three. Nothing else."

"Why?" Thorin asks while slipping past me to stand on the front porch.

"Well…" The sheriff looks behind him at the mercenaries, and I know that despite what he claims, they make him uneasy, and I realize why when he says, "They were hired by Marston George."

"Tell me this is not fucking happening," I groan as soon as the front door closes behind us. The sheriff and the men Aurelia's uncle hired just fucked off, and now the three of us are frozen in place, wondering how the fuck we're going to get out of this one.

The sheriff came all this way to introduce us to the men who will be searching our mountain with a fine-tooth comb for Aurelia. He knows it wouldn't have ended well if we'd come across them ourselves. The mercenaries also came with a hefty offer from Marston George for us to act as their glorified tour guides. We, of course, sent them packing with an offer of our own—to go fuck themselves.

Our hostility toward perfect strangers baffled the sheriff, but he knew better than to ask us for answers we'd never give.

Nothing worth having is ever easy, and damn if Aurelia isn't making us work for her in more ways than even she knows.

Thorin fakes a sharp cutting motion across his neck, silencing us, and then he waves us out onto the deck in case Aurelia is eavesdropping from the basement. The moment the upper deck door is closed behind us, he tips back his head and roars, "Fuuuuuuck!"

"I don't see what the big deal is," Seth says from his causal lean against the railing. "Let them look around. They won't find her, and then they'll be gone in a few days."

"Marston George has access to his niece's endless resources. With or without our help, he can hire a hundred teams and drag the search out for years if he wants to, and trust me, *he will want.*"

"That's fucking stupid. Does Aurelia's uncle really think she could have survived out here on her own?"

"No. He definitely thinks she's dead, but the fucker wants a body to prove it."

"For what?"

"Because right now, she's still considered missing," I tell Seth. "Without proof that his niece is dead, Marston George can't inherit her fortune. It will be years before she's declared deceased."

"And apparently, the greedy bastard can't wait that long."

Until now, I hadn't truly thought about what Aurelia was giving up when she chose us. But now the answer is staring me down like a ravenous void ready to consume me with guilt.

Everything.

She gave up everything. Her life, career, and wealth—even her very existence. The least we can do is give her everything in return—starting with our loyalty and honesty.

"We should tell Aurelia," I decide.

Thorin snorts, and when I raise my brows at him for acting like a salty bitch, he returns an equally withering look of his own. "You don't think that scheming wench didn't already know her uncle would send someone looking for her?"

That gives me pause while needles of apprehension prick at my skin. Great... Now I'm as bad as Thorin. "What are you saying?"

"I'm saying… What if she's been lying to us and biding her time? Getting us to think she's really falling for us so we'd let our guard down."

"Thorin, come on. Do you realize how paranoid you sound? Aurelia is many things, but she isn't manipulative. Don't do this shit. Not now. Don't let your paranoia ruin a good thing. A fucking *great* thing. Aurelia isn't your mom. She's not going to break her word."

"Right."

"*Wrong*." Seth pushes away from the railing and shoves Thorin back. The surprised look Thorin gives him is almost comical. "Sunshine told me she loves me. She wouldn't have said it if she didn't mean it." Thorin just stares back at him. "And she loves you too, Thor. She hasn't said it yet, but she feels it. You just have to stop being so…" Seth searches for a kinder word than what he's probably thinking and settles on. "You."

"Oh, is that all?"

"Enough of this shit. Go see her, Thor."

"What?"

"You're spiraling. Go see her right now. Touch her. Hold her. And then look into her eyes and tell yourself that she isn't yours. That she isn't mine. And that she isn't Seth's. I fucking dare you." When the stubborn ass doesn't move from the spot where he's standing, I shake my head. If Thorin can't get past that voice in his head that says Aurelia can't be trusted—that she is his past come back to haunt him—we're doomed. "Fine. If you can't do that, do yourself a favor and get the hell out of my sight before I fuck you up."

CHAPTER FORTY-ONE

SETH | ZEKE

"T he promise that it ends is what makes life beautiful."

I'm careful not to react as I sweep up the glass, wood chips, and other debris on the floor of Zeke's bedroom. Well, I guess it's Aurelia's now since she laid claim to it and suckered us into clearing it out to make room for her.

"You wrote this, didn't you?"

I can feel her eyes on me as I continue sweeping. "What makes you say that?"

"Fine, Cura. Keep your secrets. Will you at least tell me what happened in here?"

Thorin is in and out of the room, hauling the ruined furniture out, but every time he returns, he lingers, waiting for Aurelia to acknowledge him before tucking his tail and leaving when she ignores him.

It's been a few days since Sheriff Kelly and the death squad came knocking, and Sunshine's been giving him the cold shoulder ever since. It's not that he doesn't deserve it. He does. But it's better for everyone when Aurelia is happy with all of us.

Khalil is busy outside building a bed for our girl—one that's bigger and fancier than his, per her demand.

"Which time?" I muse as I finish sweeping and cringe when I look around. Fortunately, I don't have to imagine what Aurelia must have thought when she saw it.

"It looks like someone let a wild animal loose in here," she mutters.

I crack a strained smile as I dump the full dustpan into the trash. "That would be Bane. And a little of me."

"Why would he do this?"

"Because the only way to stop Bane is to kill him. Since Khalil and Thorin can't do that without killing Zeke, too, they either tranq him or trap him until Zeke or I wake up."

"How long does that take?"

"A few hours. A few minutes. It depends. The moment Bane no longer feels like Zeke is in danger, he splits, and one of us takes over."

Aurelia pauses scrubbing the blood from the walls to look at me. "So if Bane only comes when Zeke is in danger, why didn't he stop Isaac from torturing him and hurting you?"

I shake my head to free myself from the clutches of the dark memories that try to take hold. "Because Bane wasn't born until after Khalil and Thorin came for Ezekiel." Sucking in a breath while an internal war rages on, I force myself to meet Aurelia's gaze while I deliver the blow that might cause her to never look at me the same again. "He killed Tatum."

"What?" Aurelia drops the sponge into the bucket, causing soapy water to splash onto the floor. It goes unnoticed as she walks over to me, her wet fingers curling into the bottom of my T-shirt. I can tell Bane freaks her out already, and she hasn't even met him yet. "Why would he do that?"

Not wanting to relive the events of that day, I give her as much of the truth as I can part with. The rest is Zeke's to tell anyway. "Because there is no reasoning with him, Aurelia. If Bane wakes up, he'll kill on sight. He won't ask questions, and he won't care who you are." Reaching out, I stroke her soft cheek with my thumb. "He won't care what you mean to me."

Aurelia searches my gaze before she grabs my hand from her cheek and rests it over her chest where her heart beats. "You won't let him hurt me," she says with a finality that fills me with a deep sense of male gratification knowing that my girl trusts me to protect her.

But on its heels, carving a hole into my stomach and filling it with dread is the question that keeps me frozen.

What if I fail?

I obviously won't be around if Bane wakes up. How the hell can I keep him from hurting her?

"I can't control him," I try to explain while my stomach churns. "No one can. He's a kill switch in Zeke's mind, and once you flip it, there is no taking it back."

"Then I guess we better keep Zeke safe." Removing my hand from her chest, she places her palm flat against mine for the contact she seems to need as much as I do. "Any more nosebleeds?"

"No." It's a lie. The nosebleeds are not only becoming more frequent, but they're also accompanied by migraines.

"Seth…don't lie. I don't like it."

"Okay."

Nodding, Aurelia flips my hand over, and her gaze zeroes in on a similar scar on the back of my hand. "Tell me how you got this," she demands while softly tracing the raised skin with her finger.

"You're full of questions today."

"Seth."

"The same way I got this one," I say while pointing out the three-inch scar high on Zeke's throat near his jaw. "I tried to kill Zeke. Bane stopped me."

"He *stopped* you?" she exclaims. "How?"

"He overpowered me, took control of Zeke's left hand, and stabbed me in the right with the same knife I tried to use to cut Zeke's throat open. The knife went through the kitchen table, and I had to wait for Khalil to find me and free me."

The shattered look in her eyes says that if Aurelia could, she'd weep for me. The worry that I might still want to off Zeke swims in her eyes, but she doesn't allow herself to ask, and since she told me not to lie to her, I say nothing as well.

"I guess that explains the gouge in the kitchen table, but wait… The two of you were awake…*at the same time*? You can do that?"

Aurelia's gaze is a cross between wonder and weirded out.

"Sure. It hurts a hell of a lot worse than being stabbed—quite literally like being split in two, so it's not something we do for party tricks."

"Why did you try to kill Zeke?"

"Because…" I have to swallow past the knot in my throat before I can say another word. "Being in his head feels like I never left Isaac's table. He's in pain all the time, except I can't help him. There's nothing I can do to bear it for him. Nothing except making sure he never has to feel anything ever again."

"Seth…"

"It's fine."

"No. It's *not*. Maybe it's a good thing I'm staying because the first thing I'd do if I ever went home is find Zeke's brother and make him wish he'd never been born."

I smirk at that. "If anyone can do it, Sunshine, it's you."

She peers up at me. "Can I ask you something?"

"Anything."

Aurelia chews her lip like she thinks I might regret it once she asks me whatever is on her mind. "Are you sure those thoughts were Zeke's and not yours?"

I stagger back a step, breaking our connection. "What?"

"I don't want to upset you. It's just that… It sounds like you suffered just as much as Zeke did. Maybe even more. Everyone's worried about Zeke and what Isaac did to him, but what about you?"

"What about me? I'm just a door in Ezekiel's head that he pulls open when he can't deal."

"Not to me. You're real to *me*, Seth." Aurelia sighs and shakes her head with a somber look in her eyes. "It's just not fair."

"What's not fair, beautiful?"

"Zeke had a mom and a dad, he has friends, he had a childhood, he has memories outside of the cult, but what about you? What do you have?"

I stare at this beautiful girl and wonder how she still doesn't know what she means to me. "I have you," I tell her openly. "And you love me. I don't care about the rest. Just don't go, Sunshine, and I'll be whole. Stay for me, and I'll stay for you."

"I won't go, but Seth… I want you to live whether I'm around or not. You can't put this on me—"

I wrap my hand around her neck, and she doesn't blink an eye when I tighten my hold. "Ever, Aurelia," I say through gritted teeth. "You can't leave me. You promise?"

"Yes, Seth. I promise."

That damn mouth of hers drives me delirious even when she's being sweet, so I don't hesitate to devour it. At some point, I back her against the wall and sneak my hand into her leggings. Aurelia's not wearing panties, so there's nothing keeping me from petting her sweet pussy until she purrs. I'm still lazily toying with her clit when Thorin walks in. I can tell it's him because he brings his fucked-up, hating-ass mood into the room with him.

"Do you two want to fuck or help me clean?" he snarls.

Aurelia and I pay him no mind as I quickly make her come before freeing my fingers and licking them clean. Pulling away, I catch the taunting smirk she tosses Thorin's way before giving him her back.

"Be nice," I whisper with a pinch on her ass.

"He started it," she mumbles while swatting my hand away.

"Wolf."

"Seth, did you hear something?"

My gaze bounces between Aurelia and Thorin. The former is back to scrubbing the walls, washing away the words Bane wrote in our blood.

Death to the immortals.

The suds and blood run down the wall, soaking the line under it. The one Zeke wrote.

Bless the Savior.

The rest trickles down to the last line. My line. The one that Aurelia seems fixated on.

The promise that it ends is what makes life beautiful.

"Actually, I think I'll go see if Khalil needs help," I tell them before backing away for the door. Aurelia and Thorin are already bickering by the time I reach it.

"Stop following me, Thorin."

"Then stop walking away every time I come near you! Why won't you talk to me?"

"Because…" Aurelia hisses so spectacularly that Thorin actually takes an astonished step back when she whirls around to face him. "You're an *ass.*"

"Baby, I said I was sorry for doubting you."

"And I'm sure you meant it, Thorin. Until the next time it happens and you make me feel small again!"

I cover my ears while their arguing follows me out of the room, up the stairs, and out of the cabin. I find a shirtless Khalil outside, hovering over the workbench he dragged out of the woodshed. There's a sliding miter saw on the surface and a piece of wood about ten feet long poised under the blade. Hearing me coming, Khalil looks up from the measurements he's making on the lumber we picked up from town this morning while Thor babysat Aurelia.

Or maybe Aurelia babysat Thor.

Keeping him from hunting down the mercenaries and killing them all has been a full-time job, so when Aurelia proposed we clean out Zeke's destroyed bedroom, I think we were all relieved for something to take our minds off our uninvited guests.

It makes me wonder if it was her plan all along.

It wouldn't surprise me if Aurelia was already learning how to manage us.

"We need to talk."

Returning his focus to the wood, he shrugs. "So talk."

"Look. I know I don't have the right to ask you for anything considering how many times I tried to end you, but I need a favor. It's…it's important."

Khalil's brown eyes return to me, and then he tucks the pencil behind his ear as he turns to face me. "What's up?"

I shake my head when words fail me, and when it feels like my legs will, too, I take a seat on the front steps. My head is down while my hands grip my hair, so I don't see Khalil walk over or sit beside me until he nudges me.

"Zeke is going to wake up soon," I blurt.

Khalil doesn't immediately react, and when I look up, he's staring at me with a calm expression that hides what he's truly thinking. "You sure?"

"Positive."

Nodding, he rests a hand on my shoulder. "It's going to be okay, Seth."

"How do you know?"

"Because when you're this happy and when you have everything, you'll do anything to keep it that way."

"You have to promise me you'll have her back, Khalil. No matter what."

Confusion crosses his expression. "What are you talking about?"

"Protect her. From Bane, from Zeke, from Thorin, and even you. Aurelia's the priority. No matter what happens, you have to choose her."

"Of course," he readily agrees, relieving some of my fears. "But why are you telling me this?"

"Because Zeke won't go down as easy as we did, and Aurelia still doesn't get that yet. He won't allow himself to trust her, much less fall for her—not after Tatum. And then Thorin and his paranoia... Zeke is very convincing, you know that. It will be two against one. Don't make it three."

Khalil blows out a breath because he knows that I'm right. "I'll do you one better. I won't just have her back. I'll be her armor. Nothing will touch her without going through me. You have my word."

My next breath punches out of my chest. "Thank you."

"You don't need to thank me for that. It's always been the plan, but for you, I'll make that vow a thousand times if it's what you need to hear."

My eyes narrow suspiciously at the sincerity in his voice. I can't help it when Khalil has every reason to hate me. "Why are you being so nice to me? I tried to set you on fire."

"Yeah, I haven't exactly forgotten, Seth, but I forgave you a long time ago."

"Because of Aurelia?"

He tilts his head at me like I should know better. "Because you're my brother."

"Thanks. I guess you're marginally more tolerable too."

Khalil cuts his gaze at me. "Man, fuck you." We snicker at that, and then Khalil says, "It almost feels weird admitting this, even after the last couple of months, but I'm going to miss you, man."

I frown at that despite feeling funny in my chest when I hear him admit it. "You don't have to lie."

There's sadness in Khalil's eyes now, but he holds my gaze when he speaks again. "Despite what you think, Thorin and I care about you, Seth. We always have, but you wouldn't let us in. After a while, we realized trying would not only get us killed, it pushed you further away, so we backed off, but we never stopped hoping you'd come around and warm up to us."

"Oh."

"Yeah...*oh*."

"Full disclosure... If it wasn't for Sunshine, I probably wouldn't have." I shrug.

Khalil smiles a little and claps me on the back. "I'm well aware, Seth."

The front door opens, and Aurelia saunters out, bearing two cold beers and a bright smile for us. "What are my favorite boys talking about?"

"I heard that!" Thorin snaps from inside.

"You," Khalil and I answer at the same time.

Cleaning out Zeke's bedroom, and I guess mine too, turned into spring cleaning the entire cabin. It's early evening by the time the four of us collapse into an exhausted heap in the living room.

"Oh, God. I still have to make dinner," Aurelia groans from where she's sprawled on top of Bruce.

"I can make it," I offer.

Sunshine perks up at that, and I cock my head at the surprise in her eyes. "You can cook?"

"No, but neither can you, and you manage." I don't realize what I've said until Khalil chokes on the water he's drinking, and Aurelia shoots up into a sitting position with a gasp and wide eyes. Her lips tremble, and I have a feeling if she were capable of crying, she would be. "Ah, shit."

"Yes!" Thorin cheers because he'll no longer be in the doghouse alone after this.

I rub my brow while Aurelia stands before I can find the words to un-fuck myself.

"You know what? Make your own damn dinner. I'm going to take a nap. Do *not* follow me." She storms into Thorin's room and slams and locks the bedroom door.

"But that's my room!"

"And?" she shouts back.

"Is it me, or is she crankier than usual?" Thorin's grin spreads when he looks at Khalil and me. "You think it's the baby? It's definitely mine if it is."

Ignoring him, I grumble as I stand and head into the kitchen to start dinner.

It can't be that hard, can it?

As it turns out, cooking is kind of…therapeutic.

I have no idea what I'm doing, but I like it. I'm too busy focusing on manipulating ingredients into an edible meal to think about Zeke or death squads or Isaac or the fact that Aurelia is mad at me. Before long, I'm being overrun by hungry assholes.

I stand back as Thorin and Khalil pile their plates with the chicken fajitas. Neither of them move from their spots before digging in.

"Well?" I ask once Thorin eats his first fajitas in three bites and immediately starts in on the second. The only time I've seen him eat Aurelia's food that fast is when he's trying to shovel it all down without tasting it, so I have no idea what to think.

Khalil is the one to answer after finishing off his first. "What the fuck? Are you trying to piss her off more?"

"What? What did I do?"

"This tastes *amazing*, Seth."

"Okay, so? Isn't that a good thing?"

"You just hurt Aurelia's feelings and then showed her up."

"Oh. I wasn't trying to make it good. I just followed the directions!"

Khalil's eyes blow wide. "*Definitely* don't tell her that."

"You're being ridiculous."

"Man, I'm telling you," he warns with a shake of his head before going back to devouring the food.

I put a couple of fajitas on a plate for Aurelia and carry them to Thorin's bedroom where the door is still closed and probably locked. I'm holding my breath when I knock lightly. I don't breathe until I hear her quiet voice.

"Go away, Seth. I'm not hungry."

I want to ask how she knew it was me, but I don't. Instead, I stand back, lift my leg, and kick the fucking door in. It flies open, slams against the wall, and bounces off as I walk inside to Aurelia sitting up, her stunned gaze staring back at me.

"Are you serious right now?"

I don't realize I've been followed until I hear Thorin grumble, "My thoughts exactly." He's standing on the threshold, inspecting his door. "For future record, *I have a key*."

"You burned a lot of energy today," I tell Aurelia while ignoring Thor. "You need to refuel." I set the plate on the nightstand, but Aurelia doesn't acknowledge it as she glares up at me.

"I'm a grown woman, Seth. I can decide when I eat, thank you."

"Fuck that. If you're not going to take care of yourself, I'll damn well do it for you."

"Oh, goody!" She smiles and claps her hands together before resting them on her cheek. "Now all of my problems are solved!"

My gaze narrows when I feel my patience drain. "All right. What the hell is your deal? You've been kind of a bitch all day." I reach out and grab her chin in a possessive grip, yanking it toward me when she looks away. "Where did my Sunshine go? Hmm?"

Her pretty lips curl. "I've always been a bitch, Seth. You're just now noticing?"

"You've never been mean without cause. What's the matter, baby?"

Aurelia looks tormented, and then her gaze softens after a while, becoming less sharp and more vulnerable, even as her pout remains. "My stomach hurts." She releases a whimper like she's been holding it in and hiding the pain all day. "It's been cramping all day."

"Okay…" I nod my understanding. "Is that all?"

She shrugs. "I guess."

I sit down next to her and rub my palms together to warm them up before slipping my hand under her shirt to rub her belly. I have no idea if it's actually helping, but when Aurelia's lashes flutter closed, I think that it might be. "How's that?"

"Better," she whispers back, resting her head on my shoulder.

Khalil appears and stands over us with two pills in one hand and a tin cup full of water in the other. When Aurelia lifts her head and tries to take them, he shakes his head. "Open."

Dutifully, her lips part, and she sticks out her tongue. I sigh when my dick twitches in my sweats at the sight because I don't think I'll be getting any tonight.

Khalil places the aspirin on her tongue and then holds the cup to her lips for her to drink. If she's cranky about being handled so delicately, she knows better than to complain. There will always be times when we're rough with our girl, but we will never *ever* be careless.

When she drains the cup, Khalil sets it on the nightstand next to her dinner and takes a seat on her other side to join me in rubbing her stomach. Aurelia sighs and lays her head on Khalil's shoulder this time, but I don't mind. Thorin returns to the room, bearing a small mug with steam curling from the rim. When he offers this olive branch to Aurelia, I see that it's tea. "I put a little honey in. I didn't know how you took it."

Aurelia isn't able to hide her surprise, and I swear the three of us exhale all at once when she curls her delicate fingers around the mug. "This is fine. Th-thank you."

"You're welcome."

Thorin drops onto the floor while she sips her tea. He takes her ankle and peels off her sock to massage her bare foot. The paint on her toenails is chipped and nearly gone, but her feet look so soft and pretty even from here.

"Have we been demanding too much of you?" Khalil asks.

Aurelia whips her head his way. "What? No."

"Will you tell us if we do?"

"Will you listen?" she tosses back.

Khalil struggles with an answer to that one because, let's be honest, Aurelia needs a firm hand, and we're not going to suddenly turn into less demanding assholes overnight. "We'll try," he promises.

Aurelia hums like she expected that nonanswer and sets her tea aside. She pauses when she notices the plate of food, and then she picks it up after a moment of contemplation. "Baby, you made this?"

"Yup."

Aurelia lifts the fajita and takes a tentative bite before glancing at me in surprise. "Oh my God…"

"That bad?"

"Are you kidding me? You knew how to cook this whole time?" she yells.

"No." I snort as she takes another bite. "I wanted to impress you."

"Well, you succeeded."

Khalil and Thorin release a collective sigh.

The three of us are content to watch Aurelia eat, and it's how we pass the time with some mindless chatter in between until the plate is empty. I take it from her, and we all stand.

"I think we should make fajitas a regular thing," she announces as she stretches. "Fajita Fridays?"

I nod while staring at her tits. "Sounds good."

Aurelia chews on her bottom lip as she peers up at me. "Will you show me how to make it?"

"Of course."

"Good. Now beat it. I'm going to shower."

Khalil slaps her ass as he passes, and then the three of us leave Thorin's bedroom while Aurelia heads into his bathroom. Khalil disappears to get the tools to fix Thorin's door while Thorin helps me clean up the kitchen. Afterward, we return to the living room with a couple of beers while we watch Khalil curse and struggle to fix the door.

And that's where we are when we hear Aurelia squeal. "Yes! Yes! Yes! Yes! Yes!" Thorin and I are already on our feet when the bathroom door opens. "Oh, boooooys!"

She dances out of Thorin's bedroom, past a stunned Khalil, and into the living room. Her skin is wet, and the only thing she's wearing now is a towel.

"You want to let us in on what's got you dancing around naked in our living room?"

"See for yourself. You probably wouldn't believe me if I told you anyway."

She drops the towel.

At first, I don't see anything out of the usual. Just one fine, curvy piece of ass.

And then I see it.

A drop of crimson between her thick thighs. It runs down the inside of her leg, and my eyes flare, but she's too busy smirking at Thorin to notice my panic.

"What happened?" I say as I pull my knife and stalk across the room to reach her side in two steps. "Why are you hurt? Who did this?"

"Seth, I'm okay."

"You're *bleeding*."

Aurelia gapes at me before shaking her head. "God, you're precious. It's just my period, Seth. I'm fine."

I'm still frowning despite her insistence that she's okay. "You sure?"

"Very."

"Oh." I take a step back and sheathe my knife. "Okay then." I look her over once more just to assure myself she's in one piece. "Does it hurt?"

"Only the aforementioned cramps. Actually, I've never been this happy to see it before. Score infinity for womanhood." Her gaze wanders past me to Thorin. I can feel him brooding behind me because he lost. Aurelia isn't pregnant, but that won't keep Thorin down for long. Especially when it means he gets to keep trying.

Glancing over my shoulder, I see him tip his beer to her. "Impressive."

Aurelia's smirk transforms from triumphant to secretive when it shifts my way, and I wink. I guess the birth control pills I've been slipping her worked after all.

"I want a reward," I rumble in her ear so the others don't overhear. "I want you."

"I'm afraid you'll have to want me for a few days, Seth." She places a hand on my chest and tries to push me away, but I don't budge. "Period means no sex."

Smiling, I dip my head to kiss her jawline. "Says who?" Aurelia stiffens against me while I continue kissing down her neck until I reach her shoulder. That peaches-and-daffodils scent is back now that she has her own body wash again, and all I want to do is climb inside her fucking skin and live there. "I've been fantasizing for weeks about getting your blood on my cock without hurting you, Sunshine. This is happening."

Done talking, I lift her in my arms and she wraps hers around my neck as I turn toward the stairs. At the top of the landing, I pause to look over my shoulder at Thorin and Khalil, who seem rooted to the spot.

I lift a brow, and they both burst into action, following us downstairs to the basement and into Khalil's room since his bed is the only one big enough to fit all four of us.

"You *cannot* want me that bad," Aurelia whines when I lay her down, and the three of us begin to undress. "It's only for a few days."

"You really think that a little blood would change a thing when all three of us have had our tongue in your ass at least once, Goldilocks?"

Of course, she has no retort for that, so she settles for pouting while we finish shedding our clothes.

I'm the first to finish, so I join Aurelia on the bed. The moment I do, she snaps her legs closed. I pry those thick, sexy motherfuckers right back open and settle between her thighs while she stares up at me like I might eat her alive. Sometimes, I think I might.

She's just so fucking…

Diving in, I press my lips against hers and force her to feed me her tongue while I swallow her moans.

Delicious.

There's no better feeling or taste than Aurelia George.

While I'm kissing her, I hear the top drawer of the nightstand slide open, and I have a pretty good guess what Khalil is searching for. I peek an eye open in time to see Khalil toss Thorin a small silver key before removing a bottle of lube and setting it on the nightstand. On the other side of the bed, I hear the metal cuffs rattling and shift my gaze to see Thorin freeing them from the headboard.

I still have my tongue twisted around Aurelia's when my gaze connects with Thorin, and he climbs onto the bed to lounge on his side next to us. On the other side, Khalil does the same. Breaking the kiss, I return my focus to our girl as I lift my body into a plank with my hands planted on either side of her.

When her eyes fly open, there's a haze there that wasn't present before. Her head falls to the side, and she eyes Khalil and then Thorin.

"Look at me," I order. Her gaze flies back to mine. "Put me inside your pussy, Sunshine."

Gulping, she reaches hesitantly between us and wraps her small hand around my cock. I've been hard ever since I saw that first rivulet of blood on her thigh, so when she feels it, she gasps her surprise. She still runs her hand up and down the shaft a few times, playing with my goddamn dick instead of doing what I told her. I can't help but smirk at her bullshitting ass.

If there's one thing Aurelia loves to do, it's fuck. She wouldn't have been able to wait either, and now she doesn't have to. Once again, she gets her way while accepting none of the blame—just like our spoiled little brat.

Finally, she slots my cock against her slit and holds my gaze as she uses me to tease her pussy. Almost simultaneously, Thorin and Khalil both reach for their own cocks and begin stroking to the same pace and rhythm, probably imagining that she's doing the same to them while they wait their turn.

"Shit," I grumble when a little pre-cum eases out of the tip just as it lodges against her swollen clit. Knowing I'll come prematurely if I don't get inside her soon, I nip her jawline. "Enough. Do as I say, Sunshine."

Glaring at me for ending her stalling, she guides me to her little hole once more, and I press my hips forward. Her brows furrow as I breach her cunt, but she doesn't ask me to stop. She's tight and hot as usual but slicker than normal, and the reason why has me fighting for control on a razor's edge. Aurelia keeps one hand around my cock and the other on my ass, her fingers digging into the muscled globe as I slowly sink inch after inch inside of her until she's forced to remove her hand so that I can get balls deep.

Once our middles meet, we both release the breath we were holding.

"God, Seth."

"Tell me you want my dick. Tell me you want me to fuck your little red pussy."

"I want your dick. I want you to fuck my little red pussy, Seth."

"Yeah?" I say as I begin to move. Gradually, my pace increases until I'm pounding Aurelia into the mattress. "I knew you wanted it, you fucking cocktease. Our fucking slut. You knew what you were doing when you came out of that bathroom. You knew we'd take it, didn't you? Answer me!"

"Yeah! Oh, God, yeah! I knew! I knew..." Her huge tits sway wildly from our rough movements, drawing Thorin's and Khalil's attention. Their coordinated attack is a thing of beauty as they each latch on to her brown nipples at the same time while tugging furiously on their cocks.

Aurelia brings her hands up to cradle each of their heads, holding them to her while I brace my hands against the headboard and pound her gushing middle.

I make the mistake of looking down and glimpsing a red smear during a backstroke.

"Goddamn," I mutter when I can't resist the temptation anymore. I pull out to the tip and feel my balls tighten immediately once I see her blood coating my cock. "Fuck yeah." I slam back inside, and Aurelia slides toward the head of the bed from the force. Thorin reaching out to wrap an arm around her waist is the only thing that keeps her head from crashing into the headboard. "Fuck yeah, fuck yeah, fuck yeah, fuck yeah," I chant as I bully that pussy into coming for me.

Whatever reservations Aurelia had are blown wide open once her walls contract around me, and she comes on my dick. That vise grip of hers is what has my back stiffening as I spill inside her. Once I'm spent, I collapse on top of Aurelia while Thorin shifts away.

I don't know if Thorin or Khalil came yet, but I know this night is far from over when I hear him lift the cuffs from the nightstand.

Slowly, I pull out of Aurelia and sit back on my heels as I admire all the cum and blood staining my veiny cock. When I look down, I see the same combination marking Aurelia's thick thighs, and my cock gives an interested twitch.

"Oh, baby," I coo in awe. "Look at the mess you made."

"Let me see," Khalil demands.

Even though her thighs are still gapped open, I push Aurelia's knee out a little further as Khalil leans over. He's got one hand cupping his balls and the other wrapped around his shaft, and he leisurely works them both as his gaze bounces between Aurelia's bloody cunt and my equally red cock.

"Fuck," he breathes out. "That's a pretty goddamn sight."

"Indeed."

Rolling away, I take Thorin's spot on the other side of Aurelia with an arm tucked under my head. My dick is limp but throbbing against my thigh, and I know it's only a matter of time before I'm hard and ready to go again.

Thorin threads the thick chain between two of the twisted branches in the center of the canopy, leaving no way forward or back. Aurelia won't be able to free herself until one of us allows it.

At the moment, she has her eyes closed and is barely responsive when Khalil lifts her top half from the bed and raises her arms above her head so that Thorin can secure her wrists inside the cuffs. There isn't enough slack in the chain for her to lie down, so it forces her onto her knees with her arms above her head.

The moment she's in position, kneeling in the center of the bed, Khalil swipes the lube from the nightstand. He flips the top and squirts some onto his fingers before tossing the bottle away.

"Aurelia," he calls out expectantly.

She jerks awake. "Hmm?"

"Thorin's going to take your pussy now... I'm going to fuck your ass, baby."

"Mkay," she answers sleepily, looking like she might pass out again. Khalil's words finally register, and Aurelia jerks into full awareness. The chain on the cuffs scrape across the bark as she shifts nervously. "Wait… what? You're going to…what?"

Thorin is the one to answer as he kneels in front of her and presses a hot, quick kiss to her lips. "He said he's going to take that gorgeous ass, songbird, and you're going to let him, aren't you?"

"I've never…" She loses her words when Khalil gets into position behind her. Aurelia's sandwiched between them, and knowing what they intend, she's suddenly skittish. She calms a little when Khalil starts kissing her nape since her hair is pulled up and out of the way with only a few curly wisps left out. "I've never done it before."

"We figured," the three of us answer at the same time.

Aurelia jumps when Khalil spreads her ass to expose her puckered hole where he spreads some of the lube.

"Khalil's not going to hurt you," I say to her as I grab the lube and pour some onto my palm. With the way she's facing, I can see all three of their profiles from my lounge at the head of the bed. "He's going to take real good care of you. We all will."

"So you'll both be inside me…at the same time?"

Khalil answers. "It will feel a little something like this…" Aurelia's breath hitches when they both sink a finger inside her from each end. Leisurely, I stroke my cock back to life as I watch her lean her head back against Khalil's shoulder and squirm from the pressure. "But a hundred times more intense."

Thorin dips his head and swirls his tongue around her nipple while she combs her fingers through his hair. I'm just reaching full hardness again when Thorin removes his hand and replaces it with his dick. Because he's so much taller than her—even while kneeling—he ends up having to lift her up and wrap her legs around his waist. My eyes are glued to their centers as I watch him carefully seat her on his erection. Before she's even halfway down, I spot a bright red rivulet of Aurelia's blood running down the side of his pale shaft, and I nearly blow my load right then and fucking there.

Everything about this woman is designed to turn me inside out.

The moment her greedy pussy finishes sheathing Thorin, he begins thrusting upward, causing the chain to rattle above them while Aurelia moans like she's as close to death as she is to another orgasm.

And no matter how loudly she cries out, Thorin keeps going, suckling her breast while serving her long, hard dick.

Khalil eventually takes mercy on her and reaches around to rub her clit, which sets her off and leaves her limp in Thorin's arms. Afterward, Khalil withdraws a little to grab the lube and quickly slicks his fingers once more.

Aurelia is leaning forward with her forehead resting on Thorin's shoulder when Khalil begins working two fingers inside her ass to finish stretching her out. She barely stirs as he sinks to the second knuckle, so I sit up and grab the lube, pouring some into my palm again.

It's not my cock I reach for this time, but Khalil's.

While Aurelia is perfectly pliable, I reach between them and wrap one hand around his base and the other right over the mushroom tip and begin to spread the lube over his long, thick shaft as thoroughly as I can. Khalil is hung, and hurting her is the last thing any of us want when she's trusting us so completely.

I know they're both ready for each other when Khalil starts thrusting in my hand with his gaze pinned on our girl's puckered hole. Aurelia starts pushing back against him, so I let Khalil go and recline back on my elbow. I take my own dick in my hand once more while Khalil presses himself against her back once more.

Thorin is still inside Aurelia and keeping her thoroughly distracted with his tongue and mouth, so Khalil is able to line up his cock and press forward before Aurelia is even aware he's there. He has both hands on her ass, spreading her cheeks, so I can see the moment that puckered hole stretches around his flared head.

Aurelia tenses up immediately and makes such a perfect sound of distress that my hunter instincts stir, raising the hairs along my arms. I don't know how much longer I can settle for being a spectator. I already had my turn, but there's no such thing as not wanting more when it comes to Aurelia George.

Her ass is certainly tempting, but it's her blood that calls to me.

"Relax, baby," Khalil croons when his crown breaches her rim, and she cries out again and starts yanking on the cuffs. "Relax, relax, relax. I got you…" Khalil rears back only to push forward again, sinking even deeper upon his return. He repeats the movement several times until half of his thick cock is buried. "Yeah, that's it. Look at this pretty little ass opening up for me. God…" He slowly sinks the rest of the way inside her until his Adonis belt is flush with her perfectly round ass, and then he drops his forehead onto her shoulder, closes his eyes, and exhales hard. "Damn."

Thorin, who's been remarkably patient so far, checks in with Aurelia. "You okay, wolf?"

"I think so," she answers quietly. "It doesn't hurt. It just feels like if I breathe, I'll explode." She makes the mistake of squirming against the discomfort she must feel, and—head still down—a strangled sound leaves Khalil as he tightens his grip on her hips to keep her still. "Can you feel each other?"

"Yes," Thorin and Khalil answer at the same time.

"Oh." She tries to play it cool, but I can tell it excites her to know that only a thin wall separates Khalil and Thorin's cocks.

"When we fuck you," Khalil rumbles in a low tone after lifting his head to speak against her ear, "we'll feel each other then too. I'll feel him sliding inside your pussy, and he'll feel me taking your tight little ass…" Khalil retreats and slides forward slowly, causing both Aurelia and Thorin to groan. "See what I mean?"

Thorin mimics Khalil's move, and the same thing happens again, but this time, Aurelia turns her head to lock lips with Khalil, moaning in his mouth while Thorin fucks her.

When Khalil and Aurelia come up for air, she wraps her arms around Thorin's neck and feeds him her tongue.

"How does she feel?" I ask Khalil while Thorin and Aurelia kiss.

"Ah, she's tight," Khalil says as he begins fucking her too. "So fucking tight. I'm not going to last. Fuck."

"Then you better make the most of it," I suggest.

Thorin grunts as Khalil loses control and quickens his pace. His shove drives Aurelia forward, and Thorin matches his thrust, sending her back onto Khalil. They don't go easy on her, which of course, means Aurelia is in heaven. Before long, they both have a rhythm, and all Aurelia can do while trapped between them is hold on to that chain for dear life as they ride her ass and pussy.

Khalil uncuffs her once they all come together, and then he drags her into his lap with her back to his chest, where he cuddles her while they catch their breath. "You okay?"

Aurelia gives a sleepy nod while her head rests on his shoulder.

"How's your stomach?"

"Better, actually." She yawns. "The cramps are gone."

Khalil smirks like he expected that answer while Thorin climbs off the bed and prowls his naked ass out of the room. He returns a minute later with a soapy cloth, and Aurelia watches him nudge her thighs apart through lowered lids.

My gaze snaps to her pussy smeared with blood, cum, and her own arousal, and I hear myself speaking before I'm aware of the direction my mind has gone. "Wait."

I feel all three sets of gazes on me as I reach out to blindly grab the lube. I can't look away from all that slick, and Aurelia... She's so relaxed right now. So trusting and pliable. I can do whatever I want to her right now, and she'll let me.

The only other feeling that compares is knowing she loves me.

She loves me.

She loves...me.

"What are you going to do?" Aurelia asks with a shudder.

I shift until I'm lying on my stomach between her legs and peck her knee as I look up at her. "Do you trust me, Sunshine?"

After a moment's hesitation, she answers. "Oddly, yes." A heavy sigh follows like she doesn't quite understand why. "Don't make me regret it."

Fuck yeah.

"Go slow, Seth," Khalil warns after peeping the eager glint in my eyes. Thorin uses the cloth to clean his dick since I'm obviously not done before tossing it aside. He then leans his shoulder against one of the bedposts at the foot of the bed and crosses his arms to watch.

Since Aurelia's already aroused, I pour some more lube onto my fingers while Khalil palms one of her breasts and thumbs her nipple to make sure she stays that way. Holding her gaze, I slowly sink two fingers inside her with my palm turned up. Thorin and I were thorough stretching her out when we fucked her, so I ease right in, feeling her warm walls flutter around me.

When her lashes lower, I pull my fingers out nearly all the way and add a third. Aurelia gasps at the stretch, and the three of us watch her closely for any discomfort while I work to get my pointer, middle, and ring finger inside. She's fucking tight, even while dripping and thoroughly fucked, so I don't rush it and listen to her body until I'm three knuckles deep.

"How's that, Sunshine?"

"Fuck," she whispers while sitting up a little with Khalil's help to get a better look. Her pussy lips are flared around my fingers while streaks of her blood and our cum help ease the way. Aurelia whines the moment she sees it.

"Do you want Seth to stop?" Thorin asks.

"N-no." She gasps again, and then her hips and ass writhe a little into the mattress when I curl my fingers and use my knuckles to massage her. We stay like that for a while—until Aurelia is used to the stretching.

"Wouldn't it be nice if he added one more?" Khalil suggests, picking up on my cue while rubbing the inside of her thigh. "You've been such a good girl. He just wants to reward you. Would you like that?"

Her sensitive pussy strangles my fingers the moment Khalil calls her a good girl, but then she catches on to the rest of what he said and tenses. "One more?"

"It's just my pinky, baby. You'll barely notice it, but it will make you feel so fucking good."

After her nervous gaze travels between the three of us, she relaxes once more, as if finding some comfort in knowing that all three of us are focused on her instead of our own pleasure. She nods and licks her lips. "I can try."

Khalil lifts her knees to her chest to help stretch her spine and relieve the pressure on her pussy while Thorin reaches over and begins circling her clit with the pad of his fingers. Aurelia quickly becomes putty in Khalil's arms while I withdraw enough to add more lube.

Aurelia's eyes are closed while she chases the orgasm that Thorin keeps just out of reach, so she doesn't see that all of my fingers are bundled together like a duck beak when I push inside again.

But she does feel it the moment the tip of my thumb breaches her cunt.

Aurelia's eyes fly open once I'm past the first knuckle. "Oh, God. Oh, God. Oh, God. What are you—"

"Fuck," Khalil interrupts. "Seth, is that—"

"His hand," Thorin answers hoarsely.

All five of my fingers are now inside Aurelia's pussy, but I'm only up to the second knuckle, so I keep going, feeling her muscles stretch more than ever before to accommodate me.

"Seth. Oh, God. Seth…"

"Shh," I soothe when she gets inside her head and starts to panic. "You're doing so good, baby. Fuck." I watch through wide eyes as my third row of knuckles disappear inside Aurelia.

I'm only distantly aware of my cock spurting cum.

It's trapped between my body and the mattress, so no one else but me knows I just blew my load. The rest of my hand eases inside Aurelia until I'm wrist-deep. Thorin curses at the sight and fists his cock. Behind Aurelia, Khalil does the same.

The two of them fuck their fists while mine rests inside of our girl.

I don't dare move for fear of hurting her, and Aurelia seems to be frozen herself as she stares down at our connection.

"How does it feel?" I ask in a quiet voice.

She searches for words and settles for unintelligible sounds instead. If I could, I'd reach for her heart, so I could feel it beating inside my fist. Eager to see how far I can push Aurelia I give my fingers a testing wiggle as if I really might do just that.

Sunshine tosses her head back, coming so abruptly that her sharp cry ends in a silent scream. I can feel her pussy contracting around my fist while Thorin props a knee on the bed, aiming for Aurelia as ropes of cum escape the tip of his cock and land on her glistening brown skin. Khalil wraps his hand around her neck while he deposits his own on her back. I slowly remove my hand with a plop, and Thorin hands me the cloth he used to clean my hand.

Afterward, we all collapse into a tangled heap, where we stay for half an hour.

Thorin recovers from his doze first, rising from the bed and leaving the room. I hear water running in the tub moments later, and he returns after a few minutes. "The bath is ready."

Nodding, I stretch and rise before carefully lifting Aurelia from the bed, as if she's fragile despite what we just put our queen through. I carry her out of the room and into the bathroom with Thorin on my heels. Khalil joins us once he's done changing the sheets, and it's cramped inside the small bathroom, but none of us seem to mind. Once we're all clean, the four of us return to his bed.

Khalil wraps Aurelia's gingham headband around her hair to protect her curls, while Thorin gives Aurelia aspirin since she'll no doubt be sore in the morning. He then makes her drink an entire glass of water and asks twenty-one questions about how she's feeling before finally letting her lie down.

I don't remember falling asleep, but I do remember whispering how much I loved her before she fell asleep in my arms.

CHAPTER FORTY-TWO

AURELIA

Today is graduation day.

Thorin has taught me to shoot and hunt almost daily, and my aim has improved immensely. But after Seth said none of it's useful if I don't kill anything, I bet them all I could catch and kill our dinner tonight.

Of course, they hadn't gone for it.

The death squad. I'm too recognizable. They can't risk me being seen. Blah, blah, blah.

When I asked if this was how the rest of my life was expected to go—hiding in this cabin with the three of them as my only source of human contact—an uncomfortable silence followed, which is how I found myself sneaking out of the cabin an hour before dawn.

I made sure to sleep in my loft last night under the guise of being too pissed with them to sleep in one of their beds. It's easier than trying to crawl from under them since my mountain men turned out to be as overbearing in their sleep as they are when awake.

The lingering cold from winter is nothing more than a comforting breeze in the early spring morning. The warmer season has taken over most of the Cold Peaks, but there are still many places where the sun doesn't reach, so the snow lingers on top of exposed rocks and precarious slopes. The guys warned that the risk of avalanches is even higher now, but I'm pretty sure it was another excuse to keep me inside. Still, after what happened to Tyler, I'll be the first to admit that I get a little jumpy at the slightest sound of snow shifting and falling from the branches above me.

I keep going, focusing on the grass, flowers, and bees as I cross the clearing with my pack, compound bow, and the hunting knife Khalil gave me. When I reach the tree line, and my mountain men don't come bursting out of the front door to drag me back inside, I slip the uncomfortable wolf mask over my face and start into the wilds.

I'm nearing the first hunting spot—a maze of blowdowns just before sunrise, and I can't believe my luck when I spot a buck lying down with its back against the largest tree that has been knocked down.

The buck's head is down, its nose tucked under its hind legs as it sleeps.

The bow is a close-range weapon, so I have to get really fucking close.

Thankfully, it rained last night, so the ground is soft, muting my steps as I approach from downwind. When I'm about a hundred feet away, I slowly draw an arrow from my pack and place it on the shelf before nocking it on the string. I don't fumble with it as much as I had in the beginning, which is a damn good thing because deer—which I learned the hard way—can hear really fucking well.

I don't have time to overthink my aim, knowing it won't be long before my arms and shoulders tremble under the weight of the bow and the tension in the string. Khalil's been helping me with that, too, coaching me through some strengthening exercises. For now, I tell myself that my aim is true when I pull back on the bow and peer through the peephole that acts as a sight.

The moment I whistle, the old Aurelia tries to make a comeback, and I hear her screaming at me to leave the deer alone. *No, don't! Look how cute! It's just a helpless animal!*

Shut up.

Exhaling nice and slow, I release the arrow once the startled deer lifts its head, and I watch it sail through the sparse trees and pierce the buck broadside.

It's a swift kill.

But I don't see the deer when it takes its last breath.

I see me.

I'm slumped against the fallen tree and bleeding out. My face is painted, my hair is primped, and I'm draped in diamonds and dressed to stun in the designer gown I wore the night I won my first Grammy. A meaningless fucking award that countless others likely wanted more and probably deserved. I still have that plastic fucking smile on my face, even in death.

When I see the arrow piercing my false heart, I tip back my head and roar my victory.

Birds burst from the canopy, giving my position away, but I don't care.

The puppet is dead.

I take one step toward my kill when I hear a low growl.

A giant paw appears on top of the fallen tree where the buck made its bed, and then a furry head and pointed ears appear as the wolf climbs over with its gaze locked on me.

It's the pregnant, tawny wolf Thorin and I spotted during one of our hunts a few weeks ago.

The same one Seth petted like it was a damn domesticated dog.

Well, it's not pregnant now, and seeing it up close, I'm convinced Seth is fucking nuts. The wolf is huge, with flesh-shredding claws and teeth. I've seen up close what it could do with them—how quickly and viciously wolves can kill.

It's a testament to this mountain trying to kill me several times that the natural terror I once had for them is muted. There's only respect from one hunter to the next as I watch it leap over the dead buck and growl again.

I still see flashes of Cassie dying in the snow, surrounded by more than just one. But I've since learned that wolves are not the scariest thing in these wilds. And now they're mine.

"What the hell do you want, mutt? I'm not in the mood."

She bares her teeth, so I reveal mine by reaching for an arrow.

I swear her eyes follow it when I pull it from my pack. She retreats a step, and I mistake it for submission until she turns back the way she came.

I still don't catch on to the fact that I was never her intended prey until she sniffs at the buck before wrapping her jaws around its neck.

My eyes are blown wide when she starts dragging it off.

"Hey, you bitch! That's mine!"

Raising the bow again, I aim and fire a warning shot, hoping to scare it off. It lands with a thud inside the tree near its hind. The wolf snarls but doesn't let go of the deer as it rounds the trunk and torn-up roots of the fallen tree, so I nock another arrow.

I aim for the wolf this time, but after a full minute, I still can't bring myself to take the shot. I stalk it around the tree when I lose sight of the wolf, but my arms start to quake, and I know I can't hold it for much longer.

Her den must be nearby.

The den where her cubs await their mother's return.

All things die.

Not today.

Lowering the bow, I let it fall to the ground as I helplessly watch the mother wolf and dead buck retreat.

"Ooh!" I punch the air when the wolf disappears. "You're lucky you're a single mom!"

I swear I hear her growl again.

Alone again, I debate my options. Thorin, Khalil, and Seth will be pissed that I snuck off either way, but will they be more so if I return empty-handed?

I'm almost sure they'll be happy that their fuck toy returned at all, but if I'm going to take their shit either way, I might as well make it count.

An hour later, my ass hurts from sitting in a tree, and I have to pee. I wait another ten minutes for something to kill to walk by, but when I don't spot anything, I sigh and climb down.

Unable to accept defeat, even though the sun is up and my chances have dwindled, I start toward a rocky hill nearby that Thorin took me to a few times.

I get a little turned around, though, and after another ten minutes, I realize I'm lost.

Damn it!

I should have searched harder for a radio. Maybe then I could have called them to come rescue me. I bet they'd *love* that. Thorin will enjoy the hunt, Khalil will use it as an excuse to keep me locked inside the cabin, and Seth will appreciate being needed.

The guys let me have the bow and knife, but they're still keeping me on a leash—albeit a slightly extended one.

Trust has to be earned. I get that. But it goes both ways.

So yeah, maybe sneaking out was my way of punishing them for not trusting me. I'm also proving that I can be trusted and useful.

Makes a ton of fucking sense.

After staring at my map for ten minutes to no avail, I'm forced to retrace my steps. I've lost count of how many times I've gone in a circle before I stumble onto a terrifying sight.

My stomach bottoms out as I stop in my tracks.

About a hundred feet ahead of me is a bear.

A fucking *brown* bear.

I've never seen one before, so I'm rooted in terror where I stand. It's fucking huge. Five or six hundred pounds, maybe? Its fur is grizzled and different shades of brown. Chuffing sounds come from the bear as it works.

An image of Thorin and the scars left behind from his encounter with Bruce flashes in my mind. I'm chilled to the fucking bone, and for a few life-threatening seconds, I can't move.

The bear's back is to me—dirt, grass, and roots flying up as its massive paws dig into the south face of a grassy slope.

It doesn't know I'm here, but I'm upwind. My advantage won't last long.

Slowly, I back away as quietly as possible. I don't know what has the bear so distracted, and I don't want to know.

Whatever the hell it's after, it wants it bad.

After I put enough distance between us, I hold my breath as I turn to leave, but then a tiny sound makes me pause, and my stomach turns.

Yipping, squeals, and whimpers.

Desperate calls for a mother who's somewhere devouring my damn dinner.

Oh, nature, you petty, heartless bitch.

The hole isn't just any hole.

It's the tawny wolf's den, and those are her helpless pups inside. There's a creek full of fresh water not ten feet away and plenty of cover from the elements.

If there was a pack, they'd be here defending her pups.

Instead, there's only me.

I guess that makes me her pack.

Fuck.

Fuck, fuck, fuck!

All I have is this damn bow. How many arrows will it take? What if I miss?

I'll be mauled by a damn bear, that's what.

If I can get around it, maybe I can get a headshot—or one to the heart if I time it right.

Stupid.

Fucking stupid, fucking idiot.

I continue to scold myself as I move around the bear.

It can't fit inside the hole to get to the pups that must be huddled at the back of the den, but it's only a matter of time.

It isn't too late. Just leave. This isn't your business. It's nature. It's the circle of life. You are Black, Aurelia!

None of it penetrates my stubborn will.

But…

Killing the bear for trying to survive doesn't seem fair. How many nests has the mother wolf raided? How many young has it taken?

Ignoring that logic, I get downwind of the bear but forget to pay attention to where I step as Thorin taught me. A twig snaps underneath my heel, and the bear stops digging immediately.

Oh, shit.

It snorts as it backs out of the den and turns toward the sound. Once it sees me, it twists its head and roars.

I'm gonna die.

I force myself to hold my ground even when it takes a step forward and swipes a paw bigger than my head over the ground in warning.

"Yeah, yeah, I get it. You're big and scary, and I'm lunch. Let's get this over with." Reaching over my shoulder for my pack, I don't go for the arrows. I unclip the nonlethal bear spray Thorin packed for me. "Listen, I don't want to hurt you, and I know you probably feel the same. I surprised you, and that was rude." *Fucking idiotic, more accurately.* "You have every reason to maul my face off, but we can both still walk away."

The bear roars again and charges but stops after two steps.

Okay, okay, okay. Ignore your sweaty palms and knocking knees and *focus.* What did the books say?

Bluffing.

The bear is bluffing.

That's a good sign, right?

"You're probably hungry and cranky from sleeping all winter, am I right?"

He whines like that is indeed the problem.

Remembering something else I learned in one of the survival manuals I read out of sheer boredom, I say, "I saw some juicy-looking berries not far away. Bears like berries, right? It's not so bad being a vegetarian. I tried it for a couple of weeks. It was...an experience."

The bear clacks its teeth, and I can't remember what that means, but a moment later, it whines again before turning and running off.

For several seconds I can't do anything but stand there and question if that just happened or if I made it up.

I can't feel my legs.

I can't feel my brain either.

Finally, it feels like I've been rebooted, and my next breath rushes out of me. I fall to my knees, feeling like my stomach is about to drop out of my ass. Instead, I lift my mask and throw up in the grass.

My hands are shaking uncontrollably when I swipe the back of my hand against my mouth.

What the hell just happened? What the fuck was I thinking?

"Holy shit!" I exclaim. "That was a goddamn bear."

"Yes, it was." I'm startled enough by the unexpected voice to scream as I shoot to my feet. I'm lucky enough to have the forethought to pull my mask back down before I whirl around because I stop breathing abruptly, choking on my spit and vomit when I see the sheriff standing there, holding a rifle by his side. His bushy brows are raised in surprise while his thick mustache twitches when he chuckles. "But I have to say that was impressive, young lady. Foolish and dangerous, but impressive."

Now I know why the bear ran off.

It saw that I had backup and probably decided a few scrawny pups weren't worth the effort.

I understand the feeling.

"Forgive an old man's memory. Aurora, was it?"

I take off running in the opposite direction.

"Hey! Hold on there! Wait!" he calls after me. One glance over my shoulder shows him giving chase. *Shit, shit, shit, shit, shit, shit, shit!* "I just want to talk to you!"

I don't wait. I don't slow, even for low-hanging branches, logs, or the rabbits and squirrels that scurry out of my path. I keep running as fast as I can in the direction I *think* the cabin is in.

The sheriff's old. Maybe I can lose him.

Whatever I do, I can't lead him back to my guys. I can't let him piece together why I was never found.

"Stop...*Aurelia!*"

The sound of my name brings me to a screeching halt.

No. No fucking way. I'm wearing the mask. He can't see my face. How?

My hair.

My golden locks.

They aren't covered like when we met in Hearth all those weeks ago.

Still, anyone with access to a pharmacy and a decent hairstylist could have the same. It doesn't explain how the sheriff pieced together my identity that fucking fast. When I turn around, the sheriff and I are facing each other down once again. There's barely twenty feet between us now, allowing me to see exactly what he's thinking.

The kind sheriff's expression is shattered—as if he'd taken a stab in the dark and his worst fear answered.

"What did you call me?"

"Christ. It is you, isn't it? You're Aurelia George. The...pop star. I know who you are. I've been looking for you." He steps toward me, but I back away, and he pauses in shock like I'd slapped him. "Don't be afraid." He holds out his hands. "I'm here to help you."

"I don't want your help." When it looks like he won't let this go, I try begging, "*Please.* Thank you for your concern. Now forget you ever saw me."

"You know I can't do that. You have no business being out here. God knows what you've been through. Just come with me, and I'll get you home. I'll take you back to your uncle. Everything will be all right."

I shake my head and take another step back. "You're too late, Sheriff. I have no interest in being saved."

His bushy brows turn down even as a determined glint enters his eyes. "Why the hell not?"

"Because I'm trying to save *you.*"

"Save me... What the devil are you talking about? Save me from what?"

"You *know* who." To the sheriff's credit, he doesn't look away or balk.

He doesn't pretend he hasn't already suspected that his precious "boys" are fucking monsters. I bet it would horrify him to know that they're *my* monsters now. It would baffle him at least. "Do as I say, Sheriff. Forget you saw me."

"And I told you I can't do that. Look…whatever they did—"

"Whatever they did? Whatever they did!" That incredulous look is back on his face now at the fury in my tone. "Trust me, you old fool. You can't handle knowing what they did to me." The sheriff's weathered cheeks turn stark red, proving me right. "Now go your way, and I'll go mine."

I'm already turning away to leave when he says, "You're right. I failed you."

"That's not what I—"

He holds up a hand, and I fall quiet. "Let this old fool make it up to you now. Please."

I grumble and look away. "That was mean. I shouldn't have called you a fool."

"That's quite all right."

"I'm still not going with you."

"Aurelia—"

"It's my choice."

"Actually, it's not. You just implied that you were held against your will and…mishandled. I am a man of the law, and I must uphold it. Whether you come with me or not, Thorin, Khalil, and Ezekiel will answer for what they've done."

I file away that he said Zeke and not Seth and cross my arms. "And they've been waiting for the day to come when they have to disappear again. If it's justice you're looking for, you're not going to get it. You'll be too late, and I'll be the one to pay the price. No thanks." The sheriff isn't any less deterred, so I add, "And then there's the other obstacle."

"What?"

"Me."

"I don't understand."

"However it may have happened, however many times they've tempted me since to smother them in their sleep, they're mine now, and you just threatened them." Quicker than I've ever moved and smoother than I've ever managed, I lift my bow, draw an arrow, and slide it in place. The sheriff isn't expecting it, so he doesn't think to lift his rifle before I aim. "Now turn around and walk away."

His visage becomes enraged while disapproval marks his tone. "Young lady, I am an officer of the law."

"Does it look like I give a shit, old man? Last warning."

The sheriff makes a humming noise, studies my bow and form, and sighs heavily when he realizes I've been trained well. By the best, in fact. By Thorin Thayer himself. "Very well then. I'll be seeing you again, Ms. George."

I can hardly believe it when the sheriff leaves.

Once I'm sure he's gone and I'm not being followed, I circle back to the creek and find a tree downwind where I climb until I have a bird's-eye view of the den. For hours I sit and wait.

I'll admit I grow antsy watching the sun moves across the sky. My mountain men will have long ago realized I'd snuck out and are no doubt hunting for me.

If I had a *radio*, I could tell them I'm okay, but noooooo.

Serves 'em right. Let them squirm, I say.

However, if they run into the death squad before they find me, my guys will probably shoot first and ask questions later.

And then there's the sheriff.

What if he goes straight to Khalil, Thorin, and Seth? They won't go quietly, and the sheriff is naive enough to think he can talk them into turning themselves in. He hasn't said as much, but it's obvious he's developed a fatherly affection for them. Things will inevitably get ugly if I'm not there to stand between my guys and the well-meaning sheriff.

Okay, where is this bitch?

As if I summoned her, I see a flash of tawny fur.

The mother wolf darts from the tree line with something clutched in her mouth. She drops the bloody piece of carcass near the den and starts sniffing around. I do not doubt she can smell the bear when she whines. Sympathy twists my stomach.

I have no idea if her pups are okay.

They haven't made a sound or emerged from the den in the entire—I check my watch and grumble at the time—*three hours*—I've been waiting for their mom to return.

She's back, which means my babysitting duties are over, but I stay where I am with my gaze focused on the mouth of the den.

I feel the mother wolf's pain as she whimpers and whines before disappearing inside the den. Three minutes later, she emerges again with one… two…*three* pups running, tumbling, and pouncing at her heels.

The largest one is black with a small tawny patch at the top of its snout. It paces anxiously between the mother wolf's front legs while the other two—a gray wolf and a white one tussle and bite into each other.

The pups can't be more than two feet long from snout to tail and weigh no more than a gallon of milk. They're at the age when their heads and paws are too big for their small, wiggling bodies.

They're *adorable*.

And very much alive.

Most importantly, the pups are safe now with their mother to watch over them.

I can go home now.

My stomach growls, and I realize I haven't eaten yet, so I climb down as quietly as possible, but it's no use.

Wolves have exceptional hearing.

The moment my feet touch the ground, and I turn, I see the mother wolf staring at me through the trees while her babies tear into the buck she'd stolen from me.

I'm not close enough to present a threat, but I still back away slowly, waiting for her to growl or bare her teeth like she did the other times we've crossed paths. After a long and intense stare-down, the tawny wolf turns away and trots over to her ruined den. She plops down inside at the mouth of the hole where she can watch over her young. Only then does my stomach unknot itself, and I can breathe again.

Holy shit.

I guess it's fortunate she stole my kill. I have no doubt the wolf would have fed me to her kids if she wasn't full of Bambi's father.

The moment I turn to leave, I walk straight into the jaws of another predator, and I scream.

Green eyes, olive skin slick with sweat, and a furious expression stare back at me. "What the fuck are you doing out here?"

"Seth! God!" I punch his chest, and he grunts. "I was almost eaten twice today. Don't scare me like that, you jerk!" Lifting my mask until it rests on top of my head, my nervous gaze moves behind him, expecting to see the others. "Where's Thorin and Khalil?"

"Pissed and looking for you." *Of course, they are.* "Now answer me. What are you doing out here?"

I hold up my compound bow. "Hunting." Seth immediately looks skeptical. "Seriously. I caught a buck with one shot. You should have seen it. I was *so* badass."

Seth's subdued gaze studies mine carefully, and then he turns me around, checking me over for injuries. I swear he even *sniffs* me as if he can scent out the lie about where I've been.

See what I mean? My boyfriends are feral.

"Seth, I didn't try to run," I say when he takes my bow from me and straps it to his back.

"You were gone for hours, Sunshine."

"Because you bitches wouldn't give me a radio, and I got lost!"

"You have a map."

I roll my eyes. "Yes, but it was pretty much useless without a starting point. I don't know this place as well as you three."

"All right." Seth stands back and slips his hands inside his pockets. "So where is it? Where's the buck?"

"I…she stole it."

"Who?"

"The wolf…Meera." It's the first time I've said her name out loud. I'd been toying with it while watching the lone wolf nurture her pups, so I'm surprised by how right it feels.

Seth doesn't even blink at the ridiculousness of me naming a wild animal. "Seriously? A dog ate your homework? That's the lie you're going with?"

"*I'm not lying,*" I grind out.

My frustration and panic are at an all-time high right now. If I can't even convince Seth, who worships the ground I walk on, that I wasn't trying to run, I have no hope of convincing Khalil and Thorin.

Thank God I added the "no punishment" clause when I agreed to stay, but that doesn't mean they can't find other ways to make me sorry. I'm still a little torn about the "Blood Rite," as I call that night I got my period a week and a half ago.

Seth gives an exasperated shake of his head and takes my arm. "Come on."

I follow him happily like a good pet and pray his mood improves before we meet up with the others. I need him on my side or it will be three against one, and I won't stand a chance. I hadn't planned to stray so far or be gone for so long, and I damn sure wasn't expecting to return empty-handed.

It looks *really* bad.

Seth radios Thorin and Khalil to tell them he found me and we're heading back. Twenty minutes later, we're a mile in, and Seth is still brooding. His eyes are fixed straight ahead as we travel inside a dell—a dried-up streambed with steep hills on either side. Seth's expression is stormy, so I wrestle my arm free of his hold and take his hand instead.

The feel of my fingers linking his longer ones snap him out of whatever dark thoughts have taken over his mood. Seth looks down at me, and I tilt my head and smile. It's a small reassurance, but the best I can do without giving my true feelings away.

"I know what you're doing," he says in a rumble so dark and terrifying, it sends a chill down my spine.

That voice...

It doesn't...

That's *not* Seth.

I falter a step when the realization hits, and I snatch my hand away. Seth stops walking immediately and stands there like a statue.

A whimper tears from my lips. "S-Seth?"

After a few heart-pounding seconds, he blinks slowly, curses, and then shakes his head violently like he's exorcising a damn demon or something. I get the feeling that he's locked in some kind of power struggle, and I take another step away while eyeing my bow strapped to his back.

"It's me," he finally confirms. There's five feet of forest between us now while my stomach caves from the weight of my fear and uncertainty. "It's me." His voice sounds strained, as if he's holding onto a ledge by his fingertips, but... He sounds like him.

He sounds like Seth.

Still, I keep my distance because whatever the hell just happened was too intense to merely shrug off. Seth still doesn't quite seem like he has full control. It's the only explanation for why he stays where he is when he turns around to face me.

"Are you okay?" I don't realize I'm throwing self-preservation away and inching forward until he takes a cautious step backward. I stop and stay where I am. "What the hell was that, Seth?"

His eyes are pinched with worry even as his lips curl, and he spits out the name like a curse. "Bane."

My blood turns to ice. "I thought you said he doesn't come out unless Zeke is in danger."

"He doesn't. I don't…I don't know what that was." Seth curses again when he sees the terror in my eyes, and then he rips the radio off the clip at his hip. "Change of plans," he spits out. "I need you to meet us two clicks south of the she-wolf's den."

I hear the crackle of the radio, and then Khalil's voice comes through loud and clear. "Everything cool, Seth?"

"No." Seth's gaze flicks toward me and then he speaks into the radio again. "Thorin… You're going to need the tranquilizer."

Again, Seth doesn't bother to explain, but maybe he doesn't need to with them because I hear Thorin cursing through the radio a moment later before confirming he's on his way.

"What's going on, Seth?"

"You have to stay away," he pleads when I try to come closer again. "You're not safe with me."

His words are land mines that stop me in my tracks. I can see how much the admission pains him and find myself rebelling against it.

"Don't say that. I don't believe you," I immediately deny. "You—" My eyes blow wide, and the rest of my words disintegrate like ash when Seth pulls his gun. "What—"

A twig snaps behind me.

Before I can turn to search for the source of the sound and whatever new threat has descended upon us, I spot movement in the trees behind Seth while he stares behind me at whatever put him on his guard.

452 · B.B. REID

Surrounded.

The grim, silent men dressed in tactical vests and helmets and armed to the teeth have us surrounded, and even worse, they have the high ground. We're fish in a bowl. Sitting fucking ducks.

"Sunshine."

I obey the unspoken order and return to Seth's side, pulling my mask back over my face. Seth doesn't resist when I free my bow from his back. We have a shot in hell of fending off the death squad, but neither Seth nor I will go down without a fight. I nock an arrow, and the forest itself stills.

It's survival of the fittest, and it looks as if the mountain is about to test us once more.

CHAPTER FORTY-THREE

SETH | ZEKE

They're here for Sunshine.

I know it the moment another merc appears inside the dell while the rest of the death squad stands sentry above us. It makes my trigger finger a *tad* less itchy to see their rifles pointed at the ground and not at Sunshine, but it won't change their fate.

The mercenary blocking our way home holds up his hands in mock surrender and stops ten feet away while slowly reaching for his helmet. The moment his head pops free, revealing a mop of short brown curls plastered to his forehead, blue eyes, and a full beard, I immediately get the urge to shoot him. The look on his smug face says he already thinks he's won.

I can't wait to turn his intestines into a neck scarf.

Maybe we'll use his bones for our Halloween decorations this year.

In a weird twist of fate, Thorin, Khalil, and Ezekiel have been waiting for this day for ten long years. They've been waiting for the day Isaac hunted us down and tried to take Zeke back. And now I'm starting to wonder if we've been waiting all this time in our self-imposed exile for *this*.

To protect our fallen star.

The commander keeps coming with his gaze locked on Aurelia, and I feel Bane's rage rising to amplify my own as I shift to stand between the mercenary and Aurelia. If I let Bane free, this thing gets infinitely more fucked because he's not just a danger to the mercenaries but to Sunshine too—so I push him back down while keeping a close eye on the merc.

The commander's grating smile widens, and then he shifts like he might try to come closer—to get within grabbing distance—but Aurelia lifts the bow, stopping the commander with an arrow aimed at his face. He really shouldn't have taken off the helmet.

"You can take that mask off now," the douchebag orders. "We know it's you."

He doesn't say her name, so maybe he's bluffing. Either way, Aurelia keeps it on, her annoyed gaze staring back at the mercenary through the holes in the mask. It reminds me of the day we met. Only this time, I'm not on the other side of her ire.

"Who are you?" she inquires coldly.

Having no doubt that she can handle that asshole, I let her do the talking while I survey the situation, marking each of the mercenaries' positions on either side of the streambed.

If I'm quick enough, I could maybe take out two of them and send them all into a frenzy since they won't expect such a rash and stupid move. It will give Sunshine and me just enough time to run and take cover in the trees, but I find myself hesitating.

It's too huge a risk.

All of their bullets will be focused on me, but if one should find Aurelia, even by mistake...

"Patrick Finnegan," the leader replies. "At your service."

"Okay, Finnegan. I don't mean to be rude, but what the fuck do you want?"

My hackles rise when the commander doesn't answer immediately. It feels like he's weighing his words, and why the hell would he need to do that unless he plans to lie? "We're here to find you and return you to your uncle. *Aurelia*."

So, it's not a bluff.

"Okay. Well, you found me. Now run along and tell my uncle I'm doing fine and thank him for his unnecessary concern."

Finnegan shakes his head. "I'm afraid that won't be enough. We were hired for a particular task, and delivering a message was not it."

"Either you're as dumb as you look or hard of hearing, so allow me to clarify a few things. It was *my* money my uncle used to hire you, which means you work for *me*, and my first order is for all of you to fuck off. Go on," she says when they all just look at one another. "Shoo."

The mercenary visibly bristles at her dismissive tone while all the rage and suspicion I was feeling earlier evaporates until I'm the one left feeling like an ass.

I shouldn't have doubted her.

Once I figure out how to kill them all and get Sunshine back to our cabin where I can keep her safe, I'll find a way to make it up to her.

"I was afraid of this," the commander replies in a concerned tone that feels staged.

"Afraid of *what*?" Aurelia snaps.

"Do you know what Stockholm syndrome is?" Aurelia doesn't respond, but I notice her aim waver just a little. "It's when a hostage or someone who's been abused forms an emotional attachment to their captor or abuser. It's a survival instinct, Aurelia. Nothing more. What you're feeling isn't real."

At that last statement, her gaze narrows, and she steadies her aim once more. "What are you? My therapist? Did you read *Psychology for Dummies* on the plane ride here, Patrick Star?"

"Ms. George, you might want to look around you," the commander says, finally dropping the act. "You're outnumbered and outgunned. If your boy toy had a move to get out of this, he would have made it by now. We know you're stalling. We know the other two are probably racing like hell to get here in time, but it won't make a difference. You do have a choice here, though. You can come with us and save your little harem, or we can kill them all and return you to your uncle anyway."

"You forgot option three," I say, speaking for the first time since they arrived. "The one where I kill you because there's no chance in hell I'll let you take her. Either way, someone dies, and it won't just be me."

Finnegan's smile returns, and it's no longer friendly as he signals his men. "If you insist."

The sound of several rifles rising and the safeties switching off follows, and then I have several red dots covering my chest at center mass. When Aurelia gasps, I tear my glare away from Finnegan, expecting to see red dots covering her, too, but there are none. Her watery gaze is locked on my chest while her mouth is open in horror.

"Seth…"

The urge to tell her everything will be okay rises, but I can't bring myself to say the words. I can't bring myself to lie. Instead, I whisper, "Don't look, Sunshine." Aurelia's gaze meets mine, and then she whimpers and shakes her head like she knows what I'm about to tell her. "The moment I'm down, you *run*. As fast as you can. As hard as you can." I risk being turned into Swiss cheese when I raise my hand to cup her soft, brown cheek. I can't resist touching her one last time. "Thorin and Khalil will find you." Trusting that much, if nothing else, I finally let the words free. "Everything will be okay."

"I'm not leaving you."

"Take care of Thorin and Khalil," I say, ignoring her vow. "They're not so bad."

Sheer desperation rises up in her eyes when she realizes I'm telling her goodbye.

"Seth, I swear to God, if you die, I'm going to fucking kill you."

The hollow feeling in my chest heals a little more, and my response is tumbling free before I'm even aware of what I'll say. "I love you, Sunshine."

"I know that!" she snaps like a brat. "That's why you can't really expect me to let you die."

"You've got ten seconds to decide, Ms. George!" the commander yells while Aurelia glares at me.

I turn my head to roar at the mercenary, "She's not going anywhere with you!"

My heart is pounding too fast to catch my breath when I close my eyes. I keep them shut even when I feel Aurelia pull away from me. Every part of me is focused on searching for that steel vault in the deepest recesses of Zeke's mind—the cage that barely holds Bane at bay anymore. Once I find it, I let the only key that will unlock it from this side form on my lips. "Chrysa—"

"Fine, assface. You win. I'll go with you."

My eyes fly open to the sight of Aurelia already approaching Finnegan. The merc had even managed to sneak closer, getting within grabbing distance while I attempted to free Bane. I lunge to grab Aurelia first when one of the mercenaries fire a warning shot into the ground near my feet. Finnegan uses the opportunity to grab her arm and start pulling her away.

"Take your fucking hands off of her!" I roar. Charging forward, I follow after Aurelia, ignoring the barrage of warning shots the death squad fires at will but to no avail.

"Stop, Seth!" Aurelia pleads with terror in her eyes. Terror for me. "You have to stop! Please!"

"No."

"Go home before they kill you!"

I shake my head as another bullet too close for comfort whizzes by me and hits the exposed bedrock on the other side. "Not without you."

"Just forget you ever knew me."

"*Never.*"

"You better do something about him, or I will," Finnegan warns as he backs away with my girl in one hand and a gun pointed at me in the other.

I can tell by the panicked glance she gives him that Aurelia takes his warning to heart.

When her eyes return to me, something crumbles inside both of us.

"I overheard the three of you," she stumbles to tell me. "Out on the deck the day they came. I was eavesdropping from the lower deck." I'm barely listening as I continue to close the distance between us, but then she says, "Seth, I knew all along the real reason they came. I knew the three of you were lying to me again. You played me."

My blood turns cold as I shake my head. "No, baby."

"*Yes,*" she insists. "You still didn't trust me. I knew then you never would, and I can't live like that. I can't be bound to that cabin and only the three of you forever. I need more. I need my old life back. I need to matter again."

"You matter to me, Sunshine. You're everything. Isn't that enough?"

She tilts her head back and gives a derisive laugh. "Seriously? You weren't even enough for Thorin and Khalil to stick around. How could you ever think you could make me happy? I'm Aurelia George. Get fucking real."

Her words burn through me like acid, bringing me to a screeching halt while every fear I've had since Aurelia told me she loves me comes to fruition. What if she lied? What if she stops? What if she wakes up one day and misses her old life?

"I don't believe you," I grind out, returning her words from earlier.

Please…please say it's not true, I beg her silently.

"What about this morning when I snuck out?" she challenges instead. "Open your fucking eyes, Seth. You were right. Can't you see that? I was running again. I was looking for their camp, but you found me first, and I knew what would happen when you got me back to that cabin. I knew you wouldn't keep your promise, so I lied. There was no damn deer, and I *don't* love you."

No.

My heart doesn't listen to the denial my soul screams back at hers in response. It shatters inside my chest while my footsteps grow heavy.

I still continue to put one foot in front of the other, though.

"That's enough warning. Put one in his leg," Finnegan orders.

"Noooo!" Aurelia screams just as a bullet tears through the skin in my thigh.

The shot echoes around the forest while I grit my teeth in agony and fall to my knees. Aurelia struggles to break free of Finnegan's hold to get to me, but the mercenary quickens his pace until he's practically dragging her away while Aurelia screams obscenities at him.

The pain and the bullet don't stop me, though.

I crawl.

Through the mud, rocks, and dirt… I crawl to get to her. Even if she doesn't want me. Even if it was all a lie and she doesn't love me. I crawl to Aurelia because it was real for me, and I can't let them take her.

I know why they're really here.

CHAPTER FORTY-FOUR

AURELIA

F uck, that asshole doesn't quit."

"Did you see the way he crawled after her? Jesus. I don't love my wife that much."

"Forget her voice. Her cunt's got to be lined with gold."

Keeping my gaze straight ahead, I walk and ignore the raucous laughter around me at my expense.

Truthfully, my body is present, but my mind is still back in that dell with Seth. The things I said to him… I don't have to wonder if he believed them. I saw the defeat in his eyes and the crushing hopelessness I left him with.

His heart's broken, but at least it's still beating.

"Ignore them," Finnegan says somewhat amicably. "Most of them have only felt that kind of devotion from the warm mouth of a two-dollar whore."

"I want to talk to my uncle," I demand.

"I'm afraid that won't be possible."

I stop walking to face him. "Why the hell not?"

"No cell reception out here, darling."

"Why did my uncle hire you?"

"I told you. To find you and bring you home."

"You're saying my uncle thought I was still alive after all this time?"

"No. We were tasked to find your body or proof that you were dead. Luckily for us, we found you alive, so I get to triple my fee."

I roll my eyes and resume walking. This time, I let my gaze wander the forest, hoping for some sign that Thorin and Khalil have caught up, and it doesn't go unnoticed.

"You don't want them finding us, darling. It won't end well for them."

"Call me biased, but I'd say this won't end well for *you*."

Finnegan grunts but doesn't argue. We hike for two hours before I realize we're nearing the base of Big Bear.

Home.

I don't know how close I am to the cabin, but I find myself looking back, seeking out that lonely cliff for a glimpse of it. When I don't see it, my eyes travel the way we came—up the steep, craggy, snow-packed slope to the sun high in the sky right above it. It's sandwiched between two forest lines like a frozen stream, and about five hundred feet ahead is the ledge where all this lingering snow piled so precariously could fall over at any moment.

One wrong move could send it all sliding.

The climb down won't be easy, and I realize I might have underestimated my mountain men's knowledge of these wilds because they would have known a better, safer way down.

Perhaps time is of the essence for the mercenaries since Thorin and Khalil will be hot on our heels. I've done what I could to slow our progress, but when Finnegan threatened to hogtie and carry me, I decided I'd rather have my hands free for when the time comes.

The mercenaries stop once we reach the ledge, and I figure they're trying to figure out a way down, so I inch closer to the edge to see if there's a possible escape route while Finnegan argues with some of the other mercs I caught staring at me a few times.

Apparently, even battle-hardened killers get starstruck.

Two of the men are sent off to scout while another unnecessarily announces that he's going to take a shit.

One peek over the side of the ledge, and I know I wouldn't survive the fall. All those sharp rocks waiting to break me in half will ensure it. Maybe I can make a break for the trees while the mercs are distracted and take cover there.

Unfortunately, I take a little too long to shit or get off the pot.

Finnegan breaks away from the other mercenaries and approaches me. "Hey, so this is a little awkward," he says while rubbing the back of his neck, "but some of the guys have daughters and girlfriends who are fans of yours." When I just stare at him, he huffs his irritation at me for not making this easier for him. "They were wondering if they could get you to sign some autographs."

I cut my gaze at the men in question, who pretend they're not eavesdropping and waiting for my response, and then I sigh. "Sure. Got a pen?"

Having complete strangers ask for my autograph isn't new to me, so why does this feel weird? I guess because I stopped thinking of myself as *that* Aurelia weeks ago. The star. The celebrity.

The Aurelia I am now feels more human. She feels real and flawed. I can relate to her.

"Yup. Here you go." Finnegan hands me a notepad and pen and tells me who to sign the autographs for. Once I'm done, he takes them back and slips them inside his tactical vest with a smile that feels slimy, so I turn away to face the ledge again. "Thanks."

"Don't mention it."

"I didn't expect you to be so cool about this after what happened with your boyfriend. It almost makes what I have to do now difficult."

I turn my head to see him standing closer than he was before. Much too close. I look him up and down, not bothering to hide my displeasure. "What are you talking about?"

"I'd have made it quick," he continues to ramble, "but your uncle wanted us to make it look like an accident."

"Excuse me?"

I feel a heavy hand on my back a moment later, shoving me toward the edge…

A sharp whistle is the only thing that keeps me from going over.

"Hey, asshole!"

Finnegan's hand disappears from my back, and I spin around with a surprised gasp, my heart racing with hope and disbelief. It can't be…

It is.

Seth is here. And he's not alone.

When I follow the sound of his voice, I see all *three* of my guys standing together. Thorin and Khalil are holding the two scouts at gunpoint while Seth has the shitter kneeling at his feet with a gun pressed to his temple.

I fall to my knees into the rocks and snow with a grateful sob.

Seth looks a little manic, but he's here. He's *okay*.

I notice the bandage around his thigh at the same time he yells, "You missed, bitches!" Seth pulls the trigger without warning and the mercenary drops at his feet. "I didn't."

I can't bring myself to be horrified at the cold-blooded murder of the merc. I don't even think I'm capable of guilt anymore. If I could cry happy tears at seeing Seth again, I would.

He's *okay*.

Maybe the bullet only grazed him, or perhaps he was only pretending to be hurt so he could gain the upper hand.

Seth definitely has it now.

I can tell by the way these "hardened" mercenaries are scrambling for their weapons. I can tell by the way Finnegan removes his hand from my back to grab my arm in a tight hold instead. He brings me in front of him to use me as a human shield, and I let him because I don't want him to die just yet.

"What the hell are you just standing there for? Kill them!"

"But, sir! Roberts and Sanders!" one of the men reminds their leader. He gets a bullet to the brain, and pandemonium ensues when the rest of the squad realizes it was friendly fire.

Finnegan killed his own man.

It motivates the rest to start shooting.

Realizing there's no loyalty or brotherhood among their ranks, Khalil and Thorin use the mercs as human shields as they take cover.

Roberts and Sanders are dead by the time Thorin and Khalil take cover behind two of the boulders, leaving only Finnegan and three other mercs alive.

Seth has also taken cover, but only after Thorin shouts at him to get down.

Khalil raises his head to return fire, and he's so focused on dropping the others that he doesn't notice Finnegan drawing his handgun.

The wolf Thorin sees every time he looks at me raises her head, and I grab Finnegan's arm with both hands. Lunging forward, I sink my teeth into his wrist.

"Aaaaargh! You fucking bitch!"

Finnegan starts shaking me around like a rag doll, trying to turn me loose, but I don't let go—not even when his skin gives, and I taste blood. And not when I remember how close we are to the precarious ledge.

We could both fall, but at least Khalil will be safe.

Finnegan finally gets desperate and punches my temple hard enough to make me see stars. I drop to the ground while the shooting continues, and I curse Finnegan for tossing my bow.

He kept my axe, though.

It's currently hooked to a D-clip on his back.

When he tries to grab me, I spit my mouthful of his blood in his face, and it stuns him long enough for me to lunge for his gun. Finnegan recovers the moment I grab it, and our struggle for control of the gun ends with us both tipping over the edge of the cliff.

"Aureliaaaaa!" one of my guys *screams*.

Khalil, I think.

He must have seen me go over.

My heart stops when I see the sharp rocks below rushing up to meet me, but then my next breath punches out of me when the ground reaches me much sooner than expected, and I slam chest first onto the hard surface.

The first thing I notice is that I'm not dead.

Unfortunately, neither is Finnegan.

He's hanging onto the tiny ledge protruding from the cliff face with one hand clinging to the missing chunk in the rock, while the other dangles unseen next to his body.

"Wow, you're really strong. You must work out a lot. I'm guessing you can hold that just long enough to answer my questions, and then I'll think about letting you up. What do you say?"

"I'm all ears, *Aurelia*."

"You said my uncle wanted it to look like an accident."

"That's not a question."

"Exactly what did he hire you to do?"

"To find your body and bring it home for burial, and believe me, princess. He spared no expense."

But even if Finnegan hadn't already tried to push me off the cliff, I would have smelled the bullshit. My uncle has never been particularly religious or

464 · B.B. REID

sentimental. There's no way he would have gone through all of this trouble for a funeral if there wasn't something in it for him.

"And what were your orders if you found me alive?"

Finnegan isn't quick to answer, and I can see by the distant look that flashes in his eyes that he's weighing his chances between lying and honesty.

I'd say he has fifty-fifty odds.

Realizing the same, Finnegan chooses the honest route, and while his answer doesn't surprise me, my nonreaction to it most certainly does.

"My orders were to bring back your body. It didn't matter if your soul was still attached to it when I found you."

I'm still processing that my uncle wants me dead—even if I suspected it a time or two this past year—so when Finnegan raises the hand that's not holding the cliff, I'm caught off guard in more ways than one. There's a gun pointed at me now.

What a fucking idiot.

"Not so fast, Finnegan. This one is for all the marbles…" Finnegan's curiosity wins out, and he keeps his finger off the trigger. *Bad kitty.* "When did my uncle hire you to kill me?" I know by his minute pause that he wasn't expecting me to ask that question. My gaze narrows, and his widens in return. "When did…my *fucking* uncle…hire you…to kill me?"

Finnegan blows out a defeated breath. "Fuck it. Three months ago, okay? A few weeks before your plane crashed."

I'd always wondered how my uncle was able to arrange everything so quickly—particularly the ranch he purchased not far from here that I still haven't seen. My exile from public scrutiny had nothing to do with my leaked sex tape. The blizzard, the crash, finding the cabin…

This was always going to happen.

"Our orders were to wait a few days and follow you. We were going to make it look like an accident then too. Your uncle thought he got lucky with the plane crash, but then your body was never recovered, so he sent us to find you. This will have to do."

Click.

Finnegan gapes at the gun and then glowers as he stupidly tries again. *Click, click, click, click, click, click.*

Placing my hands on my hips, I lean most of my weight on my right leg. "Seriously, you're a gun-for-hire and can't even tell the difference in the weight when there's no mag inside? I want a refund."

"How? When?"

I twirl the end of a curl around my finger. "During our little tussle. I ejected the clip and emptied the chamber while you were too busy trying to cop a feel. Yeah... I noticed. My *harem*—as you called them—showed me a few tricks. Can you believe they're good for more than just delivering the D?"

"You fucking bitch." He throws the gun away and grips the ledge with his other hand. Still, his face turns red from the strain of holding himself up.

"You're about to be murdered, dude. At least try an insult that *bites*."

This goddamn wasted cum-juice-turned-human-mold-spore looks me dead in my eyes and says, "I like Tania's music better."

I guess I had that coming.

I still shift forward and step on both of his hands in case he gets any ideas about grabbing me while I unclip my axe from his back with quick fingers.

A few weeks ago, the mere mention of Tania would have sent me into a rage, and I probably would have done something idiotic, giving Finnegan the chance to regain the upper hand, but not today.

I'm already pretty fucking pissed, and I've been harnessing that rage ever since he had Seth shot.

"Well then... No need to hang around on my account. Get it?" I giggle and snort at my own joke. "*Hang around?*"

Raising the axe, I bring it back down as hard as I can, cutting off four of his fingers from the second knuckle down. Finnegan releases a bloodcurdling scream as he stares at the gruesome gap between what's left of his right hand and his severed fingers.

"You fucking bitch! You fucking cunt!"

"You have to do better than that if you want to hurt my feelings, Finnegan!" I bring the axe down a second time, severing the fingers on his left hand. Finnegan continues to scream as he falls down, down, dooooown...

SPLAT.

Blood sprays across the powder-white snow when he lands on the rocks below, and for a while, I'm frozen. I can't do anything but stare down at the body to assure myself that he won't get back up, even though I know no one can survive that.

When a full minute passes and Finnegan remains unmoving—a macabre black and red stain in the distance—I feel my shoulders slump.

It's not until I hear feathers rustling and wings flapping that I realize I'm not alone. I turn around and see an owl resting in its nest with its back to me and head fully rotated while staring at me through wide, yellow eyes.

"Uhh…"

Rocks tumble over the side of the upper ledge, and my heart drops.

Someone's coming.

Fearing the worst, I press myself against the wall to hide while my murder witness flies away.

"Goldilocks!"

Khalil.

My lips part to answer his call, but I don't allow myself to make a sound and stay hidden for some reason. Before I can examine the reason, Khalil yells again.

"Fuck!" he explodes, and I imagine him looking over the ledge and spotting Finnegan.

"What?" Seth demands. "What do you see?"

"I don't know, I don't know! It's…she's… There's blood, man. A lot of it. Someone's down there. It's too far to tell…"

"AURELIAAAAA!" Thorin roars.

My chest caves with relief while my stomach churns with dread. I have no idea which reaction to trust while the three of them lose their shit thinking I fell to my death.

Finnegan's words about my feelings for them not being real have been replaying in my head on a constant loop. What if he's right? What if I'm just coping through surrender? What I tricked myself into believing I loved them?

And then there's Seth…

I don't know what he's told Thorin and Khalil or what they'll do to me once they find out.

Closing my eyes, it takes me a few seconds more to swallow down the uncertainty clogging my throat.

It was real.

So when I feel my heart calling out for them, I finally let myself push away from the wall until I'm visible. "I'm here!"

"Goldilocks!" The stricken look on Khalil's face morphs into crippling relief when he sees me alive and in one piece. Fortunately, he doesn't stay incapacitated for long. "Hold on, baby. We're going to pull you up." When I nod, he quickly disappears back over the upper ledge. A couple of minutes later, a thick red rope is slung over the side. The long length pools onto the ground by my feet, and I grab it.

"Tie that around your waist," Khalil instructs. "And make the knot as tight as you can. I'm going to pull you up."

"Okay."

Once I have what I hope is a decent knot tied around my waist, I hold on to the slack, and Khalil begins to pull me up. Thorin grabs me the moment I clear the lip of the upper ledge, and he pulls me over until I collapse on top of him while breathing hard.

This feels familiar.

When I look around, I see dead bodies everywhere, but my gaze doesn't linger on them. I search for Seth and find him standing back with his hands in his pockets like some passing bystander.

"Seth…" I climb to my feet with Khalil's help and go to Seth. He doesn't back away from me, but I can tell he wants to. "What happened? Are you hurt?"

"My leg is fine," he answers evenly. "The bullet grazed me."

I nod with a hard exhale. "Good. That's good."

I can feel Thorin and Khalil watching our exchange closely, and I'm again left wondering what Seth told them. Had he believed my lies when I said I didn't love him, or am I living in a fool's paradise thinking he might have seen through them?

"Is something up with you two?" Khalil inquires when the awkward silence stretches on.

I can't bring myself to answer while Seth just stares at me blankly with blood on his shirt like he hadn't just killed for me.

"Seth?" I decide to ask him instead. I need to know that he knows it was all real for me too.

Instead, he turns away, giving his back to me. "We should go," he suggests while starting the hike back up the slope. "We need to get the supplies to clear these bodies out."

I stand there feeling like my heart is splintering in two while Thorin and Khalil give us both weird looks.

So Seth didn't tell them, and yet, he obviously believes all those things I said in the dell. The only question is... Why didn't he rat me out?

"Come on," Thorin softly orders while taking my elbow.

I force myself to put one foot in front of the other as I make my way back up the slope. Khalil lingers behind, making sure the mercenaries are all really dead. He's over by one of the larger slanted rocks, checking Sanders when I hear it.

The horrifying familiar crack like thunder and the sound of heavy rain pouring down...

Except the sky is clear and there is no rain.

The snow beneath our feet begins to crack and slide, slowly heading for the ledge where it spills over the side. I imagine the image from below where Finnegan lies dead is that of a waterfall except with snow.

The ground starts trembling, and it feels like a stampede heading straight for us.

Seth, who had stopped to pick a flower turns to face us with a confused frown. "What is that?" he calls out from fifty feet ahead.

The blood drains from my face as I gape at the horrifying image behind him. Mist crests the hill that leads home, and then a wall of white so thick and high it blocks out the sun follows as it heads straight for us.

The answer to Seth's question spills from my lips in a horrified shudder. "Avalanche."

Fuck, it's cold.

I stopped feeling my fingers and toes hours ago, but if I complain again, I have a feeling I'll perish from strangulation instead of exposure.

The storms have finally stopped, but the sun still hasn't appeared as snow slowly falls, making visibility poor. Today, the wilds are cloaked in fog and mist that blanket the forest floor and wrap around my ankles.

"So I'm guessing you've realized life is too short to spend it guarding a soulless witch, and you're planning to quit once we make it out of here, huh?"

I peek over at Tyler, who is currently trying to use the hands on his grandfather's watch to determine our direction. Caught off guard, his head snaps toward me, and his brown eyes widen when he finds me watching him. Amusement breaks through his surprise, and then he snorts.

"Or I realized the soulless witch needs me more than I thought, and I'm asking for a raise once we make it out of here."

"No need to wait. Done. Doubled." Wrapping my arms around one of his, I rest my cheek on his strong shoulder. "I know I can be hard to deal with."

Laughing, Tyler shakes his head. "What is it you told Joanna? Better hard to deal with than easy to play with?" Smiling, I nod. "Besides, how could I leave you? You'd be lost without me."

"Literally."

I'm rewarded with another snort, and then he says, "Come on. The beacon is this way." He points to the other side of a ravine forty feet below us where the forest continues.

I immediately wrinkle my nose. "But how are we supposed to get down there?" Please don't say climb. Please don't say climb.

"We climb, princess."

I groan. "Can't we go around?"

"That could take hours and cost us another day to reach the tail. Another storm could hit, and we may not be lucky finding shelter again."

"We could also fall to our death, Ty."

Tyler's jaw ticks, and I know he probably wants to take control and tell me we're doing this, but he's also remembering that he works for me, which means I'm in charge.

Technically.

After watching him struggle with indecision, I decide to cut the only person in the world who actually likes and gives a shit about me some slack.

"So how do we do this? We don't have any rope."

Tyler looks relieved that I'm not going to go Godzilla on him, and then he's frowning again as he trudges over to the edge of the small cliff and peers over. "Slowly. I think I see a way down. I'll go first, and then you follow. Step where I step. Hold what I hold. We should be fine."

"Piece of cake," I tease. We're gonna die.

Pushing away from the tree I'm huddling under, I take one step toward the cliff's edge when I hear something like a clap and a boom. Startled, I look around *in confusion, but before I can ask Tyler what it could be, the ground under my feet begins to shake. It trembles so hard I have to hold on to the tree I abandoned for balance.*

"Earthquake!"

The rumbling grows louder, and I follow its direction through the trees from the north. There's a wall of white that seems to get closer and closer. At first, I assume my eyes are playing tricks on me because it looks like the air is moving.

"Aurelia…" The horror in Tyler's tone has me looking away in time to see his deep-dark skin turn gray as he looks through the trees, bending and swaying from the quake. "Fuck! That's not an earthquake! Run!"

Ignoring his order, I hold my hand out for him as he makes a break for the tree that I'm still clutching. My head swivels back and forth as I measure the distance between us and the distance between Tyler and all that white.

He's naturally fast, but the deep snow slows him, forcing him to take giant steps to cover more distance, which also slows him down. Each step costs him precious lifesaving seconds. Meanwhile, the mass of snow gets closer and closer, and I realize with impending doom that I'm just out of its reach. If Tyler can get to me, he'll be saved too.

The mass of snow rockets by me and sucks all the air from my lungs from how biting the cold is. My shriveled fingers become impossibly stiff, but I keep my hand out for Tyler, and I wait for the brush of our fingers that never comes.

Tyler is still too far away.

"Aurelia! Ru—"

The mass swallows him up, and I scream as it hurtles him back toward the ravine, back toward the cliff's edge. Helplessly, I watch as it carries my bodyguard over. The snow keeps spilling over the edges like a frozen, deadly waterfall, and then, as fast as it began, it ends.

Ignoring the numb seizing control of my body, I crawl through the snow to the cliff's edge and scream over the ravine for my bodyguard.

"Tyyyyylerrrrrr!"

CHAPTER FORTY-FIVE

AURELIA

I t feels like a building fell on top of me.

My ears are ringing, and I can't feel the rest of my body. I'm choking on something cold and powdery, and whenever I try to breathe, my lungs scream that there's no air. Meanwhile, something keeps beeping, and it annoys me.

Where am I?

What happened?

The last thing I remember is…

A massive wall of snow, ice, and death racing toward the four of us. I remember how there was no time to run. Seth was swept up first, followed by Thorin and me.

God, I didn't see what happened to Khalil.

He was the farthest away from us. The avalanche would have hit him last. He would have watched us get swept up like I had to watch Tyler.

I whimper, and it sounds like Khalil's name to my ears. The beeping grows more rapid and louder, and then I hear my name.

"Aurelia!"

The voice is muffled, but I'd know it anywhere.

It's Khalil.

I try desperately to move my arms and limbs to get to him, but I can't. There's too much snow, and I'm buried deep. I can't even cry out to him.

Khalil seems to know because he shouts, "It's okay, baby! Stay still and take small breaths. I'll get you out!"

I do what he says, conserving my air, and not a moment later, I hear the muffled sound of him digging. It feels like a lifetime before the snow thins enough for me to see the sun piercing the powder.

The only problem is I've just taken my last breath, and I'm officially suffocating. Panic claws at my chest as I silently plead for Khalil to hurry.

The snow above my face finally parts, and I suck in a ragged breath. The sun still hovers above the slope, blinding me until I look away and into Khalil's relieved yet worried gaze.

"Baby, I have to leave you for a moment. Thorin and Seth are still under."

"Go," I urge him immediately.

Khalil managed to free one of my arms while looking for my head, so I use it now to claw the remaining snow from my chest and arm until I'm free enough to sit up.

Khalil is holding the avalanche tracker, and I realize it's causing the beeping I heard. Thorin would only take me hunting if I agreed to wear it, so it's around my ankle again.

Yes, even after I made a huge deal about it.

Whatever.

I'm starting to believe Khalil was right… I clearly have nine lives. How many does this make now? How many more times will the mountain test me?

The tracker starts to beep rapidly again. *Beep beep! Beep beep! Beep beep! Beep beep!*

Thorin.

He was next to me when the avalanche hit us, so I'm not surprised to find him close.

I quickly dig my legs out while Khalil begins unearthing Thorin.

By the time I crawl and wiggle free of my own snowy grave, he finds Thorin's chest. I scramble over on my hands and knees since I'm not strong enough to stand just yet, and I start clawing away the snow from where his head should be.

"How?" I can't help but ask despite us racing against the clock to free Thor.

Khalil flings a hurried arm out, and my gaze follows its muscular line to the slanted boulder where he'd been checking the dead. He would have had just enough time to duck behind it before the mass came for him.

I can see snow piled around the back and sides of the boulder even now, but it doesn't crest the tip of the slant.

Focusing on my task again, I silently thank the mountain for sparing him and dig *faster*.

Finally, I see pale skin and blond hair.

Please, please, please.

My heart crumples with relief when I hear Thorin inhale deeply. Grateful tears spring to my eyes, blurring my vision just as his blue ones spring open.

I keep shoveling to get the rest of him out, but Khalil moves off.

Seth.

Oh, God, he's still buried.

The avalanche took him first. How much air will he have left?

Don't.

The tracker is still beeping a heartbreakingly slow and steady rhythm.

Beep…beep…beep…beep.

I keep one ear open while digging Thorin out, waiting to hear that telling tempo increase. I have to get to Seth. I have to do something.

"Can you get yourself free?" I ask Thorin once both of his arms are finally free.

Thorin nods in answer and waves me off.

I want to kiss him for not dying. I want to kiss them both. Instead, I spring to my feet only to collapse again when I try to step through the deep snow.

"Where is he?" I beg more than ask Khalil. "Where is he!"

"I don't know!" he roars back.

His face is pinched with worry as he turns this way and that.

"Was he wearing his tracker?"

"I don't…" Khalil's voice breaks. "Fuck, I don't know." To himself, he mumbles, "Seth, you fucking idiot."

Snatching the tracker from Khalil, who's gone catatonic, I stumble and crawl through the snow. I point the little device in the last place I saw him.

"Seth!" I trip again when I try to run in another direction. "Seth, you answer me!" I demand even though I know he can't.

No time. No air.

We're running out of time. Seth's running out of air.

My fault, my fault.

If I'd just stayed in bed. If I hadn't snuck out. If I hadn't felt the need to challenge and push their buttons for the promise of a hot and dirty fuck.

Once again, I'm responsible for people dying.

"Seeeeth, pleeeeease." My stomach suddenly cramps, and the crushing pain of losing him forever sends me to my knees, where I double over.

When it subsides, all that's left is anger.

The only thing more useless than me is this fucking tracker. In a fit of rage and hopelessness, I chuck it as far as I can and scream.

I don't watch where it goes, but I hear it land in the snow a few feet away.

Beep beep! Beep beep! Beep beep! Beep beep!

My head snaps up with a gasp.

Beep beep! Beep beep! Beep beep! Beep beep!

I surge from the ground and back onto my feet. Khalil and Thorin must hear it too. They sprint past me and beat me to the tracker as we all race for it at the same time.

Their cleated boots help them navigate the extra feet of snow a little better, though they still struggle, losing precious seconds. They're already digging by the time I reach the tracker.

None of us speak as I join them.

The only thing we can do is dig.

Khalil and Thorin dig for their brother. I dig for the man I love. *One* of the men I love.

It feels like forever before we see even a small part of him.

His glove.

He's still holding onto that purple flower he picked for me as if he still wanted me to have it even through death. My smile is wobbly as I take it from him and tuck it into my hair.

We manage to find his head and get his face free, but Seth doesn't take a breath. It's eerily silent, his face wholly still as Thorin and Khalil keep digging.

I...I can't.

I'm stuck staring at his frozen face. His beautiful, taunting, sweet face. Seth's eyes are closed, but no matter how long I wait, they don't open.

No, no, no.

I'm clutching the front of his coat and shaking him before Thor and Khalil can finish getting him free. I don't realize they've dug him out completely until Khalil starts dragging me away. When I punch and scream at him, he simply locks his arms around me, holding me immobile as much as comforting me while Thorin rests his head on Seth's.

No. Not resting.

His ear is hovering above Seth's parted lips.

Thorin's checking for breathing.

I don't get a chance to delude myself into thinking that maybe Seth's just unconscious before Thorin places both hands over Seth's chest and starts compressions.

My heart hiccups inside my chest as I look on helplessly.

I feel as useless as I had when I watched Tyler go over the cliff. Had this been what the end felt like for him? Alone in a snowy grave, suffocating to death?

"Come on, Seth," Khalil encourages when Thorin pauses the compressions to push air into Seth's mouth.

"Please," I whisper in turn. "Please, please, please."

I lose sight of him for a second when my vision blurs, and then it clears again once I feel something hot and wet trailing down my cheeks. It happens again—like a dam that's been broken. The salty liquid spills into my mouth and over my chin. I still don't comprehend what's happening until Khalil swipes his thumb over my cheek.

"Goldilocks... You're crying."

More tears fall, and I have no idea what to do with them. Unless they're life-giving, they're utterly useless to me now. Khalil nudges my head with his own to comfort me and let me know he's here, and he has me. I clutch him harder as I turn to tuck my tearstained face into his neck.

I can't watch anymore.

Seconds later, I hear Thorin start compressions again.

I don't know how many times he attempts to resuscitate Seth before Khalil murmurs, "Thorin."

"No," he gruffly snaps.

I peek over my shoulder as Thorin pauses pumping to give him two measured breaths again.

Seth's chest still doesn't rise.

Through my despair, an untimely question pierces my mind, and I wonder who Thorin is trying so hard to save? His frenemy turned unlikely ally or best friend? Seth or Zeke?

I haven't met Zeke yet, but I highly doubt the alters are one and the same to Thorin and Khalil. Seth is as real to them as he is to Zeke.

He's real to *me* too.

I hear a cough, and it doesn't register where it came from until I clock movement and see Seth rolling over toward Thorin.

Alive.

Seth's *alive*.

A sharp sound of relief tears from my throat, and then I push away from Khalil and claw through the snow to get to him.

Thorin's brows are turned down as he peers closely at his friend. Hearing me coming, his blue gaze snaps to me, and he holds out a scarred and callused hand.

"Aurelia...wait."

Ignoring Thorin, I place a hand on Seth's shoulder and turn him around to face me. The moment I see his handsome face and sad green eyes, I kiss his frozen lips. Seth stiffens, but I'm too overcome with gratitude that he's not dead to care. I just want to hold him and let him feel how much I love him.

Seth curls his hands around my arms, and I wait for him to pull me into him and nuzzle and scent me like he always does.

Instead, he shoves me back.

I'm thrown off him and into the snow while Seth scrambles away from me.

His chest is heaving as he stares at me like I've grown two heads. His hair is no longer slicked back. Instead, it falls over his forehead and around his ears. It's grown longer over the last couple of months, so it shields his eyes, which are no longer flirty and adoring but shifty and distrustful as he watches me like he thinks I'll eat him alive.

"Seth..." He stiffens at the name. "Baby, it's me. What's wrong?"

Seth's green eyes narrow with suspicion rather than swim with mischief.

In hindsight, it should have been my first clue that something was off, but I can't help but remember the dell and the devastation in his eyes when I left him there. It feels like my soul is reaching out, making a desperate grab for his.

Ignoring the warning bells, I inch forward, trying to close this emotional and physical gap. Right now, it feels like the entire mountain is between us, so I reach out a hand, hoping it's in my head and not reality.

"Goldilocks, don't," Khalil warns. "That's not—"

Seth flinches away from my touch and finally speaks in a voice that isn't his. "Who the fuck are you?"

WHO THE HELL JUST WOKE UP?

If you're dying to know, stay tuned for *Chrysalis*, the final book in the Men of the Wilds duet. You're going to meet Zeke and Bane, find out who Thorin and Khalil will choose, uncover what Aurelia plans to do about her uncle, and meet some of your favorite characters from other books (yay to cross-overs). If you were paying attention, I've already hinted which two worlds *Crucible* takes place in. I am already so eager to get back to the Cold Peaks and just in time for Aurelia's first summer in the wilds. See you soon!

Thank you so much for seeing Aurelia, Thorin, Khalil, and Seth's story through to the *almost* end. I had many worries while writing this book. My biggest was that Aurelia wouldn't be "likable" enough. And then I had to laugh at myself because it was just as much fun reading about Aurelia as it was writing her. She's a capital B, but she had her reasons. She was also a refreshing change from my usual heroines. Aurelia's resilience and bravery were truly something to behold. I hope that you were able to resonate with her, and if not, I hope one day you do. She was written for anyone who found their voice after a lifetime of silence, who dared to chase their autonomy, who's been used until they finally had enough and ended up the villain in someone else's story.

Make sure you subscribe to my newsletter so that you don't miss important updates. My website is also the best place to find my scheduled appearances, bonus scenes, frequently asked questions, and more: bbreid.com

ABOUT THE AUTHOR

B.B. Reid is a bestselling author of several romances, including *Crucible*, the imaginative retelling of Goldilocks. She's most known for her dark and contemporary romances, but began her career writing new adult. B.B. currently resides in Atlanta with Ivan, her moody tuxedo cat. When she's not being a nomad, she enjoys gaming, white chocolate mochas, home decor, and retail therapy.